IN THE NIGHT

MELISSA SINCLAIR

DARKNESS FALLS PUBLISHING

First Edition

Cover design by Render Compose

www.rendercompose.com

ACKNOWLEDGEMENTS

First and foremost, I would like to thank my amazingly supportive husband. Without you, I would not have completed self-publishing this book. In addition, I would like to thank my three young children who've been exceptionally patient while Mommy wrote this book. One even asked to buy a copy.

On to my technical support and people I consider friends. Thank you to Mitzi Carroll, copy and line editor, and Marisa Nichols, proof-reader. These two ladies helped make my words shine. They did an outstanding job, and I couldn't recommend them more. They fixed every comma, and I hate commas; right, Mitzi? But the biggest compliment came from Mitzi when she messaged and asked if this was my first book. When I said yes, she told me that she couldn't believe it was my first. In fact, she felt I wrote like a veteran. Thank you for the words of love; if you only knew what they meant to me.

To my police expert, Officer Jody Breider, thank you for helping me with the police information. Any errors or embellishments are mine and mine alone.

If you picked this book up because the cover drew you to it like any good cover does to a book addict (like so many covers have drawn me to pick them up and read the back) then all accolades should go to the amazing Lucy Rhodes of Render Compose. Her covers are an art. Check her out at www.rendercompose.com. You won't be disappointed.

To my parents who have been supportive of my writing, I love you. And to my dad, yes, I plan to write that book you keep asking me to take on. Also, to my sisters, Nikki and Amanda, growing up you were always there for me. I would like to also send a special thank you to my sister Amanda, who wrote a book at the same time as me and encouraged me to finish this book. Whether it was through competition or love, we'll never fully know. I tend to believe it was a little of both, with a large focus on love.

Finally, to my small, but mighty street team. Erin Gray, my longest and most amazing childhood friend, I know you will make me laugh no matter how stressed I am. Joy Schabow, my book buddy and confidant, I was most worried to let you read this labor of love. You were the one I expected to be brutally critical, so imagine my surprise when you sent me your review. I could have cried, and for those who don't know me, it's amazing that I didn't. I think I was in shock. Sue Lopp, it's not possible to say thank you enough for letting me bother you relentlessly with name ideas, plot ideas, and just about anything else. You are one of my best cheerleaders. A special thank you for letting me "kill you off." I hope I did it justice. Darla Pinkerton, after I got a couple thumbs up, I asked you to read my book. Thank you for taking the time and for also turning into a name expert for me. I'm pretty sure I'll come back for more.

To any family members who read this, please don't judge me by the content alone. I love all of you!

For my Family

1

Ten Years Ago

The air was heavy with the promise of rain. It had been one of the driest months of May that the state had ever seen, and Mother Nature was ripe for one wicked storm. Kara could almost feel the static electricity in the air. Fidgeting, she tried to focus on the book she was studying. Next week was final exams, and then she was out of here. On her way to medical school.

Come hell or high water, she was going to the school she wanted for medicine. Not some degree her parents picked for her. Her intention was to study neurosurgery.

Tapping her pen on the desktop in her bedroom, she thought about what it meant to be almost done with high school. For her, it meant freedom from her parents. She couldn't wait to be out from under their constant scrutiny, their ridiculous expectations, and their lack of interest in who she really was. She was more than the dutiful daughter they demanded.

She hated always being the good little girl who was too scared of her parents to disobey them. Just once, she wanted to piss her father off and do something he would hate. Just once, she wanted to get a reaction out of her mother to make sure that she wasn't actually encased in ice. Just once, she wanted to be treated like they treated Ethan. But she didn't blame him; he was the only one who treated her like she mattered, and the last four years sucked while he was away at college.

Ethan didn't care about Father's rules; he was always bucking them. Maybe tonight would be the night that she did. She envied that he did what he wanted, but she could never be jealous of her brother; he was the only one she had, and she was proud of him. He was a genuinely great person, even if her parents had done their best to try to turn him into a pretentious snob.

And yet, he was still a little bit of the dutiful son. After all, he was about to graduate college at the top of his class in prelaw, with his choice of any law school in the country, and Kara knew that he didn't want to be a stuffy corporate lawyer. She could see him as a DA, someone who would bring down criminals, but not a corporate stooge. But, he still made his own path; she smiled when she thought of her parents' reaction when he chose a law school closer to home versus the one they had handpicked for him. Even their threats of cutting him off didn't stop him; he simply told them that he would follow the career they wanted, but he got to choose what school. He knew how hard it had been on her the last four years with him away at college and not able to be there. She felt like a shadow of herself as if she didn't exist. He would always feel guilty; she knew that about him because he was a good man.

Crash! The sound snapped Kara out of her reverie, and she jumped about a foot in the air. At the same time, the vase fell off her night-stand, a crack of thunder split the air and sent Kara's pulse skyrocketing. She loved a good storm; it helped to block out the noise of her parents arguing. But tonight, her parents were gone to a fundraising extravaganza as a last-ditch effort to gain support for her father's run at the Governor's Mansion. She figured they were knee-deep in shit from all the ass kissing. Kara giggled at the image of her parents kissing some rich person's butt, unable to tell where the butt ended and their head began.

Finding herself anxious, Kara moved to go clean up the shards of glass. The wind was blowing violently through her window, and it was causing the curtains to billow, which had knocked the vase off the nightstand to begin with. She placed the glass in the ugly, floral-print garbage can she had in her room. Her whole bedroom was decorated in her mother's taste, not Kara's. Really, what eighteen-year-old wanted a 1980s floral motif?

Glancing out the window, she saw that the night sky was liquid black; no stars were present and the tree branches were whipping around like they were in a frenzy, beckoning her to come out and play —as if they were dancing to a melody only they could hear. Lightning lit up the sky, and Kara shivered.

Who was around to tell her to stay home? she thought. Her parents would be out until the wee hours of the morning, and if they happened to get home before her, they wouldn't check on her when they got home. They would never know Kara had disobeyed them. What's more, they'd never expect Kara to disobey them, because of their indifference to her. To gain attention, she always did what they said. However, it normally backfired because they just ignored her further. Maybe if she snuck out they'd give a damn; even if they were angry, it was better than nothing. Right?

She had made up her mind. She was not going to sit home and miss the last and biggest party of her high school life. She'd never gone to a party, and tonight, she was going to go. After all, what could her parents do to her? Ground her? She was about to leave for college in three months and would be out from under their watchful eye soon enough. Her brother proved that once you were out from under their thumb, you could have a life of your own.

Kara grabbed her garbage can; she would throw away the shards of glass from the obscenely expensive vase in the downstairs garbage. Less chance her mom would notice right away; not that she ever visited her in her bedroom out of love. Usually, she just snooped. She didn't know Kara knew about the snooping, but she knew. It was unlikely her mother would ever empty the garbage. In Constance Vanderbilt's mind, that was what their house staff was for; however, she knew her mom would notice the missing Tiffany vase on one of her snooping visits and her mom would be pissed that she broke it. They had so much money, they would buy another ridiculously overpriced vase somewhere. But it would be the "principle" of the matter, that she had been careless and irresponsible as to break it—never mind that the wind broke it. She wouldn't be given the chance to defend herself.

The lights flickered as she was walking toward the stairs which, for some reason, really creeped her out. The house was far too big for the four of them, and there were too many shadows as it was without flickering lights. Shaking off the absurd feeling, she was almost to the top of the stairs when she heard a noise that set the hairs on her arm on end. She paused at the top of the stairs, and after a couple of minutes, she was confident that it was just her mind playing tricks on her. Her conscience was making her feel guilty for sneaking out. She squared her shoulders and continued down the stairs. Kara was almost to the door when she saw the shadow of someone standing by her father's study.

"Who-who's there?" she stammered and breathed a sigh of relief when the shadow emerged. "Devon, what the hell are you doing here? Shouldn't you be at my father's fundraiser? And why the hell are you lurking in the shadows?" she demanded.

Once again, she had to shake off her nervous feeling when Devon, one of her father's campaign volunteers, just stood there looking at her. He had always creeped her out, and at that moment, she knew that those feelings had been justified. She went from creeped out to terrified in less than ten seconds and started to back away from him. He finally spoke after what seemed like an eternity of time had passed.

"Your father wanted me to stop and make sure you weren't trying to sneak out. Looks like he had good reason for concern." The smile he sent her way was borderline evil. *Thank him and tell him to be on his way*, she thought.

"All right, well you've done your civic duty. I learned my lesson, so you can go now," she whispered. She had tried to sound confident like a Vanderbilt was supposed to but had come up terribly short. Instinct told her not to turn her back on him, so she was still slowly backing up when she realized he was approaching her. Panic began to rise; Kara had just decided to run when she backed into the stairs and stumbled.

Losing her balance, she dropped the garbage can, and shards of glass flew everywhere; simultaneously, she fell backward and landed hard on the bottom stair. As she tried to catch herself, her arm twisted at an odd angle as she fell on it. Pain shot up her arm and into her shoulder.

Everything went into fast forward, because once she lost her balance, Devon took the opportunity to lunge at her. She tried hard to kick and squirm her way out of his grasp, but he was too strong. Glass was everywhere, and she was conscious of getting cut as she thrashed in an attempt to get away from him.

Desperately scratching at his face while trying to scramble backward, she was knocked half silly when he punched her square in the face. With stars flashing in her eyes, Kara was barely conscious of the fact that he had pulled something from his pocket. She had only seconds to compute that it was a syringe before he plunged it into her skin. She realized the battle to stay conscious was futile as she slipped into darkness, but not before she felt pure, unadulterated fear course through her veins.

WHEN SHE WOKE UP, her head was throbbing and felt like it was in a fog. As a matter of fact, her whole body was in considerable pain. Even though her head was full of cobwebs, she knew two things: that she was in the trunk of a moving vehicle and that she was bound and gagged. It took her several moments to remember what had happened, and then it all came rushing back. Devon had jumped her and injected her with some kind of drug. Where was he taking her? And why?

Kara struggled to free her hands and feet. If she could just get one or the other free, maybe she could maneuver herself enough to kick out one of the taillights. She must have been sweating from the exertion because the ropes became slippery, but then the smell of copper filled the air, and she knew it was blood. Maybe she could use that slipperiness to get her hands out. After a few minutes, she gave up; it was no use, the more she struggled, the tighter the knots became.

She began to feel herself panic, and her breath came more rapidly. Knowing she was hyperventilating, she tried to calm herself. *Think, Kara, think! You're smart; you can get yourself out of this.*

She was still trying to regroup when the car slowed, and judging by the sound of the rocks, it was a gravel road they had turned onto. They had left the main road, of that she was sure, but where was he taking her? Kara told herself to keep a mental log of any turns they took, and she tried to calculate the length of time they were on each road. It would be useful knowledge if she escaped. A noise rose in her throat, a strangled cry as if her mind was saying: yeah, right—like she was going to escape this nightmare.

No! She would escape! Kara made herself repeat over and over the word *when*. Meaning *when* she escaped, it would be useful to know which route they had taken. The car slowed again and turned onto another road; this one was not gravel, but it was bumpy. They were not on the road for long before the car slowed one last time and the engine stopped.

Kara felt herself begin to panic again. What was Devon planning to do to her? *Get it together, remember your surroundings, and look for an escape route*, she told herself. The sound of keys rattling put her senses into overdrive. *Be alert!* When the trunk lid opened, she noted that it was still evening so they couldn't have driven that far unless the drug he'd given her had knocked her out for longer than she had thought. Devon didn't look like the man that she remembered coming to her house to help with campaign plans with her father. He looked like a crazed man; the word monster sprang to her mind, and that thought sent chills racing down Kara's spine. He stood before her, and she had no idea what to do to get away. All she knew was, she was going to try.

"Home sweet home, little lady. I know it's not much, but it's only temporary. What do you think?" He looked at her earnestly, and she knew at that moment that she was dealing with someone who was, without a doubt, insane.

"Oh, dear, I seem to have forgotten your mouth is taped shut. I suppose I can take that off now. I don't think anyone can hear you all the way out here. I just didn't know when you'd wake up, and we simply could not have you be able to scream to another car to alert them, now, could we?" And with that, he tore the duct tape off her mouth. She flinched from the pain.

"Devon, please, let me go. My father has a lot of money; he will compensate you well if you just let me go." She knew her mistake right before his hand snaked out and connected with her cheek.

"You stupid little bitch. You think this is about money? I went to a lot of trouble to get you here, and you think this is about money. Typical Vanderbilt. I bet you think you're too good for me. Well, we'll just have to see about that." He jerked her out of the trunk and dragged her across the driveway the rest of the way into the house.

All right, Kara, he's not after Father's money, now what? Once inside the cabin, she scanned her surroundings noting that it was a simple, rundown, one-room cabin. There was a terrible smell in the air as if something had crawled into a hole in the cabin and died; she only hoped it was animal and not human. She was able to figure out two things on the way in: they were in the middle of the woods, and the cabin they were in appeared to have been abandoned.

"The drugs I gave you should be fully worn off soon. I hope you aren't upset that I had to use them. I knew you might be resistant to coming with me. But now that your father and mother aren't here to watch your every move, you don't have to play so hard to get."

"Hard to get? Devon, what are you talking about? I had no idea you were even interested."

"Oh please, give me a break. The little cock tease that you are surely knew the hard-on you gave me—you gave everyone—every time you came in the room. What with all the short shorts and almost-see-through tank tops, it's a wonder any man can keep his dick in his pants around you."

"Maybe you're right; maybe I did unfairly tease you. I didn't mean to lead you on. Why don't you take me home and we can go out on a proper date?" She swallowed hard, hoping her new tactic would work with him.

Kara looked him in the eye and smiled the most innocent smile she could muster, but when his eyes narrowed, she knew he hadn't bought it. Before she could blink, his hand had collided with her cheek again; this time it was so hard she had to blink back the tears that stung her eyes.

"You little bitch, you manipulating little bitch!"

He threw her on the bed in the middle of the cabin. It was the only nice thing in the whole building, and she knew he'd brought it there for her. It was a four-poster bed in a rich mahogany, and the sheets felt like butter. He'd obviously spared no expense on them. He quickly untied her hands and placed them in restraints that were attached to each corner of the bed, and then he repeated the process with her feet. She was spread eagle on the bed, but she was still clothed.

No longer able to control her emotions, she began to sob uncontrollably. Why was this happening? Surely, she didn't deserve this.

"Please, Devon, please stop. There's still time to let me go." She sobbed.

"Feel free to scream. The nearest house is miles away; no one will hear you."

2

Oh, God, please help me, please. I won't ask anything of You ever again. She strained at her bindings, but they were secured too well. Devon had clearly thought this out, planned for this moment, and that fact terrified Kara more than anything else. If he had planned things out, then he had taken precautions to keep her hidden. She bucked like a wild animal, desperate to get free, but all she managed to do was physically exhaust herself until she was panting from the exertion.

"I love a spirited woman. Keep fighting or crying; it will only make it that much better."

The words sent ice through her veins, and she stopped immediately and looked at her captor. Maybe not moving would deter him. But, no, she knew that wasn't going to help either, because Devon looked her up and down, his eyes lingering between her thighs. Bile rose and burned the back of her throat; she nearly threw up but forced herself to push it back down. She searched his face for any sign of humanity but was terrified at the empty eyes that met hers. He reached forward and started to unbutton her shorts; she reflexively flinched, and it was as if what little self-restraint he had snapped.

He grabbed a pair of scissors and cut her shorts and shirt off; he glared down at her from where he stood. His tongue darted out of his mouth to lick his lips, and he slowly ran his hands up her legs. Then he savagely tore her panties and bra off and climbed on top of her. The stink of his breath against her cheek had the bile rising in her throat once again, and again, she had to fight to keep it down. Her mind was still trying to find a way out of the situation, but when she felt his erection pushing against her belly, she knew there was no way to stop the inevitable.

"Please, please don't. I'm a virgin."

"I know."

He penetrated her with such force that she had to bite her lip to stop from screaming out in pain—the taste of blood filled her mouth. Tears burned her eyes and slid down her bruised face; his tongue darted from his mouth, and he lapped up her tears. He thrust into her repeatedly, tearing her so badly she could feel blood run down her legs. Finally, he thrust one last time before collapsing on top of her, panting. After a couple of minutes, he climbed off her and stood while zipping his pants.

When he looked down at her, he seemed to have regained his composure. She closed her eyes and tried to block the images of what had just happened from her mind. But all she could see behind her lids was the crazed look he had had on his face when he climbed on her. And all she could smell was his breath on her cheek. She wanted to vomit; she wanted to scream; she wanted to cry, but she did none of those things. Instead, she lay numb.

KARA WOKE to whimpers coming from the floor. When she looked down, she thought she was hallucinating. Devon was sleeping on the floor, and apparently was having a very upsetting dream; but the point was, he was *sleeping*. It was the first time in four days that she had seen him sleep when she was awake, because for the last four days when he hadn't drugged her, he had been raping and torturing her repeatedly. Over the course of those four days, she had noticed his personality change several times. Sometimes he was cold and calculated in his torture, and other times he behaved as if he really thought he loved her. He was almost tender when he violated her as if he truly believed it was consensual and that they were a couple. And he had appeared to have an endless supply of energy—sexually as well as physically.

Of course, it was possible he had slept, and she hadn't noticed. There were parts of the last four days she didn't remember, times when the drugs had taken her to a blessed oblivion. Many times, she blacked out from the drugs he would inject in her, other times from the intense pain. But she was awake and alert now and conscious that this would be her only chance. This was the opportunity she had been waiting for. He had to be exhausted, she knew she was. She might be killed trying to escape. But if she didn't try now, she would certainly die for sure.

If the monster was asleep, then she had to find a way out of there. She looked around the room, and slowly her mouth turned into a grim smile. He had left one of the scalpels he'd used to intimidate her on the mattress close enough that she might be able to reach it. Huge oversight on his part, especially given how flexible she was from years of ballet training. She strained to reach it and sucked in her breath when she bumped it.

It had nearly slid out of her reach, but she could just barely touch it with her fingers. She stretched as much as she could and finally was able to get the handle between her thumb and index finger. Now she just had to figure out how to twist her hands to cut the ropes. After a couple minutes, she realized that wasn't an option. But the ropes were looser than normal, and if she put the scalpel in her mouth, she could reach the ropes—but just barely.

The first attempt to slice at the ropes caused her to nick her wrist and blood started to drip down her arm. She didn't stop to see how bad the cut was, because, quite frankly, she would rather bleed to death than stay one more second in that cabin with the monster sleeping on the floor beside her.

Finally, after long minutes in an agonizing position, she was able to cut through the ropes on her wrists. Kara slid to the edge of the bed, silently placing her feet on the ground. She had to climb over Devon's inert body to get to the door, which was going to be a challenge because every bone in her body hurt and every muscle screamed in pain. This caused her to be extremely clumsy, almost falling on him twice as she finally maneuvered around him and tiptoed to the door.

Beads of sweat had formed on her brow from the exertion of freeing herself. She wasn't sure how she'd get away if he woke, but she had to try. Quickly, she opened the door, and as soon as the fresh air hit her face, she broke into the fastest sprint her body would allow. Running around the side of the cabin, she saw the car she had been transported in. Kara had two seconds to decide if she should stop and try the car handles and hope the door is unlocked and the keys were in the ignition or to keep going. Logic dictated that even with her being tied up, Devon wouldn't be stupid enough to leave the keys in the car. However, she had to take the chance. Breaking stride only for the second it took to stop to try the handle and find the car locked, she took off as fast as she could down the dirt road.

Which, unfortunately, wasn't that fast at all. She was used to muscle aches, but this was different. While her muscles burned and she pushed herself harder than she ever had, she knew she couldn't move faster than she was. But, in the end, it didn't matter; she was going to run until she couldn't run any farther. Never once did she turn to see if he had woken up and was following. Instead, she ran until she thought her lungs would explode, and then she ran some more.

Along with the ballet training—because her parents insisted she be diversified—Kara had run on the long-distance track team all four years of high school and had competed at state level, but she had never run in the pain she was in at that moment. While endurance was something she had built over those years, what her body had been put through, the lack of food, water, and sleep, made it difficult to continue. But she forced herself to go to the place she had gone the last four days every time he had touched her, forced herself to ignore the pain and pretend she was numb to it. For the most part, it worked, and even though every inch of her was on fire, she was able to continue in her escape from the cabin.

It had been a hasty decision to run down the road versus through the woods. Her mind had dictated to go that route because there would be less chance she would get lost and less debris to run on with her bare feet. Even though it made her easier to find, she didn't care. But while the road was dirt, it was still painful to her feet to run on. It was just one more thing she had to ignore, one more thing she had to block out.

Finally, she came to an intersection. She remembered turning from a gravel road to the dirt road, but which way had they come from? The right! Should she go the way they came from or go the opposite way in case he woke and came to look for her? She knew the way they came would bring her to a main road, so even though it might be the way he would look, she decided to go that way. As she turned, she heard a vehicle approaching from behind her, and an all too familiar feeling of panic rose inside her. Had he awoken and found her missing? There was no way on a good day she could outrun a vehicle, and today was not a good day.

Running with every ounce of her soul, she tripped on a large rock on the ground and tumbled to the gravel below her. Struggling to get up, she heard the vehicle stop behind her. Maybe if she waited until he approached, she could throw sand in his eyes to buy herself some time, and then she could make a run for it again. Knowing it was a ludicrous plan, she clawed her way across the road, trying to get up, but her body wouldn't allow her to get to her feet. It was as if the tumble had sapped out every last bit of energy.

So, this is how it's going to end, she thought. *Please, God, just let me get away. I will do whatever you want. And if you won't grant me that, please make it quick. I am done, I can't fight, and I can't go through anymore. Please.*

"Young lady, are you all right?" Once again, Kara thought she was hallucinating because the voice behind her was not Devon's, but rather a deeper and older sounding voice. When she looked at the shadow looming over her, she breathed a sigh of relief and finally let her body completely relax before everything faded into black.

WHEN HE WOKE, he was startled to see that Kara was missing. How had she gotten loose? He tore through the cabin and ran outside; she was nowhere to be seen. Running back inside, he knew he had to go. He didn't know how long she'd been missing, but he knew he had to flee and regroup.

And when he found that little bitch, she was going to pay for running off on him, after all he had done to bring them together. He was still trying to gather his wits when he heard a helicopter overhead. He didn't have time to clean the cabin properly, so he decided it would be best to leave and hope that he could go back to destroy evidence. He had taken precautions—rubber gloves, condoms. But sometimes the smallest things could be enough to bring you down. Still, it was too late to worry about it; he didn't even have anything to burn the cabin. Never looking back, he ran to his car and tore down the road. Grabbing his cell phone, he made an important call. He waited impatiently until finally, someone answered. No time to be subtle, he blurted out the latest development.

"She escaped."

"What do you mean 'she escaped'?"

"What part is hard for you to understand? The word she or the word escape? I woke up, and she was gone."

"You fell asleep?"

"Yes, damn it. She must have cut her ropes with one of the scalpels; there's blood everywhere. You don't have anything to say about that, do you?" When there was no response, he continued, "I didn't think so."

"Let's not dwell on the circumstances of the escape, let's just figure out damage control. Meet me at the rendezvous point. We'll figure out what to do from there, and figure out how to get the bitch." The phone disconnected.

Yes, he knew one thing for sure. When he found that bitch, she was going to wish she had died. He would make sure it felt like she'd died a thousand deaths by the time he was finished with her. If she thought she had felt pain in the last four days, she was sadly mistaken. What he had in store for her would make that look like a walk in the park.

ONCE AGAIN, Kara woke up in a strange place, but this time, she was in a very white and very sterile room. It didn't take long for her to realize she was in a hospital; she closed her eyes as tears slid down her face. *Thank you, God, for answering my prayers.* Kara struggled to get up and nearly screamed in pain.

"Dr. Brenner, Dr. Chiglo! She's awake. Can we do something for her pain?" she heard a familiar voice ask. Ethan! Her brother was there. She really was safe, and Kara began to sob uncontrollably.

"Heather, will you give her another dose of morphine?"

Once the pain subsided a bit, she tried to sit up again.

"Don't try to sit up yet. Your body has been through a lot. We'll need to take baby steps," a woman's soft and soothing voice said.

After another moment of silence, she opened her eyes and glanced around the room. There were two doctors in the room and Ethan.

"Now that her pain is under control, can we have a moment alone?" Ethan asked.

"Only a moment, she needs her rest."

Still very much out of it, she looked at him, searching his eyes, searching the room again to see if she was wrong and that her parents were also there. However, scanning the room once more, it was easy to see that they weren't there waiting for her to wake up, and she was not surprised at all by that revelation. Once they were alone, Ethan pulled a chair next to her bed and sat down, holding her hand. She flinched at the contact and hated herself for that. Hated herself for the look she saw in his eyes, the look that said he knew what had happened to her— at least the obvious things that had happened to her.

"I can't tell you how good it is to see those beautiful green eyes."

"Ethan, am I really safe?"

"Yes. You really are safe."

"How long have I been out?"

"A few days."

"A few days!"

"Your body needed a considerable amount of recuperation after what you went through. You almost didn't make it. They induced a coma to help you heal. Then they tried to wake you up. And, it...it wasn't happening. You were in and out all day. This is the first time that you've really woken up." Kara could see he tried but couldn't fight the tears as they flowed down his face. "You lost so much blood by the time the helicopter got there to bring you here. And then you coded in the helicopter. They had to bring you back in the air—more than once —and they started giving you a transfusion on the way. If Mr. Stanford hadn't found you when he did, you'd have died on that road."

"Where am I?"

"Mercy Hospital."

"Is...is the man who saved me here? I would like to thank him."

"He was here earlier, and he was hoping you were awake, but you were still sleeping. He told me to tell you when you woke up that he would stop back to see you when you were up for visitors."

She nodded her head slightly, and even that small movement hurt. Her injuries were so numerous that she was scared to ask anything more about them. Not today, but someday, she would insist on every gory detail. Today she would simply be grateful for Mr. Stanford, the doctors, and Ethan. Before she dozed off, she had to know if they had caught Devon, if he was in jail where he belonged.

"Did they find him? Did they catch that monster?"

"You mean Devon?"

"No, that wasn't Devon. That person was pure evil. A monster. Did they catch him?" She realized she sounded crazy, she also realized she was about to slip under into blissful oblivion again.

"Yes and no."

"What do you mean?" she mumbled, almost incoherently.

"He's dead."

"Dead? How, when?"

"He died about two hours after you were found. The police had a lead on where he was going, and when they got there, they found his car. He appeared to have missed a corner and crashed; it was already on fire when they got there. They weren't able to get him out in time; he burned to death, Kara. He got what he deserved."

She struggled to process the information. It was all she could manage to keep her eyes open while she searched his face.

Dead? Devon was dead. She was equal parts happy and angry. Happy he was gone, never able to touch her or anyone else again. Angry that he was gone without a chance for her to see him rot in prison.

"I hope he suffered," she whispered, and then the drugs took full effect, and she fell back into unconsciousness.

3

Ten years later

Shit, it was hot today. And he had gotten stuck walking the stupid dog in the frickin' heat once again. Damn his sister always tricking him into doing her chores. At least he was able to bring his fishing pole so he could go fishing for a bit. Bobby was so absorbed in his thoughts that he hadn't noticed his dog, Cheddar, had run ahead of him; that is, until he heard him barking. He knew he was supposed to keep him leashed when he walked him, but he didn't care. No one was going to tell him what to do. Anyway, Cheddar was a good dog, and he wouldn't run away.

"What you got there, buddy?" he asked when he realized Cheddar was busy trying to pick something up. Bobby frowned when he got closer. *What the hell is that?* he thought. It wasn't until he was about five feet away that he was able to identify what it was, and he promptly threw up the beef stroganoff he had eaten for lunch.

Digging in his pocket, he pulled out the cell phone his mom made him take with him everywhere. *Just in case*, she would say, and he would roll his eyes and say, *Ah ma, I'm twelve now, I'm practically a man. I don't need to be treated like a baby.* Yet he was secretly thrilled that she gave him a phone to have. It made him feel like a man, but he didn't feel like a man as he dialed 911, glancing at the fresh vomit on his shirt.

"911 what's your emergency?" a calm, female voice asked.

"My name is Bobby Smits, and my dog just found a woman's body in the river by my house."

CALEB MONTGOMERY SAT behind the wheel of his department-issued vehicle, drumming his fingers on the steering wheel, waiting for Ethan Vanderbilt to get his ass in gear. They had just gotten called in from a much-needed vacation that had lasted a whole half a day. Apparently, there was a floater in the river that some kid had found while on his way to go fishing with his dog. Why did a kid always have to find the floaters?

Just the luck of the draw, he supposed. Captain had called them in because he knew they were the best two detectives he had, and apparently, they had an idea of who the floater was. He had been told that the victim was a female, and she was fresh. Captain Bob Wickman only called people in from a much-needed and well-deserved vacation when something big was happening. Which meant that Caleb had a pretty damn good idea who had been found.

Ethan flung open the door and settled in next to him, hair still wet. Ethan was tall, dark, blue-eyed, and sculpted. The man was who most women drooled over. Caleb was comfortable enough in himself to admit that his partner could get his pick of women. Caleb didn't do so bad himself in that aspect; he just didn't have time and had not found a woman patient enough to date a cop. Ethan and Caleb both knew one thing: in their line of work, it was easy to get a woman who was interested in dating a cop; just not easy to keep the woman interested when they were gone at all hours of the day and night.

"So, what we got?" Ethan asked from next to him, jarring him from his thoughts.

"Captain called and told us to get our asses back in. A body was found floating in the water. Most likely the vic is Andrea Vincent."

"He actually said that?"

"Not exactly, I added that part. But you know as well as I do that with budget cuts the way they are right now, the only way Captain would call us in for more overtime is if somebody important has been found floating in the river."

"Yeah, I suspected the same thing. I was already thinking that the body is Andrea Vincent."

"We are in for a very shitty afternoon."

Andrea Vincent was the daughter of a local Senator who had gone missing a few days back. After days of searching, they'd come up empty. She had last been seen leaving a small get-together at a friend's apartment at the university, much to her parents' disdain because the friend's apartment happened to be the boy she was seeing that they didn't approve of. Speculation was that she had wandered off drunk and had possibly gotten hurt. Of course, the other working theory was that she had run off with the guy her parents hated or they had gotten into a fight, and he had done something to her. But he had been the one to call her in missing and was checked and cleared of any wrong-doing. The third theory was the possibility it was something more sinister that had caused her disappearance. If it was her, one thing was for certain, they were about to find out how sinister her disappearance was.

The only thing that was clear at this point was that, if it was Andrea Vincent, she had met an untimely death. At only twenty years old, she was the apple of her parents' eyes and set to follow in her father's foot-steps. By all accounts, everyone loved her, and everyone wanted to be her. She had the whole world at her feet and a bright future in front of her.

When they approached the crime scene, Caleb's stomach sunk. The place was swarming with media, which meant someone had already gone to the press. Floaters weren't found every day, but they also weren't uncommon, so for the media to be this interested meant that the body found was that of someone high profile enough to leak the information and important enough to bring the vultures to the scene.

Scanning the crowd, Caleb immediately found Captain Wickman on the sidelines fielding questions. Captain being there sealed the deal, so to speak, on Andrea Vincent being the body. There was no doubt in his mind that she was who had been found.

As they approached the cordoned off area, the captain put his hand up to signal to the media that he was done answering questions. Turning, he moved toward the two of them.

"Captain," Caleb said. Ethan stood quietly next to him, assessing the area just as Caleb was. It was common for murderers to stand on the sideline in the crowd to watch the festivities after their victims were found. While the captain hadn't said as much on the phone, his body language said it all as he approached them. Andrea Vincent was found, but not only that. She had been murdered.

"Montgomery, Vanderbilt. We have ourselves a serious situation here."

"Have her parents been notified yet?" Caleb asked, indicating he was aware of what kind of situation they had.

"I am about to go over there right now. I'm hoping that they don't get wind of this until I get there. I made some calls, and one of his aides said he's in a meeting for another thirty minutes. After which he and his wife are scheduled to do another television plea for any help in finding their daughter. I came down to identify her so her parents wouldn't have to."

Captain Bob Wickman fought back tears. Caleb felt like someone had punched him in the gut at the sight of this six-foot-five man, who was ex-military, fighting the onslaught of tears. Everyone knew that the captain was childhood friends with Senator Vincent and that Andrea was his goddaughter. So, yes, it was understandable that he would want to be here to identify her body.

"Captain, we have everything under control on this end. Go be with them. They're going to need to hear this from you, not them," Caleb said. Ethan and the captain didn't have to ask who he meant by *them*; they knew he meant the media.

With a nod of his head, he made his way to the tape sectioning off the crime scene and once again had to field questions from the media. *Damn vultures*, Caleb thought. The captain was grieving and had to hide it with every bit of strength he could muster so he wouldn't give away anything to the media before he was able to tell the senator and his wife that their only daughter was killed; not only killed, but most likely killed at the hands of someone else.

Caleb and Ethan made their way toward ME Shirley Hottenstein and CSI Brett Albrecht. Brett was standing behind a tarp that had been erected to hide the body from the media. Hottenstein had been with them for a long time and was still able to be compassionate when examining a body. Albrecht was newer to the team but seemed solid and capable. In their line of work, sometimes people became immune to the discovery of another body. But after a quick look at all the team that had been assembled, Caleb knew that was not the case here.

Once they'd made their way to the tarp, both men stood with their backs toward the cameras, blocking the camera's view of their faces as well as the two people collecting evidence by the body. No need for the media to be able to read their expressions, or worse, their lips. With a glance back at the cameras, Caleb knew they were well out of earshot of the media.

"What you got for us, Shirley?" Ethan asked, speaking for the first time since they'd gotten to the crime scene.

"I am sure it is no surprise to you who we have here."

"No, no surprise," Caleb said somberly.

"How's the captain doing?" Albrecht asked.

"Holding his own. But he's shaken. She was murdered?" Caleb asked, already knowing the answer.

"It would appear so."

"How?"

"I can't really say for sure until I get her back to the morgue. But it appears strangulation. It also appears she was raped."

"Shit, does Captain know that?" Ethan asked.

"No. I don't know for sure, and he was hurting already. I wanted to be sure before I gave him that news."

"She looks...preserved. She couldn't have been in the water long. And there appears to be no decomp."

"Very good eye. It appears she was dumped probably early this morning."

"What makes you think that?" Caleb asked, recognizing that Ethan was deferring the question and answer portion of this conversation to him while he canvassed the crowd some more.

"According to liver temp, she's only been dead for about twelve hours. Like I said, it looks like she was strangled, which would indicate she was dead when she was dumped. If not, there'll be water in her lungs. If there *is* water in the lungs, then she was dumped antemortem."

"That bastard had her for a while before dumping her, and we have a small window of time from death to dumping to discovering her. Which begs the question, how was she found so quickly? The perp didn't try to weigh her down?"

"No. As a matter of fact, we found this attached to her." Albrecht pointed to the flotation device lying next to the body.

"What do you mean?" Caleb asked, confusion slowly turning to stark anger when he realized what he meant. He had assumed the flotation device was from the boy witness. "Are you trying to tell me that whoever dumped her wanted us to find her and ensured that by using this flotation device? Why would someone do that?"

"I'm not sure. What I can tell you is, she was found so quickly because she was wearing this flotation device. And she was tied to that big rock," he said, pointing to a huge boulder on the shoreline. "Whoever did this doesn't appear to have tried to weigh her down; in fact, they seem to have done everything short of putting a spotlight on her to help us find her. Finding out why is *your* job."

"You're telling me that not only did he tie her to the rock so she couldn't float away, he put a bright flotation device on her to keep her above water and noticeable."

"That's what I'm saying."

"Where is the boy that found her?" Ethan asked quietly.

"Cathy has him over there away from the media. She's questioning him. She had to wait for his mom to get here, but it doesn't look like he has any information that's going to help us. He's doing pretty good, considering. About as solid as a child witness can be. One more thing before you go," Shirley said as they were about to turn to go find the boy.

"What's that?"

"Albrecht, want to give me a hand?" Carefully, they rolled her to her side. She pointed to the left buttock. "The bastard carved some letters on her buttocks. It looks like DB and XII. Could mean dead body or it could be initials. I am not sure about the XII—"

"The fuck! Are you sure?" Ethan's startled exclamation had both men looking his way. They watched as Ethan came closer to the body and knelt beside it to view the carved letters.

"What's wrong?" Caleb asked, knowing that Ethan's pale face meant something was terribly wrong.

"I need to go see my sister. Let's check on Cathy to make sure she has everything under control and doesn't need help interviewing the boy, and then I'll fill you in on the way."

"The way? Where are we going?" Caleb asked, concerned by the alarm on his partner's face.

"I told you, I need to see my sister." Ethan glanced down at his watch and then looked back up at Caleb. "She should be pulling in anytime now."

4

It was sweltering outside. Kara hated the heat; she rolled up the window in her car, opting for air conditioning over fresh air. Judging by the skyline ahead of her, there was a storm brewing, and there was one thing she hated more than heat, and that was when it stormed. Once upon a time, things had been different. Once upon a time, she had loved the warmth, loved storms, loved running in the rain. Now the change in weather made her body ache and reminded her of those days.

She felt a shiver go up her spine at the thought of where she was going. She pulled her car off the highway and headed home. *Home.* That is if you could call it that. Seeing as how she hadn't returned in ten years, it was hard to think of the town she grew up in as her home. And it wasn't like when she lived there it felt like much of a home anyway.

What *had* possessed her to agree to return to this horrible place? The place that had irrevocably changed her life forever? She had just started to feel like she had gained control of her life again, and then she let Ethan convince her to at least *consider* moving back here. She must be truly crazy to return to this place; she could feel her blood pressure rise the closer she got to her parents' house. Now that her father was governor, they lived in the Governor's Mansion, but they had kept their abundantly opulent house.

She didn't realize she was holding her breath until after she passed the monstrosity of a house that she used to call her home or, rather, where she used to live with her family. Ethan was her only family now, and she wanted to be closer to him. She would just have to adjust to the move back. If there was anything she was good at, it was adjusting to changes. Anyway, things would be different this time. They had to be. Other than being near Ethan, working at the hospital that she could thank for her current path in life was probably the easiest part of this move.

She looked in her rearview mirror at Samsonite sleeping on the backseat of her car. Samsonite had been with her for five of the last ten years. Once she was out of that hideous dorm and able to get a place of her own, the first thing she did was research guard dogs. Then it was just a matter of finding the right one, and Samsonite had claimed her from the moment she laid her eyes on him. He was her best friend and one hell of a guard dog. Sure, he looked innocent enough, but he was deadly if need be. Thank God, he'd never had to be.

Kara felt her pulse quicken again at the thought of being here in the town her parents had raised her in. She hadn't seen them in nearly ten years, ever since she had left that place right before her father's election. She had said goodbye to this town, goodbye to them and vowed to never step foot in that house again. She moved on and tried to forget the events of that summer. She moved far away and hoped no one had heard of her. Of course, that was a ridiculous idea. Everyone had heard of her. She went to the college she had chosen for herself, not the one her parents had wanted her to go to. Of all the schools she'd been accepted to, it had been the farthest one away.

But no matter where she went, someone recognized her, and she would hear the whispers. You couldn't blame them; she was hot news back then. After all, it wasn't every day a gubernatorial candidate's only daughter was kidnapped and tortured. And it wasn't every day that same daughter publicly denounced said father in front of dozens of reporters, telling them that she didn't endorse her father as a candidate and would not be voting for him. It also wasn't every day that someone with her name and her parents' money walked away from it all. But it happened then, and it made for a lot of gossip.

And, yet, her father had won that election, and it was shortly before his win that she left. She had never told anyone why she left; she had never put any of the rumors to rest. She had never even told Ethan. It was something she never cared to discuss, and something she preferred to ignore had happened. Much like a lot of the events in her life.

Now ten years later, most of the gossip had stopped. She was sure there was still plenty of gossip around the local garden clubs, but it wasn't like she intended on joining any of them. Her hands clenched on the steering wheel, causing her knuckles to go white as she got farther away from her parents' house. The air in her car suddenly felt stifling, and she rolled down her windows to let some fresh air in.

She had always hated her parents' ostentatious house. She had always hated the way they held their money above everyone's head. It was one more reason to leave them all behind. And one more reason she decided to do it all on her own the last ten years. After a small loan from Ethan, that is. A loan she had paid off, with interest, as soon as she could afford to.

Kara had taken a semester off college because she needed to recover physically as well as emotionally. The dean had been willing to allow her to enter late, because of what had happened. Her parents had pulled strings to allow her to take the semester off. At the time, she had appreciated it, until a few weeks later. Then everything hit the fan, and she left. Once she left and was out from under Stanley and Constance Vanderbilt's thumb, she finally felt some freedom. Kara decided to go to the school she had picked for herself, not the one her parents chose. They had also allowed her to start late.

She'd been accepted to all of the schools she had applied to. Her parents had insisted she apply to all the Ivy League schools in the country. They wanted to be able to say she was accepted to them all, but that in the end, she had chosen their alma mater. It was all about appearances with them. Thankfully, her parents could have cared less to know anything about her. And they didn't know about the extra college she had applied to. The elite college, that wasn't Ivy League, so it wasn't deemed good enough by their standards.

Kara had known she would get into any school of her choice, and later she knew that she had a good chance at getting a late admittance. Even if the school had limited spots. Her parents should have known that, but they were less than interested in anything she did, so they had been oblivious to her drive to get as far away from them as possible. They also chose to ignore how gifted Kara was. Therefore, they felt the need to pull strings for her at the college they had chosen. They didn't feel there was any other way as if the school wouldn't look at her SAT scores and IQ and the fact that she was kidnapped and brutalized and let her have a semester off.

Before she was abducted, she had secretly rebelled and had accepted at both schools—their choice and her choice. She was trying to work up the nerve to tell them that she didn't want their future for her. They wanted her to major in business; she wanted to major in medicine. She knew it wouldn't matter that it was one of the best schools for the field she wanted to go into because her parents hadn't planned on her having a career. She was to marry someone they picked out and be the proper little daughter. The degree was not to get her a job; it was to land her bragging rights and a husband.

Too bad for them that she had different plans, and too bad for them that they had forgotten about her full scholarship. So, when the shit hit the fan, she told them to fuck off and said she was going to her school of choice. Her father had told her he would cut her off. She had told him to go to hell. And he did cut her off, so two years later, after a lot of hard work, she graduated early, number one in her class. Then she was accepted to med school. Once again, she graduated early and at the top of her class. The only person from her family who had attended her graduation was Ethan. Dr. Brenner, Dr. Chiglo, and Mr. Stanford had also attended. What did it say that the strangers who saved her were more vested in her life than her own parents?

Ten minutes passed before Kara saw her much more modest home come into view. Sure, she could have bought something more impressive, but that wasn't what Kara was about. She was momentarily startled to see a car in her driveway but quickly relaxed when she realized it was the realtor who had helped her find the house. She had only seen a picture of him online, so she had not recognized him at first when he climbed out of his flashy car.

"Miss Vanderbilt, I presume? It's so good to finally meet you," he said, approaching her with his hand outstretched.

"You must be Mr. Abfall. You can call me Kara." She shook his hand, trying not to flinch at the contact. After all these years, she still had a hard time allowing a man to touch her without wanting to shy away from the contact.

"All right, then you can call me Marshall. I think you will find this house is as beautiful as the pictures show. Here are your keys."

"Thank you. It's hard to believe that I finally own my first home. After all these years of renting, it's nice." Kara hoped that she didn't sound as awkward as she felt.

She was just making polite conversation and hoping he would leave. It was hard not to notice how he had looked her up and down when she got out of the car. She assumed it was curiosity. Of course, it could have been that he was checking her out for more physical reasons, personal ladder climbing reasons, maybe, but not physical. After their first conversation, he had asked if she was any relation to Stanley Vanderbilt. She wanted to deny the lineage, but she knew it was pointless to deny he was her father. And judging by his appearance and his vehicle, he was materialistic and flashy and someone who liked to "network" to get ahead.

"I remember those days. Well, here are your keys. Are you interested in going out for a celebratory bite of lunch?"

"That is very kind of you to ask. But I just drove a long way and would like to settle in. Maybe some other time."

She hoped that she didn't sound rude, but she really wasn't up for lunch with someone like him. It was clear to her that he thought he was something special and she wasn't interested in men like that. *Be honest with yourself, Kara, you haven't been interested in any man in a long time. Because you choose not to date, because you can't get intimate.*

Judging by his body language, she knew that he didn't take kindly to rejection. He nodded and held his hand out to shake hers one more time.

"Well, then, I'll be on my way," he said curtly and spun on his heel, climbed into his car, and peeled out of her driveway.

Temper, temper. It really was a strong reaction to a simple rejection to lunch. She shrugged her shoulders; obviously, he wasn't used to being rejected. She turned and walked up the sidewalk to her new house.

For the first time all day, she felt excited to be there—apprehensive, but excited. This was going to be a new chapter in her life. She had told Ethan when to expect her because she always had to have someone who knew where she was. Freedom to be spontaneous was not something she was at liberty to take for fear that something would happen and no one would know. However, she had not told Dr. Brenner or Dr. Chiglo when she was coming, and she had wanted to surprise Mr. Stanford at the assisted living home where he resided now. That was another draw to moving home, visiting the man whom she literally owed her life to. But she wasn't expecting any other visitors; she had no one else she was close enough here to invite over. And very few people back in Baltimore where she had gone to medical school, but she did have friends, all of which were women.

She had almost made it to the door when she remembered Samsonite. She had left him in the car so she wouldn't startle the realtor. Sam was a large dog and very intimidating. But now that Marshall Abfall had left, Sam should really be with her to see the house. He was her only real confidante, and he would also check it out to make sure it was indeed safe. It was important that Samsonite get a feel for the house and all the surrounding property. As she turned around to go get him, she collided with a brick wall, the force with which she ran into the solid wall of muscle was enough to cause her to fly backward and fall on her butt. The landing was not graceful and was painful enough to make her wince.

"Are you okay?" she heard a deep, male voice ask.

5

___

Kara looked up and then up some more. When she met his eyes, her breath caught in her throat. She was staring into the most beautiful, clear blue eyes she had ever seen. Deep blue like the sea, and at first glance they seemed open and honest. Even so, Kara was trained to be hesitant around almost everyone she met. Therefore, when he reached to help her up, but before he could get close to touching her, she had scrambled to her feet. She took an attack stance just in case he tried to approach her. She couldn't help but notice the laughter in his eyes. Which aggravated her further.

"I'm all right. Can I help you?" she stammered, her heart in her throat.

"I should have waited in the car, but E is on a private call, and I wanted to give him some space."

"E? Excuse me, who are you?" Other than the most attractive man she had ever laid eyes on. All 6' 4" of the tall, dark, and muscular man was hot as hell but also intimidating as hell. "And who the hell is E?" She looked him up and down, trying to figure out if he was a threat. Surprisingly enough, she found herself intrigued by what she saw. He really was the epitome of the romantic book cliché.

"Kara!" Came a booming voice from behind the tall, dark stranger.

"Leave my little sister alone, Montgomery! She's too good for the likes of you!"

CALEB WAS SLIGHTLY FRUSTRATED. Ethan had been just about to tell Caleb why he had gotten so agitated at the crime scene and why he had insisted they go see his sister right away when his cell phone had started ringing.

Caleb quietly got out of the car, deciding that Ethan would prefer the privacy as he argued with his latest girlfriend. Not that she was really a girlfriend, it hadn't gotten to that point yet, and Caleb suspected that it wasn't going to. It was hard to call someone your girlfriend when you had a hard time keeping your second date with them. And in their line of work, it was hard to get to a second date. It wasn't getting there that was the hard part; it was keeping the date and not having to cancel it. While a lot of people romanticize police, it's harder to want to be part of the lifestyle.

So, at that moment, Ethan was cancelling a date. Which wasn't going over well. He had to give the lady credit, though; she had tried to be understanding. But this was the fourth time they had gotten called out on a homicide case, and Ethan had had to cancel their plans. Of course, in Caleb's opinion, Ethan didn't try all that hard to make the dates work out. Ethan usually picked times when he knew he would get busy; it was his way of dodging a serious relationship. Caleb suspected that Ethan's parents had done a number on him when it came to relationships.

Therefore, Ethan had parked a little down the block so he could finish his conversation before he got out to see his sister. Not interested in hearing the nitty gritty details, and knowing he would want space if the roles were reversed, Caleb had decided he should give Ethan some space, so he climbed out of the car and had been slowly walking up the sidewalk when he saw a tiny little knockout that was having a conversation with a man that Caleb didn't like the looks of. The jerk appeared to think he was something spectacular.

The situation became interesting when the woman said something to upset the man, and he tore out of her driveway. Caleb decided to check out the situation to see if everything was all right and to get a closer look at the tiny little woman standing watching the man peel away.

He was walking up the front walk and was right behind her, when she paused and turned, running smack into him, then promptly falling to the ground. Before he could react, she was up and ready to attack— which he found mildly entertaining. She looked as if she were ready to battle when she demanded to know who he was. He didn't have a chance to answer when Ethan's voice boomed behind him.

"Kara! Leave my little sister alone, Montgomery! She's too good for the likes of you!"

Little sister? So, this was the famous baby sister that Ethan talked about with such pride, but was secretive about. Her face lit up with a smile that didn't quite reach her eyes, but transformed her face from beautiful to stunning. He wondered what made her look so sad.

"Ethan, I missed you! I can't believe I didn't realize E was you."

"For such a smart girl..."

"...I'm pretty dumb," she finished, laughing at what was clearly an inside joke. And, boy, what a laugh. It was deep and throaty and sent a spike of warmth through him, which landed square in the groin.

"You go in yet?"

"No, I was just about to, and then I realized I had forgotten about Sam."

Caleb stood quietly to the side, assessing the situation. He knew Ethan hadn't seen his sister in a long time and was thrilled to see her. But Caleb could see that there was a lot of tension in Ethan's shoulders over whatever he had to tell her. Caleb could also see that Ethan's petite knockout of a sister could sense something bad was about to happen.

Ethan had always been very protective of his little sister, and while Caleb had seen pictures, it was obvious the picture Ethan had on his desk was quite old. This was not the little sister Ethan talked about; this was a full-grown, beautiful woman who would make any man drool. And he couldn't help but be jealous of the man named Sam.

"Care to give your big brother a tour?"

"Don't even bother pretending you came here for a tour. What's wrong?"

"Why don't we go inside?"

"Sure, but only if you wait just one second. I'll be right back, and then you can introduce me to your friend here," she said over her shoulder as she walked toward her car.

The woman had an incredible body and curves that wouldn't quit, even though she could not be more than five feet two. Her dark hair swept her shoulders, and her eyes were green, almost like a cat. She opened her car door and out lumbered a huge, furry beast of a dog. Her dog was at attention the minute his feet hit the ground, and it was clear that he wasn't just a companion, but a full-fledged protector, as well. Caleb knew a guard dog when he saw one. Which begged the question why this spitfire needed one. In Caleb's mind, the guard dog, along with the sad eyes and overprotective brother, added up to Kara being a victim of some crime.

"Is this the Sam I've heard so much about?" Ethan asked.

"The one and only. Now, will you please introduce your friend?"

Okay, Sam was a dog. If Caleb would have been paying attention to anything other than her, he would have noticed no one was sitting in her car, except the behemoth of a dog. Caleb wasn't sure which emotion he was supposed to feel, but relief over Sam being a dog was not the one he was expecting. He knew he had to tamp down the obvious attraction he was feeling for his partner's sister and in a hurry. Being interested in your partner and best friend's sister, one that he was overly protective of, was not a good idea. Especially if she was a victim of a violent crime. A person like that couldn't be a fling. Someone like that would need to be able to trust whomever they became involved with.

"This is my partner, Detective Caleb Montgomery. Caleb, this is my little sister, Kara."

"Nice to meet you. But I'm not so little anymore. I am quite afraid that Ethan seems to have forgotten that I'm not ten anymore. But that happens when you rarely see each other."

"The road goes both ways, Kara," he said softly.

"I know. I just...you know how I feel about being back here."

"Then why did you come?" he asked testily.

"It was time."

"I saw a car pulling away when we got here, who was it?" Caleb blurted out, intending to change the subject that had become private. Normally, he was much more charismatic than that, and he realized too late that this question was private, and that it came off sounding borderline jealous.

"That was the realtor."

"He seemed upset; any reason?" Caleb asked.

Where in the hell had that come from? First, he asks who the guy was, and now he asks why he was upset? He regretted it as soon as Ethan looked at him with a warning look, but Kara's eyes seemed intrigued by the question. Which meant, what? That she found him as attractive as he found her? Would it matter if she did?

She shrugged her shoulders.

"I'm not really sure. He asked if I wanted to go out for a celebratory lunch because this is my first home. But I told him I wanted to settle in and relax a little. I drove a long way. I would like to unpack and maybe stop by my new work."

"An attractive man asks you out, and you turned him down? No wonder he tore off. It's damaging to a male's ego to be shot down. And judging by the way the car peeled out of here, he was not pleased," Ethan stated.

Caleb couldn't help but notice that Ethan sounded a little relieved that she had turned the realtor down. This peaked Caleb's interest. Ethan always gave the impression that no one was good enough for his little sister. He understood that feeling; he felt the same way himself about his sister. But this was a little over-the-top in enthusiasm. Maybe he was happy because he had gotten the same first impression—that Mr. BMW was too absorbed in himself to take care of a woman the way she needed to be taken care of.

"I'm sure he just was trying to be polite. Why would a guy like that ask me out? Other than to get close to Father, and that wouldn't work, would it?" she answered, sounding very annoyed.

"And I guess there is just no way that he was interested in you because he finds you attractive?" he asked cautiously.

"I doubt it. There was something you came here to tell me, so enough beating around the bush and tell me already."

"Let's go inside first."

"Fine. I will warn you, though, the place is probably a mess, and the movers got here this morning and dropped everything off."

The three of them walked to the entrance in silence, both men waiting patiently as Kara unlocked the door. With a subtle motion that most would have missed, Kara signaled for Sam to go in ahead of them. Kara took a few cautious steps into the house and waited patiently until Sam returned, apparently given the all clear sign.

"Good boy, Sam," she said, rubbing his ears. "All right, boys, spill it. Why are you here?"

"Why don't we sit down?" Ethan asked. Caleb noted it was more of a demand than a suggestion. With a roll of her eyes, Kara moved to the living room and motioned to the sofa and loveseat.

"Have at it. I, however, would prefer to stand. I have been sitting in my car for long enough, and my body is..." she paused, "...not able to sit still like that without it wreaking havoc on me. Now, enough with the cat and mouse game, damn it."

"Fine, be stubborn. A body was discovered in the river this morning. A young woman, twenty years old. She appears to have been raped and murdered." Ethan winced after the words came out of his mouth, clearly regretting the way he delivered them.

"And you're telling me this because...?"

"What I am about to say is confidential. Meaning it does not leave these walls."

Rolling her eyes, she responded, "I know what confidential means."

"The woman found was Senator Vincent's daughter." Caleb was surprised that Ethan would disclose that to his sister, but he went with the flow.

"I'm very sorry for their loss, but I'm still waiting to see why you're telling me this," Kara said, her calm demeanor betrayed by the subtle tremor in her voice.

Caleb noted that while Kara was trying to sound tough, the mere mention of this woman being found had shaken her to the core. The question was, why?

"Kara, you know why I'm telling you." This time Ethan spoke as if talking to a frightened child. Pausing, he sucked in a deep breath before he continued. "There are some similarities."

"Similarities?" Caleb noticed her face drain of color, and he suspected she was merely trying to delay what Ethan was about to say, and that she, in fact, knew what similarities he was talking about. Even if Caleb didn't have a clue what was going on.

"I know you never intended for me to find out about it, but I need to talk to you about the marks on your left buttock."

"H-how did you know about those?"

"Before you woke up, I heard the doctors telling Mother and Father about your injuries," Ethan said calmly.

"Why are you asking me about this?" Kara's voice was a mere whisper. "What does that marking have to do with this victim?"

"Kara, the young woman had the same initials on her left buttock, but instead of DB II, the marking was DB XII."

6

Kara noticed a few things at the same time: the room felt suddenly too small, the men standing by her suddenly seemed very far away, and it felt like all the blood in her body had either rushed to or away from her head. She had suspected Ethan had something horrible to tell her, but she wasn't expecting what had come out of his mouth. She began shaking her head back and forth, barely conscious of the hand that had softly taken her arm and led her to the couch.

"But that's not possible, it's just not possible. Why would they make that subtle change? Was it intentional or accidental?"

"At the time, they assumed it was Devon Bristol II. But it is clearly DB XII on this victim."

It was a battle to maintain control, but slowly her head cleared and her breathing returned to normal, and that was when she realized that the hand that had led her to the couch wasn't Ethan's, but rather, his partner. Kara carefully pulled her arm out of his grasp. She was surprised to find that she was okay with the contact. Her brother speaking grabbed her attention once again.

Sam sensed her distress and whimpered beside her. Needing the contact, she reached out to rub his head.

"Andrea Vincent. Don't refer to her as a victim." Regretting her tone, she took a deep breath. "I don't understand why there's an extra letter. But there has to be a reason."

"He's dead, he died. You told me that." She knew she sounded accusatory and unhinged as the words bubbled and flowed out of her mouth.

"He is dead."

"My God, Ethan, why would anyone copy that? And for what reason? It has to be a copycat, right? Everyone knows that Devon Bristol died. What could they possibly hope to accomplish by making it appear he's responsible for her murder?"

"Unless there's something we're missing, something that was never disclosed that whoever did this wants us to find out. Perhaps a partner or someone who wants revenge for his death?"

"Then this is not the beginning." Kara swallowed and tried to calm herself. "If I had an inkling that I would have been coming home to witness it all again, I would have stayed away. But it's too late now, and what I have tried to put behind me for the last ten years is about to blow up in my face."

"Or it could be a coincidence," Ethan said. Kara knew he was grasping at straws, trying to find a way to calm her.

"You once told me that there are no coincidences," Kara said, her voice devoid of all emotion. "Why would this be any different?"

"I think we should just take this one step at a time. You both are going to have to fill me in on a few details," Caleb said.

Kara knew the look she gave him was one of complete disbelief. She had never met someone who hadn't heard of her abduction, so surely, she was misunderstanding him when he asked to be filled in. Perhaps he meant he needed to know intimate details, which was not going to happen.

"I'm not going to go into details about that summer. I spent a long time trying to forget about that, and I am not going to go into it, at least not here and not right now."

"You have to give me more than that or I can't help you out. What happened ten summers ago?"

"You're not serious, right? Tell me he is not serious." Kara looked to her brother, clearly shocked.

"Kara, Caleb isn't from around here. I can fill him in if you want," Ethan said quietly.

"No, I can tell him. Ten summers ago, I was abducted and held for ransom for four days. Unfortunately for me, the man who abducted me used those four days to the fullest extent. Also, unfortunate for me, is that he died after I escaped."

"Why would his death be unfortunate?" Ethan asked slowly.

"Because it wasn't by my hands," she said coldly.

Kara knew that her voice sounded cold and devoid of human emotion, but it was the only way she could handle speaking about what had happened to her. Judging by the look on both men's faces, they recognized her behavior as very superficial and weren't buying for one second that it didn't still affect her very profoundly.

"So, ten summers ago, Devon Bristol abducted you and did some things you rather not mention. You got away, he died, and now ten years later, a young woman washes up, dead, with eerie similarities to your abduction. And I am going to guess that the initials were presumably not released to the public. Does that about sum it up?" Caleb asked, sounding matter-of-fact, but also as though he empathized, which was important. Kara hated the looks of pity she got.

"That about sums it up. I buried those demons a long time ago. Or, so I thought," she said, lying through her teeth.

"Sure, you did," Ethan said quietly.

"Believe what you will."

"All right, for now, we need to react offensively. This may be nothing more than someone playing a sick joke on the ten-year anniversary of your abduction. I would think they could get a lot of information about it online," Caleb said.

"There are a number of sites that have information on it." She paused, and a thought dawned on her. As she was putting the pieces together, she could feel her face get pale.

"What is it? Did you think of something?" Ethan asked, his voice laced with worry.

"She went missing on the twenty-fourth? After leaving a small get-together around ten o'clock, she had left early because she had to be up early for class, right?" The details of the news broadcast she had heard and turned off on her ride suddenly clicking into place.

"Yes," Caleb answered.

"And she was found today? When did she die? Have they determined that yet?"

Caleb looked at Ethan as if he wasn't sure if he should answer her, and after a silent nod from Ethan, he told her the estimated time of death.

"They figured she died within the last twelve hours."

Sinking to the couch, she sucked in a deep breath and put her head in her hands. Counting to ten and taking a breath with each number, she calmed herself enough to explain her line of questioning. Though she knew Ethan was already doing the math.

"I went missing on May twenty-fourth at about ten o'clock. Same time as the senator's daughter. And I escaped on the twenty-eighth at ten o'clock, exactly four days later. Add twelve hours to that, and you have ten o'clock this morning. So, she was killed at the hour I escaped. And was found with the same initials that I have on my buttock or damn close. Are the initials a mistake, the X an error?" Kara was shaking badly. "The only way it could have been planned better would be if she would have been found at the time I was found."

"Shit!" Ethan said. "The motherfucker is copying it down to the last detail, but how could he know?"

"Like Caleb said, you can get a lot on the internet these days. Some sites are more factual than others, and some are just speculation. But most of the details are out there."

"But the markings are limited knowledge," he said.

"Oh, really?" she asked sarcastically.

"Well, other than Mr. Stanford, the doctors and nurses and cops. Our parents and I are the only other ones that know about them."

"And you believe for one second that none of them would leak that for some cash? I know it was not released to the public, but that doesn't mean that the public didn't find out. Believe me, I have toured some of the murder sites that glorify that asshole, and the initials are out there."

He opened his mouth, and clearly struggling, he closed it and then opened it again.

"That detail was classified; they were all told to not say anything."

"Right, well somebody did because there certainly are a lot of pictures of it online," she said.

"What?" Ethan roared. "Some sick son of a bitch took a picture of that and put it online?"

That really caught their attention. She didn't want to divulge how she knew the pictures were online, that someone had actually e-mailed her the link, and that the link was the reason she had discovered all those murder sites. That someone over the years had made it personal to taunt her. If she hadn't known Devon was dead, she would have thought it was him. Sometimes she did think it was him, haunting her from the grave.

They also didn't need to know that the reason she had come home was because it was time to exorcise her demons, once and for all. Sure, she was pretending she had already done that, but she had never left that summer ten years ago. So, she had moved home to find answers to a lot of questions she had. But for now, it was in her best interest to let both men think she had overcome all that. That she wasn't here for revenge against those who never saw justice. And over the years, she had realized there were more involved with the days before and after her kidnapping than even she had known. Realizing she had checked out of the conversation, she tried to focus.

"All right, so we have some serious similarities here. What do we want to do about it?"

"Kara, damn it, you know changing the subject isn't going to cut it with me, right? I can google those pictures without your help."

"But you won't. All you need to know is that they were nice and bloody and they showed the initials perfectly."

Ethan was steaming. Kara could see that, but she couldn't let herself care. She was about to say something when Ethan's eyes widened and he looked at her with questions in his eyes.

"What do you mean bloody?"

"Have you gone insane?" Kara frowned at him.

"Damn it, answer me, what do you mean by bloody? Describe it."

"I'm not sure I'm following you."

He pinched the bridge of his nose. She looked at Caleb for help, but he could only shrug, equally confused by the line of questioning.

"I mean, was the picture of a fresh wound or a healed-over and scabbed wound?"

"Fresh. But why does that...?" It was her turn for her eyes to widen. "Oh my God, Ethan, the picture was of a fresh wound. Are you telling me that it wasn't fresh when I was found?"

"No. It had begun to heal over, and the scab had already formed. Montgomery, I know you might not like this, but for now, I would prefer not mentioning the connection to Kara. If someone else figures it out, fine. But for now, and until we know for sure there is a connection, I think we work as status quo. Are you okay with that?"

"I have your back, bro. And if they get wind of it before we're ready to let them know, we can just plead the fifth. Kara never filled you in on the markings. But I hope you know if another girl goes missing..." Caleb said.

"We will say something right away. For now, it might just be some sicko who saw the pictures online."

Kara was surprised at how quickly he was willing to cover Ethan's back. She knew in that instant that he was a man she could trust. Both men were willing to put their careers on the line to keep her name out of the mix until necessary.

"You know you don't have to do that," Kara said weakly, knowing that both men could pick through her words and hear the appreciation.

"As far as I'm concerned, we didn't have this conversation until we know more," Caleb said.

"Thanks, Caleb," Ethan responded.

"You had my back once; now I have yours."

"Unfortunately, we have to go, Kara. We left in a hurry, and if we don't get back to the crime scene soon, we will be missed."

"I understand. Once I get everything unpacked, you should come over for supper." Ethan wrinkled his nose at the invitation. "You might be surprised; I'm getting pretty good at cooking. So, I would appreciate you coming with an open mind. Both of you. I would like to get to know the man who has my brother's back, under friendlier circumstances."

"I would like that."

"Even under these circumstances, it was nice meeting you, Detective Montgomery."

"You can call me Caleb. And the pleasure was all mine."

It suddenly got very quiet; Kara realized she was staring at her feet. Taking a deep breath, she looked up and into the eyes of the man that had literally knocked her on her ass—the most handsome man she had ever met. The fact that she could even think about the way she was attracted to him was amazing, considering what she had just been told. It showed that she had come much further than she thought she had. Her stomach did a cartwheel when she realized he was as intrigued by her as she was by him. Which both scared and excited her. Kara jumped when Ethan cleared his throat.

"Here is my new cell number for work. Call me at any time if you need to get a hold of me," Ethan said.

"I will."

As they turned to leave, Caleb paused and looked her in the eye, long and hard.

"Don't just say you will. If you get scared or something feels off, call. Until we figure out what's going on, you need to watch your back. And here's my number, in case you can't reach Ethan."

A bad feeling enveloped her, and as they turned to leave, she stopped them. It wasn't rational, but she just knew this wasn't the only victim.

"We all always assumed the II was for Devon Bristol the second," she said quietly.

"What was that?" Caleb asked.

"What if the II is a Roman numeral and the XII is as well, that the X isn't a mistake by a sloppy copycat. Can you both do me a favor? Can you check around? I have this bad feeling, call it intuition, that this person has been copying my abduction for a while. My guess is, if you look around throughout the states, you'll find other abductions."

"Kara, as high profile as your abduction and this one is, don't you think we would have heard if any similar cases had happened in the last ten years?" Ethan asked.

"Not necessarily, not if the killer picked less 'important' victims, homeless teens, et cetera, just to satisfy his thirst. Not to mention, some of them might not have been found. Or perhaps they weren't found before the similarities like the initials decomposed." She involuntarily shivered at the thought.

"She might be right," Caleb said. "It's worth considering." And with that statement and a quick hug from Ethan, they left.

Once they were gone, Kara was jumping out of her skin with fear, but she also couldn't help but feel disappointed. She'd spent too much time alone in the last ten years and was starting to get tired of it. Her life had been stagnant for far too long. She had been swimming through a wasteland, and it was time to move on. Time to live.

So, they finally found the body. About time. He had hoped it wouldn't have taken so long, that it would have been truer to the actual timetable. Oh well, couldn't be helped; he had to do it the way he did. It wasn't like he could have really dropped her off at that time of night; the chances would have been much higher that he would have been seen. There was no way he wanted to show his hand too soon; after all, he'd left enough breadcrumbs on this victim. Surely this time they would notice? He had wanted to do things differently, and not be too obvious, but in the end, he figured it was best this way, and in the long run, it worked out perfectly. With sweet Kara Vanderbilt back home, he couldn't have planned it better himself. It was a pleasant surprise when he found out she was coming home, finally, after all these years. Although, it wasn't like he hadn't spied on her the whole time she was gone.

As private as the Vanderbilts were, he knew they'd not be going to the press with the similarities between the two cases; that is, of course, if they even realized there were similarities. Let's face it, the only smart one in the bunch was Kara. Ethan was clever, but nothing compared to his sister, and she certainly proved over the years that she didn't want to relive those days. He certainly liked messing with her. He had thought she was smart, but not smart enough to tell the authorities about his taunting her.

Of course, who would believe her? He was just as smart as her and had covered his tracks well. No one would believe her story anyway; he had made sure of it. Maybe she was smart for not saying something? That way she could go on in her world of false pretenses, that she had moved on from that summer. After all, if she had gone to the authorities with the emails, they would have treated her nicely and laughed behind her back. The man who abducted her had been killed. How could he possibly be taunting her from his grave? This was going to be so much fun, resurrecting the ghost from her past.

He laughed at how quickly Detective Vanderbilt had run to Kara's side. So that must mean he saw the markings on her all those years ago. It wasn't like they were kept the secret their parents had wanted. Nope, everyone who could use Google would know all about those initials, another thing she could thank him for. But he still hadn't expected the brother to know about them; he was kept out of the loop throughout the whole investigation ten years ago. And he wasn't the type to go on the websites that he had uploaded those pictures to.

No bother, because he knew the brother would keep his mouth shut, too. For now, at least. The Vanderbilts were built that way. But for him to make the connection, maybe Kara wasn't the only one who had gotten the brains in the family. The introduction of Detective Montgomery did present a problem, but only on a small scale. An interesting problem; it wasn't hard to see, even from his vantage point, that Detective Montgomery was interested in little Kara. Of course, she wasn't that little anymore; she had filled out in all the right spots. It would be hard for any man not to want a little action where that one was concerned.

He was sure they were trying to figure out the significance of the girl. He wasn't sure himself if there was any significance; he had only done what he was told to do, and he had a hell of a time doing it. Yep, little Andrea Vincent put up quite a fight. She wasn't his best, but she sure wasn't his worst. If he had to rank her, he'd say she came in at a distant second to his best conquest ever. One he could still taste, one he still dreamed of every night. Andrea hadn't broken as fast as some of the others, and none of them could hold a candle to Kara.

But all good things had to end; he had learned that the hard way in his life. And now he didn't wait for good things to happen, he took good things any way he could. Life was short, and he was damned sure he would live it the way he wanted, even if he had to play the game for a little while longer. And who said he couldn't have a little fun in the meantime? No one, because, in the end, he made the rules. They just didn't know it yet.

7

Kara wasn't sure what she'd been thinking inviting her brother's partner over for supper. At least she had made sure to invite her brother, too. It was completely out of character for her to be so forward. To be honest, she had never asked anyone other than Ethan over to her place in Baltimore. Her home was her sanctuary. But this was her brother's partner, so it was expected for her to be cordial, right? Who was she kidding? If she were being honest with herself, she would admit that she didn't invite him over to be cordial; she invited him over because she wanted to get to know him better, plain and simple. For a woman who didn't trust easily, she found it incredibly easy to trust Detective Caleb Montgomery.

Obviously, his relationship with Ethan helped score him points in her mind. But there was something else, a kindness that was predominantly featured in his eyes. And what an amazing pair of crystal clear and honest eyes. Eyes that had showed, what? That he was interested in her?

Kara found herself dismissing the thought as foolish; a man that looked like him would not be interested in someone like her. Especially someone who had gone through what she had, someone who'd been tarnished. Even so, Kara thought she had seen something in his eyes when they'd locked with hers right before they left. Something completely foreign to her, but if she had to describe it with one word, the word would be what? Curious? Obviously, he was curious about her background only. Sighing, she decided she needed to clear her head, so she decided there was no time like the present to unpack.

The next several hours flew by as boxes were emptied one after another. Kara had made sure to have the movers come ahead so she wouldn't have to be alone with them in the house. It had taken a lot out of her to be alone with them at her old apartment, and the only reason she had managed was because it was an apartment building, and she had told herself people would hear if something went wrong.

Arranging for the realtor to meet the movers had been slightly irritating; Mr. Abfall had been hesitant to let them in until she had expressed her discontent at his attitude. Finally, he had relented but insisted on waiting for her to give her the keys. Kara had tried to convince him to let her meet him at his office, but he had insisted on meeting her at the house, his excuse being that he wanted to see her reaction to the house, but she suspected he had more nefarious reasons. Like wanting to meet the freak that had been abducted so he could tell his friends a good story. As the sun set, Kara quietly looked at the clock and counted the hours until the alarm company came to install her new state-of-the-art alarm system. That was the one thing she couldn't get done ahead of her arriving.

At least she had Samsonite there to protect her. Even so, she would be on edge all night, and he would not leave her side for a second unless she instructed him to do so. The whole while she unpacked, he lay lazily in whatever room she was in. He was so incredibly well trained that the smallest of motions or the most innocuous of words, he was at her side ready to protect her. She would forever be grateful to the amazing Judy Trippilo for training Sam and her. Just having him there put her at ease and made this easier than she had expected. She was calm enough that she found herself enjoying unpacking and arranging everything just so.

As she unpacked the last item from the last box, she glanced at her clock again and was surprised at the time. Her intention had been to make an appearance at her work, but even if hospitals were open around the clock, it was far too late to visit now. It was just as well. She needed to regroup before she showed up. Prepare herself for the whispering that was sure to happen. Suddenly, she felt very weary and decided she might be tired enough to sleep, which would be out of character for her.

Kara climbed into bed with Samsonite right behind her to warm her feet, and it only took a few minutes before she fell asleep. And it only took a few minutes for the same nightmare to come. The nightmare that had haunted her for ten years. The details sometimes varied, but it always ensured that she never got more than a few hours of sleep a night.

Kara was bound, and the ropes were tight around her wrists and ankles as she bounced down the old dirt road. Sweat dripped into her eyes, and she blinked to clear them and suddenly she was in an old relic of a cabin. In the center of the room was a bed fit for a princess that had a table adjacent to it full of scalpels, flogs, whips, paddles, and other instruments of torture. She blinked again and found herself naked, bound to the bed in the center of the room. A shadow was in the corner. It was him. He was there; he was always there. She trembled with fear and pulled at her restraints. The shadow moved out of the corner toward her.

Slowly, the features of the shadow came into view, and he was smiling, walking toward her with a scalpel, eyes pinpoints of evil, teeth gleaming. Eyes that were dead, devoid of emotion. No lights on at home. She squirmed, trying to get away from those eyes. The eyes terrified her more than the scalpel. Suddenly, his teeth elongated, and his nails turned into razors. Another slow blink and he leapt at her. She screamed and screamed until his hands were around her throat and she couldn't scream anymore.

Kara woke up startled, struggling for breath. *Block it out*, she told herself, but it was too hard. Too hard to block out everything. There were times when she had prayed someone would find her and times when she had prayed for death. Dark times—times in which she had lost herself and was not sure she would ever find herself again. Evil, vengeful times where she knew, given the opportunity, she would kill. And most nights, all those memories would come flooding back, crushing her in her sleep.

Sometimes, the monster that had abducted her didn't want to rape her; sometimes, he just wanted to torture her. And torture her, he did. He would beat her, bring her outside in the dead of night when it was cold and dump buckets of ice cold water on her, or worse, bring her outside in the heat and cut her to attract bugs.

Then there was the strangle game; he liked to choke her while he had sex with her, and he would choke her until she passed out. She would fight it, which would get him more excited, and then, slowly, she would accept it, hoping that she would die this time, hoping she wouldn't wake up, that it would be over this time for good. Only to come to again with him still on her, ready for round two.

And the choking game started all over again. She would fight again, while her lungs burned, kicking and bucking with all her strength until the black took over. Until he won, and he always won. And when she would come to, he was sometimes different.

Sometimes, he looked almost as if he cared, but he was distant and not there; other times, he was pure evil. When he was evil, he was so evil, it terrified her. When she would come to, she would find herself hoping for the distant version of her captor. When it was that version, she knew it would be another round of rape, but nothing more.

When she woke to find pure evil looking at her, it was a different story. The only question was which one he would be, and tonight, in this dream, he was the purest evil. Tonight, she dreamed of the strangle game.

Kara was trying to calm her ragged breathing, counting to ten repeatedly. Just when she had finally calmed down, she heard a noise that made her blood turn ice cold. A window had shattered downstairs. Quickly, she gave Samsonite the command to put him on alert and reached for her phone. She hit the number she had programmed into her speed dial that evening. The phone rang several times, and the whole time she repeated over and over in her mind, *please pick up, please pick up*. Finally, on the sixth ring, someone answered.

CALEB WAS SITTING at his desk, waiting for Ethan to come out of their boss's office. He had been in there longer than Caleb had expected it to take. They should have called Kara to explain that the situation had changed. Even though they'd told her only a few hours ago that they would keep her out of the investigation, they could no longer promise that.

Which fucking sucked. Caleb had no desire to involve Kara more than she already was. He had been beyond impressed with her, but, at the same time, he knew that she was still fighting the past. How could she not be? While he didn't know the nitty gritty details, he knew what she went through was beyond horrific. Lost in his thoughts, he nearly jumped when his phone rang. Glancing at the readout, he recognized the number Ethan had given him to program into his phone. It was Kara.

"Montgomery, here."

"Detective Montgomery, is my brother there?"

"He's in a meeting, but I can get him."

"Can you just tell him that I think someone is in my house?"

"Are you sure?"

"Damn sure, please believe me. I-I heard a window break downstairs." Her voice sounded desperate.

"I believe you. Ethan! It's Kara; she thinks someone is in her house."

Ethan tore out of their captain's office, and without skipping a beat, grabbed his jacket as he flew past his desk.

"Please hurry." Her anguished whisper tore at his heart.

"We're coming." He could hear her breath becoming labored, and it was clear she was beginning to panic. "Can you go to a safe place without being heard? Like a closet?"

"Sure."

"Good, just stay very quiet. All right? Bring Sam with you wherever you decide to hide."

"Please don't hang up."

"I won't, just stay as quiet as possible. If someone is in the house, we don't want them to know you called someone or your location in the house. Ethan and I are on our way; we should be there in less than five minutes."

"Why did you answer?" she whispered. He could hear rustling and breathed a sigh of relief that she had listened to his advice and hidden, most likely in her closet. For some reason, he had been worried that she would try to take on the intruder. Hopefully, her big barrel of a dog was snuggled in next to her, on full alert if anyone should come near her.

"Shh, be very quiet. I answered because Ethan was having an important conversation with the captain, and you called my cell phone."

They were coming in hot with sirens and lights.

"You should be able to hear our sirens; we're less than a block away. We can see your house. Stay on the phone with me, and do not move from your hiding place until I tell you otherwise." They skidded to a stop in front of her house, and he was out and running before Ethan had put the car in park. "We're walking up the sidewalk, all right? Are you still there?"

"Yes."

"Stay where you are until we give you the all clear."

KARA MET them at the door. She reached for the door, startled to find it open and unlocked. When she pulled it open farther, she almost hit the floor when she met the two men with guns drawn. Samsonite was at her side on full alert; a low and menacing growl emanated from him and was aimed at the aggressive stance of the two men.

"What the hell, Kara? I told you to wait until we gave the all clear," Caleb angrily spat out.

"I got antsy, and Samsonite was with me."

"She can take care of herself, but having said that, you should have waited like he said," Ethan stated. "Caleb, why don't you check the inside, and I'll check the perimeter."

"The door was open when I came down here."

"We noticed. The window pan in the door was broken, and they were able to get their arm in and unlock it. Don't touch anything," Caleb said. "Stay here while I check all the rooms. And listen to me this time," Caleb reprimanded, his voice showing that he meant business if she disobeyed.

Well, he can stuff it. She had taken care of herself for ten long years. In all honesty, she wasn't sure why she called them. Two days ago, she would have called a locksmith and dealt with the intrusion on her own. Home for one day and already she was relying heavily on two men that meant well and were ready to take care of business where she was concerned. She would deny it if someone asked, but she was secretly grateful for their overprotectiveness and for their proximity.

Of course, two days ago there wasn't a murder weighing on her conscience. Not just a murder, but one that had scary similarities to her own abduction and narrow escape of death. The only difference—and it was a huge one—was this girl hadn't been so lucky. The question was, what did it all mean? Was it a message to her, or was it a mere coincidence? She didn't believe in coincidences. She believed in well-thought-out plans.

"Everything is clear here. Unless whoever broke in unpacked all your boxes, it looks like everything is where it should be."

Kara jumped at the sound of Caleb behind her; clearly, she wasn't as calm as she thought she had been. Slowly, she turned and looked at him, her face flushed from the male magnetism that he threw off. An unfamiliar sensation began to spread through her—a sensation she couldn't exactly define at first, but then she suddenly realized what it was. Her body was reacting to the sight of Caleb, chest puffed out, gun drawn. But she wasn't scared. She was attracted to him.

8

Kara couldn't even be embarrassed at the mention of all the boxes being unpacked, even though she found it all too revealing because she was too busy being embarrassed by her reaction to him. It made her feel naked like he could see into her. Could he see the way she was reacting to him? Did he see that she was unpacked because everything had to be in order? Because she would rather stay up than sleep and have horrible nightmares. Unwilling to analyze her reaction to him, she opted to focus on his statement.

"About that; I was just too excited about the new house, found myself having a hard time falling asleep. First house and all, I wanted it to look just right. Not to mention I have to report to work soon, so I wanted to be settled in." She rambled on and on, wanting to stop, but not being able to.

Kara found her lie sounded transparent and knew he could see right through it, but she was infinitely grateful he didn't let on. He merely nodded in quiet acceptance of her lie, signaling that he knew if she wanted to discuss anything further, she would on her own time.

She wasn't sure why she had felt the need to lie. So what if she never got more than two hours sleep a night? There were a lot of people like her. Although, most people didn't develop insomnia the way she had. Not many people found it hard to sleep because they were scared when they woke up they would be tied to a bed in a dilapidated cabin.

"Ethan come back yet?"

"No, not yet. Do you think I scared whoever it was off?"

"Not sure, maybe. Maybe they heard the sirens."

"Kind of strange how I have been home for less than twenty-four hours, and this happens. I researched this area very closely and chose it due to its low crime rate."

"And its proximity to the police station?" he asked knowingly.

"I am not embarrassed to say that was a factor in my choice, as well. And I may be a jumpy person, even a tad paranoid, but I find it awfully suspicious that this happened today."

"It could be a coincidence. The intruder might have been watching this house when it was vacant and knew you had moved in. Thought it would be an easy B&E since you showed up alone." Samsonite let out a small sigh. Caleb chuckled, and Kara found herself enveloped in the warmth of the sound. "I don't think Samsonite agrees with that theory. At least she had you with her. Feel better, tough guy?" he asked as he rubbed Samsonite's head.

"You are lucky I released him from the attack command, he would have ripped off your arm otherwise," she said quietly, mesmerized by the man rubbing the head of her treasured dog.

Ethan walked through the door looking grim. Kara's heart sank a little when she saw him. Judging by the look on his face, there was more to this break-in than met the eye. Kara felt weary again and decided she needed to sit down before she heard whatever her brother had to say. She wandered into the living room and sat on the couch, drawing her legs up and pulling a blanket over her to try to warm her from the sudden chill that had seized her body. Both men stayed in the entryway for a moment. She could hear them whispering and knew they were trying to figure out if she could handle what Ethan had discovered. Kara wasn't going to let them sugarcoat it for her.

"Would you two just get in here?" As she spoke the words, they had already made the short distance from her entryway to the living room. Samsonite climbed up on the couch next to her, successfully warming her and comforting her at the same time.

"I am not going to tiptoe around this," Ethan began.

"Well, that's refreshing," she said sarcastically.

"There are footprints all around outside; I found some pretty disturbing things, especially by your bedroom window. It appears whoever broke in had been waiting quite some time, most likely for you to fall asleep."

"What else?" she asked, even if she didn't want to hear the rest, she knew she had no choice but to hear it.

"It appears whoever was out there ..." He paused, obviously rethinking telling her.

"For God's sake, after everything I've been through, I'm sure I can handle it. Just tell me already."

"It appears that whoever was watching you made it a peep show. There is evidence of ejaculation on the side of your house."

Kara felt her stomach flip over; surely, she heard him wrong. But for the life of her, she couldn't think of how she would have heard the word wrong. She laid her head back against the couch and closed her eyes to steady herself. Someone had been watching her—someone who had masturbated while watching her unpack. Who would do that and why? Exhausted, that was what she was. Completely exhausted.

"You're sure?" she asked without lifting her head from the couch.

"Not a hundred percent, but it certainly looks like semen, and it's dark outside. I'll have to have someone analyze a sample to make sure. Are you okay with my asking the boys and girls at the lab to run it?" Ethan asked cautiously.

"Do what you have to do. I'm going to guess that whoever it is doesn't have their DNA in any database, but it's worth a try, right? And even if he isn't in the database, now we'll have a sample in case he comes back. To be honest, I'm getting tired playing the reclusive victim," she whispered, her eyes still pinched tightly shut, trying to block out everything just a little longer. "Guess it was dumb to not put some blinds up right away."

"You okay?" Caleb asked.

"Just peachy. I have been home for less than twenty-four hours, and I have regretted almost every second of that time. No offense to the both of you."

"None taken," Caleb said. "Do we want to run this through the station or do the analysis on what you found off the books?"

"No. Don't even suggest that; just do it by the book. I don't want either one of you losing your job trying to protect me. Not to mention that if he's connected to the recent murder, which I suspect he is, we'll have evidence."

"We wouldn't lose our jobs, but if that's what you want, then that's what we'll do," Ethan said. "I'll go call it in." He walked away to make the call, leaving Kara alone with Caleb.

"This whole situation is screwed up," she said after minutes of silence passed.

She was still sitting with her head on the couch and her eyes closed when she felt the weight of someone sitting down next to her; no small feat, considering Samsonite was taking up a large portion on the other side of the couch. He had his head resting on her shoulder and thumped his tail once to make sure she was fine with Caleb's proximity to her. She rubbed his head and opened her eyes and saw Caleb sitting, staring at her, concern evident on his face. She took a deep breath and braced herself for the cursory questions. When it appeared that he wasn't about to ask her anything, she found herself talking.

"Who do you think was out there? Just a peeping Tom, or am I right, and he's the one who killed Andrea Vincent?" she asked, hoping that she wasn't grasping at straws and it was a coincidence.

"I'm not going to lie to you, but I don't think this was a random occurrence. It would be too odd for that to happen on your first night back."

"Why do I keep coming back to the awful prospect that this is all connected to what happened ten years ago?"

"What *did* happen ten years ago? The real story, not the sanitized and G-rated version you tell your brother to spare him."

And there was the proverbial question, followed by the most on-target statement ever. Still, it didn't mean she had to go over what happened. Maybe if it became pertinent to the case, but not now, not tonight. She knew it was supposed to be part of the healing process to talk about it, but that was bullshit. In her mind, she needed to block it out as best as possible. And she didn't want this man to hear the details any more than she wanted Ethan to. She didn't want him to think any less of her, for some reason. She didn't want him to see her as the dirty and sullied woman that she saw when she looked in the mirror, and if she told him what had happened to her in detail, he would forever look at her as a victim, an image she had fought hard to rid herself of.

Although he probably already thought of her as a victim, he was doing a good job of looking at her as anything but. And really, the only thing she was getting off him was concern, not pity.

"What makes you think that's why I don't talk about it? Have you considered I don't talk about it because it's behind me?" Her voice sounded cold and detached, with her defenses fully up to protect herself.

"Actually, no. You know as well as I do that you haven't put whatever happened those four days behind you. No one could put it totally behind them. Sure, you go on, but you don't forget."

"Maybe I have."

"There is nothing wrong with talking to someone." He paused. "You had no control over what happened to you. No one on this planet would think less of you, and if they did, then that's their loss."

Kara couldn't hide the surprise on her face. He had nailed it, nailed what her mind had been stuck on. It was as if he had read her mind. But that didn't change anything; she just wasn't ready to tell details of that time in her life. She was pretty sure she would never be ready. She had tried to work through it, and she wanted to move on. She had even been contemplating seeing a therapist, but the little bit of Vanderbilt genes she *did* inherit were stubborn and proud.

Seemingly from nowhere, tears stung her eyes, and her throat burned from trying to hold them back. Brutally, she shoved those tears and the feel-bad-for-herself emotions down, back into the cellar they had been locked away in. She was disgusted with herself for appearing so weak. Fighting it with every inch of her being, she regained her composure. She had nothing to cry about. She was alive, she had made it out, and the person taunting her would not win.

"Yeah, well, easier said than done. You may think someone could hear all the details about what was done to me without looking at me differently. But that's just not possible." She took a deep breath. "How can you tell anyone, especially a man you might be interested in that you were raped repeatedly, that you were soiled, and not expect his opinion to change? No one worthwhile would want damaged goods."

"That's where you're wrong. If I was the one you were interested in, I would want to know what you went through because I would want to be there to support you, and it wouldn't change my opinion of you. What kind of person would that make me if I blamed you for something you didn't ask to happen to you?"

"Ah, victim blaming is common, though. I heard the whispers, had I led him on, maybe I should have dressed differently, behaved differently. Am I wrong to say that I'm damaged goods? Am I wrong to feel soiled? Am I wrong to say no man can look at me and see me as anything other than a victim?" she asked, suddenly feeling very emotional and damn if she wasn't feeling self-pity at that moment.

"You have no idea how wrong you are. First and foremost, you are not damaged. You shouldn't feel soiled, and most importantly, anyone worthwhile would want you no matter what happened, no matter where you came from. Anyone worthwhile couldn't possibly look at you as a victim if they truly wanted to be with you. Because it wouldn't matter. You are a package deal, and that's what matters. All of what happened made you who you are."

"Nice story. But I live this life, and every man I've ever dated has heard of what happened to me. They stick around a little bit hoping to...I don't know, maybe fix me, maybe hoping to get ahead because of my dad, and in some cases, to find out about what happened. But they all leave," she said sadly.

If she was being honest, there weren't a whole lot of men she had tried to date. She could count on one hand how many men she dated in ten years. And half of them didn't last past one date. Hell, she'd only tried to be intimate once since the abduction. Once. In the end, no man had ever been able to be there for her. No man had ever gotten her to open up at all or have her wanting to be normal, until this man. This man whom she had only met that day. His voice broke into her thoughts.

"That's because they couldn't separate what happened to you and who you are, and because they went into the relationship with the wrong goal in mind."

"Find me a man who could separate me from the victim."

"Me." Kara's eyes widened in shock. She had to have heard him wrong; she'd just met him. Maybe he meant that he could separate the two, but it didn't mean he was up to the challenge. She opened her mouth and closed it, opened it again, trying to find the words that wouldn't come. She was just about to ask him what he meant when Ethan walked back into the room.

"Dispatch is sending over a couple of uniforms to take your statement, and I called in a favor and asked Cathy to come out to collect the samples," he said, looking between the two of them. His eyes widened slightly, and then, as if sensing he had interrupted something, added, "I'm going to wait for them outside a minute." He stalked out of the room, and Kara could not help but think, *uh-oh.*

9

Caleb sat quietly, looking at the beautiful and brave woman sitting beside him on her couch. Had he just implied that he would be interested in exploring things with her? Yes, he had. And he knew that he meant it; he hadn't spent one minute after meeting her not thinking about her. She had infiltrated his innermost thoughts, and he wasn't sure how that had happened.

Like he didn't know how it happened. It had happened because he was intrigued as hell to get to know who this stubborn and private woman really was. Other than a knockout. Caleb knew there was a lot more to her than met the eye. Just from spending an hour with her, he could tell that she was extremely intelligent and so full of pride that she was exceptionally good at covering up how she really felt about what had happened to her.

It was not hard to figure out that she had never opened up to anyone about those four days, and that tonight was a first for her. Even if she had not gone into detail, she had offered up key information that helped to shed a little light on the woman who had been stunned into silence. She was terrified but would rather die than show it.

What she was terrified of was more complex. Was she terrified of opening up because people might look at her differently, or was she terrified of opening up because that meant she would have to face what happened? Because it was apparent that she had done a very good job at pretending she had moved on. He was guessing that it was a little bit of both columns. The silence suddenly became deafening, and he was just about to say something to ease the tension when her voice stopped him.

"What were you doing when I called?" Her voice was so quiet he could barely make out the words. He knew she was trying to change the subject, so he allowed the diversion.

It was okay if she wanted to pretend he hadn't showed interest and ask about him instead. Normally, he might give up, move on. Caleb had no problem with finding women to entertain him for short times. He did, however, find it hard finding a woman who was worth the effort for more than just a casual fling. And he had a feeling this woman was worth the effort. That she was worth taking his time over, building her trust. That it would be worth it to take his time in showing her how a real man would treat a woman like her.

When Kara cleared her throat gently, he looked at her and remembered she had asked him a question.

"We were meeting about the young woman we told you about earlier today. I had stepped out to grab Ethan's cell phone. He'd forgotten he took it out of his pocket and left it on his desk."

"But you said I called your phone?"

"You did. Our numbers are only a digit off."

"But I programmed both in; I must have hit the wrong speed dial number in my haste."

"Hearing someone breaking in could do that."

"That, and I had just woken up from a horrible nightmare, so I was still groggy from that."

He didn't ask what the nightmare was about; it was obvious what it would have been about. They sat in silence for a minute until she looked at him and breathed deeply as if deciding.

"Why were you still there?" She paused then looked at him closely. "Or were you called back because they found something else?"

He paused, knowing that he had discussed with Ethan what they should and shouldn't disclose to Kara. Both men were unsure of how much she could handle all at once. But he knew from the ten minutes he had just spent with her that she was much stronger than Ethan had given her credit for. Part of Ethan still thought of her as his broken little sister, and while she was still lost, to an extent, she was not broken. Although to give Ethan credit, he really did think she was strong, and he was so incredibly proud of her. He just wanted to shield her from the ugly in the world.

Unfortunately, there was too much ugly to shield her from. Because he would want to know as much information as possible if the roles were reversed, he decided he would fill her in, whether Ethan approved or not. In all honesty, she had a right to know what had been discovered.

"We were called back in; Ethan said if any new evidence was found to call us. There isn't an easy way to tell you, so I'm just going to spit it out. There was a note discovered that appears to connect the case to you. We hadn't wanted to involve you, but it became evident we were going to have to. Ethan was filling in our boss about your past, though he already knew most of it. I went to get his cell phone, and then you called."

"What did the note say?" she asked, her voice the same monotone from their visit earlier.

"Maybe I shouldn't tell you. Maybe this isn't a good idea after all," Caleb said, regretting bringing it up. Maybe in the light of the day she'd be able to handle it better. But she made up his mind for him about four seconds later.

"Just tell me, damn it. I think I deserve that. If it pertains to me, I deserve to know about it." Her voice was edged with a little bit of anger, but for the most part, she sounded completely prepared for him to drop a big bomb, and a big bomb he would drop.

"#12 wasn't as sweet until once again we meet." To her credit, she handled it much better than he had expected. Her face tensed ever so slightly, but that was it.

"So, I was right." It wasn't a question, and she sounded so sad that it broke his heart, like she was reserved to her fate. "This isn't the first one since me."

"It looks that way. Ethan was trying to convince our boss that you didn't need to be involved. But he's a smart man and had the same mindset I do; we shouldn't protect you from this because you need to know what's going on."

"I appreciate that. Ethan means well, but he still just sees me as this little girl who he should protect. Worse than that, he still sees me as the victim in that hospital bed. I can't blame him; if the roles were reversed, I would do everything to keep *him* safe. But he thinks that I can't handle anything on my own. He sees me as a fragile little girl who will break if anything challenges me."

"I'm not sure you're completely right on that one. He wants to protect you from anything bad happening again, but he knows that you can handle things and that you're extremely strong because of what you went through. But that doesn't stop him from wanting to lock you in a tower somewhere to protect you from anything else happening. I understand that feeling."

"Because you're a brother?"

"Yes, but also because I know that you're strong and brave. And I know that you would never admit any weaknesses or that you might need someone to lean on. I suspect that other than your brother, and a few others, you don't let people in. Although, I sense that you don't lean on anyone as much as you could. I also know that even though I just met you, I would do anything to stop you from ever being hurt again."

"That doesn't make sense to me. You think I'm strong and brave, but you don't think I can handle anything bad."

"No, I don't think you should ever *have* to handle anything bad again, and I don't want you to. I don't believe anyone should go through what you did, and since you've already seen more bad than any person should ever have to, you deserve to never be put through anything like that again. You should be allowed to move on and have the rest of your days be happy."

Silence ensued after his statement. Kara looked down at the floor and then took a deep breath before looking up at Caleb and locking eyes with him. He saw a resolve in her eyes, and it tugged at his gut. He wasn't sure what she had made her mind up to do, but he knew it was something big. He held his breath as she moved her face closer to him and delicately kissed him on the cheek. Just as slowly, she pulled away.

"Thank you."

"For what?" he asked, after taking a deep breath.

"For being honest with me. Maybe—" Ethan walked back into the room, cutting her off mid-sentence.

"Kara, this is Cathy Weaver. She's going to collect the samples we talked about."

Kara scrambled to her feet like she'd been caught doing something she shouldn't have and shakily held out her hand to the other woman. Caleb wanted to reach out to steady her, but he knew that would insult her. It was after midnight, and it was hard to believe that it was only yesterday that he had reached out to her, and she had allowed him to.

"It's nice to meet you," Kara said, sounding very genuine in her statement.

"Likewise, though it would be nice if it were under different circumstances. Well, I better get to it. The faster we get done here, the faster you can go back to bed."

"No worries there. I couldn't sleep if I wanted to. I don't sleep much anyway." She shrugged, embarrassed.

"I'll be right with you Cathy; I just want to talk to my sister privately," Ethan said pointedly.

"If it has anything to do with the note that was found, I already know. Don't get mad at him; he was only doing what he thought was best." Ethan nodded at Caleb, a silent thank you rather than an angry gesture. As he turned to leave with Cathy, Kara's hand reached out to stop him. He and Cathy turned to look at her.

"Ethan, thank you for believing in me enough to tell me about the evidence that was discovered."

"I have always believed in you. I just wanted to shield you from this whole mess." He smiled sadly, kissed her on the forehead and looked at her long and meaningfully.

"I understand but don't shield me. Keep me in the loop; I deserve to know what's going on. I think I earned that right all those years ago." Ethan nodded and hugged Kara close.

"I love you; you know that, right?"

"I know, and I love you. So, let's get this guy. You're going to need my help into some insight on this whole damn mess. After I go make an appearance at my new job tomorrow," with a quick glance at the clock, she said, "or rather, today, I'll stop by the station and fill your team in on everything that happened. Maybe it'll be of some help."

Ethan looked shocked, but Caleb now knew what Kara had resolved to do. She had resolved to exorcise some more demons by making what happened to her public. And he could understand her wanting to do it, but at the same time, he was concerned for her. She had gone through so much, and he was already fiercely protective of her. He would do everything in his power to help Ethan to protect her, but at what cost? The cost of another life?

"You're sure?" Ethan asked, and was met with a look that said it all and then some.

"I'll be there at one. How does that work for the both of you?"

"If that's what you want, that works for us," Caleb said, answering for the concerned and shocked Ethan.

"Why are you looking at me like that?"

"I just ... you're different today than you were a month ago; hell, even a day ago. It's the first time you haven't flinched when I've touched you in...I don't remember how long."

Kara blushed, clearly embarrassed by the statement.

"Don't be embarrassed. It's understandable that you would struggle with the physical contact. It's just...I don't know...nice being able to hug you." He hugged her again as if to emphasize his statement.

"If you both don't mind, I'm going to go up and get ready for the day. I have a lot to do. When you're done, you can let yourselves out."

Both men looked at each other as if they were about to object but thought better of it. It wasn't even dawn, and she was going to go get ready for the day. She was functioning on the bare minimum of sleep and had been for a decade. She knew her limitations, and she had an iron resolve. That, of course, didn't stop him from voicing his opinion.

"Your front window is broken. I think one of us should stay with you until you're ready to go to work. It's not even four a.m., so you have a while until you need to leave."

"Suit yourself, but I work at the hospital, so they're open 24/7/365. I have someone coming to install an alarm system this morning; they should be here by eight. I guess I'll have to see about a new door, too. But for now, I'm going to take a shower."

Both men, plus Cathy, watched her walk away. Cathy took her absence as a cue to step outside, sensing the two men needed to talk. Taking a deep breath, Caleb turned to meet the questioning eyes of his partner of six years.

"Montgomery, I don't think I need to say what I'm about to say."

"But you're going to say it anyway," Caleb finished for him, preparing himself for Ethan to tell him to back off and leave his sister alone. The hell if he would leave her alone. What man could leave a woman like Kara Vanderbilt alone? He would if that was what she wanted, but he hoped that she wanted to explore what he was feeling and what he sensed she was feeling, too.

"Be careful with her. Don't hurt her. If you're going to go the route I think you are, then treat her good. She isn't just some skirt you can chase for a bit. She needs someone to help hold her up, even if she doesn't know it. She's been through enough."

Whoa! That was *not* what he was expecting to hear. And Caleb felt as if he was supposed to deny he was interested, but he just didn't have it in him. It would be a bald-faced lie. Before Caleb could comment at all, Ethan had turned and walked outside to help Cathy, leaving Caleb to mull over his statement. He was giving him the green light if he was in it for Kara and in it for the long haul. Caleb knew he was in it for Kara and that he would not hurt her. The big question was whether he was capable of being in it for the long haul. His parents had been blessedly happy their whole marriage, and Caleb wanted that. Could he have that with Kara?

Before Caleb made it to the door, he knew the answer. Yes. Yes, he could have that with Kara; she just didn't know it yet. He knew it sounded ridiculous because he had only known her for a matter of a day, but he also knew a good thing when he saw it. And Kara was a good thing. He wanted to explore his feelings and see where they went.

10

Kara felt marginally better after she got out of the shower. For a minute or two, while she was in the shower, she could forget everything that was happening. But once the water turned off, everything came crashing back. As she stood there, cops were downstairs collecting evidence. On top of that, there was a young woman who had been murdered and whose blood appeared to be on her hands.

The weight of everything was almost overpowering, but Kara was certain she could handle anything. After her parents' betrayal, there wasn't much that could surprise her in life. If anyone else knew what she knew, her parents would not be so revered. And over the last ten years, she had learned a lot about Stanley and Constance Vanderbilt. Much of it was learned to try to figure out why they had done what they had and not because she wanted to be involved with their lives. In fact, the more she found out, the more she knew she made the right decision regarding her relationship with them.

While the information gathered was valuable and worthy of pause, it was still no help in figuring out how her parents had turned into such deviant people. In the end, she knew she would never figure out what made them what they are. The important thing was to find out what role they had or didn't have in her abduction. She was no closer today than she was ten years ago to finding any answers, but when she decided to move home, she hoped to solve the puzzle. She had figured out a long time ago that there was much more to the story of her abduction than met the eye.

In all honesty, she had hoped her move home would shake some people up and maybe someone would slip up. So far, it looked like her plan was working, and she hated herself for her desire to find answers. Maybe if she hadn't desired revenge so badly, Andrea Vincent would not be dead. She kept telling herself she could not have known her move home would result in a young woman's death. But it didn't make it any easier.

Kara knew there would be repercussions to her return; she had just hoped it would be toward her alone. It appeared that was partly the case. It was just a matter of how much she could handle before she turned tail and ran away. She wasn't on a suicide mission; she just couldn't live anymore without answers. The closure she desired wasn't there.

Down deep, she never really believed it was over, even when Ethan had told her Devon was dead. She just hoped that when she figured it all out, she could handle the truth and that it wouldn't destroy Ethan. Because deep down Kara knew—she just knew—her parents were hiding something from her.

The question was, how many people would she allow to be hurt to get the answers she desired and to get the revenge she was cheated? The warnings in the back of her mind to stay away had drawn her home instead of keeping her away. She felt that this was her one chance to find out what she had spent every day for ten years trying to get answers for. Now it was too late to turn around. It was time to make a stand.

Kara took her time getting ready, telling herself it was because she wanted to make a good impression on the employees she would be supervising but knowing full well that it was more for the handsome detective that she should not be so attracted to. Kara could list at least a dozen reasons why she shouldn't allow herself to be attracted to Detective Caleb Montgomery.

Namely, because she didn't want him to be caught in the cross fire of whoever was behind the mayhem that had suddenly become part of her life. The other reason being that she was certain she could never be the woman he would need, a woman who could be free and be intimate. And if she was alive when the dust settled, would he really be able to handle her baggage? She found herself hoping he would be up to the challenge. She found herself rooting for the tall, bronzed man she found standing in her entryway when she emerged an hour later.

"What are you still doing here? Did you draw the short straw for protection duty this morning?" She knew he would be there, but she didn't want him to know she was anticipating it. Unfortunately, she went too far and realized her tone sounded sarcastic at best and venomous at worst.

She knew that because she wanted him to fight for her if she should push him away. Because no good could come of it, and she could not live with herself if something happened to him because of her.

When she tried to push past him, his hand reached out and grabbed her by the arm, carefully turning her to face him. Kara averted her eyes and stared at a spot just past him. Tenderly, he placed his forefinger and thumb on her chin and lifted her face until her eyes met his. And her resolve melted at the look in his eyes. One that told her that she was not going to get away with the game she was trying to play.

"You damn well know I didn't get the short straw. I'm here because I want to be, because I am worried for you. I don't know what's happening here between us. What I do know is even though I met you only a day ago, I couldn't live with myself if something happened to you."

"Don't you see that I feel the same way? I'm caught up in something very serious. Something I have no control over, something I didn't ask to be part of. I can't allow anything to happen to you, and I can't be distracted with worry for you."

"You know what's really funny?"

"What?" she asked, trying to look away.

"I can take care of myself. I've been doing this cop thing for a long time."

"Yeah, but..." The rebuttal she was forming was cut off when he dipped his head down and gently touched his lips to hers.

"No buts. I'm with you every step on this one. Ethan has accepted that, so it's time for you to accept it. There comes a point in everyone's life when it's time to stop being so stubborn about doing things on your own," Caleb whispered. His mouth was so close to hers that she could feel his breath as he spoke.

"It's not that simple," she whispered back.

"It can be if you let it."

"I'm a mess. You know that, right?"

"Wouldn't have it any other way." He pulled back ever so slightly and looked deep into her eyes. "Here's the deal: Ethan and I agreed on something while you were upstairs getting ready."

"And what might that be?" she asked with a quirked eyebrow.

"We decided that you are not to go anywhere without one of us until this is figured out. So, I am going to take you to your work, and when you're ready to leave, you can give me a call. Ethan had some things he had to tie up at the station."

"Things?" she asked, not even bothering to argue with this incredibly stupid plan because she knew it would do no good.

"Namely, he has to convince our boss why he should be allowed to continue on the case."

"Why wouldn't he be allowed to?" She paused a mere second before it dawned on her. "Because of me? Right? Because somehow, I'm involved in all this, and the evidence could be considered tainted?"

"That and the emotional aspect of it all. If his head isn't in the game, he could mess up. Bob was Andrea's godfather. He's taking this personal. And right about now, Ethan is trying to convince him that if he doesn't touch any of the evidence, and if someone else is with him every step of the way, it'll be fine. He just wants a cursory role in the investigation, for you. He knows if he's at least in the loop, you'll feel more comfortable."

"Do you think he'll agree?"

"I hope so. It would be better for both ends if he does. Ethan won't sit idly by, and Bob isn't an idiot. He knows that Ethan will investigate on his own if he's not involved. And Ethan is one damn good detective. Not having him on the case could be more of a hindrance than having him on the case."

"I hope he sees it the way you do. I don't want Ethan to get in any trouble over this whole chaotic mess."

"He can handle his own; I'm guessing he and you are pretty similar in that regard. So, are you ready to go to your work?"

"I guess as ready as I'll ever be."

When they walked out her front door, she noticed an officer standing guard outside on her front porch. Confused why he was there, she turned to ask Caleb what he was doing, and before she could ask, he was giving her the answer she sought.

"Until the alarm company and locksmith show up, Officer Black will wait here. Once everything's set up, he's going to call me to let you know, and I'll bring you back to get instructions on how to use the new alarm."

She nodded her appreciation at the officer and walked down the front steps. Caleb put his hand on her lower back as they walked to his car. She liked the feel of his hand on her back; it made her feel safe. She realized she liked having someone there to lean on. Realizing it and letting it happen were two different things though, and she wasn't sure she was capable of letting it happen.

CALEB WASN'T sure where everything was headed, but he knew one thing for sure—he was just going to go with the flow. And right now, the flow had them headed to Kara's place of employment. On the ride there, he realized how very little he knew about her, but it didn't seem to bother him. He hoped that they would have time to tell each other their interests and hobbies.

Caleb knew now was not the time to learn that. There was a killer on the loose, and he had an agenda regarding Kara. An agenda that could end up harming her if she didn't listen or if they didn't find him in time. So, that meant Caleb had to stay focused, and hopefully, along the way, he would learn a thing or two about the woman sitting beside him.

The first thing he was about to learn was what she did for a living, but it appeared that Kara didn't want to talk about anything at the moment. The only words she spoke were directions to him; she had locked herself up inside her head and had forgotten that she told him she worked at the hospital. It hadn't occurred to her, in her current state, that all she had to do was tell him which hospital and he would know how to get there. Too much had been thrown at her, and she was starting to approach a critical overload. The woman certainly was a mystery.

Lost in his own thoughts, he didn't process that they were at Mercy Hospital until they pulled in. It made sense she would work there; it was the closest hospital to her house. Which left him wondering what role she had at the hospital. Kara was smart enough to be a doctor, but at only 28 she would have to still be a resident. His aunt was a general surgeon, and she told him she'd been in school for eight years and then had five years of residency before she became an official doctor. One of the things he remembered her telling him was that not all fields of medicine required the same years of residency.

"I'll give you a call when I'm done meeting some of my staff. I want to get a tour and such so it might be a while. You can probably figure on about noon. Then we can head over to your station, and I'll tell my story."

"You know you don't have to do that. At least, you could just tell the CliffsNotes version."

"No. No, I think I have to."

"You don't owe anyone anything. The details aren't necessary if it doesn't pertain to the actual abduction or Devon himself."

"Perhaps, but I think I need to do this. I've spent too much time hiding everything. You were right earlier."

"About?"

"Anyone worthwhile won't care about the details." With that statement ringing in his ears, she got out of the car.

Caleb watched until she was safely inside. He thought about what she said for a long moment before pulling away and into traffic. By the time he was on his way to the station, he had decided that her parting comment was a good sign. And for now, it would have to be enough, because he needed to focus on the task at hand. And the task at hand was keeping her alive and out of trouble. Which meant he better do his job and do it well.

When he got to the station, he was working on almost twenty-four hours with only a few hours' sleep. While it would seem ridiculous that he was in bed at such an early hour, he had learned early in his career, that when a case like this broke, you needed to get sleep while you could. So, the night before he had only been in bed for a matter of two hours before he'd been called and told to come back in. That was when they'd found the letter, and the case was bumped up a notch on the priority list. As if it could have gotten any higher. And then came Kara's frantic phone call.

It wasn't every day that a senator's daughter was murdered, and when that case was linked to the governor's daughter, it made it about as high priority as possible. Which worked just fine for him. It meant they'd get the resources they needed when all too often resources were cut to a bare minimum.

When Caleb got to his desk, Ethan was walking out of their boss's office. He had a surly look on his face, which meant that the conversation didn't go as well as they'd hoped for.

"So?"

"I'm pretty much benched on this one. I'm allowed to be in on the meetings and given all the details, and I can look for other cases that are connected, but that's it. I think I only got that much because of my bloodline, and apparently, Senator Vincent and my father want an inside man. No investigating without explicit permission or I am out of the loop entirely. For now, he's allowing me to look for other victims."

"Well, at least we got that much out of him. Did you find out anything new?"

"Only that we are supposed to get our asses in the conference room for a briefing. Did Kara get to the hospital okay?" One look at Caleb's face had Ethan quickly adding, "Shit, sorry man, of course, you got her there safe and sound."

Caleb blew it off; he knew the stress Ethan was under. Hell, he was under the same stress, but he wasn't related to someone key to the case. His interest in Kara didn't negate the fact that Ethan was her brother. It also didn't negate the fact that Ethan was the only family that she could rely on. Ethan didn't talk about his parents much, if at all. Therefore, it didn't take much for Caleb to deduct that his relationship with them was strained, as well.

Both men knew that Captain Bob Wickman had made the only choice he could have under the circumstances. Caleb and Ethan were his two best detectives, and he clearly didn't want one sitting on the sidelines only able to listen and offer up his opinion. But if he allowed Ethan to be more involved, it could taint the case. And it didn't matter who his father was. If the media even got the slightest whiff of misconduct or inappropriate investigation techniques, they would all be fucked with a capital F.

11

When they walked into the conference room, they were met with the grim faces of Cathy, Brett, Bob, Shirley, and DA Gloria Finnegan. Surprised at the small gathering, Caleb moved farther into the room. He knew instantly that this briefing would be for their ears only. Which meant that right now, they were going to try to keep a low profile to keep the chances of leaks to the media out of play. Caleb knew it was all hands on deck for this case. Therefore, many other officers and detectives would be involved; they just wouldn't be in on certain information.

"Sit down," Bob said sharply.

No one in the room took offense to his sharpness because everyone knew that this case was personal to him. The only reason he hadn't been removed as well was because he was the captain and he had friends in very high places. But he was skating on thin ice for the moment. If he crossed the line, he would most likely be removed from the case, and they would bring in an outsider to run the show.

Everyone in the room would hate to see that happen. The team worked best with each other, and no one wanted to see the team split up. Even if some of the team was only allowed to be involved in a cursory manner.

"All right. So, we have some new developments. Shirley, do you want to take the floor?" Bob asked.

"We've confirmed time of death as approximately twelve hours before her body was dumped. Which is what I thought. She died from strangulation. I believe she was with the killer since the night she disappeared."

"Why do you think that?" Ethan asked.

"There were many cuts over her body. The cuts were methodically placed, and both the cuts and bruising on her body were in different stages of healing. I would say she was held for the full four days before she was killed."

"So, it follows the timeline, then. That will make what Kara has to tell us even more important."

"Want to fill everyone else in on what you told me earlier?" Bob asked.

"As I told you earlier, my sister will be coming in to help us out. She might have information that's pertinent to this case. She and I both feel that she'll be extremely important to the investigation."

"She'll be coming in this afternoon," Caleb said.

"This is huge and for our ears only," Ethan said, looking around the table. Once everyone nodded in agreement, he continued. "Kara was held for four days before she escaped on the fourth day. She escaped in the evening and was found by a middle-aged farmer that was on his way home. The farmer called for help. She was evacuated by air. In the air, she flatlined before they got her to the hospital. She flatlined at ten p.m."

"So, the killer is following the timeline of her abduction and escape," Bob said, making it more of a statement than a question.

"To the letter," Ethan said. "My thoughts are this: whoever is doing this is very ritualistic in his killing process, and he knows detailed information that only Devon Bristol should know. He's trying to make a point—that she should have died all those years ago, and that he's going to make sure she knows he's coming for her. Kara also felt we should look for similar cases in other states, and I've already found another one."

"The man responsible died. I remember he was killed in a car accident. So, who would be behind these murders?" Cathy asked.

"Kara always suspected someone else was involved."

"Why don't I remember that?" Bob asked.

"I'm sure it had something to do with my father trying to close the book on it all. Once she was found, and Devon was dead, he didn't want to discuss it any further. But she always swore that she had heard Devon talking to someone on the phone. And that he had an accomplice. Not in all the torture, but in the kidnapping itself. Our father and the investigators were certain that with all the drugs he injected in her, she was confused—that she had heard him talking to himself and not on the phone. So, my father convinced her that there was no accomplice. And she seemed to accept it and move on."

"Or did she?" Caleb asked. Everyone looked at him. "Something tells me she never gave up on the theory. It might account, at least in part, for why she stayed away. It might also account for why she's still so terrified."

"Wouldn't you be terrified if this happened to you?" Cathy asked.

"Yes, but this is different as if she's looking over her shoulder. At first, I just thought she didn't believe Devon died. But this makes more sense. The idea that there's someone else out there, this has caused those memories to resurface," Caleb said.

"Makes sense to me. I know there was a falling out with our parents all those years ago. But she never told me about what caused it. Maybe this is what it was. Maybe she wouldn't let it go, and they gave her an ultimatum. In their eyes, it was open-and-shut, and there was no use crying over spilled milk."

"Harsh," Brett acknowledged.

"Hopefully she can shed some light on it all today when she comes in," Gloria finally spoke up. "Before we leave, Ethan, this other murder that you discovered, what makes you think it's the same unsub?"

"Disappeared on the same day two years ago, found four days later, and there was a note sealed in a bag and left in her vagina, as well. The note said *#10, now and then, I wonder where you been.*"

"Shit. All right, time to start digging. If we don't count Kara, that means we have nine other bodies to link to this sadistic SOB." Bob said.

"And that means she wasn't the first victim," Caleb said, and his stomach felt like there was a rock in it.

KARA KNEW that not everyone would be thrilled about her being the new attending—some because of rumors they'd heard and others because of her age. But eventually, they would have to come around or find a job elsewhere. It sounded harsh, but that was the reality of the situation. She would be a fair boss but hoped she wouldn't have to deal with anyone undermining her.

The drive over to Mercy wasn't as long as she thought it would be, but she had gotten distracted getting ready and lost track of time. She'd wanted to come during shift change so she could meet as many people as possible, but shift change had already happened. So, she would meet who she could. Walking into the ER brought back a lot of memories. Kara had spent over a week in this hospital recovering from her injuries. She probably should have spent longer at the hospital, but as soon as the doctors said she was able to go home under the care of a private nurse, she did. No one wanted to mess with the Vanderbilts. However, two doctors certainly did their best to keep her there. It was against their opinion for her to leave the hospital so soon, but they couldn't force her to stay, and her parents wanted her away from the doctors that cared about her more than they did.

When she had heard they were looking for an attending doctor for the ER, she jumped at the opportunity, hoping she'd be able to give back to them the way they had for her. It had been Dr. Brenner who had performed lifesaving surgery, Dr. Chiglo who had been there the moment she was brought in and assessed her injuries, and a nurse named Heather who had been like a mama bear protecting her cub when it came to Kara's care. Those three people made her feel like there was hope. Dr. Chiglo was the one who had called to tell her they were looking for another attending, and if the job hadn't become available, she would still be in Baltimore with her head in the ground, hiding.

She expected some people to recognize her when she walked in. But no one seemed to look at her twice, and that was just fine by her. Of course, someone would eventually remember who she was, and then the rumors would fly, but she could handle it. She had to; her future depended on it. There would be no way she could ever have a life of her own if she couldn't handle a little idle gossip. She wasn't sure if anyone had announced that she was taking the position, but she'd assumed there was a formal announcement. If that was the case, then the talk had already started.

"Kara? Kara Vanderbilt?" she heard a familiar voice from behind her say. She turned around to find Dr. Vanessa Brenner smiling warmly at her. "I thought that was you. I didn't know you would be starting today."

"Vanessa, it's so good to see you. I start on Monday, but I thought I'd stop by to see if I could meet some of the staff. I thought shift change would be a good time to meet a lot of those I'll be working with, but I seem to have come late for that. How have you been?"

Hesitating only briefly, Vanessa approached her and hugged her. Kara hugged her back. The hug was fierce, and it felt good. After a moment, Kara regrettably backed away and was shocked to see tears in Vanessa's eyes. She looked away quickly and then looked back when Vanessa spoke.

"Well, I'm good and you, something is different, you've never been able to..." the statement hung in the air.

"Hug you? Ethan said something similar when he hugged me this morning." She shrugged and breathed deep. "I've been so closed off; it's just time not to be. How are Tom and the kids?" Kara had gotten to know Vanessa over the years and considered her a friend on an exceptionally short list. In all honesty, there were times Vanessa was like a surrogate mother to her. Hell, Vanessa was more involved in her life than Kara's own mother, making her one of a handful of people Kara trusted.

"They're doing just fine. It's hard to believe, but our oldest is graduating this year," Vanessa said. "I think I can help you meet some people if you would like? That way we can do a little catching up. I haven't heard from you in so long."

"I've been doing a lot of soul-searching."

"And what did you find out?"

"That I didn't much like the way my life was turning out, so I decided to change that."

"And that would explain the big move back home. How's it going so far?" Concern furrowed her brow.

"I'll let you know in a few days. I just got here yesterday. I met a man, Vanessa."

Vanessa hesitated for a moment before responding.

"And how do you feel about that?"

"Apprehensive, terrified, hopeful, and excited." The words were spoken quietly and to the ground.

"All normal emotions." She paused. "Are you ready for tonight?" she asked, changing the subject. For now. Kara knew she'd ask her more later when she had time to assimilate her feelings.

"I think so. I can tell you this much, I'm bound and determined to make this center work. It isn't just about the grand opening tonight; getting people willing to fund it is crucial. But there is more to it. This center is my hope for a future, not just for me, but for so many others. Care to give me any last-minute advice?"

"Kara, you are going to do just fine tonight and fine here. Most of the people here have no idea who you are; a lot of them are transplants. And those who do know who you are, are not of the kind of nature to give you a hard time."

"I hope you're right," Kara murmured.

"I know I'm right. Anyway, any talk will be of the curious nature, not the vicious kind. And you might have to endure some gossip, but I have faith you can get through that. It's not like you haven't had to listen to people whispering before, right?"

"I guess you *are* right about that." They walked quietly for a little while, and then sucking in a deep breath, Kara prepared herself to meet the staff she'd be working with.

About an hour later, exhausted from the effort of meeting new people, she was about to call for her protection detail to pick her up, when her cell phone rang. She didn't recognize the number and assuming it was Caleb or Ethan calling to check on her, she answered the phone sharply.

"I'm fine. You don't have to check in on me."

"Are you sure about that, Kara? Welcome home, bitch; I have been waiting a long time to have you here, in my hunting ground. You better watch your back."

Before Kara could respond, the line went dead. She pulled the phone from her ear and stared at it a moment. Shaken, she sat on a nearby chair. She'd known there were no coincidences when it came to everything that had been happening, and after the impromptu call, she was less likely to argue about her overprotective brother arranging for protection for her. The fact that only a handful of people had been given her phone number was not lost on her.

She was still staring at her phone when it rang again. Jumping, she looked at the caller ID and once again didn't recognize the number. Second-guessing whether she should answer the phone, she squared her shoulders and tapped the answer button.

"Who the hell is this?" she demanded.

"Kara? It's Caleb. What's wrong?"

"Nothing. I just got a strange phone call. Why didn't I recognize the number you were calling from?" she asked, feeling stupid.

"I called from my desk phone."

"Oh, yeah, that makes sense, I guess. I will need to program that in, as well. What did you need?"

"Are you done at the hospital? There've been some developments on our side, and it sounds like there may have been some developments on your side, too. Care to fill me in?"

"Not really, but I will when you get here."

"I'll be there in about fifteen minutes. Where can I meet you?"

"I'll just wait outside where you dropped me off this morning."

"No way! Under no circumstances should you wait outside. Wait inside, and I will meet you there. Understand?"

When she didn't respond right away, he asked again.

"Do. You. Understand?"

"Yes. Geez, calm down. What happened?"

"I don't want you alone, and Ethan doesn't want you alone. We'll fill you in when we get there."

Kara stood, confused as the other line went dead again. What was with people? She wandered to the entrance by where she'd been dropped off this morning. After about ten minutes, she had had all she could take of people staring at her and decided to go outside. Once outside, an eerie feeling fell over her, and she couldn't shake the feeling that her mystery caller was there, hidden somewhere, watching her. Deciding it might be better, after all, to wait inside, she turned to go back in the building.

Something in her peripheral vision caught her attention as she turned to look, and before she could use her ten years of self-defense classes, she was pushed to the ground, her head making a loud thunk as it hit the concrete.

12

Kara's head hit the ground with a sickening crack. She connected so hard, she saw stars. On the outer edge of her awareness, she sensed someone standing over her as she struggled to sit up. Her stomach rolled with nausea, and she slumped back to the ground, as if an afterthought, and before the figure ran off, he grabbed the purse she'd been carrying.

She was still struggling to sit up when she heard tires squealing to a stop behind her. Blinking back what she initially thought was tears, but was actually blood, she struggled to see. Her medical training kicked in, and she had enough presence of mind to lift her hand to her head to stop the bleeding. Delirious, she was on her knees swaying, trying to stand when someone knelt beside her and softly touched their hand to her shoulder and then scooped her to their chest.

"Kara! What the hell happened? What are you doing out here? I told you to stay inside."

"I-I don't know. I came out to get some air; it was stifling inside. I got a little weirded out like someone was watching me and decided to go back inside. I had just started to turn to go inside when someone threw me to the ground. I hit my head and was dazed, so I didn't get a look at him, but it was a man. He took my purse."

She was about to stand up when his hands urged her to sit back down. Thankful, she fought back another wave of nausea.

"Sit down. Ethan is inside getting help. Why did you go so far from the entrance? No one can see you over here. If you were set on going outside, you should have stayed within distance of someone's vision."

"I needed to get away from all their stares. I know it was stupid."

Caleb had taken a handkerchief out of his pocket and gently removed her hand from the wound and placed the cloth to the cut. Kara leaned against his strong frame, still dizzy from the blow. She had her eyes closed, but she could hear footsteps approaching. No doubt Ethan and a nurse to bring her inside to get the cut looked at.

"Kara, what the hell happened?"

"I fell. When someone pushed me," she finished, knowing he would have asked how.

"Ethan brought a wheelchair for you to get a ride inside."

"I can get there on my own two feet."

Kara stood up and almost went down again when everything got fuzzy. Clearly, her head wound was worse than she had thought. Strong arms steadied her.

"Okay, tough girl. Want that ride now?" Caleb asked.

"I guess I don't have much choice." She allowed herself to be guided to the chair and wheeled inside.

Thirty minutes and six stitches later, she was feeling better and had been given the green light to go, if she took it easy. She promised she would, but she didn't believe for a second that anyone in the room bought what she said. It wasn't like she didn't have some work cut out for her. She was in a race for her life to uncover the mystery that surrounded her abduction. And it wasn't as if Kara didn't know what to watch for when it came to head wounds and mild concussions.

"All right, time to go to the station. Have you heard anything about the alarm system progress?"

"How about we just take you home?" Ethan suggested.

"No way. I'm in this, and the least you can do is let me be involved. I'd think you would prefer that to my investigating on my own."

Caleb chuckled softly at her outburst.

"What the hell is so funny, Montgomery?"

"Nothing. This whole situation sucks, but the lady has a pair of brass ones, and you have to admit, she sounds just like you."

"Stuff it," Ethan mumbled as he climbed in the car.

As Caleb navigated the streets back to the station, no one spoke a word. Which was unfortunate because it gave him time to think back to the moment he and Ethan had pulled up to the hospital and seen Kara on the ground in a puddle of blood. He couldn't get to her side fast enough. Without verbally communicating, Ethan had gone inside for help.

Good God, he hardly knew the woman, and he felt as if someone had sucker punched him in the stomach every time he looked at her in the rearview mirror. She was sitting stick straight, trying to hide how terrified she was, and she still looked gorgeous. Even with the black and blue bruise that was starting to form on her temple and the dried blood in her hair that the nurse was unable to clean up, she was the most alarmingly beautiful woman he had ever seen.

What he wouldn't give to be able to wake up to her every day. It was truly amazing that one woman could look so vulnerable and so strong at the same time. He had never in his life met a woman like her. And he was more certain than ever that he wanted her to be in his life, because as soon as he saw her on the ground with blood dripping into her eyes, he wanted to rip the throat out of the person who had caused her injury. An injury that was minor and paled in comparison to what she'd been through when she was abducted.

Caleb knew he was in trouble; his feelings were more intense than any he had ever felt for a woman. The primitive instinct to protect what was his, was so strong that he struggled not to scream out in pure, vicious anger at the bastard who had deemed himself worthy to touch her.

As if her morning wasn't bad enough, now came the hard part, they had to tell her that Andrea Vincent was not the only other victim. She had already suspected as much, but to have the confirmation would surely rattle her. On top of that, she was about to bare the darkest details of her ordeal ten years ago. He knew he could handle the details. He knew Ethan could handle it, and he was sure she would get through it.

He just hated that she felt the need to air it out to everyone and that they needed to hear the details. Because while he knew it was good for her to talk about it, he didn't want her to air her dirty laundry out to everyone—for it to become part of the official record. It was part of what made her who she is, but he didn't want her to feel degraded, and he knew Kara felt they didn't have any other choice.

Once they got to the station, both men turned to her to make sure one last time that she was sure this is what she wanted to do. And once again, she surprised him by being strong and adamant that this was the right thing to do. That even though it might be ten years too late, she was going to make an official statement. Her head had to be splitting, but she stood there with a look of determination etched across her face. A look that said, *This is me; I am a force to be reckoned with.*

Caleb was not oblivious to the looks when they walked into his department. It was obvious it was a mixture of concern and...something else. He could see the looks of interest on most of the men's faces. It was clear that many of the men found Kara as attractive as he did. Which made Caleb feel jealous and possessive. He couldn't help but think that they had better back off. A couple of the guys smirked and nodded, message received. A few others were clearly reacting to the injury she had sustained.

Before he knew what he was doing, he'd put his hand on her lower back. It wasn't the first time he had felt the need to touch her. Surprised by his territorial attitude, Caleb tried to focus on the task at hand.

But it was useless because not only was he having a hard time ignoring the men checking her out, now he had to ignore the feel of his hand to her body. And now was not the time to get aroused, but touching her and smelling her combined with the spike of testosterone from seeing other men look at her was causing just that reaction.

"Montgomery, Vanderbilt. What took you so long?" Bob barked, clearly agitated.

No one could blame him; everyone was hoping Kara had the key to this case. It only took a glance at Kara for him to change his tone.

"What the hell happened?"

"Someone shoved her to the ground, and she took a solid hit to her head. They took her purse. My guess is it was as much to make it look like a mugging as it was to see if they could get information from anything in her purse," Caleb said.

"They wouldn't learn much from my purse, and they already have my cell phone number."

Caleb was still fuming that somehow the bastard had gotten her private number and had the balls to call and harass her. The question was, how had he gotten the number? His guess was that it was somehow obtained through the hospital personnel records.

"I would tell you to go home and get some rest and come back later, but we need you. Are you good to go?" Captain Bob Wickman asked.

"As ready as I can be." It was evident that she was pleased by the way the Captain had addressed her. He could tell that she was trying to show confidence in the inflection in her voice, but there was a barely discernible tremble to her words.

With a nod from Bob, they moved to the same conference room as earlier. Ethan and Caleb walked directly to the wall where pictures of Andrea Vincent's body and the crime scene were pinned up, but Kara stopped them before they could remove them.

"No, leave them up. I've seen dead people before, and I might see something in the pictures that you missed."

Knowing she was right, they left the pictures up. Caleb pulled a chair out for her to sit on, and with a slight touch to her shoulder, let her know he was there for her and she could stop at any time if she wanted.

"I apologize for not introducing myself. I am Captain Bob Wickman. We can start whenever you're ready. But we're still waiting for one more person. If you could just wait a little bit longer?"

"Kara Vanderbilt," she said, shaking the hand he had extended to her. "That would be fine. May I ask who we're waiting for?"

"DA Gloria Finnegan. We just want to have everything as legit as possible. Is that all right with you, Miss Vanderbilt?"

"Please call me Kara. Of course, I want everything to be done by the book. Once we find this bastard, we need to make the charges stick. I just hope we find him as soon as possible. Before we start, can someone fill me in on what new development sparked your wanting me to come in as soon as possible?"

All three men looked at each other and shared a pained expression. They hadn't gotten a chance to tell her when they picked her up because of the scene they found when they got to the hospital. Ethan nodded to Caleb, giving him a gesture that relinquished the task to him. He sighed heavily. If Ethan was unable to bring himself to tell her, he preferred to be the one to tell her versus one of the others.

"When we were meeting this morning, the victim's time of death was confirmed."

"Andrea Vincent. I want everyone to say her name, she was a person; don't refer to her as the victim. Please." Kara's eyes were stripped naked at the near admission of how she felt about being considered a victim.

"All right. Andrea Vincent went missing for four days before she was found, and she died just as we had speculated, around the exact time you coded."

"Is that all? I mean, I thought you had already figured that out. So, this is just confirmation?"

"We wanted you to hear that it's official before it hits the press," Ethan said. "But there's more. We have reason to believe that we have linked another murder to this unsub."

Kara's shoulders sagged, and she looked at her hands. They were tightly linked, and her knuckles were white. And then she shook herself slightly and squared her shoulders and looked at the men in the room.

"So, I was right, which means there'll be more. And the number on the note is, what? The number of victims?" She looked around the room at the people assembled and sighed. "The word 'victim' is only offensive to me if we actually know the name of the person who was brutalized. Once you know who they are, you should give them back their identity." They all nodded once.

"Our working theory is that the number coincides with what number victim and the rhyme that accompanies the note is directed at you."

"That doesn't make sense, though, because with me it would be eleven victims. The note you found on Andrea said number twelve. Unless..."

"We're working on the premise that you were not the first victim," Caleb finished quietly.

"But I am the only one that got away. Then, in my opinion, the key to this case is finding victim one," she whispered. "He'll have made mistakes with the first woman he took."

"We are going to do our best to keep as much as possible out of the papers. So, anything you tell us today is between us, unless we absolutely must tell someone else," Captain Wickman said.

"Captain Wickman, I assure you that I will not do anything to jeopardize this case. As it appears at this point that I'm a target, it would be foolhardy for me to go to the media."

"I know that. I'm just letting you know that from our end; we plan to keep you as close to a confidential informant as we can. Obviously, the media can be sly and eventually will figure things out on their own. But for now, we don't plan to help them out. And please, call me Bob."

"Understood." Her voice faltered a little, and she looked down at her hands as if searching for the strength to tell them about that May.

"I thought there would be repercussions to my psyche if I came home. But even in my worst dreams, I didn't think that other women were in danger all these years. The monster that did all those things to me is dead. How could I have known that someone else had picked up where he had left off? If I'd known, I would have done all I could to stop it. I would have made myself bait, something, anything to save those other women."

13

"The hell you would have! This isn't on you; this is on the bastard killing those women. He's responsible for the deaths, not you. And we are responsible to locate him and put a stop to him. Our responsibility and ours alone, not yours!" Caleb exclaimed sharply. His outburst caused shocked expressions to form on everyone's face, including the tall and attractive woman who had just walked through the door.

"All right, what did I miss?" the woman asked. Kara assumed she was the district attorney they'd been waiting for.

"Kara was talking out of her ass," Ethan snapped, clearly as upset by her statement as Caleb was.

"I was not talking out of my ass, as you so eloquently put it. I was merely stating that it might be better for all of us if I talked all those years ago, been bait, something. I can't allow anyone else—especially someone I care about—to get hurt because of me." She knew her voice sounded pathetic, but she didn't care.

"I'm DA Gloria Walker, but you can call me Gloria." The beautiful woman smiled softly at Kara and shook her hand.

"Please, call me Kara."

"Kara, none of this is your fault," Captain Wickman said.

"I wouldn't be so sure if I were you," she said, knowing she sounded miserable.

"Kara, there's no way you could have had the foresight to know that this would happen. Bob has brought me up-to-date on all the details. The person who attacked you died. There's no way you could have known someone else was actively taking women in the same method," Gloria stated.

"Let's just start at the beginning."

"All right. You have the floor," Gloria said, her voice soothing.

Kara couldn't help but think that Gloria Finnegan was very good at her job. She had the sympathetic voice down pat. Kara only hoped that she was as sincere as she made herself sound.

"Tell me something, Gloria."

"Sure."

"Have you had training in social behavior?"

"Very intuitive. I knew from an early age I wanted to be a DA. I also knew that I would have to talk to vic...people who were subjected to horrible ordeals. Therefore, I decided that a minor in psychology would be beneficial in helping me to be more compassionate, understanding, and forthright when cross-examining or having a simple conversation."

Kara nodded slowly. Her suspicion was correct, and her feelings that Gloria was a person that could be trusted helped her immensely. She took a deep breath and then another, focusing on what she was here to do.

"Is this all, just the four of us? You don't want Cathy, Shirley, and Brett here?" Gloria asked.

"No, I didn't want to have too many ears in the room, and I want Kara to feel comfortable."

"If there are more people that are part of your team, then you should have them come in. Honestly, the whole team should be here. I don't matter. What matters is that we find this person—this unsub—before it's too late."

Ethan nodded once and stood to leave the room, presumably to get the other team members. Kara was ready. As hard as it was going to be, she was ready to share her story. But she didn't want to hesitate. The longer they waited, the more likely she would get cold feet and run screaming from the room.

And just when she was about to jump out of her skin, Ethan returned with two women and a man. Obviously, the aforementioned Cathy, Shirley, and Brett. As she watched everyone take a seat, she focused on each person intently. They all appeared to be solid, open, and honest people. People that were going to help take down this monster.

SHIT, he hated this. He didn't want to have to make her tell her story; he didn't want to have to hear it, not because it would change what he thought about her or how he felt about her, but because he knew it would make him so angry, and he'd want to wring the man's neck who'd hurt her. But he would never be able to do that.

There was a quiet knock on the door and Lois, the office clerk, brought in a folder for him. He had requested the file on Kara's case before he left to go pick her up. But he found himself frowning at the size of the file; it certainly didn't appear to be very large. He would have expected the folder to be huge, even if Devon Bristol had died and made it an open-and-shut case, there should still have been some due diligence in the investigation. Which would have resulted in more paperwork than the single sheet he found when he opened the folder.

The sheet of paper merely consisted of a case number and nothing else. No evidence. No statements. There wasn't even a statement from Kara, the farmer that found her, or the officers on the scene. It was the most obvious lackluster attempt at building a case he had ever seen. Was this all the officers assigned to the case managed to pull together? If so, they deserved a kick in the ass. Was the evidence lost? It seemed unlikely. If that were the case, surely the whole file would be missing. Or did something more nefarious happen? Was the evidence destroyed? Whatever the answer was, it wasn't good. Somehow, all the evidence was gone or had never been collected. It wasn't merely a case of bad filing because that, too, would result in the whole file missing, and not just 99% of the legwork.

"Before you start. Um...I took the liberty of requesting the folder from your case." He paused before continuing and then cleared his throat. "However, it appears we have a problem."

Every set of eyes in the room looked at the folder. Kara was the only one who didn't have a startled look on her face.

"What do you mean? That's the folder? There should be more than just one piece of paper," Ethan's voice roared. Kara's hand reached out to touch his.

"Surely, you aren't surprised? After all these years, how can you still be surprised about anything that surrounds me or that case?" Caleb was certain that her voice was colder than she had meant it to be; once again, she was deflecting her pain by portraying herself as cold.

"What do you mean?" Ethan asked.

"Come on, already. Why can't you just see it for what it is? Our sweet old parents had that file disappear, and you know it. Since I know for a fact that I gave a statement, even if it wasn't very detailed, and I also know that Henry Stanford gave a statement. I have maintained a relationship with him; he would be disgusted by the lack of papers in that file. I also know that the officers gave statements. In fact, when I last saw that file, it was brimming with papers."

Now all eyes turned to look at Kara.

"First, when did you see the file? Second, what would make you think our parents had anything to do with it? I know they can be pretty horrible, but what purpose would there be to make it disappear?" Ethan spat out, angrier than Caleb had seen him in a long time, and he was sure Kara had never seen that anger directed at her. And to her credit, she never flinched because she could see that Ethan wasn't mad at her. He was mad at the situation and the knowledge that he knew she was right.

"You find it so hard to believe that dear old Dad and manipulative Mommy wouldn't have a reason for that to disappear? Maybe, just maybe, if you sat back and considered all the pieces to the puzzle, you might be able to put a few things together. And to answer the question about when I saw the file, that would be a few days before I left our home. I saw that file in our dad's hands."

"The hell you say?!" Ethan's voice squeaked.

"I'm not following you," Caleb said, trying to diffuse the situation.

"My dad was talking to two officers the night I left. They had my file and Father was looking at it. You see, our parents only like publicity when it serves to help them, and I have no doubt in my mind that they made that folder disappear that night so that the pictures taken of my injuries wouldn't be leaked. Once I was found and the usefulness of my disappearance to get my father the seat as governor faded, it turned into damage control. After all, we couldn't have details of what had happened to me become public knowledge. How could they possibly marry me off to the highest bidder?"

"Why would they do that? What are you implying?" Ethan asked.

"Mother and Father never wanted me to speak to the police. They wanted it to all get brushed under the covers. I refused. Back then, I wanted to explain everything. I wanted to tell what had happened. I let it appear to them that I didn't want to give a statement, and then I went to the police station and gave one. I allowed them to think I hadn't talked to the police. Because they had encouraged me to not talk to them."

"But why would they do that?"

"To hide the fact that I was raped. They wanted the media and the public to believe I was only kidnapped and held for ransom. They didn't want anyone to know that I had been soiled."

"But..."

"Believe me or not, but that's the case. I heard it from their own mouths when they visited me in the hospital when they were trying to bribe the doctors not to say anything to the police. Dr. Brenner and Dr. Chiglo are consummate professionals and didn't take the money and told them to get bent. They had to hand over the evidence of my rape."

Ethan looked shocked by the statement and at a loss for words. He just stared at his sister for a moment. "Is that why you left?"

"It wasn't the catalyst. Trust me, they are not good people. It was just one of the many straws that broke the camel's back, so to speak.

But we are not here to discuss that. We're here to discuss what happened while I was held." Her voice had once again grown cold and distant.

Caleb knew there was so much more to the story than met the eye. There was some kind of deep-seated hatred for her parents that she wasn't willing to share with anyone. At least, not yet. Which made him wonder what they could have possibly done to make her hate them so much. He knew one thing for sure: he intended to find out what it was.

KARA TOOK A DEEP BREATH. She had to control her temper; she wanted to shield Ethan as much as possible from what her parents had done. They didn't deserve it, but she just felt like she needed to protect him. Granted, he knew they weren't perfect people, but he had no idea what they were capable of. She cleared her throat and her mind and decided it was time to get this whole story over with, and the faster, the better. There was somewhere she needed to be, and it wasn't at the police station reliving her messed up past.

"So, everyone is pretty much aware when I was kidnapped and all the logistics, as far as how I was kidnapped and for how long. What most people don't know are the details of the kidnapping. Which was fine with me, but if it can give some clue into identifying this person, then I'll talk."

She looked down at her hands, uncomfortable, but forged forward.

"For those who don't know every detail, I'll start from the beginning," she said pointedly, looking at Caleb. She had hoped she'd never tell anyone this—especially not the man she was interested in. But what had to be done, must be. A small part of her wanted to tell him. The question was, did she want to tell him in hopes of scaring him off or to see if he *did* have staying power? Maybe a little of both.

"It's just simpler to start from the very beginning, so we're all on the same page. Ten years ago, I was at home studying for my finals. My father and mother were at a fundraising event for his bid for the governor's seat. I was brooding over my parents telling me I couldn't go to the big end-of-the-year party that was going on that night. I was having an internal war about whether I should stay home and be the dutiful daughter, or disobey and go to the party. It was storming. I remember so vividly the way the sky looked, and how the air smelled heavy with the promise of rain. My window was open, and the curtains had knocked over a very expensive and rather flamboyant vase. I determined that I was going to go to the party, and I picked up all the glass and was going to throw it in the garbage on my way out, to delay Mother from finding out it had been broken. When I got to the base of the stairs, I found Devon Bristol hiding in the shadows.

"He had a look in his eyes I'd never seen before, and it terrified me. I backed away from him but backed into the stairs and stumbled, sending the glass flying, and he was on me fast. Fast enough that I had no time to react. I landed hard on my arm, and I tried to get away, but he injected me with something, and I lost consciousness. When I woke up, I was in the trunk of his car, bound and gagged. I woke up just around the time we left the main road and turned onto a bumpy gravel road. We turned down another dirt road and then we were there.

"I made sure to remember as much as possible, so when I got away, I would know which way to go. When we got to the cabin, he dragged me inside." She paused and swallowed.

"Inside, the cabin was old and unkempt. There was a large bed in the middle of the cabin. It looked brand new. It was huge and had a princess canopy over the top. I tried to convince him that Father would pay well for my release. It angered him. He called me a lot of names and accused me of being a cocktease. I tried a different tact by telling him he was right, and if he let me go, we could explore his feelings. And it was like I had thrown a match on the fire. That was the first time he raped me. It was brutal and earth-shattering to me. Until then, I had been a virgin. But I survived it, and I decided in that moment, I *would* make it out of there. I just didn't know how. I thought the worst had happened. But I learned over the next four days that much worse things could happen." Pausing again, she reached for the glass of water on the table in front of her and took a long drink.

"I went into what must have been survival mode and tried hard to block out everything. He liked to strangle me while he was raping me until I would pass out. Then he would revive me and do it again. At first, I was terrified, then I was numb, and finally, I was resigned to my fate. Which was, in my opinion, to die. The belief and determination that I would make it out alive faded until I didn't care that I would die. I just wanted the pain to be over. It was around day three or four that I gave up. I had been raped more times than I cared to count. He had cut me and beat me. He liked to cut me and tie me up outside in the heat to let the bugs come feast on me. Sometimes he would douse me in water and hang me outside in the middle of the night. Sometimes I was tied upside down, and other times, he strung me from my hands. He'd play mind games by telling me I could go home if I complied. He was very sadistic. I passed out from the pain often, and when I woke, he was always there, but sometimes he was different."

"Why do you say that?" Caleb asked, leaning forward as if something she had said piqued his interest.

"I don't know. He was always scary, but sometimes he was completely evil. There were times he would rape me while he choked me and that was all. That was the mild version. And then there was the evil version that liked to do other things to me. That was the version that cut me and hung me outside. That was the version that had all the toys to use on me." Once again, she paused, not wanting to say what other things he had done.

"Was there anything else that made you think he was different?" Bob asked softly as if to say that those details weren't pertinent, and at the same time, encouraging her to continue.

"I'm not sure. Like I said, he was always mean. But sometimes he was crazy, bona fide insane. It was like no light bulbs were on; that was the man I saw the night I was abducted. I was kept pretty drugged, so I didn't usually know which version I was going to get until he started playing with me."

"These other times, do you think it was a dissociative disorder? Forgive me if I use the wrong word, but could it have been another personality?" Gloria pushed.

"If I had to categorize it, I would say one version was sociopathic. No remorse. When I woke up to that version, I would be petrified. I could handle the crazy version, the version that swore undying love, but I never felt threatened by him when he was like that to the point that I was in fear for my life. The other version liked to use foreign objects, and he was clinical about it. Like he was experimenting. No matter what version showed up, I was instructed to say he was the only one for me. He would force me to say things to him, and I was only allowed to call him 'Master.' He was cold. I knew when he was like that, he could kill me in a second. He had a table of things next to the bed I was tied to that he used on me. Pincers, scalpels, a shocker, among many other things. Like I said, he was clinical about it all. I think he was experimenting to see how far he could take it before I died, but my death would not have been intentional at his hands; it would have been part of the process he was putting me through. He took notes throughout."

Kara paused to regain her composure. She'd been staring at the table with her hands folded in her lap. As if Caleb had sensed her need to find a power source, he found her hand under the table and held it in his. It was all she needed to get her back on track. If she just told it like it was fiction, maybe she could get through it.

"Maybe Gloria is right about the dissociative disorder?" Ethan pondered out loud.

"I thought of that, even did some research on it. It just didn't seem to fit, but it isn't my area of expertise, so it was certainly possible. With him being dead, we'll never know; but, Ethan, you know I have always thought he didn't work alone. Maybe the two personalities were two different men, and I was just too drugged and in shock to realize they were not the same person. It's what I've always thought, what I tried to tell the police after all the drugs wore off. They told me I was mistaken."

"I don't think you were mistaken. It fits with how he's still actively killing. I think it makes a lot of sense that Devon had a partner," Caleb said.

Kara couldn't stop herself from shuddering.

"Kara, if I had known this, I would have fought for them to investigate it further. I am so sorry I didn't listen to you." Ethan looked down to hide the pain on his face from her. After what she deemed a successful attempt, he glanced up. "Are you ready to tell me how you got away?" Ethan asked. Kara knew he'd wanted to know all those years ago, and she had refused to tell him. She had refused to tell him anything back then. She was fine with telling the police, but for some reason, she couldn't get the words to come out for Ethan. But even with the police, she sanitized the details. Now was different. Now he *was* the police, and she would tell all the necessary information.

"He never rested; I wondered how he managed on no sleep. If it was two people, I guess I would have missed when they switched shifts, because of the drugs. I was never alone. When I woke up, he was always there. Most of the time, he was the one waking me up with some new method of torture. On the fourth evening, whimpers woke me up after a particularly brutal session. I looked around and saw he was sleeping. It was the only time I had been left with an opportunity to escape. And I was going to do everything in my power to get away. I knew I would rather die trying than spend one more second there. And it was like God had left me a present. There was a scalpel within reach of my hands. I was able to grab it, but I couldn't use it at first, then I realized the ropes were looser, and I was able to put the scalpel in my mouth and saw through my restraints. I nicked myself once because I could feel the blood run down my arm."

"That was the wound that had caused all the blood loss. They wondered if it was self-inflicted," Ethan said quietly.

"They thought I tried to kill myself."

The room fell silent at her statement. Little did they know, she had wanted to.

14

"The doctors weren't sure what to think. They weren't sure if you'd done it intentionally, or if Devon had done it, or if it was a wound from your escape. I defended you and told them you wouldn't have tried to kill yourself; if so, why were you found naked and running down the road? And you weren't talking to me about it."

"I bet Mother and Father were willing to accept that I would kill myself. I bet they secretly wished I would have done exactly that. That bit of the conversation makes sense now," she whispered, and then, shaking her head, she said, "Never mind about that. I apologize for not talking to you, but I just couldn't share the details with you. I was willing to with the police. Hell, I went to them. But with you, I had to pretend it never happened. It was the only way for me.

"Anyway, I'm not sure how I was able to cut myself loose; it just should not have been feasible, and I don't know how I managed to sneak past him. But somehow, it all worked to my favor. The car had been locked, and I wasn't about to try to find the keys. I ran until I didn't think I could run anymore and that was when I heard the car behind me. I thought for sure it was Devon."

"But it was Henry. It was amazing you had been able to run that far.

I remember hearing the police tell Father that they found the cabin by following your blood trail; you ran a mile before you collapsed. Henry saw you just as you fell and watched you crawl another hundred yards to the middle of that dirt road before he was able to get to you," Ethan said quietly, pride etched on his face.

"Adrenaline does an amazing thing. When I woke up, I was at the hospital, and you were there. Noticeably absent were Mother and Father. Did you ever wonder why?" Kara asked, looking at Ethan.

"I did."

"So did I. I mean, sure, they weren't loving parents, but, where were they? Later, I saw in the papers and on the television repeatedly where they were. They were too busy playing up to the media to come to my room. Mother's crocodile tears and Father's arm wrapped around her. The most contact I'd seen between them in years. It was all too much, and I decided there was something off. So, I tried to look into it. As you can imagine, I was blocked at every turn."

"What caused the fallout between you and our parents?"

"I'm not sure if it's relevant to this case. And without evidence, it doesn't matter. Our parents' behavior was not normal after I was found. They were more secretive than ever and very interested in sweeping everything under the covers."

"Other than their behavior, what makes you think they were involved?" Ethan asked.

"Father with the file wasn't normal. I know a man with his power can get what he wants, and he may have just wanted to view the file. But then I overheard him talking to someone about whether it was done."

"Done?" Bob asked.

Kara had almost forgotten he was in the room. She wasn't sure she wanted to disclose everything about those days leading up to her moving out of her parents' house; in the back of her mind, she knew her parents were hiding something from her abduction. Kara just didn't know what it would be and how she would be able to find out or convince anyone else once she did find out. For now, she would hold back a little bit of information—until she was sure it was relevant that they know. Kara wasn't dumb. She knew she needed to share the information, but she wasn't going to go after her parents until she had irrefutable proof. It would be an impossible battle to win if she didn't have evidence against them. For now, she would present the information, only leaving out one key element.

"I think Father has something to do with that folder only having one sheet of paper in it. But like I said, he could just say he was viewing the file." *Or he could be the exact reason it is all missing.*

"But who would have helped him?" Ethan asked sharply.

"Are you sure? You realize what you are saying, right?" Bob asked.

"Father has a number of people on his payroll that are 'off the books.' Is it really that much of a stretch to believe? There have been whispers for a while about how 'clean' my father's hands are—or rather, aren't. Do you find this so hard to believe?"

"He definitely isn't the kind of person Cal Vincent is, so I guess not," Bob said. "Shit, this has the potential to blow up in our faces."

"You're telling me," Kara added.

"This means that we might not just be trying to find out who murdered Andrea Vincent. We also might have other people coming after you. People who are scared you'll talk, people who are scared you might know they're beholden to your father. That, coupled with the fact that someone might be copying your case or that there was an accomplice after all, means we have our work cut out for us," Caleb said, squeezing her hand.

Kara looked both Ethan and Caleb in the eye, lingering on Caleb's longer than she had intended. In his eyes, she saw worry and frustration, but there was something else that she saw in Caleb's eyes that had her anger melting on the spot. It was the same look that she'd seen earlier in the day. A look that was all consuming, it was almost too powerful to comprehend. With one look, Kara knew that she wanted everything he was promising in his eyes.

CALEB WASN'T sure what he had expected to hear, but he knew that wasn't it. It was not without reason that her father would be able to bribe someone to destroy evidence. But why would he destroy the evidence of an open-and-shut case pertaining to his own daughter?

Caleb didn't just suspect there was something she was holding back. He knew there was much more to the story. However, he let it be. He knew she would tell when the time was right; he just hoped it wasn't too late when she finally decided it was time. It was obvious that she was aware of the dangers of holding back. Therefore, he knew that the risks of telling were also a danger to her safety. Every person in that room knew there was more to this story, but because it was involving a sitting governor, they would have to tread lightly. Which is why Kara was holding back. Caleb's suspicion was she was holding out until she could have concrete evidence to present, which scared the ever-living shit out of him.

Without a doubt, she was aware of whom her father had paid off. Down deep, he knew that wasn't all that was going on, that there was a much bigger secret she was hiding. For now, he would go with it, because he had no choice and he trusted her judgment.

"I'm not sure if any of this helped. The man who hurt me is supposed to be dead, so I'm at a loss to who is doing this now. Clearly, someone wants to finish what was started. Maybe it was their plan all along. Maybe they're taking advantage of my coming home. I only know that my coming home was not part of their plan. I didn't even know I would be coming home, and I only hope that we can figure out who it is and what his agenda is before anyone else is hurt."

"We all do. We're operating under the assumption that this unsub is an anniversary killer. He's very ritualistic, and that means we should have until next year before he strikes. But your coming home seems to have changed his agenda. His fixation has been on you all this time if we're interpreting the notes right. If there was an accomplice, you're the one that got away—his greatest challenge. This means we shouldn't assume anything; he's become unpredictable," Bob said matter-of-factly.

When they all stood to leave, Gloria left, followed by Ethan, but Kara hung back a second and Caleb waited beside her. He watched, openly curious, as she stopped the captain and pulled him off to the side.

"Captain—" She stopped when he would have objected. "Bob, I'm terribly sorry to hear about your goddaughter. I'm so sorry for any connection I have to it. If there's anything I could have done to stop it all those years ago, I would have. I'm determined to help finish it now." Bob lifted his hand to stop her from speaking further.

"I assure you, whoever did this is to blame and them alone. Not you. There's nothing you could or should have done differently. You thought it was buried along with Devon Bristol."

Bob was about to walk away and paused, as if considering something, then turned and pulled Kara into his arms in a tight embrace. Bob whispered something in Kara's ear and then walked away. Straightening her shirt, she turned to look at Caleb. He was touched by the scene, and he knew that she was, too.

"Ready to go?"

"Go where?" she asked, looking confused.

"Back to your house. We're late to meet with the security system people."

"That's right. I have a function I need to get ready for tonight, as well."

They walked out to his car, and once inside, she turned to look at him.

"Ethan isn't coming?"

"He's going to continue looking for other victims. Captain decided it keeps him part of the case, and it doesn't utilize resources that we can't afford to pull from other departments."

"So, he *did* get sidelined?"

"He did. He's still being allowed to sit in for input on Andrea's case. To keep him sane and out of trouble. But for all intents and purposes, he isn't allowed to touch the case. I think he pulled your father's name to get as much leeway as he did."

They traveled in silence for a couple of minutes. Caleb knew that there was something she wanted to say, so he waited patiently until she worked up the nerve to tell him what was on her mind.

"You know there's more to the story, don't you?" When he nodded his head, she continued. "Why didn't you say something?"

"I figured you'd say something when the time was right. For the record, everyone in that room knew you were holding back." He looked at her when she sighed heavily.

"Devon told me I was a terrible liar. I didn't figure I had pulled it off with people trained to see lies. I hope they understand I had to leave some stuff out for Ethan's sake. There are some things he just doesn't need to know and some stuff that I need evidence for before I open Pandora's box."

"For instance?"

"Ethan doesn't need to know that I prayed to die back then, or that sometimes, in the middle of the night, I think it would have been better. I hoped one of the times the blackness would take over. I dream of a revenge I can't have because Devon Bristol was killed and not by my hand. I couldn't stand having him look at me like I'm a monster." She took a deep breath before continuing. "He doesn't need to know that sometimes, especially at night, the blackness threatens to take over, and I consider ending it all. It's fewer and farther between than it used to be. When I first got home, all I thought about was killing myself. I-I still struggle when the nightmares get intense."

Caleb had pulled the car into her driveway, and he turned to look at her. His heart ached at the haunted look on her face; it was hard not to notice the faraway stare. She was back in that time, in that place. Somehow, she had successfully closed herself off from it at the station. But he suspected admitting it was too real right now. Gently, he reached out and touched her hand. He wasn't offended when she flinched. He knew how hard any physical contact must be for her. Especially when she was feeling the pain she was feeling.

"God, Kara, please tell me that you'll reach out to me if that blackness threatens to take over again. I couldn't stand it if you did something to yourself."

"It's been a long time since it happened last, but I can't lie to you, the last day has been one of the most challenging I've had in the last several years. But I know that I have a purpose in this life, and I can do so much good to offset the bad that happened to me."

"Kara, can I ask you something?"

"Go ahead. But I won't promise I'll answer."

"Have you ever seen someone for post-traumatic stress disorder?"

"No. I know I'm not living; I mean, I exist, but I'm not living. I want to be happy. I want to marry, have children, and have a life. I made an appointment with someone for next week. A friend at the hospital set it up for me. I'm tired of feeling this way. I hate the rage inside me. I want to feel normal. I don't even know what normal is."

"I'm glad to hear you're going to see someone."

"I know I have issues. It was just a matter of admitting it to myself. Vanderbilts aren't supposed to admit weakness. They're supposed to carry on."

"You don't have issues. You just need some help in dealing with what you went through. No one could have gone through that much and not need some kind of counseling."

"Maybe..." Her voice trailed off.

He knew that whatever he told her wouldn't be enough, that she had to figure it out on her own. Once she could accept that she couldn't change what she went through then, she'd be able to begin to heal. He had seen many people traumatized by tragic things happening to them, and he had never seen anyone weather as much as she had and come out of it well adjusted. And certainly not by doing it alone. It made him proud to know her.

"You know, you don't have to babysit me. I can handle myself. I've had lots of training in self-defense since that summer. And I have Sam. Sam wouldn't let anything happen to me. One word, one subtle gesture, and he would rip the throat out of anyone who tried to touch me."

"I know you can take care of yourself, but I would feel better if you let me watch over you. Captain feels the same as I do about watching out for you. As long as this person is on the loose, he wants protection for you."

"When did he decide that?"

"Before I picked you up. When we realized there are more victims, he decided we should put a protection detail on you. He's struggling with the loss of Andrea, and he doesn't want another murder. I suspect after meeting you, he's even more resolved to protect you."

"That's ridiculous. First of all, you said yourself that they can't afford to pull resources. I know the budget constraints that most police departments are under. Secondly, like I said, I can take care of myself. I've been doing it for a long time."

"Damn it, don't you understand? This is serious. My feelings for you are not what are propelling this. This is coming from the top. This is a high-profile case. A senator's daughter is dead; there has been a threat to the governor's daughter. You matter, whether you want to or are ready to believe it."

"All right, so I am scared shitless. And I know that I make a difference with my job and that, in theory, I matter. But that isn't the point. The point is that I would rather the person watching me be out on the street looking for this person."

"Trust me; we're all looking for whoever did this. But for now, you're going to have to deal with being protected."

"Do I have a choice?"

"No."

"And who is supposed to be watching out for me?"

"Right now, me. If I get called away, then someone else will be assigned to you."

"You?"

"Yes, me. Do you have a problem with that?"

"No. I guess if someone had to watch my back and it couldn't be Ethan, I would want it to be you. I trust you almost as much as I trust him. Maybe even as much. But they can't afford to have you, of all people, watching me and not working on the case."

"First, I'm still working the case. We've been investigating her disappearance for days, and all the leads dried up. Finding her hasn't resulted in any new leads, other than it has connected to you. We are at a virtual standstill. For now, you have me to watch over you. Answer me this, how come you trust me so easily?"

"You have my brother's back; yesterday, you said you would back him up on this. And that meant a lot to me. Can I ask you something?"

"Sure."

"How did you get assigned to watch me?"

"I wasn't assigned; I volunteered. Ethan will also help, but he's working to locate the other old cases. We're hoping we can find something there that can help us. It didn't take very much convincing. Bob understood that you would have a hard time with a revolving shift of men you'd never met watching you. You've met Officer Black, so he'll take any shifts Ethan and I can't."

"I see. So, what does this mean? That you drop me off and pick me up?"

"It means you go nowhere alone. One of us is with you at all times. And I mean *all* times. If you have to go to the bathroom, we'll stand a discreet but safe distance away so we can get to you in a snap." He snapped his fingers for emphasis.

"So...who gets the night shift?" she asked with a note of shyness in her voice.

"Me." The word came out as a growl.

"You can't be serious? When will you sleep? You haven't slept as it is."

"I can go for days on very little sleep. That isn't a problem for me."

"You won't be useful on this case if you're dead on your feet. I'll only accept you being on the night shift if you're allowed to sleep."

"How effective would that be?"

"Caleb, be serious, you need to be firing on all cylinders to catch this monster. That means you need sleep. Officer Black can do the night shift."

"You don't understand; I don't want another man here when you're at your most vulnerable. If it can't be me, the only other person I'll allow to watch you at night is Ethan. I trust Ethan and Ethan trusts me." He noticed she raised her eyebrow at the word 'allow.'

"You can sleep inside." She paused. "On my couch. The alarm system should be installed. Better protection if you're in the house with me."

"Deal."

15

They climbed out of the car and made their way up the walk. The gentleman from the alarm company was inside when they walked in.

"Perfect timing. I just finished up. I'll run through the system with you, show you how to set up the code that you'll need to use to arm or disable your system."

It didn't take long for Hal to run through all the operating instructions for the new system. Kara had shut the door behind her and was making her way to the stairs when Caleb cleared his throat. With her eyebrows raised in question, she turned to look at him. His face was very intense as he looked at her.

"What? I set the alarm."

"It's not that. You mentioned a function you have to go to tonight. I know Ethan is busy, as well; he's also going to some function as a representative of the police department. He gets sent to things like this because he cleans up well." He smiled wryly. "Would I be wrong in assuming it's the same function you're going to?"

"For the new rape crisis center?" she asked.

"Yes."

"Then you would be right. He doesn't know I'm going to be there, but if you have something you need to do or someone you need to visit,

I'm sure Ethan can babysit me. It will be a huge crowd. So, I don't think you need to worry about my safety that much. After all, a lot of the people there will be off duty police officers."

"That wasn't my point. The reason I asked was that I remember Ethan saying that he always gets asked to be the official representative to these kinds of functions because of his family name and because he owns a tux," Caleb said with a look of consternation on his face. Kara couldn't help herself, she giggled. She actually giggled at the look on his face.

"What? You don't have a tux? No worries, a suit is just fine. As a matter of fact, the invitation didn't say anything about a dress code."

She smiled at the relieved look on his face. Clearly, she found something he wasn't comfortable with—black tie events. She couldn't blame him there. Kara may have been raised in that environment, but she'd never been at ease in it, and she would avoid them at all costs, and had for quite some time. But this event was near and dear to her heart, and after all, it was stressed that it was supposed to be a dress down event.

Kara hated going to public events where she had to try to behave normally around people. It was amazing she could function at all in her work, but she'd found it incredibly rewarding. And tonight, she was going to open a new chapter of her life; she hoped that funding and spearheading the new rape crisis center would help heal some of her wounds.

She hadn't planned on the day's events or having an escort to the grand opening of the center. The center had been her baby for the last six years. After fundraising for four years, she finally had enough money to go to the bank with and to start getting the state-of-the-art center built. It was her big surprise to Ethan, the big reveal that she was doing her best to move on. She had meticulously picked the guest list and had made sure that her name was left off all the invitations.

As a matter of fact, she had made it impossible to figure out that she was getting the center together. She didn't want anyone to know until the night of the grand opening and would gladly have kept her name out of it altogether, but she knew her name would add much needed donations, and they needed all the donations they could get. Kara wanted people to donate their money and come to the grand opening for the center and not for her and her name, but she was a realist. For the most part, it had been surprisingly easy to get donations and yet hide her name from the actual center. Being involved in fundraising didn't automatically make you the one spearheading the whole thing. It helped having Dr. Brenner and Dr. Chiglo to help. Their help had been irreplaceable.

She forced herself back to reality when she saw guests starting to arrive. Tonight was supposed to be her big night; the night when she spoke openly for the first time about her own rape. She wasn't expecting having to tell her story to the cops that morning. But that didn't matter. The version she told tonight would be less detailed, and it was a sort of dry run for her. Kara felt sick to her stomach. She was happy to hear that her brother was coming tonight. She had extended the invitation to his bosses weeks prior, specifically asking for him, hoping that he would come.

Even though she'd had months to prepare for this night, she was still nervous. Taking a deep breath, she began mingling with the people who had been carefully picked to attend the opening of the center. There were many people she'd wanted there, many organizations that had helped to make this day happen. And there were some more strategic invites, ones she had invited who would hopefully be willing to help fund the center in the future. They would still need a lot of donations to keep the doors open for years to come.

Out of the corner of her eye, she saw Ethan arrive, and she quickly moved out of his line of vision. She wanted to surprise her brother. And because of that, she didn't want him to see her until she stood on stage to give her speech. With Caleb by her side, she walked silently into the corridor to wait until it was time to go to the podium that was set up and tell everyone her story. Caleb surprised her every minute she spent with him because she knew that he believed in her. And that meant a lot to her and said a lot about him.

While she stood, she fidgeted with her blouse and nearly jumped out of her skin when she heard a female voice behind her.

"Ms. Vanderbilt?"

She spun around her heart in her throat. "Yes, that's me. May I help you?"

"Quinn Sanders, we spoke on the phone."

"Oh, Quinn, how nice to finally meet you," she said. Kara felt foolish for being so startled. Quinn was the woman she had chosen to manage the center.

"Quinn, this is Detective Caleb Montgomery."

"We've met a time or two on a case," Quinn said, smiling warmly at Caleb. "Nice to see you again."

"Likewise, but I'm glad it's under better circumstances."

For some reason, the exchange between the two irritated Kara. And she felt somewhat agitated as they shook hands. Kara hadn't felt like this since high school, and it was never on this level. She knew deep in her gut that it was jealousy, even if she tried to convince her head that wasn't what it was.

"Are you ready?" Quinn asked. "It's time."

"I guess I'm as ready as I'll ever be," she whispered, trying to hide the jealousy in her voice, wondering if that agitation could be used to her advantage to get through the next few minutes.

"In that case, I'll go out and introduce you."

Kara just nodded in response. Quinn exchanged a quick glance between the two and smiled knowingly, then grasped her hand in support. While Kara had never explained her story to Quinn, she knew Quinn had heard of her. Even so, Kara was confused by the look she had given her as if she understood why Kara was agitated. Which would be impossible, because Kara herself didn't know why she was so agitated. Who was she kidding? She knew exactly why she was pissed. Kara didn't want the attractive blonde woman by Caleb.

Kara didn't have time to ask Quinn about the expression before she was walking out and politely introducing her. Quinn didn't use Kara's name in the introduction because she didn't want a big uproar before she got out there; she knew she would back out if that happened. So instead, she just introduced the speaker as the founder of A Place to Hope.

"And now I would like to introduce you to the woman who envisioned and made this center happen. Please give her a warm round of applause." The applause was the cue for her to go to the podium. She took two, deep calming breaths. Right before she walked onstage, Caleb laced his fingers with hers and squeezed her hand warmly before letting it go and walking back out into the main room where he stood off to the side in the crowd.

Being in front of the crowd was more daunting than she had expected. She searched the crowd for something to calm her and was not surprised when that something ended up being a very attractive detective who looked beautiful and supportive standing off in the shadows. *It's now or never*, she told herself.

"Ladies and Gentlemen, my name is Kara Vanderbilt..." She paused when she heard the gasps and whispers start, and taking a deep breath, she continued, "...and I would like to thank you for coming tonight to share in my dream to have an avenue for victims of abuse—whatever kind it may be—to seek help. Not just rape victims, but all victims can come to A Place to Hope for help and guidance, a place that is completely free and designed to protect those who cannot protect themselves. This dream was a long time coming, and I would be lying if I said it wasn't a dream built on a nightmare. Ten years ago, a terrible thing happened to me. Something I've never spoken about in public until today."

The crowd became deafeningly silent. One more deep breath, and then she continued.

"I was abducted and held captive for four days, and in those four days, I was repeatedly raped by a man who fortunately is dead today and not able to do it to anyone else. He did heinous and deplorable things to me that no person should ever have to endure. I was only eighteen at the time, a virgin, and I had never even been kissed. I had dreamed of my first kiss, and I had dreamed of the first time someone made love to me. All those dreams were crushed by Devon Bristol." She paused, sucking in a labored breath. Her chest tightened, and she knew she was beginning to have an anxiety attack. Finding Caleb in the crowd again, she forced herself to continue. *Keep going.*

"Not only did he steal my innocence, but he did it in the most despicable ways imaginable. I was not only raped, I was sodomized and tortured. I opened this center so that other scared women or men can come somewhere to talk when it seems there is nothing good left in life. I had many resources that I could have used, unlike many victims. And I am ashamed to say that with all the wealth I grew up in, I chose to not seek any help. As a result, my life has been lived in fear..." With a slight nod from Caleb, she continued. "At times, the darkness threatened to swallow me up, and there were many days that I considered killing myself." She searched the crowd for Ethan and smiled sadly at him; he swiped at a cheek, and Kara knew he was crying.

"A few months back when I was told that the center was almost ready, I told myself it was time for a change. I'm here today to prove to everyone that there can be a life after being violated. Once again, I would like to thank all of you for coming. Please tell anyone who you think needs help that our doors are always open for whatever reason they made need it. Even tonight." Thunderous applause enveloped her like a warm hug, and Kara felt a piece of her heart heal.

ETHAN WAS CONFUSED when he saw Caleb come out of a doorway to the left and was moving toward him when Kara walked to a podium on risers. Seeing Kara standing there had Ethan pause mid-stride. Ethan had a hard time fighting the tears that formed and eventually gave up the fight to stem them. He quietly approached Caleb and stood beside him as Kara spoke. When she was done, he heard Caleb start to clap and followed suit. He was in shock from finding out that Kara was the founder of A Place to Hope.

Obviously, equally moved by her speech, Caleb stood stoically beside him. Which ultimately scared Ethan; he had always been protective and didn't want anyone to hurt Kara. He wanted her to be able to date, but at the same time, he was terrified of her dating. Ethan could not ask for a better person to be interested in his sister. He just hoped that it worked out and neither one got hurt. And above all, he hoped that Kara would take a chance on Caleb because he knew that Caleb could make all the difference, and even though he worried, he felt in his heart that Caleb was just what Kara needed.

"I think I underestimated her for the last time," Ethan said, breaking the silence. "She definitely is stronger than I gave her credit for. And I could not be prouder of her." Ethan turned to scan the crowd, looking for Kara, and then froze. "Shit!"

"What?" Caleb asked and then followed his eyes. "Son of a bitch," he exclaimed when his eyes locked on what Ethan was looking at. Stanley Vanderbilt was there, and he was making a beeline for Kara.

"WELL, you never cease to amaze me, Kara."

Kara stopped abruptly; she had been on her way to find Ethan and Caleb when she heard his voice boom over the crowd. Slowly, she turned to find her father standing tall and regal in the middle of the room, commanding the attention of all around him. Which pissed Kara off beyond words; this center was not about him. Damn him for trying to make it about him.

"How the hell did you get in here? This was by invitation only, and you were not invited," she spat between clenched teeth. Ethan and Caleb showed up just in time to hear her.

"It amazes me how easily you forget who I am and what I can do," Stanley Vanderbilt said.

"Forget? Hardly. I don't forget, and I won't forgive. I just choose not to acknowledge who and what you are."

"This isn't the time or the place," Ethan said. Kara didn't even bother looking his way. Her father was not about to ruin this night for her.

Stanley looked around the room at the nosey eyes peering at them and grabbed her by the upper arm, but he even made that seem regal as he pulled her out of the main room where all the guests were and lead her to the same corridor she had been standing in terrified only moments before. Except, this time, she was no longer terrified—quite the opposite. She was furious and no longer the eighteen-year-old girl who was scared to stand up to her parents. She was barely aware that Ethan and Caleb had followed and even less aware of the concern in their eyes.

"What's the problem, Governor? You don't want anyone to hear what I have to say? I bet you would prefer they not hear about what I know. About who you really are and what you did that was so, so bad ten years ago that your only daughter would scream to not come near her ever again in front of a crowd of cameras. I'm sure there are enough reporters in there that would love the exclusive rights to our story. Shall we go talk to them?"

She turned to go back into the main room to talk to the reporters. Fuck the consequences of taking on her father; he had no right being there. She had no sooner turned when he had grabbed her arm again— much rougher this time. She nearly winced in pain but made herself focus on something else. Kara had gotten good at hiding pain, but she knew that she would have a horrible bruise from him and that made her even angrier.

"Kara, keep your voice down," he said angrily.

"What are you saying? You would prefer I not tell them what you did? I wonder what your constituents would say if they heard about what I know and the evidence from my case? Or should I say, the lack thereof?" *Crack!* Before she could blink, her father had slapped her. Actually slapped her! Both men took a step closer until she held her hand up. She was not going to back down, and she didn't need their help. "You son of a bitch. You think you can do anything and there are no repercussions?"

"Kara, I'm warning you..." Her father's voice roared in her ears, even though he was speaking quietly.

"Warning me?" She laughed coldly. "I'm not that scared little eighteen-year-old anymore. How dare you think you have the right to come here? This place is a good place. It's a place of healing and should not have to be tarnished by your presence. I am warning *you*; get out of my center and out of my life, while you still have a chance. Because I wasn't bluffing about the reporters. If you ever step foot in here again, you will be sorrier than you have ever been in your life."

How had she become such an angry and vengeful person? The answer was ten years in the making. Ten years of brooding over what her parents had done to her. Before Ethan could intervene, Caleb's hand stopped him, and she heard him whisper something that calmed her ever so slightly. He told Ethan that she had to do this to move on and that *they* were there for her if she needed *them*.

"My presence is instrumental in everything you do, *darling*. You are who you are because of me."

"You're right about that. I am who I am because of you. Care to tell them what I mean?" she asked, looking her father dead in the eye. "You see, you can't pay me off like Jenkins and Byrnes."

"Don't listen to your sister. She's been crazy since she emerged from the woods all those years ago. She thinks she overheard me paying off someone regarding her case. What she heard was me trying to pay off some reporters," Stanley said.

Oh, he was good, she thought. He could lie with the best of them, but she knew he was lying, and he was lying through his teeth. After all these years, he could not muster the balls to fess up to what he had done. And that angered her even more. The blood in her veins pumped through her body like liquid fire, and she had to hold herself back from physically attacking him.

"You know damn well that is not what I heard. Come on, *Dad*, we're the only ones here, admit it, just once. You forget that I have an impeccable memory, and somewhere in the back of your head you were hoping over the years I would forget. But you just keep underestimating me. Because while I don't know why you did what you did, I do know that you did it. And I will never forget, just like I will not forget the events of those four days."

"Why can't you just let it rest? Devon Bristol died ten years ago. I don't know why you insist on blaming me for what happened."

"I insist on blaming you because you are as much to blame. And I cannot let it rest. Funny you should mention how Devon Bristol died ten years ago, because you may as well have died with him for all the good you did to find me. I'm going to let you in on a little secret. Are you listening? I am taking you down, *Daddy*, so it's time to start doing damage control. Because there is a storm of whoop ass about to come down on you, and you are too dumb to know it. The way I see it, this can go down two ways—you resigning as governor and moving far away, never to contact me again, which you should be able to handle quite well—or, you in prison. Either way, I'm fine with the outcome."

"Surely, you must be kidding. You moved here; you can move back to the rock you were hiding under." She heard Ethan suck in air and saw him tense in her periphery. Kara laughed. It was a bitter laugh, and she hated the sound of it.

"Plan your next move carefully, and do not underestimate your opponent. Now, if you'll excuse me, I need some air."

She turned on her heel and headed outside, outside where there was freedom. Ethan and Caleb were hot on her heels. She didn't stop until she was outside dragging in big gulps of fresh air, her hands on her knees, bent over. The confrontation was so intense, she thought she would explode. But she had survived, and another piece of her heart healed. She had confronted the great Stanley Vanderbilt and had lived. Sure, she had threatened him, tightened the noose around his neck. But that was all part of her plan. After a couple deeper breaths, she turned to face Ethan and Caleb.

16

Caleb was worried about Kara when he followed her and her brother outside. He knew she was hiding things, and after the altercation inside, it was even more evident that she hadn't moved on from whatever had happened between her and her parents. Caleb was also certain that she had PTSD. With the anger and frustration that emanated from her, he was concerned that she might attack her father.

Of course, if she had attacked him, Caleb would have done nothing to stop her. The bastard was lucky that Caleb didn't drop his ass when he slapped Kara. He wasn't sure who—out of the two of them—was itching to drop him most. He knew if Kara wouldn't have stopped them, either he or Ethan would have taken him down.

Once outside, both men gave Kara a little space to regroup. When she finally stood and turned to face them, her eyes were more in control, but still brimmed with hatred. There was no doubt in Caleb's mind that Kara hated her father, and he knew it centered on her abduction. It was just a matter of her disclosing why. Once again, he found himself hoping that would be sooner rather than later.

"I need to go back inside."

"The hell you do. You need to explain what the hell just happened!" Ethan shouted.

"Tone it down a little, E."

"So, the gloves are off, no longer treating me like I will break, are you, big brother?" Kara's voice was laced with venom.

Caleb knew her anger was not intentionally directed at Ethan and that it was just a matter of proximity and she was projecting her hate on him. Kara was still coming down off the high she was riding when she confronted her father. The adrenaline coursing through her system would take a little bit to wear off before she crashed. And crash she would, Caleb knew. He had been there dozens of times himself.

"Kara, I just want to help. I'm not a fool; I know you're incredibly intelligent. I know your intelligence far surpasses mine. But for such a smart person, you are being a jackass. You know you need our help, but you're so damn stubborn, you're set on doing it all yourself. Let us help you."

"Help me what? Trust me, you don't want to be a part of this when it hits the fan. You should get as far away as possible."

"Not happening, so just spill it."

"Yes sir, master, sir." Kara was nearly shouting at that point.

Caleb knew he had to do something to diffuse the situation. He didn't want Kara and Ethan damaging their relationship because of their father, and he certainly didn't want them coming to blows. And at that moment, it looked as if Kara was ready to attack. Once again, anger that was badly misplaced.

"All right, you two, round's over. Go to your separate corners of the ring. I think you both need to charge down a little and regroup. We all want to figure out what's going on. So, let's just take a step back and reevaluate things in the morning."

Brother and sister both looked his way and simultaneously nodded their agreement. If Caleb didn't know better, he would have thought they were twins. Their mannerisms were the same, and they were both bullheaded. Hopefully, both would be willing to give a little so they could be useful to each other.

"Right. Fine. I need to go back in and mingle for at least a little while. The people in there are the backbone to this center succeeding, and I need to reel in a couple of big donations so the doors can stay open for years to come."

"Kara..."

"Caleb's right, Ethan. We all need to recharge. I'll talk to you in the morning. Give me the night to figure some things out. I need to go inside to make sure Stanley isn't causing any issues that'll shut us down before we even get started."

"You don't really think he would do that, do you?" Ethan asked, clearly skeptical.

"Oh, there isn't much I would put past him."

Before Ethan could respond, Kara walked inside without looking back. Caleb's heart broke for both. Ethan just wanted to help his sister get back to herself, and he couldn't do that if she wouldn't let him. And Kara just wanted to keep Ethan out of the line of fire. She had tried the same tactic with him and had finally given in to the fact that it wasn't going to happen.

"Just give her some time, Ethan. She's coming around; it's just hard to give up the demons and secrets after a decade of keeping them to herself."

"I know. I just...I just want to kill the son of a bitch who did this to her. You know? She used to be so happy. No, you know what, that's a lie. She used to be happier. Our father and mother have always treated her terribly, so she was never carefree and happy."

"I want her to be happy, too; at least the consolation prize is that the bastard is dead. But, Ethan, I think you need to be prepared for something big. We both know she's holding something back."

"I know. I just hope she tells me soon."

"Me too. Before something else happens to her."

"You really like her, huh?"

"I really do. Are you okay with that?"

"Yeah. She needs someone like you in her life. I just hope she realizes that before it's too late. Something needs to change and fast."

He couldn't agree more. Kara was on a precipice, and there was a big fork in the road. One that if she didn't navigate it correctly, she would be lost to all of them. Caleb watched him walk away and was about to go inside when Ethan called out to him.

"Montgomery? Watch both your backs. I think Kara's right—our father is capable of anything, and the shit is about to hit the fan on this whole thing."

ETHAN WAS STILL REELING from the exchange between Kara and their father. He had known that something bad had gone down all those years ago, and he was starting to think that maybe he didn't want to know the reason Kara had left and tried to never look back. It was obvious that it was something extremely bad because he had never seen anger in Kara like he'd witnessed tonight. Clearly, ten years was a long time to let that anger fester, and it was becoming clear to Ethan that, even though Kara had left, she had not left behind what had happened to her.

The anger and resentment was so profound that he had a hard time focusing on what she had said to their father. Ethan knew that their parents kind of sucked, especially when it came to her. He could never figure out the indifference they had toward her, especially their mother. While their father pretty much equally ignored them, their mother doted on him and completely ignored Kara unless she was in the mood to belittle her. When he was young, he was too self-centered to really pay attention. The older he got, the more he noticed it. He loved his mother, but he hated her for the way she treated Kara, and he became his sister's lifeline.

As Ethan walked to his car, the words she had spat at their father as the exchange between father and daughter had ensued slowly began to sink in. Kara had given a small hint that might help him figure out what had happened to cause the huge rift. She had mentioned a couple of names that he had discarded as familiar and nothing else until it clicked why he knew the names.

You can't pay me off like Jenkins and Byrnes.

The statement repeated over and over in his head. He knew the two names, but he didn't know why. Ethan decided to go to the station and see if he could find anybody connected to his father, mother, or Kara with the name Jenkins or Byrnes. He was grateful that Caleb would take Kara home; he was beginning to worry about her for a far different reason than he was used to.

Ethan had always worried about Kara being fragile. But it was becoming clear that there was more to her than met the eye. A different side of his sister emerged tonight, a side that was angry and full of hatred, combining that with her admission of fighting through the darkness, and Ethan was terrified that she would harm herself. It was something he'd never even considered a possibility; maybe at first, but not now. Kara had seemed well adjusted. Now, he wasn't so sure; now, he was scared she was about to self-destruct.

Maybe, her coming home wasn't a good idea after all. Maybe, being so close to her parents wasn't good for her, because it was clear to him after tonight that Kara wanted revenge. Whatever she had on them was so bad that it had turned his beautiful kid sister into someone he barely recognized tonight.

Ethan was going to have to do whatever was in his power to stop her from waging an all-out war with Stanley and Constance Vanderbilt —a war she didn't stand a good chance of winning because their parents had their hands in every cookie jar in the great state of Wisconsin. Ethan wasn't dumb; sure, Kara was the genius of the two of them, but Ethan was also extremely intelligent and had realized that if Kara was not going to fill him in on what happened all those years ago, he would have to find out himself.

At the time, Ethan had found it odd that his sister, the dutiful daughter, had walked away from their parents and had refused any contact with them. Not that Stanley or Constance had reached out to her, but she hadn't reached out to them, either. He would have walked away, too, but down deep, he knew there was something there that he needed to know. The detective in him wanted to scratch away until he found the answers. But out of respect to Kara, who had told him to let it go, he had backed off. However, over the last decade, he had stayed in touch with his parents, for the sole purpose of finding out information on them. He would have loved to have washed his hands of them years ago, especially after some of the dealings he had found their hands in, but he hadn't hit the mother lode yet. Meaning he hadn't figured out what they had done to his sister, and he wouldn't stop until he knew—no matter how bad it was. He was pretty sure he had enough evidence of extortion to bury them both, but not until he knew everything. It would be easier not knowing, but he had to find out.

Ethan was pulling into his precinct when he remembered why the names were so familiar. He was almost certain the two men were cops —partners. He was going to have to play this very carefully because he needed access to personnel files. Personnel files that were behind a locked door. He was not concerned about how to get into the files; there was more than one cop who'd help him out there. He was more concerned about getting caught in the act because that would tip his hand to his father, who was well connected in the police department. After only about a minute of negotiating, he had convinced a rookie, whose name badge read Hernandez, to let him into the vault with the records.

Once inside, he moved instantly to the file cabinets. He found Byrnes' file first and whispered a cursory *shit* under his breath when he found that Byrnes had been killed in the line of duty during a drug bust eight years ago. The hairs on his neck stood at attention when he located the file for Jenkins because he knew what he would find before he opened the file. Jenkins was killed the same night in the line of duty at the same drug bust.

Ethan now knew why he recognized the names. He hadn't been on the force for more than a couple of years before they had been killed, and there was a huge cloud of suspicion that had surrounded their deaths. There had been whispers throughout the department that they were dirty cops, and Ethan recalled mention of Internal Affairs opening files on them. Pieces to the puzzle started to fall into place.

The two cops had to have been among the officers that were under his father's payroll. The question now was, what were they paid to do for Stanley Vanderbilt and what had Kara discovered? He suspected they were paid to get rid of evidence, but for what reason?

17

Kara stood, watching from a window at the taillights of her brother's car as he pulled away. She'd lost her cool, and she knew she had. Seeing her father tonight—of all nights—had her seeing red. Tonight was about healing, not about rehashing old drawn-out stories about her parents. But that was what she had found herself doing. Rehashing that day in November that could have destroyed what little was left of her, but it was somewhat easier than she had thought it would be.

However, if those memories hadn't been brought up, not once, but twice in the same day, she may have handled things better. Right now, she knew her brother, and probably Caleb, too, thought she was stark raving mad.

Kara should have been grateful to her parents. Because if they wouldn't have been so cocky—so foolish—she would have stayed there and maybe never gotten out from under their thumb. She was what she was because of her parents; her father had gotten that much right. She was stronger, strong enough to walk away from them and their power and money. She was more driven. Driven to make the center come to being. She was more compassionate. Compassionate enough to think of Ethan before she went to the reporters, which she desperately wanted to do. Admittedly, that was a bad example of compassion, but she was certain she was more compassionate than her parents. And she was working on being less fearful; sure, she was scared of every noise and any man that looked at her in a suspicious manner, but tonight showed her she was no longer scared to take on her father. And for that, she could, albeit grudgingly, credit him for.

Why did she hate them so much? It was easier to hate them than to forgive them. And she just didn't think she could forgive them. She was strong enough to endure their betrayal, but she didn't love them enough to forgive them. If that made her a selfish person, too bad. She deserved to be selfish about this one thing.

She also had her father to thank for her discovery of a couple things tonight. One thing was, while she knew she hadn't put that night behind her, she had *not* realized how much anger had grown in her about it. The other thing she had discovered was that she was tired of the whole sordid mess. Tired of being scared, but trying to appear strong, tired of being angry over things for which she had no control, and she was exhausted when it came to her parents.

The dirty truth of it all was she could care less what happened to them. Kara had realized tonight she was tired of hiding what they'd done, tired of continuing to be the dutiful daughter even when she no longer talked to her parents. She was tired of being a masochist, tired of taking the brunt of what had happened on her shoulders, and it was time they paid. Oh, it was time, all right. It was time for their judgment day here on earth. She wouldn't compromise herself—or her standards—for them.

Kara had had enough and knew she had to tell Ethan everything before she turned into an evil, bitter, hateful person like her parents were. Kara only hoped it wasn't too late. Slowly, she turned to look at the tall, dark man standing beside her. Quietly, she sized him up. In another life, on another day, she may have had a chance with a man like him. But Kara was certain there was no hope for that; even so, she found that she wanted to try.

It felt like an eternity before she finally felt like she could go home for the night. Kara was certain she'd done enough mingling with the right people that she would have some lucrative investors for the center. And it appeared her father had left without tarnishing her chances at donations. He probably assumed it would hurt him more than help him to ruin her center. Searching the crowd, she located Quinn and made her way through the throngs of people so she could ask her to finish up for her.

"You did wonderful tonight!" Quinn exclaimed.

Caleb hung back a few feet, giving both women some space.

"I don't know about that. I just hope I did enough."

"I think you just may have done exactly that. Are you about to leave for the night?"

"If you don't mind. I'm exhausted; it's been a rough day."

"I imagine it has."

If she only knew the half of it, Kara couldn't help but think. Makeup was a wonderful invention, and Kara had been able to hide the bruise. It was a little trickier to hide the big gash on her head, but parting her hair just right had done the trick. Kara knew that Quinn's comment was aimed at the speech she had given and the mingling to get sponsors, so she didn't feel the need to explain where the injury had come from.

"Well, I'm going to be off, then."

"You have a good night." Quinn paused, seemed to be considering something and then continued. "What's the story with you and Caleb?"

Kara was taken aback by the question. She wasn't expecting it, and she realized she wasn't sure how to answer. It didn't take her long to decide, though. While it was none of the woman's business, Kara felt the need to answer. While Kara wasn't sure where she and Caleb were headed, she wanted the other woman to know that this was a territory that Kara planned to explore and that the other woman should back off.

"I'm not sure there is a story. I hope there is."

"Me too. Caleb's a good man; he needs a good woman. I saw the way he was looking at you all night," Quinn said.

"And how was that?" Kara asked.

"You don't see it, do you? He can't take his eyes off you. He looks at you like you're already his."

Kara wasn't sure what she expected the woman to say. But she knew it wasn't what she had just heard. She had been certain that the woman was going to try to stake a claim on Caleb. Not that she was going to tell her to go for it with him. And she certainly wasn't prepared for Quinn to tell her that Caleb looked at her like she was his. They hadn't even had time to tell each other about themselves. It would be presumptuous to make it out to be more than it was.

Yet, Kara got a little excited at the idea of it all. To have a man like Caleb look at her—and only her—would be remarkable. For him to see her and not the victim would be even better. Kara said good-night, trying to make herself sound composed when her stomach was doing flip flops. Her emotions were on a roller coaster, and it felt like she was fighting to keep her head above water.

"What did you and Quinn Sanders talk about?" Caleb asked as they walked to his car.

"I just asked her if it was okay if I left early. And then she asked the weirdest question."

"What was that?"

"She asked what our story is."

If Caleb was surprised, his face didn't show it. Kara carefully studied him in the dark. It struck Kara at that point that Caleb was as good at hiding his feelings as she was. Which made for an interesting future, if there was one.

"What was your answer?" Caleb asked, sounding nonchalant.

"I told her that I wasn't sure there was a story." Kara stopped walking and turned away from him for a second, contemplating about leaving out the rest of her answer, and then changed her mind when she saw a flicker of disappointment flash across his face. If she was going to move on, she had to really move on. She hoped she hadn't misread his face. She turned to look at Caleb and added, "And then I told her I hoped there would be."

"Thank God." Kara was happier than she thought possible by hearing just those two words. Caleb's mouth formed into a smile, and he went from devastatingly handsome to breathtaking. He pulled her close, and she stiffened slightly, which caused him to loosen his hold, but he didn't entirely let her go as he kissed her tenderly on the lips.

"What do you like to do to burn off energy when you get frustrated?"

Kara was confused by the question but figured out quickly what he meant.

"I like to run. When I get angry, I run for miles. Sometimes, I'll go to the gym and run, since I'm not willing to risk running outside at certain times of day by myself. Other times, I will just punch the bag for an hour."

"Let's go. You need to work off some angry energy. I happen to have a friend who has a gym. We can stop there and burn off some steam."

ETHAN PICKED up his cell to call Caleb. He'd made a decision after reading the two files. He wasn't going to wait any longer to hear Kara's story. The two officers' deaths looked suspicious at best. Ethan was starting to get a pretty good picture of what had happened all those years ago, but there were still too many missing pieces to make the puzzle complete.

"Montgomery."

"It's Ethan. I'm on my way over. Tell Kara that her reprieve is over; she has to tell us everything tonight. We'll figure out what to do from there, but it has to be tonight. I found out some stuff that's pretty unnerving, and it's time to talk."

"I'll tell her. I think she'll cooperate."

"Watch your back," Ethan said and then ended the call.

Checking his rearview mirror, Ethan noticed that the same car had been following him for a few blocks now. Shit, he had picked up a tail. All right, things were seriously getting hairy. He had to lose the tail and fast. Whoever it was, was not invited to the get together. Speeding up, he took a sharp right and got on the freeway. He knew it was out of his way to get to Kara's, but right now, losing the tail was priority over talking to her.

Glancing in the rearview, he cursed under his breath when he saw the same car still hot on his trail. They drove like a cop, and they were moving in fast. Really fast. Ethan accelerated, but the car behind him kept up with him. Both cars were traveling at speeds of over a hundred miles an hour when the bastards behind him opened fire. His back windshield shattered.

Fuck! Whoever was following him wasn't messing around. They were going to ask questions later after it was too late for him to answer. He had to get out of Dodge and fast because apparently, his snooping around at the precinct hadn't gone unnoticed like he'd planned. Whoever was following him had the advantage because they appeared to have a passenger who was doing the shooting.

Hopefully, his years of training could get him out of this mess. Ducking in and out of traffic, they flew down the freeway that was still busy for that hour of night. Misjudging one of his lane changes, his car veered to the right and hit the shoulder. He almost hit the ditch and had just gained control of the vehicle when the car following him hit his bumper and sent both cars into a tailspin.

Ethan knew he wouldn't be able to pull out of it; he prayed he could hit the ditch at the right angle. He was peripherally aware that the other car had not regained control and was cartwheeling down the highway when his own car hit the ditch, and then all his focus turned to crushing metal and shattering glass as it rolled several times before landing upside down. When the car stopped moving, everything became deathly silent. In the distance, Ethan could hear sirens. Knowing the cavalry was coming, he stopped fighting the blackness.

18

Caleb looked at his watch; it had been thirty minutes since Ethan had called. They had been at the gym hitting the bag when he'd gotten the urgent call that Ethan was on his way to Kara's to talk to her. Something in his voice told Caleb to listen. He told Kara they had to go, that Ethan had found out some important information and they left. Thirty minutes ago. Ethan should have beat them to Kara's house, and yet they waited. Something was gnawing at his stomach; he was worried. He didn't like that he wasn't there yet. He didn't let on to Kara; he knew it would be bad to jump to conclusions.

"Why won't you tell Ethan what happened between you and your parents? I assume it's bad, but Ethan has a right to know and decide for himself how to process the information."

Kara had been rummaging around in a cupboard trying to find something and stilled immediately. Obviously surprised by his question. And he was equally surprised. He had expected her to tell him to mind his own business.

"Because my life was already ruined. What was one more ugly detail?"

"How do you feel now?"

"The same way, but now I'll at least concede that it might be in the best interest of all to explain what happened."

Caleb was standing behind Kara, leaning on her counter watching her as she began to rummage through the cupboards once again. He found it mildly entertaining and a good distraction from his worrying about Ethan to see her trying to keep busy, especially considering her height and the cupboard she was trying to retrieve something from. He knew that she was trying not to show how nervous she was about having him there. About the prospect of him spending the night. But she was failing miserably.

He was trying just as hard to not look at her round ass as it bounced while she continued to look around in the cupboard. *Trying* being the operative word; trying and failing miserably. Yep, Kara Vanderbilt was something else. It was obvious before they had gotten to the gym that she took care of herself, but Caleb was still surprised to see how fit she was.

Shit, all he could think of was how she looked all sweaty in an outfit he had borrowed for her because she had nothing with her to wear. An outfit that she nearly drowned in. Fortunately, she had a hair tie in her purse that she was able to use to tighten the shorts. He wasn't sure what he would have done if she would have gone in with them that loose on her with all the men in the gym working out. The thought that there could have been a wardrobe malfunction and all those testosterone-filled men would get an eyeful was almost more than he could take. It was worth his anxiety about drooling Neanderthals to see the look on her face when she hit the punching bag. The woman wasn't going to lie down without a fight. Kara clearly had been preparing herself over the last ten years in case the occasion ever arose again, and she would need it.

A sense of pride swelled his chest yet again at that thought. That she had been working to prepare herself so she would never be a victim again said a lot about her character. It said she would not lie down and die. Deciding he needed a distraction before his thoughts brought him back to her tush on display in front of him, he moved forward to stand behind her.

"Do you need help finding something?" he asked.

He instantly realized his mistake; the proximity had him inhaling her scent and had done the opposite of what he wanted. Instead of distracting him, it had made his senses acutely aware of her. Suddenly hypersensitive, he needed to put some distance between his body and hers. He didn't want to scare her with his sudden reaction to her.

But he moved too late, and Kara moved too soon. The split-second difference was all it took for her to collide with him. His closeness and the huskiness in his voice had startled her, and not realizing he was standing so closely behind her, she ran backward into him. With their bodies locked flush against each other, it would have been hard for Kara to miss his arousal. He could have punched himself for not being more careful.

"Um, I was trying to find something to put some iced tea in. But, for the life of me, I can't reach the pitcher. Not sure what I was thinking putting it up so high."

Caleb was surprised to hear her voice sounding just as husky as his. Which only added to the already sensitive situation.

"How about we skip the iced tea and sit down and talk?"

"About?"

"This, us, what's going on between us. The obvious attraction we feel for each other."

"It's just...I just don't know what to do around the opposite sex."

"I know. That's why we should both take a few steps apart and go sit down and talk. Maybe get to know each other a little. Sound good?"

Kara didn't say anything more. She just brushed by him and made her way to the living room. With a glance over her shoulder, Caleb nearly swallowed his tongue. Her eyes were black with desire, and he knew that she wasn't sure what to do about that. Caleb knew he was treading in sensitive waters; he knew he should be careful.

"So, what do you want to talk about?"

"You. I want to know who you are, where you've been. What motivates you? What makes you cry?"

"I don't cry. Haven't in a long time."

"Why not? There's nothing wrong with crying; it's an outlet necessary to release pent-up emotions."

"You might be right. Sometimes I want to cry, sometimes I get
close, my eyes fill up, but I force them back. I haven't cried since the
first night Devon raped me."

"Why do you think that is?"

"I don't know. Maybe because I didn't want to show emotion; that
was the reason at first. Then as the hours went on, I stopped crying
because I was angry at God for letting it happen to me. Then as the
hours stretched into days, I was too numb, too dehydrated to cry. After
I was rescued, I cried in the hospital, cries of joy or anguish, I'm not
sure which, and then I stopped. I decided I didn't have a right to cry.
I'd made it out, just a little later than I had wanted."

"You don't cry because you don't think you have the right to?"

"Like I said, at first, I was angry with God, then when I was spared,
by God or whomever you believe in, I decided I didn't have a right to
cry any longer because I made it. Every day people are abducted, and
they're not as fortunate as me."

"Just because you made it doesn't mean you can't cry about what
happened. It certainly doesn't mean you can never cry again, that you
don't have the right to cry."

"Oh, yeah? So, when was the last time you cried? I would think
with your job, you would want to cry all the time."

"Touché. I do want to cry, but with my job, I have try to bury those
emotions. I wouldn't have a life if I let the cases I work get to me, but
occasionally, a case gets to me, and I go home and cry. Especially if the
case involves a child."

"There are many reasons a person buries their feelings. Please try
not to judge mine."

"Kara, I would never judge you. Please believe that. I just want to
know you. The good and the bad."

"It really isn't worth the effort; I'm not worth the effort." He was
still trying to figure out a response to her ludicrous statement when her
eyes darted from his and landed on the clock. Her shocked eyes flew to
his. "Shouldn't he be here by now?"

Caleb looked at the clock, and even though his stomach knotted, he was about to tell her not to worry, that Ethan must have been delayed, when his cell rang. For a brief second, he thought about ignoring it. Then his instincts kicked in. It had been an hour since he'd talked to Ethan; dread filled him as he hit the answer button.

"Montgomery."

"Caleb, its Bob." Caleb's stomach dropped to his knees when he heard his captain's voice. "There's been an accident."

"How bad?" he asked, not needing the captain to say who was involved.

"It's pretty serious. Two vehicles. The other vehicle had two off-duty officers in it—both DOA. I need you to get Kara to Mercy as soon as possible. Things don't look good, so hurry." Bob paused. "And Caleb?"

"Yeah?"

"Watch your back. Preliminary witness 911 calls are indicating that he was intentionally run off the road by the two dead officers." For the third time today, he was told those three words. *Watch your back.*

Caleb took a deep breath and looked down at his hands, ironically fighting tears.

"What is it? What happened? Is it Ethan?" Kara fired a round of questions at him.

"We have to go. That was my captain; Ethan was in a bad accident."

"How bad?"

"I'm not going to lie to you. It doesn't look good."

Kara's face paled as she flew to her feet. Caleb could only follow her as she ran out the door, nearly setting off her new alarm. By the time he armed it, she was already in the car waiting impatiently for him.

"Do you know any details?"

"All the captain told me was that it's serious." He handed her the shoes she had neglected to put on in her frenzy and started the car. "Kara, he may have been run off the road intentionally by two off-duty officers, both of whom are dead."

Caleb's heart broke when he heard the small whimper come from the woman sitting next to him. He wasn't sure what he could do for her at that moment. And to make matters worse, time seemed to stand still as he negotiated the roads as fast as possible to get them both there in time. Ethan had always been like a brother to Caleb. His family felt the same way.

Once they pulled up to the front of the hospital, Kara flew out of the car. She was running at a dead sprint, and Caleb had a hard time keeping up with her. Once inside, she stopped in her tracks, looked around, and as if deciding, headed to the front desk.

"Detective Ethan Vanderbilt was brought here. I would like to know his status."

"We can't divulge his status to you, ma'am," the nurse at the front desk responded coldly.

"He's my brother."

"Why don't you have a seat and a doctor will be out shortly to talk to you."

"I am his power of attorney; I have the right to know his status. You are not violating anything by telling me."

"Do you have the paperwork with you?"

Caleb watched as Kara grabbed the counter, her knuckles turning white. He wasn't sure what was going on between the two women, but he knew it was a power struggle. At this point, his money was on Kara.

"Listen, Nurse..." She paused to look at her name tag, "...Abfall, I normally try to be very patient. But I'm warning you, if you don't pull up the information I need from the little computer in front of you, there will be repercussions."

"Are you threatening me?"

"You're damn straight I'm threatening you..." Kara paused when a distinguished looking doctor approached. Even the nurse shut her mouth and looked down.

"Nurse Abfall, I will talk to you later. Dr. Vanderbilt, please come this way." The nurse behind the front desk paled and then flushed when she heard the doctor address Kara. Clearly, the nurse wasn't expecting an audience to her rude behavior. Caleb was stunned by her attitude and surprised and proud that Kara was, indeed, a doctor. He knew she worked there, but for some reason, he'd decided she was too young to be a doctor.

"Dr. Chiglo, how is he?" she asked the graying man.

"I don't know much, but I know it doesn't look good. They're getting ready for surgery; he has severe head trauma and some internal damage."

"Who's performing the surgery?"

"Dr. Vandehei scrubbed in."

"Good, that's good; he's one of the best. What can I do? Can I observe?"

"You know we can't let you do that; you would be a liability. Just be here for him. He needs you."

They followed the doctor to a waiting room that was already starting to fill with detectives and officers, and where they were forced to wait to hear any news.

KARA WAS GOING CRAZY. There had to be something she could do. She was tired of sitting in the tiny waiting room that was filled with Ethan's co-workers who all seemed genuinely concerned for him and even for her. The closeness of everyone was starting to become stifling, and she knew they meant well when they would attempt to talk to her or bring her something to drink or eat. But the bottom line was, she didn't want to talk to any of them. She wanted to hear how her brother was doing, period. It had been hours since they'd gotten the news. Hours since he had gone into surgery, and still nothing.

"Ethan never told me you are a doctor."

Kara stopped pacing for a couple of seconds to look at Caleb, who had followed her every step with his eyes since they'd gotten to the hospital. She knew he was trying to ease some of the tension and appreciated the effort. Of all the people in the room, he was the only one who knew what she needed, and she needed, at that moment, to think of something else.

"I suppose it probably never came up."

"What kind of doctor are you?"

"Emergency medicine. Ironically, I just accepted a job as the new attending in this ER. And, yet, here I stand not being allowed to help or do anything."

"Impressive. Any reason why the nurse at the front desk was so rude to you?"

"I just think it might be her personality. I don't think she knew who I am. I didn't get to meet as many people as I wanted today; she wouldn't have been on shift yet. If she'd known that I'm the new attending, she probably would have responded differently."

"It seemed like she recognized you, though."

"You think so? I didn't recognize her."

"Still, something was off there. Aren't you a little young to be attending doctor of an ER? I mean, it's impressive at such a young age. You couldn't have become a doctor that long ago."

"I graduated a lot longer ago than one might think. Having no social life helps those sorts of things."

"That and an above-average IQ?" he asked. She looked at him closely, couldn't put one past this guy. Because of her parents, Kara had always felt the need to hide her intelligence. Guys especially didn't seem to want to be outsmarted by a woman they were interested in dating.

"That, too. I graduated with my undergrad in premed in two years. I'd started a semester late, so I told myself I was working hard so I could graduate on time. It was all just an excuse so I could drown out the memories as long as possible. When I was taking a double course load and working full-time to save up for med school, the memories were less intrusive," she murmured. He whistled quietly.

"Double course load and working full-time. How long did that work?"

"It still works. If I keep myself busy, I don't think about it as much. Until the night."

"Which is why you don't sleep."

"Exactly." She sighed. "I am also willing to work night shifts."

"How long did med school take you?"

"I also finished med school in two years."

"So, not just a smart woman?"

"If you want to label it, then my IQ would be labeled above average. Does that scare you?" she asked. He looked at her, puzzled. "My IQ has scared a few men off. Mostly in high school; then after, well, other things scared them off."

"It doesn't scare me, but I was surprised. I mean, I realized that you are very intelligent. But premed and med school in four years. Amazing. I was still figuring out what I wanted to do after four years of college."

"I would actually call that smarter than me. I just did what I had to do to get through the day, and that meant drive myself into the ground with courses."

"Why didn't you graduate high school early? I would think you were way out of the league of your classmates."

"I could have, but my parents wouldn't allow it. I was expected to graduate valedictorian, but not that I do it too soon. Really, I'm surprised they didn't want me to graduate and leave sooner, they were so indifferent to me. They could have spun it to their advantage. Genius daughter. But they didn't. I think they didn't want their daughter to be smarter than them, and they wanted me under their thumb."

On cue, her parents walked in, hours after everyone else, and still managing to look the ever-distraught parents.

19

Kara was sure they had some kind of reason. The cynic in her told her the reason was that they had to plant a bug in the media's ear so they'd be here when the grieving parents showed up. And Kara knew she was right, especially when the media walked in behind them. She was honestly surprised it had taken the media that long to come; their scanners must have been malfunctioning.

Kara had finally started to calm down, and then her parents showed up. She knew they didn't care about Ethan. The thought made her blood boil. One might find it hard to believe that Ethan and she came from them. If you just had the facts to look at, i.e. birth certificates and family photos, you'd know they were her parents. Kara had a similar bone structure to Ethan and her father. And Ethan looked a lot like their mother, as well, but Kara didn't look anything like her. They were complete opposites. Ethan had platinum hair and blue eyes just like Constance Vanderbilt. Kara had auburn hair and green eyes. Her father had dark hair, but no one in their family had green eyes. Somewhere during her thoughts, Kara had missed Dr. William Chiglo enter the room.

"Dr. Vanderbilt?" Dr. Chiglo said. "Governor and Mrs. Vanderbilt."
William Chiglo nodded curtly in her parents' direction but never

made eye contact. Much like Vanessa, William wasn't a fan of her parents. Kara remembered a conversation ten long years ago with the beautiful older man and woman, in which the young doctors at the time had encouraged her to get away from her parents as soon as possible. Vanessa told her there was something off with them and that Kara needed to get away from them. William had agreed. Both doctors proved to be correct in their assessments and had nailed it on the proverbial head.

"William, how is Ethan?"

"He's out of surgery and in critical, but stable condition. I won't lie to you, Kara," he said, deliberately addressing Kara and not her parents, "it was a surprise he made it out of surgery, and he's not out of the woods yet. The next twenty-four hours will tell us more. Right now, it's just wait and pray."

Kara ignored the gasp of shock that had come from her mother. Constance Vanderbilt was a world class actress; Kara wasn't sure if she was acting at that moment or if she was legitimately upset. It could be that she was upset; their mother was always more of a mother to Ethan than she had been to Kara, so maybe she cared. Of course, Kara was certain that wasn't the case. In her opinion, Constance Vanderbilt only cared about four things: Constance Vanderbilt, money, power, and prestige.

"Can we go in and see him?" Kara asked. The "we" being herself and Caleb.

"Of course. But only for a few minutes."

Kara stood back, agitated, but allowed her father and mother to go in first, even if they were the last to get there. At least she knew they would be in and out fast and then out of her hair. Not to be disappointed, they emerged less than a minute later; of course, the distraught parents. *Distraught, my ass*, she thought. She hung back for a second, preparing herself. Working in the ER, this wasn't the first time she'd seen someone seriously injured after a car accident, but she had to steel her nerves because she knew it would be entirely different seeing someone she loved hooked up to machines.

"Do you want to go in alone?" Caleb asked.

"No. I would like it if you came in with me. Ethan thinks of you as a brother, and I..." She stopped short of saying she needed someone there for her. Caleb put his arm around her shoulders as if he understood what she had wanted to say.

For a brief second, her legs felt like rubber, but she squared her shoulders and went into the ICU room and to Ethan's bedside. Once standing next to him, she felt her knees go weak again, but before she could fall, Caleb pressed her body into his and held her up.

"I'm so sorry for involving you in this. If anyone should be lying in that bed fighting for their life, it should be me. My life hasn't been much of a life, anyway. I'm not sure anyone would even miss me. But you—you would be missed. You need to get through this." Tentatively, she took his hand and jumped when alarms sounded. Her eyes darted to the machine monitoring his heart rate.

"Oh, God, he's coding." She darted into the hallway. "I need a crash cart, he's coding." Within seconds, the room filled with doctors and nurses.

"Kara, we can take care of this. You need to give us some room," William said as he came running into the room.

Caleb's arm came around her slowly, and he led her into the hallway as they worked on her brother. Once in the hallway, she collapsed to her knees. Caleb followed her to the ground, holding her. She rocked back and forth, back and forth, with Caleb cocooning her in his arms. *No, no, no, this can't be happening. Please God, please do something. He's all I have. I know I've questioned You in the last ten years, but please don't take him and leave me here alone.*

They knelt outside the door to Ethan's room; her eyes remained transfixed on the room as she watched them work on Ethan. She could hear the machine signaling his heart was flatlined. And there was nothing she could do, but pray, so that's what she did. Closing her eyes with her shoulders shaking with the effort to breathe normally, she continued to pray harder than she had ever prayed in her life, even harder than she had when she had been taken. *Please, God, please don't take him, he is an honest man. He needs to be here to do good. Please, I haven't asked for anything in a long time. You came through for me, please come through for him.* Caleb continued to hold her as she shook and rocked back and forth, pleading with a god she had thought she had given up on.

"Wait, we have sinus rhythm," she heard William say.

William emerged, looking concerned.

"We were able to bring him back. It's touch and go at this moment. I think if he makes it through the night, we're in the clear."

Kara turned into Caleb, and he enveloped her in his arms. Holding her tightly as her world crashed around her. *If* he makes it through the night, she promised herself she would be a better person, and stop living in the shadow of a ghost. No, make that *when* he makes it through the night. For the second time in her life, she found herself repeating the word *when* over and over, and for the first time in ten years, she found herself crying.

Damn! He thought for sure that fucker wouldn't survive that crash. But he had, and what made matters worse was that jerkoff Montgomery wasn't even in the car. He would have to be more careful of his temper. It would be his downfall, or so that bitch who raised him always told him. Well, he had the last say where that fucking cunt was concerned. She wouldn't be able to talk down to him or hurt him ever again.

If he had his way, Vanderbilt would die, and Montgomery would be out of the picture soon too. And he would make damn sure he got his way when it came to that. Patience was a virtue; it was a matter of being more careful and not flying off the handle. It wouldn't take much for the cops to figure out Vanderbilt's car was forced off the road. He was pretty sure they already knew. Fortunately, the two cops he'd paid to kill Montgomery had died, or he would be tempted to kill them with his bare hands for fucking up. His benefactor was going to be irate that Vanderbilt had almost died, might still die. He was supposed to take out Montgomery, not Vanderbilt. Next time, he needed to make sure it counted. He had to do it himself and use an ex-con to pin both of those guys' deaths on. Otherwise, there would be too many questions. It was just a matter of picking the right scapegoat.

Once they were out of the way, he could go in for the prize. Stanley Vanderbilt would be left wondering who'd outsmarted him. No fears, though; he would make sure that self-righteous bastard was aware of who had one-upped him. It was just a matter of picking the right time. These matters were delicate, and he wanted the optimum bang for his buck, so to speak. And that fucking wife of his. Don't even get him started on that bitch. She was almost as bad as the woman who had raised him.

Laughing to himself, he walked out of the hospital. No longer disappointed that Ethan Vanderbilt was alive, he could market this setback to his advantage. It was unfortunate that innocent people would have to die. Who was he kidding? He couldn't care less who he had to kill to reach his goal. Maybe people will think twice about messing with someone like him.

His phone buzzed, and he looked down at the text that had just come in from his benefactor. The message was loud and clearly angry. *WTF! You were told to get rid of CM and KV. Not EV! You better hope he lives.*

He couldn't care less who lives and dies. He liked killing, and he didn't care who he killed, but he had a certain thirst that needed to be quenched every so often. No one was the boss of him, and it was about time the person holding the purse strings figured out that bit of information.

CALEB SAT QUIETLY, holding Kara close. After Ethan had nearly died and given them both a scare, Kara had refused to leave his side. Even though the doctors asked that they leave the room, she held her ground and refused to leave. Even though she hadn't officially started working at the hospital, she had the respect and sympathy of many of the doctors and nurses. Therefore, she could stay if they weren't in the way of the medical staff. So, they stayed in the room and didn't get in the way.

Ethan made it through the night with no more scares, but he was still not out of the woods and still hadn't woke up. Kara had talked to

Dr. Chiglo and asked for a rundown of his injuries. Ethan had suffered a lacerated spleen, collapsed lung, and some broken ribs, and they had to remove his spleen and stop the internal bleeding, which they'd been able to do during surgery. The most concerning injury remaining was the massive head trauma and the swelling in his brain.

Eventually, the nurses got over having Kara hovering over everything they did and every little beep. Judging by the stance she had taken, signaling she was about to square off with them if she had to, they knew they were going to get nowhere with her. They were in what she called *the critical hour,* and she was not leaving her brother's side.

So, here they sat, Caleb holding her close, silently praying for his friend and partner to make it, not only for him but for the woman that felt so right in his arms. Ethan hadn't woken up yet, and it had been 24 hours. Eventually, a nurse convinced Kara to use their showers and change into scrubs. She refused to go unless Caleb agreed to stay with Ethan and then take a shower himself. It made him nervous to let her out of his sight, but he agreed if only to get her away from all the machines for a moment.

Eventually, she had come back looking lost and retaken her post by Ethan's bed. Once he was done with his shower, he had taken his spot back next to her and held her until she had fallen asleep in his arms. He had no heart to move her, even though his arms had fallen asleep and lost feeling a long time ago. Kara had alluded to being unable to sleep more than a couple of hours a night, and she had been sleeping for four hours. He would rather have his arm go completely numb than wake her, and he didn't have the will to remove his arms from around her.

About another hour passed before he felt her stir and looked down to see her looking up at him, sleep filled eyes blinking slowly. Eyes that were uncertain about a lot of things.

"Hey, there sleepy head. How you feeling?"

"Like I got punched in the head."

He traced around the cut on her head, and said, "You kind of did."

"How long have I been out?" she asked, trying to pull away, obviously embarrassed. But he wasn't quite ready to let her go, so he held on.

"About five hours."

"Five hours?! I haven't slept that long in…" She paused, a tear leaking out of her eye and sliding down her cheek. "Thank you."

"For what?" he asked, utterly flabbergasted.

"For being here. For holding me up physically and for helping me sleep."

"I think you give me too much credit," he said, but he felt warmth spread through him. To be a beacon of light in her otherwise dark world was an honor that he wouldn't turn a blind eye to.

"Have there been any changes?"

"Dr. Chiglo came in a couple of times and checked everything. He gave the thumbs up sign and then left. Neither of us wanted to disturb you. I figured when you woke, we could go find him."

"His shift ended hours ago, I'm sure he went home."

"Wrong, kiddo." Both Caleb and Kara turned to see William enter the room. "I'm not going anywhere until your brother is out of the woods. You should know that. I caught a few hours' sleep on the couch in the breakroom."

Kara stood and walked to the side of Ethan's bed, absentmindedly grabbing his wrist to check his pulse while she viewed all the monitors that were connected to the wires that were connected to her brother.

"Strong pulse," she said quietly.

Caleb knew that she needed to assess all of Ethan's injuries. She needed to see for herself how he was doing. So, William and Caleb stood back, letting Kara look Ethan over. Once she had completed her assessment, she turned to look at them both. With a quiet motion to the hallway, they all walked out into it.

"His stats look good. Would I be able to see the CAT scan?" Kara asked.

"I'll see what I can do. When you were sleeping, I talked to Dr. Vandehei. He is doing really well; he has a pretty serious head trauma. They're going to reevaluate in a few hours."

"To measure brain activity?"

"Correct. There is no reason to believe he won't fully recover. But he did go without oxygen for a little bit while they were trying to revive him. Not long enough to be terribly concerned. As you know, the swelling in the brain is more of a concern at this point."

"I would like to be a part of the tests. I just want to be a bystander, I won't get involved. But I just need to be there."

"Of course. Kara, about Nurse Abfall..."

Kara waved her hand.

"I imagine Nurse Abfall didn't realize who I was. I would think that if she recognized me, she would have reacted differently. I know she was doing her job. And, perhaps I should have behaved differently. After all, I work here, and I could have skipped the front desk and not caused a scene."

"She's a decent nurse. Not one of our best, but she cares about the patients. I hope that she can work with you. When I pulled her aside, I got the feeling she has bitter feelings toward you."

"If so, I can't imagine what it would be over. It would be on her end; I don't recognize her or her name."

"Abfall is her married name. Her maiden name is Pascoe."

Kara's brows scrunched together while she tried to place the name.

"Suzanne Pascoe," she said. "There is a history there, but I'm not sure why it is—she's never liked me. I just assumed it had to do with my family's money. Regardless, I plan to treat her fairly. I just hope she can get past whatever dislike she has for me and that we can work together."

William nodded and squeezed Kara's shoulder before he walked away. Caleb couldn't help but wonder what the real reason was for Nurse Abfall's hostility. Perhaps it was just about Kara's family having more than her, but Caleb got the feeling there was more to it.

20

"Kara," Caleb spoke softly so as not to startle her. She was sitting holding Ethan's hand again. "Are you willing to go home and shower, change your clothes, maybe get some rest in your own bed? We've been here for almost forty-eight hours; you need to take a break. They'll call you if something changes."

She looked over her shoulder at her brother's partner, who had stood vigil by her side through another night. Kara didn't know if she had the strength to leave Ethan—he had sat by her bed for days, waiting until she woke up after she had been brought to the hospital. But she knew he had also eventually left, gone home to shower and change his clothes and rest. When they had decided to bring her out of the coma, he refused to leave. The doctor in her knew that she was useless if she didn't take care of herself, but she didn't want to leave until he opened his eyes.

"Not yet. I just want to wait a little bit longer. I need to be here if… when he wakes up." A single tear slipped out and slid down her face. She ignored it and let it slide down her neck into the neckline of her shirt. "I can't seem to stop crying. Every once in a while, a tear leaks out," she said, sniffling.

"No reason to be insecure about that," he whispered.

Tentatively, he placed his hands on her shoulders and massaged as she continued to stare at the only constant thing in her life while he fought for his life. If she lost him, what would she have? Samsonite and her otherwise empty house. That thought made the tears slide faster. She had been so angry and so blocked off from everything and everyone. She didn't have many friends. Even Vanessa wasn't allowed to get that close.

The realization of how bleak her life had become was life altering. Slowly, she turned into Caleb's arms and cried. She wanted more, she needed more, and what's more, she deserved more. Slowly, she inched her arms up around his neck. She felt him tense, and she began to pull her arms back down.

"No, don't pull away," he said quietly. "I like the feel of you against me."

She pulled her gaze up to meet his and swallowed audibly. Slowly, he lowered his face to hers and placed his lips to her mouth. She gasped at the tingle she felt when his lips rested on hers. His tongue carefully touched her lips. Her mouth opened farther, and he cautiously slipped his tongue into her mouth and explored cautiously at first until she moaned, and then he hungrily dove in.

He tasted so good, and he smelled of musk. All of her synapses were firing, and she wanted nothing more than to melt into him. She needed more, wanted more, and deserved more. She was consumed by the need for more. She must have said the word out loud because she heard him chuckle deep in his chest before he deepened the kiss even further. Her body was plastered to his. In the years since her abduction, she had intercourse with one man, one time. It hadn't gone well. That experience had left her feeling like she would never be normal. Never be able to feel like this.

She had been wrong, oh, so wrong. Not only was she feeling normal, she was on fire. Somewhere in the back of her head, she knew it wasn't right to be doing this in an ICU room with her brother fighting for his life. But another selfish part of her didn't want to stop. Her hands spread over his broad shoulders and skimmed down his muscular biceps, landing on his lean waist, fingers skimming the hem of his T-shirt, lightly teasing the skin right above the button of his pants.

A throat cleared.

"Do you...mind...not manhandling my sister...while I am possibly on my...deathbed?" Ethan rasped out between agonized breaths.

Kara's hands dropped, and she spun around.

"Oh, thank God, Ethan! Thank you, God!" She rushed to his side, conscious of Caleb following behind her. She wasn't embarrassed that she almost undressed Caleb in the ICU. Not really. However, she was guilty that she had been doing that when her brother woke up.

"Stop it..." Ethan scolded.

"W-what? Stop what?" she asked.

"Feeling guilty...for finally...feeling..."

She chuckled while she wiped the fresh tears from her face. Tears. Again. Boy, how things had changed in such a short time.

"Try not to strain yourself. Are you thirsty? I can't give you water, but I can get some ice chips."

"That would be...great..."

She turned to get some when Caleb stopped her.

"I'll go get them. Stay, hold his hand. I'll be right back."

Grateful, she nodded at him as he walked out the door. She sank into the chair by the bed and cautiously picked up his hand as gently as possible.

"How is your pain level? I can get a nurse to administer some more meds."

"No, I'm okay...for now. Just tired and thirsty. Don't leave yet. Need to tell you..."

"Ethan, there's time to talk about the heavy stuff later. For now, I need you to rest, heal up. Doctor's orders."

"Love you..." he whispered. "But you are one...hard-nosed...doctor..."

She huffed. Always trying to make her laugh. She was about to throw something back at him when the door opened. Assuming it was Caleb, she turned with a smile on her face, only to see Nurse Abfall standing in the doorway.

"Detective Montgomery said you were awake," she said. "I just wanted to make sure you're comfortable."

"Hi, Suzanne, I'm good...for now...want to talk...to my sister...painkillers will make my head...foggier..."

"There'll be time for talking later. You shouldn't strain yourself," she said sweetly, while her eyes threw daggers at Kara.

After she had fluffed his pillows, Suzanne turned to leave, saying she would be back with ice chips. Kara knew Suzanne had some kind of hang-up with her, but she had no idea what it was. What she did know, was that Suzanne was going to have to get over it, work her schedule around Kara's, or find a new job. She was about to say something about the ice chips and the need to talk to her privately when Caleb came in, ice chips in hand and a frown on his face.

"That is quite all right, Nurse Abfall, I have some right here. Dr. Vanderbilt sent me to get some." He directed a smile at Suzanne that didn't quite reach his eyes as he eyed her warily.

"Oh, well then, I guess I'm done in here. Please make sure not to allow him too many ice chips and to let him get rest. He's been through—"

"Are you for real? I mean, are you serious?"

"Excuse me?" Suzanne stammered.

"Nurse Abfall, I would like a moment with you. In the hallway." When Suzanne didn't make a move to leave, she continued with a finger directed at the door and a vehement sounding, "*Now*."

Suzanne came into the hallway with Caleb hot on her heals. Kara held up her hand to him, indicating that he could stand down.

"I hate to pull this card on you, but did you miss the doctor in front of my name? I didn't graduate yesterday. I know how to take care of a patient. That may be my brother in there, but you will not talk down to me in front of a patient. Ever again. No exceptions. If you have a problem with me, you can file it in a file labeled *I Don't Care*, because quite honestly, I don't care. I have way more going on in my life than I need right now. I'm not going to deal with some ridiculous, childish, petty feelings. Either get it off your chest what's bothering you or move on."

Kara turned to go back in the room when Suzanne whispered, "Cunt," under her breath. She whipped around and stared her down.

"You get three strikes in my ER, and then you'll be packing up your locker and walking out of this hospital. Strike one just happened. I will ignore the insubordination in my brother's room." And with that, she turned and walked into his room.

"What the fuck is her problem?" she mumbled.

Caleb laughed, and Ethan tried to.

"What are you both laughing at?"

"You, swearing, her calling you that word. The situation is mildly entertaining..." Caleb trailed off when he saw her face and shrugged.

"I thought...they were going to...throw down in the hallway..." Ethan said, not nearly as apologetic. "You really don't know why she hates you?" he asked.

"No clue," Kara answered, exasperated.

"I suspect jealous, Valedictorian...Prom Queen...full scholarship to the school of your choice."

"Seems like it would be more than that, don't you think? I mean, she really hates me."

"Who knows, some people just have issues with jealousy," Ethan said. She could tell the medication was starting to make him drowsy.

"Sorry about Nurse Abfall being so rude to you," Caleb said.

"Bad timing on her part and small fish compared to the other mysterious person in my life that clearly has it out for me. Really not going to let it bother me."

"Still seems like an asinine reaction, to treat someone like that, the other party usually has an idea why."

"Yet, I have no idea, and I'm too tired to really care about whatever issues that woman has with me. She just better watch herself." Caleb chuckled loudly this time. The smooth baritone of his laugh warmed her from her toes to the top of her head. "What's so funny, Montgomery?" she grumbled looking at him.

"You are adorable when you are pissed off. Remind me never to tangle with you, though. Or maybe, remind me to pick a fight. It might be worth making up." Now Kara was blushing at the possibility of making up.

"No offense...love that you are exploring this...but, gross. She's my little sister..." With those words, he drifted off to a medicated sleep.

"About this making up...let me know when you want to try that," Caleb said, smiling from ear to ear.

"Of course, we have to get to that level first."

"We will; listen, about before..."

"Yeah, sorry about that. I guess I got carried away. I didn't mean to take advantage of your concern for my brother," she said, hoping that she sounded casual and not as embarrassed as she felt about her behavior. After all, she had thrown herself at the poor man.

"I can see those wheels turning in your head," he said, while he placed his hands on her hips and tugged her close. "But you can rest assured that you were not taking advantage of me, and you can bet your sweet little ass that I didn't reciprocate out of anything other than complete male interest. In other words, there was no pity in the reason behind my response. It was one hundred percent genuine."

Leaning down, he skimmed his lips against her already kiss-swollen mouth and down the length of her neck. She sighed and leaned her body into his openmouthed caress. With complete certainty, she knew she'd never felt this way before in her life. Danger surrounded her, and she melted into this strong man, thinking only of being in his arms.

"Now, about that shower and change of clothes?" he whispered. She looked up to see him smiling at her.

"A shower sounds amazing," she said with a sigh. And then something occurred to her. "Samsonite! I've been here for two days almost. He's probably about to spring a leak."

"He should be okay. I had Officer Black stop and let him out a couple times. He was the only person I could think of that had contact with him and that Samsonite wouldn't freak out around."

"Samsonite was okay? He didn't hurt Officer Black, did he?"

"I picked up on a couple of your commands and had one of the K-9 trainers accompany him in full gear, just in case. Officer Black was also in gear. Seemed like it might be best, and I didn't want to stress you out by asking."

Tears filled her eyes, and she looked at him long and hard.

"God, where have you been all my life?"

"Around, waiting for you. How about we get you home, just in case. We wouldn't want your fearless protector to spring a leak," he said with a smile on his face. He hooked an arm around her waist and led her out of the room. The relief they both felt was so palpable, it felt like a living organism in the room.

CALEB COULDN'T DESCRIBE how he felt right then. The predominant feeling, other than hard-core lust, was how grateful he was. Grateful that she had picked him to step into the light with. Grateful that he had literally bumped into her and knocked her on her ass. So freaking thankful that Ethan was his partner, which afforded him the opportunity to meet her, and so incredibly thankful someone hadn't been smart enough to scoop her up before he found her.

Even though he was feeling so incredibly peaceful, he was also consumed by fear. A debilitating fear that he would screw up, by going too fast and pushing her too soon, or worse, that somehow the bastard out there killing women would get to her. He knew with every fiber in his being that he would do everything in his power to not allow that to happen. He couldn't lose her, not now, not ever, and especially not after just finding her.

"You look so serious," she said quietly.

A quick glance at her and he realized that his silence was messing with her newfound confidence. He reached out and laced his fingers with hers. He squeezed them gently and then held her hand while he drove, striving to find the right words, words that wouldn't freak her out. Being honest usually was the best route, so he went with truth.

"I was just thinking how freaking happy I am that I met you." He paused and glanced at her as a shy smile curved her lush lips, but the smile didn't quite make it to her eyes. She knew he was holding back.

"Why do I feel a 'but'?" she asked as he pulled his car into her driveway.

"It's not like that. But, yes, there is a but," he continued quickly when he saw her eyes get shiny. "You see, I'm also scared shitless that I will lose you and I just found you. I know it sounds crazy, but I don't think I could handle losing you."

She sucked in air at his admission.

"I feel the same way. But if we both feel that way, you shouldn't worry about my leaving. Unless...oh, I see, you're worried the person killing these women will get to me." She swallowed audibly. "I'm not going to lie, that scares me as well, but I can't continue to let what happened control my life. It was far too long, and I just can't do it anymore. Almost losing Ethan made me realize that life is just so unbelievably fragile, and I don't want to live my life in fear and alone."

"I'm relieved to hear you say that. I need you to know that I will do everything I can to prevent any harm from coming your way. Not only do I owe it to your brother to keep you safe, I need to keep you safe for me. The need to protect you is so strong; it's like that need has gotten into my veins and spread through my whole body."

Running his hand up her arm, he cupped her cheek, and she leaned into his hand. Another small sigh of contentment escaped her lips. He leaned forward—he couldn't resist those plump lips—and kissed her gently. Before he could blink, she had deepened the kiss, and in a matter of seconds, they were panting like high school kids making out in their parents' car on prom night. Slowly and grudgingly, he pulled away from her.

"As much as I would love to sit in my police issued sedan making out with you, I believe we have an audience," he said and tipped his chin to the window in her living room. Sam was standing with his nose pressed against the window, slobbering all over the place, body shimmying with excitement.

Kara giggled at the sight and happiness spread through him at the sound escaping her lips. It was the first time he'd heard a genuine and carefree laugh escape her lips. She'd been so sad and angry since he met her; he liked this version of her. He could easily fall in love with this woman. A thought suddenly occurred to him, and he looked at his phone.

"I had some plans for today that I cancelled this morning. I was wondering if you would be interested?"

"What plans?" she asked, appearing genuinely interested.

"Nothing big; I was just invited over for a barbecue at my parents'."

"Why did you cancel? You could have left me at the hospital."

"I wasn't about to leave you alone, even at the hospital. Ethan was supposed to stay with you while I went to the barbecue. I didn't figure you would want to tag along; my family is big and overwhelming. And worse, they are incredibly nosey."

"I would love to go; that is if you want me to?"

"I absolutely want you to go."

"I just have one condition."

"What's that?"

"Is it possible that I can bring Samsonite with? He's a perfect gentleman in a crowd. I can't leave him here after he's been alone for so long. It would be cruel."

"If he's good with other dogs, we have a deal, since my parents have a couple of Labradors," he said without hesitating.

"What time are you supposed to be there?"

"There really isn't a set time, but everyone is probably just getting there now. They live about a ten-minute drive away. I called my mom and dad this morning when I went to get ice chips and updated them about Ethan waking up. He's spent so many barbecues at their house that I lost count. He's part of the family. They were devastated when they found out about the accident and wanted to come to the hospital. I told them visitors were limited right now. They understood."

"Let me take that shower and get changed and then call the hospital to see how he's doing. I know it hasn't been that long, but things can change quickly with someone who's been in a car crash like he was. I want to know there aren't any changes so I can feel comfortable not going back right away. If all is well there, we can head over to the barbecue. I really want to meet Ethan's surrogate parents."

That feeling of warmth spread through him again. The idea of letting her meet his parents didn't scare him at all; it felt right to bring her to meet them. Ethan was already a part of his family, and Lord knew that Kara needed a family that loved her as much as he knew she deserved. Her heart was aching to let someone in. They both climbed out of the car, and when she came around the front of the car, he laced his fingers with hers again.

It felt so right to hold her hand, to hold her against him. He had never been a believer of love at first sight, but he thought it was possible he was experiencing the phenomenon. Never in a million years had he thought it would happen to him. She looked up at him and smiled a brilliant 100-watt smile, and he knew with certainty that she was his and he wouldn't let her go.

She unlocked the door and disarmed the alarm just in time as Samsonite came bounding her way. He skidded to a stop by her and sat down, his whole body wiggling. She crouched down to hug him and ruffle his fur.

"Looks like he's happy to see you."

"Samsonite and I are pretty tight, aren't we, boy? He picked me as much as I picked him, we're nearly soul mates. I bet you are hungry and have to go take a break outside, don't you?" she said in a soft crooning voice, and in a flash, he could see her with their children.

21

Caleb knew there was a big difference between feeling like you were falling in love—much faster than normal—and being ready for a family with that person. Yet he knew he wanted it, wanted it with her, and he wanted it with all his body, mind, and soul.

"I can take him outside while you shower? Is that okay? Will he be all right with that?"

"He really can go out by himself. We walked the perimeter, and he knows where our property line is."

"Invisible fencing?" he asked

"Nope. Can't do that. I mean, I can, but I won't. What good is a guard dog if something happens and he's limited to the yard? He won't be able to leave the yard. I know some dogs can break through the barrier if they are intent enough, and I think if I was in trouble, he would blow right past the fencing. But I don't want to risk that, and he's so well trained that he knows exactly where he can and cannot go."

Caleb nodded in admiration; she really had trained the humongous dog well. He had to be splitting with the urge to pee and, yet, he hadn't moved from his perch next to her. Since the door was open, he was clearly waiting for permission to go outside.

"He is an amazing friend, isn't he?" Caleb said, rubbing his ears.

"He is. I wouldn't mind if you walked him, though, he would get used to you, and if you're going to be around like I hope you'll be, I don't want to have to keep giving him the command to be friendly. I also want him to be more comfortable here before I let him out by himself." She smiled shyly. "I mean, that is, well...uh...since you are going to be spending time here, I mean, after this case is solved, right?"

"There's nothing that could keep me away."

With a shy smile, she inclined her head to the door, and Samsonite bolted out the door. Caleb smiled and followed the monstrous animal. After Samsonite emptied his bladder, he smelled every blade of grass. If it were any other dog, Caleb would assume he was just doing his dog thing, finding the right blade of grass to sprinkle some more pee. But this wasn't an ordinary dog, and Caleb knew he wondered if he was watching the beautiful animal check for odd smells.

After about ten minutes, Samsonite headed toward the house, clearly indicating to Caleb he was done with what he came out to do. Caleb followed him to the door and let them both inside. He stood at the base of the stairs, and when he couldn't hear the shower or any other noise, he became concerned. Surely, he should at least be hearing her moving around, and he hadn't set the alarm when he went outside. Granted, he was right in the yard, but it still set his hackles up that he hadn't had her arm the system.

He made his way up the stairs two at a time, briskly walking down the hallway, his hand on the gun at his waist. He knew which room was hers from the other night, so he skipped past the other rooms and listened at the door. When he didn't hear anything, he slowly opened the door, terrified of what he would find. And when he stepped through, he froze to the floor for the briefest of seconds before two strides had him pulling Kara into his arms.

Caleb knew what an adrenaline crash looked like, and when he'd opened the bedroom door, he found Kara standing in the center of the room, wrapped in a towel, looking lost, with tears spilling down her cheeks. The enormity of almost losing her brother smacking her up against a figurative wall of emotion. Caleb knew he was crushing her to his chest harder than necessary, but he couldn't stop himself. Her body shuddered at the contact, and he had to make a conscious effort to ignore the fact that she was clothed in only a towel and pressed, nearly skin to skin, against him.

"I-I'm sorry. I just, I can't stop crying. I thought I had gotten a grip on things and then, gah, I thought about how I almost lost him. Then I thought about how I could still lose him. And for what? Because he got involved in my shitty back story." She shook with a sob that she tried valiantly to hold in.

"Shhh, come on, Kara, we all know that Ethan is too stubborn to let this stop him. It was touch-and-go, but he woke up. I consider that a win. I know he might have a long road ahead of him, but he made it through the night and then another night. Remember?"

"Yes. Yeah. Of course. I'm the doctor; I'm supposed to be telling you those things. The doctor in me knows that, but the sister in me is freaking out and struggling to find the logic in your words. You really are an amazing man." She clung tightly to him as if he were the only thing holding her together.

"Honey, please don't take this the wrong way, but if I don't step back from you, I might do something that will have you thinking I'm not that good of a guy after all." He pulled away from her and instantly felt stripped bare without her in his arms.

Sniffling, she shook her head and looked him in the eyes for a long time before speaking.

"I doubt that is possible, Detective Montgomery. I doubt that, indeed. But I understand why you would want to be careful with me. Just do me a favor?"

"Anything," he said without thinking.

"When the time comes, don't treat me like I'm spun glass. I've been through a lot, and because of that, many people treat me like I'm fragile, when in reality, they should treat me like I'm unbreakable, because I walked through that fire and came out alive."

"Fire is needed to make spun glass," he said quietly.

"Exactly," she said.

Caleb watched as she turned to go to her closet. Every minute he became more impressed and infatuated with this woman. And his traitorous dick knew it. Caleb tried to think of everything but the lines of her back and arms as she reached into her closet.

"You're staring," she said with amusement in her voice.

Clearing his throat, he somehow managed to tell her he was going to wait in the kitchen for her. He was so screwed. His dick had won the battle and was fighting his pants to stand proudly at attention. It didn't care that he should take his time, no matter what she said.

"Hey, buddy, you want some water?" Caleb asked when he walked in the kitchen and found Samsonite staring at his empty water dish. *Subtle*, he thought. He bent and picked up the dish to fill it with water. Samsonite looked like he was grinning. His mouth was hanging open, and his tongue was hanging out, tail wagging and thumping on the ground. Caleb chuckled. As he set the dish on the floor, he rubbed Sam's ears and stood up.

"I love your laugh," Kara said softly as her arms came around his waist from behind. He turned into her embrace and hugged her back. She had donned a coral sundress, and the color did magic to her skin tone. She was already beautiful, but in that color, she was breathtaking.

Without thinking, his mouth swooped down, taking her roughly as he devoured her mouth. Sipping, teasing, tasting, and marking her as his. Running kisses down her neck to the top of her dress, he untied the straps at her neck and tugged the dress down. His tongue made its way to her breast; through her bra, he sucked the marbled nipple into his mouth.

A moan escaped her, and she arched into him. Losing what little control he had, he spun her and backed her up until the counter stopped their progress. Pinning her with his weight, he continued to suck at her nipple until he realized she had tensed. Samsonite made a small whining sound. Abruptly, he stopped. If the dog hadn't alerted him, he'd still have sensed the subtle change, but that didn't make him feel any less of an ass, even as her body had already begun to relax. He knew he'd pushed too far, too fast.

FOR THE BRIEFEST OF MOMENTS, she panicked, trapped against the counter. With his weight on her, she was momentarily confused and tensed. She knew it was Caleb; she smelled him, felt him, but for a moment, Devon was there. The mind being a powerful thing, she could almost smell his foul breath as Caleb sucked at her nipple. It only took a second for her to rid the feeling from her mind, but it was all it took for Caleb to notice.

A small gesture to Sam, who had sensed her tension, had him relaxing, but not before he came up and pressed his nose to her ankle, and then he promptly dropped to the ground by her feet. This was new territory for him, too.

"Don't stop," she whispered, her voice husky. "Please don't stop. I'm sorry, I just freaked for a second."

He jerked away from her like she was hot to the touch and backing away quickly, he scrubbed his hands through his hair. Turning his back to her, with his hands still in his hair, breathing heavily, he stared at the ground. Kara felt crushed by the vision of him looking so defeated. She was reaching out to touch his shoulder when he whipped back around.

"*You're* sorry?" he asked, his chest heaving, and too late she realized that he wasn't disgusted with her; he was disgusted with himself for going, what he perceived, was too far. "God, Kara, I told myself to take it easy, and I didn't. I know you don't think you're fragile, and in many ways, you aren't. But I can't have you thinking of him while I'm kissing you. I understand it'll happen, but I am damn well determined to not push when he's there in your mind."

"You need to."

"What?"

"Push me. Caleb, he's always somewhere in my mind, and the slightest thing can trigger my remembering him. It could be a song that I heard him humming while he sliced my skin. It could be the smell of the deodorant he wore. So many things can trigger an adverse response. You need to work with me, talk to me, keep kissing me. Don't back away. After that initial panic, I knew it was you. I focused on you, and he was out of my mind."

She reached out and touched his face; he leaned into the contact and kissed her palm. The contact caused a full body shiver, and she moved into him.

"I might not be ready to go all the way, or I might be. Maybe if I take control, it won't scare me as much. It was your weight on me that had me tensing. Maybe if we try other ways." She blushed, and he fell for her a little more. "Me being in charge, on top. I don't know, I just know with certainty that I want to try with you and I have never wanted to try before. Not once. I-I mean, I did try once about a year after the abduction, not because I wanted to have sex, but because I wanted to prove I could, but it didn't go well." Her eyes darted away as she said it.

Caleb roughly pulled her into his arms and kissed the top of her head.

"Oh, baby, I am so sorry that he took that freedom away from you."

"But he didn't. Don't you see, Caleb? In all these years, I haven't found anyone that I have found myself craving. Until you."

"Craving?" he asked, and she could sense his wicked grin when her eyes finally made their way to his face.

"I want to be with you. Maybe there's still a little glass in me when it comes to this one area, but it's just a crack. I won't shatter. It'll take a little patience for me to find my groove. With that other man, I didn't even want to. I just did it to prove I could."

His big body shuddered against hers as she ran her hands up his back to his shoulders, hugging him tightly to her, her fingers playing with his hairline as she reached up on her tiptoes to lightly kiss him. After the briefest of kisses, she pulled back and stepped away, glancing down at the dog humphing at her feet. She couldn't help but chuckle. Quickly, she stooped and scratched behind his ears.

"Feeling a little neglected, buddy? You're still my number one furry friend." Her words, as much as the contact, had him drooling and wagging his big tail. "We should get going to your parents'. I think we have crossed enough bridges for now. Samsonite is still getting used to having you around. I should have eased into this situation. He freaked out a little bit when he sensed my tension."

"Understandable. He's trained to sense your emotions and to

protect you, and here is this big, dumb goof practically mauling you."
The tone in his voice showed he was still hung up on the situation. She
stood up and turned to him.

"That big, dumb goof wasn't mauling me. In fact, it was quite
enjoyable having that goof touch me. But we still need to ease into
things with Sam. As for me, I am definitely ready to continue
that later."

Another swift kiss and she sashayed past him to the door, glancing
over her shoulder at both boys she had let into her heart. One muscular
beast of a man, the equivalent to eye candy, staring at her with a
combination of lust and longing in his eyes, she would have to work on
banishing the longing and make sure there was just lust; and one furry
beast watching her every move with utter devotion while looking for
distress.

Kara hoped that one day, Samsonite could just be a dog, carefree
and happy, and not always working to protect her. She inclined her
head, and Samsonite stood, rushing to her side, pressing his wet nose to
her hand, loving her unconditionally.

"Want to go for a ride? Maybe meet some new people? Will you be
my exceptionally good boy while we are there?" The poor thing
couldn't contain his excitement at being offered a car ride. "How about
you, ready to go for a ride?" she whispered, her voice had gone husky
again.

"Absolutely." He reached for her hand, and after arming the alarm
system, they walked hand in hand to his car.

22

Caleb noticed how quiet Kara was on the drive to his parents' house. It wasn't an awkward quiet, but he knew something was running through her mind and she had something to ask.

"Just go ahead and ask what's on your mind," he said.

"You said that Ethan had your back once; what did you mean?"

Of all the things he thought she would ask, that wasn't one of them. Caleb didn't want her to think less of him, but he knew he needed to tell her the truth.

"Ethan and I started out as beat cops together. We both went into police work for similar reasons."

"He decided not to go to law school after my accident. At first, he just deferred a semester, and my parents were not happy. But when he dropped out entirely, they were furious. Then he told them he wanted to become an officer and protect people. They had blamed me for his taking the semester off. I imagine they were even more pissed at me when he decided to pursue law enforcement. But Ethan had always wanted to be a lawyer that fights the bad guys, not some corporate lackey," she said quietly, looking at her hands. Even so, he sensed she felt responsible for that decision.

"Ethan is a damn fine detective, and he never wanted to go to law school. You know that he made the right decision."

"Yes, I know. You were saying you had a similar reason."

"It isn't entirely my story to tell, but the CliffsNotes version is that someone I know who I love very much, was raped by her boyfriend when she was in high school. It changed her."

"It often does," she said sadly.

"She was no longer a carefree teenager on her way to school to become a graphic designer. Instead, she was depressed, and ended up failing her classes. She spiraled, got into drugs, and almost OD'd. That was when her family really knew how bad it was, and they stepped in and got her help.".

"Family can often make the biggest difference," she said when the silence fell over them.

"It did. She got clean, managed to go back to college, and became a graphic designer. She still has moments here and there where she struggles."

"What did you do that Ethan covered up?" she quietly asked.

His head snapped to look at her, knuckles white on the steering wheel.

"This is a judgment free zone. I know he helped you."

"I wouldn't say he covered anything up, but he kept me from killing a man one night. A man that we caught in the act of raping a woman. I lost it, completely lost it, and went after him. Ethan had to pull me off him."

"Obviously it wasn't that bad, or you would have been charged."

"I busted his nose; I only got in one swing before Ethan stopped me. It still could have gotten me into a lot of trouble, the man was unarmed. Ethan covered for me, told them that we both thought he was going for a weapon. I don't think our captain bought it, and I don't think he cared that I broke the bastard's nose."

"So, what happened?"

"Came down to the fact that the asshole would-be rapist didn't press charges against me. If he disputed anything, then it could look like he was doing something wrong and not consensual. Which was his claim. That they were role playing a rape scene and the young woman was into it. That it was her idea."

"Did she corroborate?"

"Not at first. At first, she was absolutely saying it was rape, and it most certainly appeared that way to Ethan and me, but then her story changed. She came in a few days later, said she was just mad that we caught them and was worried what her parents would say because he was married and they thought she was a 'good girl.' Told us she was leaving town."

He hesitated a moment before deciding to continue, for fear he would insult her, but in the spirit of honesty, he decided to put it all out there.

"Money can buy a lot. He paid off his almost victim, and she left town shortly after. He had a prestigious job, a wife, kids, and lots of money. She was 'just' the nanny."

"Can't say I'm surprised. This country has a problem. The rape culture is terrifying. You have some that falsely accuse men or women of rape, ruining lives, and taking away legitimacy from people who *are* attacked. Then there are those who are terrified to come forward, those that do and retract, and those that come forward and the case makes it to trial, only for a judge to give the perpetrator a slap on the wrist for it being the first offense and because they go to church." Her face was bright red now. "Even if they're caught in the act."

Caleb didn't say anything. She was aware that he already knew all of what she was saying, but she needed to say it.

"When they prosecute, the defense attorney then will victimize the person who was attacked. During the trial, the survivor then must go through a long trial where they're shamed for dressing a certain way, drinking too much, being alone at a party, giving the wrong signals. And if the victim is male, a lot of the time that isn't even reported. The rapist wins and gets to carry on, only to repeat the cycle again and again. Sometimes people spend more time in prison for recreational drug use than for rape or molestation."

He turned into his parents' long driveway and pulled to a stop. He didn't say anything; he just pulled her into his arms and kissed the top of her head.

"Thank you."

"For?" he asked.

"Telling me. I was hoping you really whooped his ass, but a broken nose is good, too." He could feel her smile against his cheek.

"I want our relationship to be as open and honest as possible. It's the only way if we want to have a chance to make this work." He leaned in and kissed her gently, and at that moment, a fist pounded on the window of his car. They both jumped like kids caught raiding the cookie jar.

"Sweet Jesus!" Kara said, her hand flying to her chest.

Standing outside his car was his niece, a precocious little four-year-old who was smiling from ear to ear and jumping up and down. He smiled at Kara, and they both climbed out of the car.

"Uncle Caleb, Uncle Caleb, you came! Grandma and Grandpa said you couldn't come. That Uncle Ethan got hurt, and you were visiting with him."

"Hey there, buttercup, how've you been?" he asked, scooping her up. His eyes met Kara's over the roof of the car; tears had filled her eyes when the little girl had said Uncle Ethan. He hadn't been lying when he told her that Ethan was part of his family.

"Good! Mommy and daddy are having a baby; I am going to have a sister or another brother!" She started off happy and ended on a hilariously serious note.

"Oh boy, were you supposed to tell me that?"

"Oops, I supposed to keep it secret. Shhh...don't tell anyone." Her eyes darted around, obviously looking for her parents. Caleb chuckled; she truly was an adorable little girl.

"I won't tell anyone," he said, pretending to zip his lips. "Do you want to meet my friend and her doggy?"

"Ooh, a doggy!"

Kara had gotten Samsonite out of the car and was letting him go to the bathroom while she watched the exchange between him and his niece. Watching for her cue, she came over with Samsonite when she heard the little girl's excitement.

"Uncle Caleb, the doggy is huge! I thought Grandma and Grandpa's doggies were huge..." Clearly, she was a little apprehensive at the size of Samsonite.

"Hi, my name is Kara, and this is my dog, Samsonite. He is big, but he is one hundred percent sweetheart, and he loves kids. Would you like to pet him?"

She nodded her head yes.

"My name is Ava. But when my mommy and daddy are mad, they call me Ava Isabelle Montgomery."

Kara had to cover her mouth to hide her giggle. And Caleb fell even harder; there was nothing about this woman that he didn't love. He watched as she told Ava about Samsonite and how he's her guard dog, which Ava was fascinated with. After a few minutes, they were about to go to the backyard when they heard his sister's voice.

"Ava Isabelle Montgomery, where are you?"

"Uh-oh. I didn't tell Mommy where I was going." Ava grabbed Kara's hand and tugged. "Come on, I want to show her Sam...si..."

"You can just call him Sam."

The two girls walked in front of him, with Sam right at Ava's side, so that she could have her hand on his neck while they walked. Kara hadn't lied, he loved kids.

"Ava...?"

"Right here, Mommy! I found Uncle Caleb and his girlfriend and her doggy, Sam. Isn't he the coolest doggy ever!?" she squealed and then looked at the other two dogs sprawled on the lawn that had lifted their head to look at her. "Sorry, Cubbie and Bear, you are cool, too." She leaned forward and whispered in Samsonite's ear. "I don't wanna hurt their feelings."

Caleb's heart thumped hard when Ava called Kara his girlfriend. It wasn't that he didn't want that, it was that they hadn't even gone on a date and he didn't know how to define them right now.

"Uh, Ava, Kara is my friend..."

"Nu-uh, I saw you kiss her like how my daddy kisses my mommy.

That makes you her boyfriend!" she said, and then promptly ran off with her younger brother.

He turned in time to see everyone standing and staring at him for a moment before they all moved into action at the same time. His mother was quicker than the rest of the group to hide her surprise. She rushed over and hugged him; pulling away, she stared at him intently.

"Caleb! We weren't expecting you to be here. Does that mean...is everything all right with...?"

"Ethan is doing well. He woke up this morning, so I convinced Kara to take a break. She called the hospital before we came over here. He was resting comfortably." He paused. "Mom, this is Kara, Ethan's sister."

Once again, he gave his mom credit for her recovery skills. She barely batted an eye before turning to smile at Kara. He knew she was surprised that the girl standing there was Ethan's sister, the sister Ethan rarely talked about, the sister that Ethan hadn't told them was moving back to their hometown.

"Kara, I am so happy you could join us. I apologize for my surprise; my son didn't mention you were in town."

"I wasn't sure she would want me to share that information." Caleb looked at Kara apologetically.

"Caleb's right, I tend to be kind of private, please don't be mad at him. I'm sorry for intruding on your family barbecue," she said quietly.

Caleb instantly felt his hackles go up. Kara was retreating. She had misinterpreted his mother's surprise as rejection of her when his mother was admonishing him for not telling her information that she deemed important. Kara returning home was absolutely important information because they all knew how protective Ethan was of her. The fact that she had been at the hospital was something his mother would have wanted to know. That information would have put his mother's mind at ease that Ethan had family there to sit vigil by his side.

"Kara—" he began to reassure her that she was most definitely welcome when his mother cut him off.

"Kara, please don't misunderstand my comment. You are very

much invited to stay. I was merely shocked that you're here and frustrated that my son didn't tell me about you being at the hospital with Ethan. That makes me feel better. Your parents are..."

"Sucky?" Kara said glibly, which got a nervous laugh out of his parents.

"That's one way to say it," Caleb muttered.

"Everything is good, though? The doctors wouldn't lie to you about his prognosis?" his father asked. It was Caleb's turn to chuckle.

"Maybe we should start over; this is Ethan's sister, Dr. Kara Vanderbilt. She is the new attending doctor at the ER at Mercy Hospital," Caleb said.

Kara threw her hands in the air, miming a stopping motion as if to halt his parents' embarrassment.

"Seriously, I know I like to be private and everything, but did Ethan tell you nothing about me?" And with that statement, the awkwardness fizzled and disappeared.

"Kara, I am Caleb's brother, Grayson, and this is my wife, Ella. We are thrilled to get to meet the elusive sibling of our other brother, Ethan," Grayson said, making light of the situation as he scooped Kara into a big bear hug before Caleb could warn him to take it easy.

Sam stood up from his perch on the ground and looked at Kara, who just laughed good-naturedly at the abrupt nature of his brother. Subtly, she motioned for Sam to lay back down. Satisfied that there was no danger, the behemoth of a dog laid back down on the ground. Ella had moved in for a much less aggressive hug, and then his mom and dad swooped in for their hugs. Finally, his sister Taylor approached.

"I'm Taylor, the youngest sibling of this group, and the only daughter. Which makes me the cutest." She gave a quick hug and went back to her seat.

"I apologize; I should have warned you that my family are huggers."

"I hope you like burgers and corn on the cob?" his mom asked, rolling her eyes at him.

"Absolutely," she said and sat in the seat offered to her. With a pat on her leg, Sam came over and sat at her feet. When all else failed, Sam was her faithful companion through thick and thin. With an exaggerated sigh, he plopped down by her feet. With his head on her knees, he gazed at her adoringly. Much the same way that Caleb was currently staring at her.

23

"That is one well trained animal you have there," Caleb's father, who wanted her to call him James, said.

"That he is. Samsonite is my guard dog. Since it appears that Ethan hasn't told you the basic of details, I would assume he hasn't mentioned my need for a guard dog?" she asked, and continued when everyone shook their head no. If she wanted to have a relationship with Caleb, she was going to have to be honest. With a quick glance around, she made sure the children were not in hearing distance. "I know Caleb isn't from this area; can I assume the rest of you aren't, as well?"

"Right, he moved here about eight years ago after Grayson moved here with Ella. Grayson told him the police department was hiring and he applied. He was assigned your brother for a partner because his had just retired. With two of our kids here and Taylor going to school nearby, we decided to move, as well," his mother said. She also insisted that Kara call her by her first name Evie and not Mrs. Montgomery because that's her mother-in-law's name.

"That's why he didn't know about my history, either. My parents put a tight lid on things and memories faded. Ethan didn't talk about it because I didn't talk about it. But it isn't healthy to bottle it all in,"

Kara said, her eyes falling on Taylor briefly. Kara scanned around to make sure that Ava and Alex were still out of hearing distance.

"There is no easy way to say this." She paused and took a deep breath. Caleb gently twined his fingers with hers. Kara noticed that his mother caught the gesture and smiled warmly. "Ten years ago, I was abducted, for four days. The sanitized version is that I was raped and tortured until I managed to escape. Until this last week, I never talked about it. Ever. For various, and unfortunate reasons, I have had to share the story. Fortunately, it's getting somewhat easier to share."

Caleb squeezed her hand, and his thumb caressed the pulse point on her wrist. His family was amazing and completely welcoming. But Kara knew a survivor of abuse when she saw one, and Taylor definitely was one. Kara had enough experience from volunteering in rape crisis centers to know what to look for, even if she hadn't experienced a similar trauma. She also knew when to leave things. Taylor would approach her later if she wanted to; Kara just needed to be subtle in her attempt to talk to the woman.

"I'm so sorry you went through that," Evie said, tears in her eyes. If there was anything Kara hated, it was pity, but Evie's eyes were not showing pity. They were showing grief; obviously, Evie was aware of Taylor's assault.

"I wouldn't be who I am today, if not for those four days. He didn't break me, he may have bent me a little, but he didn't break me. In some ways, he helped me to discover what true strength is. I'm not going to say it hasn't been tough. Hence, the guard dog. But I chose my profession because of two of the doctors who helped me after the assault," She paused, looking at Taylor before continuing. "And I learned via volunteering at the local rape crisis center that I could do something to make myself feel whole again."

"The new center in town opened because of Kara," Caleb said tenderly, hesitating, clearly unsure if she would be okay with him sharing that. She nodded that it was fine. "She raised all the money and told her story in front of a crowd of strangers. It was a sight to behold."

She found herself blushing—honest to God, blushing—again. This man brought a plethora of feelings out in her that she had never felt before.

"I heard about the center; it's about time we have something like that here," James said, covertly looking at Taylor.

That their mom and dad knew about her assault wasn't a surprise. This family was obviously tight knit. And it was equally obvious Caleb was talking up the center for Taylor's benefit. Kara now knew the story he had told was about his sister. It was clear to Kara, that in the eyes of Taylor's family, she needed some help.

"Technically, there was a center here. The person I chose to run the center is an amazing asset to this community, and she just needed the resources to expand the center she'd started out of her own home."

"I have worked with Quinn before; she is everything Kara says and more. She's a rape survivor as well," Taylor whispered. The silence felt heavy as everyone, who had banded together to, not so subtly after all, show support for Taylor, let the words sink in. "Kara, before you leave today, I would like to have a word in private with you." Kara let out the breath she had been holding.

"Absolutely. Do you—?" Kara was cut off by Ava's high-pitched squeal.

"Auntie Sa, Auntie Sa!"

Kara turned to see what, or rather who, had gotten Ava so excited and was momentarily speechless when she saw Vanessa standing with her husband in the gate to the backyard. Kara stood up quickly, confused why they would be there.

"Kara?"

"Vanessa?" they said at the same time and laughed.

"I should have realized you'd know each other; after all, you'll be working at the same hospital," Caleb said.

"Vanessa is your aunt?" Kara asked, shaking her head to clear it.

"Yep. She's my mom's sister. I wasn't sure if you had a chance to meet her, since she doesn't work in the ER. She's a—"

"General Surgeon. Yeah, I know. She's the one who operated on me all those years ago. She's the reason I'm here today, one of the many who saved me, but she is one of only two who inspired me to continue with my dream of becoming doctor. Vanessa and William brought me through it all, and after meeting them, I changed which medicine I would pursue."

Vanessa and William were what had kept her going. Their kindness, their words, everything they had done had taught Kara to fight. Because of them, Kara did just that. When she wanted to curl up in a ball and give in, their faces floated to the front. When she considered killing herself, she thought of how hard they had worked to save her. William and Vanessa were the closest people she had as friends.

"That answers how *we* know each other, but how in the world did you happen to meet my family?" Vanessa asked, laughing.

"She's Uncle Caleb's girlfriend!" a giggling Ava shouted. "I saw them kissing!"

The situation was absurdly funny. It was the second time the precocious little girl had declared she was Caleb's girlfriend, and they hadn't even discussed what they were to each other yet. Girlfriend/boyfriend sounded too premature; after all, they'd just met. But acquaintances wasn't right, either. Friends? Friends wasn't right. They were more than that, weren't they?

"Um, well..." she stammered.

"Ava's right. Kara's my girlfriend." Kara looked at Caleb in shock. "I think I mentioned my partner to you a time or two, but I'm not sure I ever told you his name. My partner is Ethan Vanderbilt, who happens to be her brother."

"Yes, yes, of course, I remember Ethan! He was so devoted to you; unlike your parents, he doted on you. How is he doing?" Vanessa asked brightly.

"Actually, he was in a really bad car accident late last night; he almost died. Dr. Vandehei operated. If you couldn't be there, he would have been my second choice. William was there and he helped save his life later when he coded," Kara said, her eyes glistening. "Sorry. I..." She blinked furiously. Vanessa understood. Vanessa had never seen her shed one tear in all the time they'd known each other.

She came quickly to Kara's side and hugged her, whispering in her ear, for her ears only, "Don't you apologize for feeling, Kara, don't you dare." And then for everyone's ears, "Come sit down, tell me about the accident."

A couple hours later, they were getting ready to leave. As they were saying their goodbyes, Kara was trying to find a discreet way to get Taylor alone. She didn't want to come right out and remind her that she had asked to speak with Kara. As she was struggling to find a way to linger behind, Caleb's cell phone rang.

"Montgomery." He glanced at Kara, indicated it was work and walked ahead a bit so the conversation could be more private. His parents were distracted talking to Vanessa and her husband, and Grayson and Ella had already left with their two adorable, but tired children. It was the perfect opportunity to talk to Taylor.

"Walk with me?" Taylor asked, and promptly started to walk toward her car that was parked in the driveway. When she got to the driver side door, she turned toward Kara. "My family wasn't really very subtle back there, were they?"

"It wouldn't have mattered. I could tell, just like I bet you could tell about me. Am I right?"

"There were some things I noticed. The guard dog was a definite sign, but you might have only been a survivor of a mugging. I wouldn't have known it was rape. I could tell from a mile away that he's a guard dog. I noticed the subtle gestures you made to him."

"Do you have a guard dog?" Kara asked.

"No, but I've researched getting one. I'm not as lost as my parents would have you believe."

"I think you misunderstand their concern for you as something less than flattering. I can tell you this; I would be over the moon to have your parents. Mine suck."

"Yeah, no offense, but I didn't vote for your dad at the last election." The revelation startled a laugh out of Kara.

"Neither did I. As a matter of fact, I moved out of state and purposely changed my voting residence. Cowardly, but there was no way I was voting for him."

"He doesn't care a hell of a lot for victim rights, does he?" Taylor murmured bitterly.

"Not a bit. Listen, if you're serious about getting a guard dog, I know a person who's amazing at finding the right one for you. I don't know what I would do without Sam. He got me through some rough times."

"I think I'll take you up on that offer. Listen, I would like to visit your center. It wasn't all the talk tonight, but I had been looking into it for a while. I went to school for graphic design and I enjoy it, but I'm starting to feel a calling to help others who have gone through what we have."

"If you would like to volunteer there or even work part time, I can certainly get you a position there."

"I didn't bring this up because I thought I could use your relationship with my brother to get me a job there," Taylor said quickly.

"I didn't think that was the case at all."

"I actually was going to call the center tomorrow, now that they're open. I guess I was telling you, because…"

"I get it. You want me to tell your brother, slip it in that you're doing better than they think?"

"Do you mind?"

"I don't mind. If it's true," Kara said gently.

"It is. I've been clean for four years now. I used to take prescription drugs. At first, it was because I needed them to help with the pain when I was healing from my attack. Then it was just because it dulled everything else, but I got sober, I fought for where I am."

"I pegged you for one. A fighter knows another fighter. It's like a secret club. For what it's worth, I knew you were holding your own before this conversation. You don't have that hollowed out look I had after it happened to me."

"I used to. I still do sometimes. Do you?"

"Sometimes, not as much in recent years. Trust me when I say it'll get better."

"When did it start getting better for you?"

"A couple days ago…when I met your brother…"

"I can tell, you know."

"Tell what?" Kara asked, glancing over her shoulder for Sam.

"He's over by the bushes going to the bathroom. I can tell that you are in love with him." She paused when Kara sucked in air and held up her hand. "Don't worry; he is helplessly in love with you, too. He's never brought a girl home to meet us, by the way."

"I don't think he had much choice; he's on duty watching me."

"Yeah, keep telling yourself that. He could have passed you off to another deputy for the afternoon." She paused and looked at Caleb, worry lines etched in her forehead. "The way he looked at you and found subtle ways to touch you. I think it's great, by the way. He works too hard. And you are just what he needs."

With that final statement, she smiled and paused as if considering something, and then hugged Kara before she walked away, leaving Kara stunned and remarkably happy, until she turned and looked at Caleb. The expression on his face was enough to take away any euphoric feeling she had just been experiencing. Taking a calming breath, she walked over to him, reaching him as he disconnected from the call.

"What's wrong?" she asked, a feeling of trepidation coursing through her. Sudden panic filled her. "Is it Ethan?"

"No, nothing like that." He paused, clearly wanting to protect her, but knowing she needed to know whatever he had learned. "That was Cathy. Since Ethan was busy at the grand opening and then was hurt, he wasn't able to dig into old cases. Cathy started digging. She found a few more young women that fit the bill. Each one had a note left in the same exact spot."

"Where did he leave the notes?" She needed to know the answer, but she didn't want to know.

"They were all placed inside a Ziploc baggie and inserted into the woman's vagina." Kara grimaced at the information. "Upon examination of the bodies, the notes were found. All of the notes have a number assigned."

"We knew they would find more. That isn't what has you upset. What has you so upset?"

"Ethan had been at the police station last night and requested some information. Information he shouldn't have been able to get his hands on. But he called in some favors and got into the personnel files. We don't know whose file he was after, but he was after something before the accident. The officer who helped him came forward anonymously because he knew that it wasn't a coincidence."

There was no way around it; everything was about to hit the fan. She wasn't trying to protect her parents after all this time. But she *had* been trying to protect Ethan, and look where that had gotten them. Ethan had almost died. Maybe if she had been open and honest from day one, this could have been avoided. She sighed, resigned to her decision.

"Jenkins and Byrnes."

"What? I don't understand," Caleb said, frowning.

"Ethan is smart; he caught my slip during the confrontation with my father. He was looking for any files with the last names Jenkins and Byrnes. My father was quick on his feet, but not as quick as Ethan was," Kara said and turned and walked to the car—shoulders slumped, feeling defeated and depleted. The emotional roller coaster of the last 24 hours was too much, and she felt like she was about to crash. "Come on. I will fill you in on the ride to my place."

Quietly, she climbed into the car and stared off into the distance. It wasn't until Caleb got in and started the engine that she was shaken from her thoughts. Her history was so fucked up and her family was a colossal mess. If this conversation didn't have him running for the hills, they just might have a chance. He reached out and caressed her cheek and, as if he could read her mind, he spoke her thoughts.

"No matter what you have to say, it doesn't change how I feel about you. About us. There is nothing, and I mean nothing, that you are responsible for in this mess." She leaned into his hand as a tear slid down her cheek. His rough thumb wiped the tear away, and begrudgingly, he started the car and pulled out of his parents' driveway.

"You sure about that? My family is pretty fucked up. Sorry for the crude language, but that is the God's honest truth."

"There is not a doubt in my mind that you were an innocent bystander in it all. You have survivor's guilt, splash in some PTSD, but you have not done anything to facilitate this mess."

A huge weight lifted from her shoulders, because she believed that he would stand by her. And, by God, she trusted him unequivocally.

"I overheard my father paying Officers Jenkins and Byrnes to give him all the information collected and then I watched from the crack in the door as he burned it in our fireplace."

24

Caleb took a deep breath and looked at Kara. She looked so sad. Completely lost, and just when he thought they were making progress. Down deep, even though she knew better, she had hoped that her brother's accident had nothing to do with her past. But the information coming in clearly showed it had everything to do with her past.

"I couldn't figure out why he would do that, other than to protect his own interests. There's more, but I would really like to tell you the rest with your captain there." Swallowing audibly, she asked hesitantly, "Do you mind if we go to the hospital after dropping off Samsonite? I want to see Ethan. I would prefer to tell him everything before I make it official, and even though it's not a good idea to share this with him in his condition, I know he deserves to know, and I think he's strong enough to hear it. Hell, I think he suspects to some degree. Tomorrow morning, we can go to the station right away. I don't think what I have to say will necessarily help your case."

"You don't have to ask. Kara, I will do whatever you need me to do."

But by the time they got to her house, Caleb had decided it would be better for her to visit Ethan in the morning. It was late and he was certain that whatever she had to say wasn't going to affect the case that much. He was equally certain that whatever she was holding onto was devastating to her and would be to Ethan, but that it wasn't the missing link. Therefore, once they got to her house, Caleb convinced her to call the hospital first to see if Ethan was even awake or up to visitors. It didn't take a medical professional to figure out from her conversation that he was resting.

Hanging up the phone, she turned to him with a smile on her face.

"His stats are good; the swelling on his brain has gone down remarkably. Memory seems to not be affected and he can move all his extremities. He's still in a lot of pain, so they have him medicated and he's resting comfortably. But all in all, he's doing well and might even be moved out of ICU in a couple of days, possibly tomorrow if he continues to improve. An amazing thing, considering he almost bled out on the operating table."

"One even might call it a miracle," he said as she came to sit next to him on the couch.

She automatically cuddled into him, and Caleb sucked in a breath of gratitude for that small favor. He had thought she would wall herself off again. But instead, she was flush against him, where she should be, with her hand on his thigh, and, oh shit, she was rubbing his thigh. Which meant Mr. Happy was suddenly very happy, and it was very hard to hide said happiness. Caleb shifted to relieve some pressure but failed miserably.

Kara ran her nails lightly up his thigh and toward the hard bulge in his pants, tentatively brushing them across the rock-hard evidence of what she was doing to him by merely touching him. He inhaled deeply, counting to ten because he wasn't sure if he was awake or asleep. Blinking slowly, he looked down at her and, yep, she was sitting there, touching his traitorous dick. Couldn't blame the guy for wanting to spend some time with someone as amazing as Kara.

"Caleb..." she said breathily.

"Yeah?" he answered, his voice husky with lust.

"I want to touch you. I-I think like I said earlier if I take charge it will be less frightening for me."

Caleb knew what she was asking of him. She was asking for him to help release her from the torture. She was asking him to be the man to make her feel whole again. It was a daunting request that scared the shit out of him. Could he be everything she was asking? He knew without a single doubt in his head that he wanted to be her everything. He wanted to be her everything—not just today, but for the rest of their lives, and that scared him more than he thought possible. Because in a short time he had decided he wanted to be part of her life forever, and he was scared he would hurt her.

Down deep, Caleb knew it would not be intentional, because he would never hurt any woman, but if he went too fast, he could still end up hurting her and that would destroy him. How could he hurt someone that smelled as sweet as heaven? He was desperate to taste her lips again, but he was worried he would scare her with the intensity that was consuming him. By her taking the reins, he could give her what they both wanted without becoming too intense for her. It pained him that she didn't know what real, honest to God, good sex was.

"Are you sure?" he asked, trying to put one last road block up, in case she wasn't ready after all.

"I understand if you don't want to." She started to pull her hand away, but he quickly put his much larger hand on top of hers.

"We haven't even gone on a date. Maybe..." He groaned as she tentatively continued to rub him underneath his hand. "Ugh, that feels...so, very good. I don't want to push you too fast." His dick was screaming *no*, as his head was screaming *slow up*.

"If that's what you think," she said, and incredibly, she was mock pouting.

"Kara..."

"What?" she asked playfully. And Caleb swallowed hard; he was going to blow the moment.

"You've had a long day; I don't want you to do this for the wrong reason."

And her hand froze, just like that.

"It's just, right now, you're working on no sleep. Running on adrenaline. I need you to be with me because that's what you want. Not just because I'm available."

Tears pricked her eyes, and Caleb felt like an ass. But he knew he did the right thing; he knew he had to give her one more chance to back out. He couldn't live with himself if he didn't.

"Kara—"

"You think I'm here, doing something I have literally never done before because you're available?" she asked, angrily swiping at the tears sliding down her face. "You know what? Fuck you. I've had sex with one man. Count it. One man, since my abduction. It was a horrible experience. It closed me off to even trying again. I came to the conclusion that there was no emotional connection. Then I met you and holy shit, I feel an emotional connection. I feel like maybe it was just that I needed to wait for the right person, and I thought that person was you..."

She stopped talking and tried to stand. He grabbed her hand and pulled her toward him until she was straddling his lap.

"Kara, you are misunderstanding me. I don't think it's deliberate, but you're misunderstanding me all the same. I just want you to be here with me. I don't want you doing this because you think I expect it. I don't want you doing this because you need to prove to me you can. I just want you. God, how I want you."

"Caleb, please, I need to know what it's like to be with a good man, a man like you."

"I'm not so sure I *am* a good guy. And I want to be with you, too..."

"You don't think you're a good guy? I'm throwing myself at you, and you're putting up every roadblock you can think of, and you don't think you're good enough for me? Caleb, if anything, you're too good for me." She paused and looked down.

"How could you think that?"

"I don't think it, I know it, and I can't be fixed. I come into this relationship if you can call it that, with all kinds of issues."

"Who said you need fixing?"

"The few guys I tried to date. I-I haven't been able to be intimate since...well, since that one failed attempt. And, we didn't finish. I panicked as soon as he penetrated me. He was so eager, and he went so much faster than I had planned on, so I freaked out, and he left, angry, called me a nut job. I have never been able to get beyond that. That was a year after I was abducted. The boys I dated tended to leave when they found out about the abduction. Initially, it was a locker room challenge to have sex with me, and then it was too much baggage, they would say. I eventually stopped trying."

"Well, maybe that was your problem," he whispered huskily. She met his eyes, confused.

"What do you mean?"

"You were going out with boys, not mature enough to take care of your needs. A man wouldn't turn away from a woman like you. A man would stay and fight for you; a man would be patient and wait until you're ready. They damn sure wouldn't rush sex with a woman like you. I will wait until you're ready and there's not a chance I'll rush. Which begs the question, are you sure about doing this now, tonight?"

"I've never been surer of anything."

"Good, because I want to show you how good it can be. I need to show you how good it can be."

Caleb knew how ashamed she felt about something she had no control over, and he hated that she felt that way. As tenderly as possible, he pulled on her chin with his thumb and forefinger until her eyes met his. He needed to see her eyes, needed to be able to gauge her comfort level as he traced her lips with his thumb.

Her eyes were clouded with desire.

"Let me show you…"

LET ME SHOW YOU… Wasn't that what she had just been trying to do? The fear of rejection was so palpable that she could almost choke on it.

"I-I wanted to take control…"

"You can still have control. Anything you don't like, stop me. I promise to not put my weight on you. I knew that was what scared you before."

He had known. How could she have thought for a second he didn't know how to handle her? She was sitting on his lap, straddling him, not sure what to do when she looked at him. Really looked at him and saw the desire in his eyes. Felt the desire evident in his pants, the desire that had not gone away in the last five minutes of conversation.

"Show me, please...and, if I freak out...just give me a second. Know that I want this. Know that I want you."

Caleb pulled her close and kissed each eye, each cheek, then her nose, and when his lips were a mere breath from hers, he whispered, "Know I want you, only you—today, tomorrow, always." And then his lips descended on hers, parting them with a grace she didn't know was possible, his tongue gently probing the inside of her mouth until he found hers.

Within a matter of seconds, dampness had pooled between her legs, a feeling she had only felt when she had indulged in her fantasies. Alone. The ache was so strong that it was almost painful. She needed him like she needed air to breathe, water to drink, food to live. Crushing him to her, she deepened the kiss, and when she thought she was about to combust, he pulled away and masterfully removed her shirt.

His mouth traveled to her bra covered breast, and he sucked her nipple into his mouth, eliciting a moan. Yes, she moaned. Her hands were tangled in his hair, holding him against her as he tugged at the nipple that was peaked and fighting to get past the satin of her bra. With a growl deep in his throat, he unsnapped her bra and removed it. His mouth found her breast once again, and he sucked her nipple into his mouth. First one and then the other, back and forth, driving her crazy. She rocked against the hard bulge in his lap, needed the sensation desperately, and arched into his mouth.

Incredibly, she felt close to climax. The feeling was so intense, and he had only played with her nipples. Was that even possible? His hands were planted firmly, one on her ass and one on her lower back, while he continued to lick, nip, suck, and tease her pebble-hard nipples. With a sudden movement, he stood her up, swiftly pulling down her pants and underwear. Suddenly feeling exposed, her instinct was to cover her intimate parts of her body.

"Don't," he said gruffly. "Don't hide yourself, let me see you." Hesitantly, she removed her hand from her sopping wet crotch and her arm from her breasts. Trembling, she stood before him, until he stood and turned her and pushed her gently onto the couch. Spreading her legs as she sat, he kissed his way up her knee to her inner thigh and then he kissed her there, in the area that was throbbing with need.

As soon as his tongue touched her clitoris, her whole body jerked in response. How was it possible that the little pressure he had placed there could cause her to orgasm so quickly? His hand was splayed on her lower belly as he laved her with his tongue, her body jerking with each touch of his tongue to the overly-sensitized nub.

Once her body had stopped trembling, he looked up at her through his dark lashes. Slowly, he kissed his way up her body until he made it to her face, gently kissing her mouth. Impossibly, warmth began to spread through her, and she moaned again. He laughed softly in his throat.

"I don't think you have a problem in this department after all. Though you may have just shattered." It was her turn to laugh, and once her lips parted, he took the opportunity to deeply kiss her.

She moved against him, rubbing her groin against his. With unsteady fingers, she reached for his belt. Caleb must have sensed she wanted to do it herself because he waited patiently as she fumbled, but finally managed to undo the belt, then the button, until she slid the zipper down and placing her hand inside his pants, finally freed the erection that had been fighting to get loose. It was Caleb's turn to groan as she wrapped her fingers around the throbbing erection.

"Oh, gah, Kara...careful. I might finish right now." She smiled a wicked smile and licked her lips. "Uh-uh, not a chance. I see where your head's going and you need to keep your mouth away from Mr. Happy for now. I need to be inside you when I come."

"Well, then, what's taking you so long?" she whispered.

It was all he needed to hear as he rummaged in his pocket and then dropped his pants and underwear to the ground. Then he was back on his knees, seated between her legs, condom in hand, and the room got smaller, and things got real—fast.

"Stay with me," he whispered, leaning forward to kiss her as he began to place the condom on his cock.

Reaching out, she stopped him. He took a deep breath and looked at her.

"Okay, just give me a second. I can stop. I just need a second."

"No. No condom. He-he always used one and the smell...and, I'm on birth control. I just want to feel you, only you." Her eyes pleaded with him, and without a moment's hesitation, he threw it on top of his pants.

She relaxed into him, and he kissed her again. Kara almost forgot what they were about to do until she felt the pressure of his cock trying to penetrate her. She tensed again, and he broke the kiss. "Uh-uh, with me, just you and me. No reason to worry." Kissing her between the words he spoke, she melted into him.

Pushing against her folds, he slowly entered the sanctity of her womanhood. When he would feel her tense, he would stop and back out; once she relaxed, he would move in again. It was an almost painstaking process, and she loved him for his patience. Before she knew what had happened, he was deep inside her, and she moaned in pleasure at the feeling. She wasn't scared; she was just ready.

"Tight," he whispered. "You are so wet and tight." She dug her nails into his buttocks and wiggled, encouraging him to move. It didn't take much to encourage him before he started to move. Thrusting slowly in and out, in and out, building the sensation that would lead her to another orgasm. She began to meet him part way, and he picked up the pace; thrusting harder into her each time he met her. It felt as if her body was about to overheat, and just when she couldn't take anymore, she crested the peak, her body convulsing with the most incredible orgasm.

"That's it, come with me." And with a final thrust, Caleb also came, his body shaking as he spilled himself into her.

Once his body relaxed, he looked up at her. His face was startled as he looked at her.

"Are you all right? Did I hurt you?" he asked, bewildered at the tears spilling down her face.

"No...no, it was amazing. You are amazing." She melted into him while kissing him fiercely and felt him start to grow inside her again. Her eyes were wide when she looked at him.

"Sorry..." he said, and he was actually blushing.

"Can we? I mean, so soon?"

"Oh, baby, can we ever. But not here. I want you in your bed, on top of me. Nothing restraining you." He stood and scooped her up, carrying her up the stairs to her bedroom.

HE WAS LIVID. His blood was boiling, and he felt like he would erupt. She had gone to bed with the detective. After all these years, she had finally fucked someone, and it had to be that fucking, pretty boy, arrogant asshole of a detective. Sure, she had tried that one time all those years ago. What would she do if she knew that he had paid that college boy to fuck her, that he had told him that she liked it fast and hard? College boy didn't know what the fuck had happened when she freaked out. It was an experiment. He had just wanted to see if she would, and she had performed beautifully when she freaked as soon as the hired idiot's pathetic dick got past the folds of her pussy.

It made him feel omnipotent, that he could still control her months later and then years later. She was pathetic. She had never had a relationship beyond one or two dates; it was exhilarating that he controlled her so completely. After all those years, she was still cognizant of the power those four days had over her. Then she moved back, not part of his plan, but he couldn't have planned it better himself.

Until that asshole moved in on her. He saw it right away, the way she looked at that detective. He could practically smell her arousal in her house the night he watched her sleeping, and that was only after just meeting Montgomery.

And now she had slept with him. Not awkward sex, which he had hoped would be the case if she went through with it. No, she went and fucked him. On her couch, in her living room, where anyone could have walked by and seen what was happening. Sure, the blinds were drawn, but come on, in this day and age that really didn't stop people.

After all, no one had found the hi-tech cameras he had placed all through her house. She couldn't even take a piss without him seeing her. He smiled briefly at the thought of the camera that looked right into her pussy as she pissed. So, at least no one had found the cameras or the tracking device he had placed on her phone. They really did underestimate him.

25

Morning came in a silent crescendo. Kara had slept better than she had in ten long years. Her rom was bathed in light, and she realized that she hadn't drawn the curtains in her room. Normally, this would have sent her into a near panic attack, but as she stretched and felt the long, lean, and warm body next to her, she had not a care in the world.

She sighed deeply. She had mind-blowing sex with Caleb, not once, not twice, but all night long. Not only that, but she had so many orgasms, she lost count. Her body ached everywhere, but all the aches were in good places. This was what it was supposed to be like. The smile on her face couldn't get any bigger as she burrowed into the blankets and the arms of the man she had fallen hopelessly head over heels for.

In that brief instance, in that cocoon of happiness, she was certain there was nothing that could ruin the moment. This was what she had longed for, had fought for the chance of having, and nothing was going to stop her from having it.

Breakfast in bed! She should make him breakfast in bed. With another stretch and a yawn, she made to move out of the warmth of his embrace but was met with resistance. The slumbering man was not slumbering at all, judging by the hardness pressing into her backside and the growl emanating from his throat.

"Where do you think you're going, woman?"

"I need sustenance; we burned a lot of calories last night. I was going to make us omelets."

"Mmmmmm, omelets. That sounds amazing, but I would rather go hungry for now than let you out of this bed."

She turned to look at him over her shoulder and laughed at the wicked grin on his sleepy face. The man appeared to be quite insatiable. And at that moment, she didn't have a care to object. Rolling into him, she kissed him deeply and knew that it would be a bit before that omelet was made. But just as his hand was making its way up her legs to her butt, a crash sounded downstairs. Startled, she sat bolt upright. Caleb was out of the bed in a nanosecond, his gun in his hand in one fluid motion.

"Stay here!" he said, grabbing his underwear and jerking them on before he darted from the room.

Stay here? No way was she going to stay there. She was staying with the guy with the gun, no question there at all. Grabbing her robe, she threw it on and was still tying it as she hit the top of her stairs. Flying down her stairs, she skidded to a halt in the entryway when she saw Caleb on her front stoop, looking at something on the ground.

"I told you to stay in your room," he said, not turning around.

"I wasn't staying up there by myself, not when you're down here with a gun. I feel safer with you. What is it?" she asked, scared what the answer would be.

"Someone threw a brick at your front door. They also left a calling card," he said, tension in his voice as he looked at her front door. In her haste to run to his side, she hadn't noticed the front door. In blood-red paint, someone had written: *#2 was my four-leaf clover and soon will be my do over.*

"Well, whoever it is, they're pretty good at rhyming," she said, her voice strained. Caleb stood and swept her into his arms. "The timing seems awfully coincidental."

"I was thinking the same thing. I need to call this in. Whoever is killing these women has continually threatened you." As he turned to move, she stopped him.

"What do you mean? I know that the note found on Andrea Vincent seemed like a possible threat and this one is definitely a threat. I wouldn't say that is continuous; it's just since I have been home. Right?"

"Of the other victims we have identified, all of the notes seem to be directed at you." He winced when she staggered and slumped against the wall. "I'm sorry, I had already thrown so much at you last night and I know I was supposed to be honest. But, I just didn't want to tell you and put more on you."

"No, I understand. I do. I just, my God, all these years, all those times, all those emails..."

"Wait, what?" he asked. "What times, what emails?"

"I have always had a sense I was being watched. I've gotten emails, links to websites pretty much since the first day I moved away. Emails that I assumed were from weird fans of infamous crimes that had somehow gotten my email address. I've changed my email so often, I lost count, but somehow the emails continue. I don't know how, and I was always sure it was someone new each time, that some new person who'd come across me and did some research found my email."

"How many emails?"

"Enough. But there was never anything in the emails that made me think it was anything to take seriously."

"And now?"

"Now? Now I am taking it very seriously. My God, this whole time...I think whoever sent those emails was the same person, not a bunch of random people, and whoever it is, has been watching me this whole time. Does that make me sound crazy?"

"Unfortunately, no. Man, what I wouldn't give to think you were being paranoid." He paused and pinched the bridge of his nose. "Go on upstairs and get some clothes on. I'm going to call this in."

With a quick kiss to her temple and a hug, he moved toward her landline. The land line she kept in case of an emergency. This was an emergency to her. Her precarious world was crashing around her, and the solidly good mood she had woken up in was gone. Obliterated by a brick to her door on a beautiful and warm spring morning. The bastard knew. Somehow, he knew that she was happy. Much like he always knew her email, but how?

She had never changed her name, wasn't willing to do that to hide from curious onlookers, because Devon Bristol died. Had he not died, well, she would have hidden herself very thoroughly. A chill raced up her spine as she thought about it, really thought about it. Terrified with the realization, she apprehensively looked up to the ceilings. Then even slower she looked down. She hoped like hell she was wrong. However, she knew she wasn't wrong. Standing, frozen to the spot, she waited for Caleb to return from his phone call. When he returned to the entry, he seemed momentarily confused by her presence, and then a look of understanding crossed his face.

"Did you want me to go up with you when you get dressed? I'm sorry, that was inconsiderate of me. Come on..." When she didn't move, he stopped and really looked at her. "Kara, what is it?"

"The timing was too coincidental," she mumbled.

"It was. For all we know, he had planned this all along..."

"No. He knew. He knew I was with you. Somehow, someway, he figured it out. That we were making love. It makes sense."

"Kara, honey, you aren't making sense to me. What do you mean?"

"Can the detectives coming check my house?"

"For what?"

"Cameras."

A FEW HOURS LATER, Kara was sitting, huddled under a throw blanket on her couch. No matter what he did, he couldn't get her to move. She was frozen to the spot where she had sat down, and she was shivering. The signs of shock were obvious. As each room was checked and multiple cameras were found in each room, she had become quieter and more despondent.

He wanted to kick his own ass for not thinking of cameras. What the hell was he thinking? But then again, why would he have thought that the maniac they were looking for would have had the foresight to put cameras through her house before she got there, and how did he know she was moving back? Kara had been getting emails the whole time she had been away. Maybe the unsub had hacked into her computer and was able to see her emails and internet searches.

Caleb didn't believe he could have gotten past the security system, but anything could be hacked. What worried him the most was that the person they were looking for had been able to follow her and get intel, like her email, without any issue whatsoever. This means whoever it was had to have a gift for hacking, which would mean he could have gotten into her house easily, but not with Samsonite here. Which meant that he had to have done it before she got here; there was no other possibility.

"Kara, they think they found all the cameras," Caleb said softly, approaching her like she was a startled deer.

Kara continued to stare into space, trembling on the couch. And it was more than he could take.

"Damn it, Kara, look at me," he said, physically shaking her.

The motion seemed to be enough, and she blinked long and then turned to look at him.

"Caleb?" she asked.

"Yeah, I'm here, baby."

"Can you hold me, just hold me?" she said as she broke into sobs.

He pulled her into his chest and hugged her tightly to him. She was still crying when his captain walked into her living room. He paused briefly, looking between the two of them. Normally, the Captain wouldn't have showed up to this scene. But he had developed a soft spot for Kara. It was hard not to. Captain Bob Wickman also walked up to Kara like she was a startled deer and knelt on the ground in front of her, holding her hands.

"Kara. The department has all their resources on this case. I will not fail you like I failed Andrea." His eyes stared intently into her eyes, and that was what really snapped her out of it.

"You didn't fail Andrea. A monster killed her, a monster that we're going to find and put down so he can't hurt another woman again. I couldn't put down Devon Bristol, but I sure as hell am going to find whoever is idolizing him. Whether it's his partner or a random fan of his." Squeezing his hands once, she stood up. "I need to make that statement now. I don't think it is going to help us one bit because this is much bigger than I ever imagined. But I need to put it all down on paper."

With that announcement, she went upstairs to her room. Caleb was about to follow her when Bob stopped him with a hand to his arm.

"Just a quick word."

"Yeah, Cap?"

"I am not a fool. I see how you are looking at her and I see how she is relying on you. I'm not saying I have a problem with it. She needs someone like you. However, if I for one second get a whiff of your head not being in the game, I will pull you from this case. I know that we're short right now with Ethan out and other cases to handle, but I will pull you. Understood?"

"Understood." Caleb was about to leave and then turned and looked at his Captain. "But with all due respect, sir? There is no fucking way I will sit idly by if this case is still open and her life is in danger. He won't hurt that woman any more than she has already been hurt; I love her too much to allow it. I want this bastard's cold, dead heart in my hands. Understood?"

"Understood, we all do, so keep your mind on the task at hand."

"No worries there." Caleb looked toward the ceiling and made his way toward the stairs.

"Have you told her yet?" Bob paused and then continued when Caleb looked at him, confused. "That you love her?"

He hadn't realized that he had admitted what had been building inside him from the moment he met Kara. A slow smile spread across his face.

"Not yet. But I will. The timing isn't right."

When he got to her room, she was standing in the center with a look of terror on her face.

"I can't do it," she said frantically.

"Do what?" he asked.

"Take a shower, get naked." She took a breath. "I was tough down there, but when I got up here and thought, what if they missed a camera. Then what? The sick fuck will see me. It isn't like he hasn't seen me already. More than once. But I can't let him see me again. He has ruined my new house for me. Fuck."

"Kara, they got all the cameras. They even got the one in the toilet."

"Toilet?" Her color got so pale that he worried she was about to faint. "He put one in the toilet?" Panic strained her features. "Who does that? Why?"

"To hold control over you. Sit down, head between your knees. You're having a panic attack."

"I-I know. I've had them before. So much for not being glass, huh?" she said between gasps for air.

"You aren't glass. No one could weather all of this." He knelt beside her, waiting for the panic to subside. "I say if you're worried we missed a camera, let's give him a real show. The only way to fight fire is with fire, and this creep wants to scare you. Don't let the bastard win; show him he doesn't scare you. You made him mad by making love to me. I say we continue making him mad until he messes up, and he will mess up. When he does, we'll be there to bring him down."

Caleb knew the moment he got through to her. She sat up straight, her breathing under control and looked him in the eye.

"I won't let whoever is behind this do this to me. I won't be a victim. I am a survivor, and he can go to hell."

"That's my girl!" He leaned forward and kissed her tenderly on the temple. "How about you take a shower and then we can go see Ethan."

"Ethan?" she asked, clearly confused.

"You wanted to talk to him before making your statement."

"Right."

He stood up and pulled her to her feet. There was no way for him to stop himself from pulling her in for a hug. Again, he kissed the side of her head, breathing in her scent, trying to center himself. He held her to him, amazed at how she had become so important to him in such an incredibly short amount of time.

"If we didn't have a full house downstairs, I'd make sure that if there was a camera left, we would give that bastard a real show."

Shaking her head, she laughed quietly. His heart filled with the small victory of making her laugh. She made her way to his mouth and kissed him deeply, seemingly throwing everything into that one kiss, as if she wasn't sure if it would be her last chance. That thought momentarily chilled him, but the heat racing straight to his groin crossed off the feeling of dread. Eventually, he had to gently push her away and send her to the shower, so he didn't fulfill his earlier statement, to hell with the crowd downstairs. Hell, most of them were men and wouldn't blame him, anyway. But now wasn't the time for what the less-evolved portion of his body wanted to do.

Once she was safely in the shower, Caleb sunk to the bed, his shoulders drooped and his head in his hands. He had spent the last hours calming himself because he needed to be strong for Kara. But if he was being honest, and he was an honest man most of the time, he would admit that he was scared to death for her safety.

One thing was for certain, Caleb didn't know what he would do if anything happened to her. He damn well knew that if this monster got a hold of her, he would be jumping out of his skin trying to find her. There was no way he could allow it. Which meant that he had to get his ass in gear and find this guy before someone else was hurt.

26

The drive to the hospital was a strained silence. Not quite awkward, just full of worry on her end, and she wasn't missing the signs of worry on Caleb's face. If she could smooth away those lines, she would. Maybe her walking away from him to spare him any pain would be what a better person would do.

Kara wasn't a better person; there was just no way she was walking away from the man sitting next to her. He was everything she wanted and more. There was no way she could walk away from the person that had helped her start to open up and leave her past behind. Everything she wanted—no, needed—depended on finding the person who had been on a killing spree for at least ten years. Deep in thought, she didn't realize they had pulled into the parking garage and that Caleb had turned the car off and turned to look at her.

"Ready?" he asked as he caressed the side of her face. She loved the feel of his fingers on her and unconsciously rubbed her face into his hand.

"Yes. It's time I air it all out. Bad timing with Ethan in the hospital, but it needs to be done."

They were just about to Ethan's room when they ran smack into her parents. Numb to any further shock, she didn't even bat an eyelash at the fact that they were there, in the hospital, apparently visiting Ethan. If they kept this up, they would visit Ethan more in two days than they had the whole time she was in the hospital.

Kara moved to go around them, and her mother's hand shot out, wrapping around her upper arm. It was all Kara could do to hold herself back from lashing out at the woman who had raised her. Instinct is a strong thing, and her instinct was screaming at her to slap the woman right across her booted face, or at the very least, to slap her hand away. Instead, she stared her down and waited for her mother to speak.

"Your father tells me you have been spouting off a bunch of drivel again. I needn't warn you about spreading rumors that have no merit, do I?" Constance wore a smug expression on her face, and Kara wanted nothing more than to wipe it right off.

"I wouldn't dream of spreading rumors that have no merit." When her mother began to smile, Kara continued. "Don't smile just yet, wouldn't want your lovely face you paid for to wrinkle; I wasn't done speaking. You see, these 'rumors.' as you like to call them, have much more than merit behind them, they have truth. So, do us all a favor, and spare me your disgusting attempts at threats. I am older and much wiser than I used to be. And like I told the man you married and call my father, a day of reckoning is coming; it would do you good to get out of my way. Right. Now."

With that final statement, Kara tugged her arm out of her mother's hand and walked down the hall to Ethan's room, Caleb's hand pressed firmly to her lower back. When they walked into the room, she was stunned to see Ethan sitting up, eating Jell-O and smiling one of his most charming smiles at one of the nurses.

"Ethan!" Her face broke out in a genuine smile. Seeing him sitting up and eating was like a dream come true!

"Hey!"

As quickly as the smile had taken over her face, it faded. She wasn't here for a happy reason, and now that she saw he was doing better than expected, she hated to set him back in any way. Yet, she knew it was time that she told Ethan everything and that he could handle what she had to say.

Ethan looked to Kara with concern in his eyes and a silent question of are you all right. And she knew the exact moment that he figured out why she was there. Ashamed, she looked to the ground. When she looked back up at him, realization and relief registered on his face.

"Kara, are you ready to tell me what happened that night?"

Caleb stood close behind her, so close that she could breathe in his scent. Somehow, he knew that his proximity to her would be something that she could use to stand tall and look her brother in the eye. Today would be the hardest day in her life, even over the abduction and repeated rapes. Today would be the day she would disappoint the one person that had been there for her through it all.

"I-I'm sorry, Ethan."

"Sorry for what?" He was going to make her say it. And she got angry, not at him, not at herself for feeling so weak suddenly, but angry at her parents all over again. She knew while behind her Caleb was there to support her because she could sense it in his body language when he came to stand beside her. But even though he was there to hold her up, to protect her, this would still be a hard conversation to have.

"Ethan, Kara is going to go down and make a statement this morning. She wanted to talk to you first, though."

"It's time I told you both everything I know. Time I let some of the demons rest. Jenkins and Byrnes gave our father all the evidence from the investigation, and I watched him burn it all in the fireplace of his office. He didn't even look at the paper that was in the file before he set it on fire. But the reason I left that November isn't solely because of Jenkins and Byrnes and our father paying them off. That had something to do with it though because, from the moment I heard father asking his goons if the job was done, I knew something else was up. Their behavior was off, even for them. There shouldn't have been a reason for him to want the evidence destroyed: Devon Bristol was dead, easy as cases could go, completely open-and-shut case. Or was it? Something else had to be going on. I didn't find out that my instinct was right until that night."

"How about you enlighten me?" Ethan asked, and she could see he no longer was going to let her get away with protecting him. Yes, his controlled anger was directed at her because she hadn't trusted him, but he was also furious at their father because he believed her. She understood the anger; she felt it every day. It just was hard to have the one person who had always been in her corner aim even a small portion of his anger at her.

"That night I was restless, like every other night since my abduction. But it was different; it was a more profound restlessness. I attributed it to what I had overheard earlier in the week, but now I'm not so sure. Now I know it was my intuition telling me there was more to the story. I knew there had to be a good reason Father would want all the evidence destroyed. I wanted to believe that he was covering up for past shady dealings, but I was terribly wrong."

"Kara, I think it's time you stop telling such foolish, made up stories," Constance Vanderbilt said, her voice dripping venom.

Kara hadn't realized that their parents had walked in, but she wasn't surprised they were hovering outside, careful to protect themselves. Kara turned and looked at her mother and mock clapped at her performance.

"Bravo, Mother. Good timing. Unfortunately, this time I won't be silenced. So, you can leave the command performance at the door." Kara looked at her mother scornfully and noticed that her brother and Caleb had both looked at each other with alarm on their faces. For the first time in her life, Kara had made her mother pause, and she was going to take advantage of the situation. "I heard arguing, which was not unusual in this household, but for some reason, I was intrigued by it more than scared of it."

Her mind traveled to that night nearly ten years ago. Kara couldn't wait to get it all off her shoulders, and once she started, the words tumbled out. It was surprising how easy it was to recount.

IT WAS A COLD, damp night, and once again, Kara couldn't sleep. Big surprise. She hadn't slept more than two hours a night since the abduction unless she was medicated, and Kara had stopped allowing them to dispense any medicine to her. Therefore, the two hours she slept were usually filled with horrifying nightmares. They weren't really nightmares, just memories of what had happened. A nightmare was something that you worry could happen, but it never actually did.

It was no wonder she was more restless tonight than usual. After hearing her father with those two cops, it was any wonder she could stomach being in the same house with him. Soon that wouldn't be a problem since she was still going away to college like she planned. Agitated, she got out of bed and decided to go grab a book from her parents' extensive library.

Surely a good book could get her through the night. Lord knew it had done the trick almost every other night since she'd gotten home. At least she was brushing up on her literature; it would be useful knowledge when she left for school in the coming weeks. Even if she'd been struggling to leave her parents' house for more than a photo op with them, it didn't matter, she wasn't staying in her parents' house forever.

Kara had always felt uncomfortable getting her picture taken with her parents, pretending that they were the happy family when the reality was far from that. But before the incident, as her parents referred to it, she could at least stand there and not feel like a freak show. That wasn't the case anymore. They expected her to act normal; no, they expected her to be normal.

Uneasy, she walked down the hallway, and when the sounds of arguing piqued her interest, she crept as silent as a whisper to her parents' bedroom door. She found herself tiptoeing, a habit that had formed as a youth so as not to be heard when arguments were occurring. Her parents had forced her to break the habit, but these days she seemed to always be tiptoeing, even though no one would be able to hear her footsteps on the plush carpet.

Kara wasn't sure what had compelled her to eavesdrop; normally, she would walk as quickly and quietly in the opposite direction as possible. But on this night, she felt the compulsion to stand by her parents' door and noiselessly listen.

Perhaps it would help her figure out her father's betrayal, the betrayal she had overheard earlier in the week because for the life of her, she could not figure out why he had asked those two cops for the evidence and then burned it in their fireplace. But for whatever reason, he had paid them to hand it over so he could make it disappear.

Whatever the reason was, she knew it was imperative to listen to the argument tonight. Leaning into the door so she could better hear, her stomach dropped to her knees, and her heart felt like it would jump out of her chest and bounce down the hallway. Kara wasn't sure what she had expected to find out, but she knew it wasn't what she was hearing.

"Would you just calm down? We are not going to go to jail. As long as your two hired guns are as good as you say they are, we should be fine. They are *as good as you say, right?" her mother asked.*

"They damn well better be. I paid them a lot of money to get me that evidence, and I am not about to go down for this whole mess."

"Don't you mean we paid them a lot of money?"

"Fine, whatever; let's argue over semantics when we should be discussing how to handle this blackmail letter we got."

"So, we pay it, what is there to discuss? We pay what he wants, and if he comes back, we pay again. I will not go to jail if I have anything to say about it."

"But you would send me to jail for you, wouldn't you? Just remember, darling, this was your idea. From the day we got the ransom call, you were calling the shots, delaying the drop so we could get some more publicity. I knew you could be a bitch, but I had no idea you were so coldhearted."

Crack! *Kara jumped when the sound of a hand slapping someone across the face echoed through the door. Apparently, her mother hadn't liked being called a bitch. It was no secret she was coldhearted. Kara guessed she just didn't like it being said out loud. She didn't particularly care at this point. If she understood what she was hearing, she didn't care about anything her parents said or did. They were unre-deemable.*

"Are you saying you don't want to be governor? Hell, she was already in their hands, and the publicity was priceless. You climbed up in the polls so fast that there's no way you can lose." Constance's voice was different now, seductive. Hell, she was nearly purring.

"Is that all you care about, being a governor's wife?" Stanley asked and then grunted, and Kara heard a zipper sliding down.

"No, but it ranks in the top five. Right behind what I am about to do right now. Don't get all sanctimonious on me; you certainly were not fighting me on this back when it mattered. You were thrilled at the prospect of using this to get you in the governor's mansion."

Kara heard the sounds of her parents having rough sex and swallowed, disgusted. Not because her parents were having sex, but because they were having sex while discussing what had happened to their daughter. As if it turned them on.

"That was before I found out what they did to her. You don't care in the least what they did to her, do you?" he moaned and grunted.

"It was unfortunate. But what would paying sooner have done? She had already been with him for two days before we were contacted; what was done, was done. Yeah, like that." Kara didn't know what that was and didn't want to know.

"She spent two extra days being raped and tortured before she escaped. That doesn't upset you?"

"Harder...which part? That she escaped or that she was there for two extra days?"

They stopped talking for a while, and all she could hear was more sounds of rough sex. She finally heard clothing being put back on.

"It should upset you. But the part about us dragging our feet, all for what, for some publicity to get me in the governor's office? How can that not upset you? How does that not keep you up at night?"

"What doesn't kill you makes you stronger. It doesn't appear that you care all that much, either. Kinky bastard that you are."

"Lucky for us, she didn't die."

"Things might have been easier if she had."

"Constance! Don't you care for her at all?"

"Oh, like you care. You're too busy bedding anything with a pulse to care about your children."

"And you should talk."

Crack*! Kara flinched again when she heard another slap connect with her father's face. Stunned, she quietly walked back to her room and packed.*

"As you can see, our wonderful sainted parents delayed paying the ransom for some added publicity. They left me with him for two extra days. All because Dad was climbing in the polls. God, I felt so loved when I heard you strategizing."

The truth came tumbling out in one breath, everything except the disgusting details of her parents having sex while discussing her kidnap and ransom. No one needed to know that part; she didn't even want to know that part. Being raped had been no contest to having such a deep betrayal from her parents. The betrayal had been felt so deep, she would never be the same. Parents were supposed to protect their children. They should have rushed the money to her captors, but they didn't.

"My God, Kara. Why didn't you tell me?" Ethan whispered.

"I couldn't tell you. My life was ruined. Why ruin yours, too? What I heard that night…it was like being raped all over again. Over the last ten years, I found myself wondering if it would have been better never finding out what they had done. But I now know it made me who I am today. I'm stronger because of it. I still had been planning to go away to school, but I may never have left their godforsaken house had I not heard them that night. I certainly wouldn't have gone to the school I wanted to and not their choice. I had been scared of my own shadow. I would have done whatever they wanted if they only showed me the simplest thing—that they loved me. But they didn't show me that, and what I heard empowered me. Not only did it empower me to leave, it helped push me to the school I wanted and to choose medicine like I wanted, so I could make a difference."

"But I could have shouldered it with you. For God's sake. Kara, the only reason I kept in touch with our parents was for Mother. And she's no better than Father. In fact, from what you just told me, she's worse. So much worse."

"Ethan, please don't be angry. I had to do it this way. I had no idea how to deal with things that were going on in my head, much less what I had witnessed. There was no way I could let you go through what I'd gone through. Your life was still livable. At the time, I kind of felt like mine was done. I know I told you I felt liberated. Which I did, but I was like a person with no country and didn't know if I would be able to pull out of the tailspin my life had gone into."

"Kara, I'm not mad at you; I'm furious at them," he said, throwing a glare to their parents. Who had been systematically ignored since the truth had broken out of its shell.

"You're not?"

"How could I be mad at you? You were only eighteen. I'm not sure anyone could have stomached what they heard. Actually, I give you a lot of credit for walking out on them. I would have done the same thing." He glanced at them again. "I would ask you if you're happy that you have lost your daughter since now you are going to lose your son, but I don't think you care. Even if you do care, I quite frankly *don't*. Some sins just cannot be forgiven."

"Someday, you are going to be sitting all alone and wonder what happened. You might even forget whose fault it was and try to contact me, but you can be sure I will not answer any kind of correspondence from you. Time cannot heal what you did, and I should know," Kara said.

Kara turned her back to them. Caleb placed his hand on the small of her back, and she finally felt protected. Even when her mother chose to show her true colors, she felt capable of handling it.

"Don't worry, dear, there won't be a time when I will be sitting around wishing I could talk to you. So, don't wait by the phone for me to do so," her mother said coldly. "But I will make you pay for turning my son against me. Mark my words."

Kara squared her shoulders, sucked in a deep breath, and turned once more to look at her mother. Locking her eyes with the eyes of the woman who raised her, who was supposed to protect her, all that she saw was hatred, and she shook her head sadly.

She turned to look at her father, pity washed over her face.

"It's a real shame that all this time, I gave you some credit. After that night, I thought you were just a product of an evil wife. I disagree with Ethan; you turned out to be worse. When you could have been salvaged, you did something unredeemable. You allowed it to happen, and then you nearly laughed about it after. For that, I am sorry. As for you, Mother, in the last ten years, I thought you might have a change of character and plead for my forgiveness. You didn't, and after you leave this room, I'm done with you. I will not think of you another second."

As if their father was truly tired, weary of the fight to continue to pretend he was the patriarch who led their family when in reality their mother did, he looked at her, and she swore his eyes were glistening when he said, "I truly am sorry, too." And then he turned and walked away.

"You always were so weak, it disgusted me," her mother spat. "At least your children got their strength from me."

"Oh, but remember, dear mother, you would have preferred I died, so maybe you would have preferred I inherited his weaknesses?" Kara asked coldly. "If I had, I wouldn't have made it out of that cabin and those woods. I would surely be buried somewhere, either never to be found or destined to be found by some poor hunter or kid walking his dog."

Kara was about to leave the hospital room, but then she realized that she didn't need to leave. They did.

"No, you know what? I am not leaving. You need to leave. You are not welcome in this room."

"You can't force us to leave; you don't have the power to do so."

"This is my hospital room, and I would like you to leave..." Kara held up her hand, effectively silencing her brother.

"That is where you're wrong, Mother. As one of the attending doctors of this hospital, it is fully in my right to not allow you to step foot in a patient's room. It doesn't matter if you've donated money to the hospital. You need to leave before I call security or, better yet, I could have Detective Montgomery escort you out. Wouldn't that be great for the evening news?"

Her mother not being one to be talked down to had one last biting remark as they walked out the door.

"You got one thing right: I would have preferred you died. If he would have done his job right, you would have…"

Once they left, she took a deep breath, and another piece of her heart seemed to heal. Even her mother's cruel remarks couldn't diminish what had happened. She had laid a major demon to rest by finally telling what she knew. It made her think of possibilities. There was life out there for her. The man standing stoically behind her with his hand on the small of her back was her present and her future. Once everything was said and done, and the dust was settled, she would put the past behind her, and he would be there. After all she'd been through, she deserved a happily ever after.

27

Caleb thought he'd heard everything in his years on the force; likewise, he'd thought his years of training had prepared him for anything, that he could handle just about anything without losing his cool. But standing there beside Kara as she retold the story of what had caused her to close the door on her parents, Caleb felt a temper rise in him that he'd never felt before.

Parents were supposed to keep the evil at bay. They weren't supposed to hang their children out to dry for power and greed. Caleb wasn't stupid; he knew things like this happened every day. And he had witnessed a few monstrosities in his line of work, but this affected him bone deep, and he knew it was because of the love he felt for Kara. He now knew more than ever why meeting his parents had put such a look of longing on Kara's face. It was because she'd never known what love from a mother and father—a real mother and father—felt like. Kara had Ethan's love, and Ethan had hers, period, until now.

Caleb was no longer surprised when he thought about how much he loved her. He knew damn well that, while it hurt to hear the details of what had happened to Kara all those years ago and now the details of what her parents had done, he would try every day to make her know nothing but happiness. It might not be time to tell her he was in love with her and that he would spend the rest of his life making her know how loved she could be, but that didn't mean he had to hide it from his own heart. She deserved to be loved. He wanted to be the one to love her; that is if she would let him.

As much as he knew he was in love with her, he also knew that it was going to be a challenge to get her to accept it. She was a complicated and headstrong woman who thought she was tarnished and of no use to any man. And that was another thing that Caleb was going to work hard to fix. Because if last night was any indication of how good it could be between them, he was willing to do anything and everything for her.

"My God, Kara, I-I had no idea the level of depravity that they both would sink to. I knew Father was guilty of bribes. But this? And Mother…"

"You were always a little blinded to how Mother really is," she said sadly. Caleb came to stand behind her and wrapped an arm around her shoulders, pulling her tightly against him.

"I wasn't blind, not entirely. At least, not to the way she treated you. I mean, I didn't think she hated you. I just thought she was indifferent. But, Kara, she literally hates you."

"I know," Kara said, and the tears that Caleb knew she had kept at bay so that her mother wouldn't see them, began to flow. "But, why? What could I have ever done to warrant such hatred? I did everything they ever asked, everything they ever wanted, and this is the way they feel about me? I would understand if I was a t-terrible person." She was sobbing now, and Caleb spun her around and tucked her into him.

He looked at Ethan over the top of her head, and his eyes said it all. Ethan was on the same page as Caleb. If either one of them could get away with it, they would teach Stanley and Constance Vanderbilt a lesson. For now, they had to be happy with doing what they could to take down a governor. Caleb knew they would eventually accomplish that goal; they just had to be patient.

"Kara, I am so sorry." Ethan's eyes were glistening, too, and Caleb discreetly looked away, not wanting to make him feel uncomfortable. He guided Kara to Ethan's bed and let her go so she could sit by him. It tore him apart to see her lay her head on the bed and watch Ethan stroke her hair. "They will pay. I will make sure of it."

"I am not glass. I am not glass. I will not break. I may bend, but I will not break. This will not define me." Kara whispered the mantra over and over until her voice became less clogged with tears and stronger with every word. "They both can get fucked, for all I care about them. But, yes, they need to be removed from power. That man has no business being in the position he's in."

"All it takes is one well-placed article in a very well-known news-paper. We just have to find someone willing to print it and we can force him to step down. Judging by the dark rings around his eyes, he isn't sleeping much these days. I think the guilt is getting to him. Not her, your mother ..."

"I know. She's pretty reprehensible," Kara said. "I almost feel bad for him. He always seemed like he was a strong man. But he's just a spineless piece of crap. Maybe he loved me at one time, but I can't see it now. There's no love there; it dried up and died the night he was complicit in not paying the ransom."

"We really don't need a statement; it doesn't appear this affects the case now. But, if you want to, we'll certainly take it. I don't think there's any kind of crime we can charge them with. The statute of limi-tations beyond passed on any charge we could have come up with."

"If you had died, I would have never known how terrible they are. Thank God that you didn't," Ethan said.

"We can still do a lot of damage by my just making a statement, especially if it were to get leaked. So, let's do it."

CALEB HUSTLED into the room five minutes late. All eyes turned to him. He had called the meeting, but they hadn't expected being delayed at the hospital. He was dreading this meeting. On the way over, he held Kara's hand, and while he'd wanted to withhold how Kara had found out about her parents' deception and their subsequent destruction of evidence, she had done the right thing, the honorable thing, by deciding to come and put it in writing.

The man who had abducted her was dead and buried, so she hadn't thought it was important to disclose the information. In her mind, what good would it have done? And, really, nothing she had told him would help the current case. However, she would do the right thing and come forward—another reason she was the woman he had fallen madly in love with.

"Nice of you to join us," Brett said with his eyebrows raised. "I mean, it wasn't like you called the meeting or that we have a gruesome murder case on our hands."

Obviously, they all were feeling the stress. They hadn't made much headway on this case, and it felt like they were just spinning their wheels. They needed a break in this case, and they needed it fast.

"You know, Albrecht, you can get bent. It's not like I haven't been busy," Caleb said, not unkindly. Albrecht smirked at him and nodded his head, acknowledging the retort was meant to lighten the mood.

"All right, now that you're here, we can start the meeting. Please tell me that someone has some news for me to help stop this nightmare," Bob said, cutting into the conversation.

"I have some information for everyone. Like I told you on the phone, Kara is here to give a statement. It does not appear it'll help us at all on this case. But it still needs to be brought to light. I am disclosing this for her at her request so I would appreciate some leniency in that regard," he said, looking at DA Gloria Finnegan who was seated next to Bob. Judging by both of their faces, he had piqued their interest.

"Where is Kara?" Cathy asked.

"Out with a uniform, writing up her statement. But she wanted me to fill you in. Today has been trying, on many levels."

"Go on," Gloria said.

"She finally confided in Ethan and me this morning about why she left town. This isn't easy for her to talk about, so I told her I would do it. I'm sure most of you are aware that she has been estranged from the governor and his wife for some time." He paused and looked at all the faces around the table. Taking a deep breath because he still could hardly believe what he had just found out, he continued. "Well, it appears that they are the reason we are unable to find any evidence."

"What do you mean?" Bob asked cautiously.

"Kara overheard her father talking to Jenkins and Byrnes, two officers at this precinct. He was paying them to deliver all the evidence for her case. Kara watched her father later burn all of the evidence in their fireplace."

"You mean to tell me that he paid them so he could destroy evidence? Why would he do that?" Cathy asked.

"At the time, she thought it was to keep a lid on details. She told me on the way over, she initially thought her father was protecting her from embarrassment. Her abductor was dead, so while it upset her, she didn't really care." He paused, and when Bob opened up his mouth to speak, he raised his hand to halt him. "It gets worse."

"You mean there's more?" Bob asked.

"Unfortunately. It appears that her parents had gotten a ransom request that they hid from the authorities for an undetermined amount of time."

"Excuse me?" Gloria blurted out.

"They had received a ransom request pretty much immediately after she was abducted. Apparently, they decided to drag their feet for a while because they were getting such good press. In her words, her father was climbing the polls, and they figured it wouldn't hurt to delay. I assume they told her abductor it would take time to get the money together."

"What kind of a parent lets their child stay a second longer than necessary in danger?" Cathy said, her voice cracking. Caleb knew it was hard for her to take as a new mother.

"Apparently, Stanley and Constance Vanderbilt are not candidates for parents of the year. And the worst of it is, her mother convinced her father to wait. He had wanted to pay the ransom right away. But she sold him on it because of the polls. It doesn't let him off scot free because he went along with it. Though he does seem more remorseful than her mother."

"Wait, were they there when she told you?" Gloria asked.

"Affirmative. We stopped so she could tell Ethan first. Since it involved their parents, I agreed. I was in the room for moral support, so I got to see and hear the whole story firsthand. Her parents came into his room, and it got heated."

"How heated?" The question came from Bob.

"Ethan won't talk to them; he's written them off and ordered them out of his room. Kara also told them to leave, *Governor* Vanderbilt didn't object, but Constance told Kara it would have been better for everyone if 'he had done his job right and killed her.'"

Every single person in the room was shocked. Cathy gasped audibly, and Brett's mouth was hanging open. Gloria and Bob looked at each other long and hard.

"Odd choice of words, don't you think?" Gloria asked.

Caleb paused and looked to Gloria. "Now that you mention it, it most certainly is a weird choice of words. I was so focused on Kara, who had threatened to get security or have me escort Constance out of the room, that I didn't really think about it too much. Maybe I remembered her words wrong; regardless, there has to be something we can do."

"You know as well as I do that statute of limitations prohibits me from prosecuting. Even if we had evidence, I couldn't."

"What were the names of the two officers?" Bob asked.

"Jenkins and Byrnes."

"That doesn't help us one iota."

"What do you mean?"

"You haven't been here long enough to know those two names. I suspect if we ask Ethan, he will tell us those were the files he was looking at the night of his accident. Anyway, they both were killed in the line of duty about eight years ago, right before his partner retired and you were brought on."

"That's convenient," Brett muttered.

"Sure is," Caleb said.

"Even better, IA had opened files on both of them the week before they were killed in a drug bust gone wrong," Bob said.

"Shit. Please tell me I'm not the only one that wants to take down her parents?"

"I think we can all agree that we would love to see them fall from their ivory tower," Cathy said.

"I wonder what would have happened if she would have come forward all those years ago?" Caleb asked.

"Probably nothing. At least, not right then. If she would have come to us, we wouldn't have believed her. Those two cops were highly respected up until the night they were killed. Hell, there are still some who are pissed IA opened files on them," Bob said.

"What about you? Do you believe they were dirty?" Caleb asked.

"Who do you think requested they be investigated?"

HIS PHONE WAS RINGING. Not the regular phone; it was the throwaway he had that only two other people knew the number to. He didn't want to talk to either one right then. But he knew he couldn't ignore the phone call. One would make him pay if he didn't and the other one, well, he was as unpredictable as they come. It was getting harder to control him these days.

While he hated to even consider it, he knew something was going to have to be done on that end. The other man had been useful to have around, but he was becoming more a hindrance than a help these days. While he couldn't allow anyone to cause any problems for him, could he do what needed to be done? He would have to wait; right now, he was too close to his goal to take on that, too.

He answered the phone on the sixth ring, which happened to be the last ring before automated voicemail would pick up.

"What?" he asked, agitated.

"You can get rid of that tone right now."

He was tempted to hang up the phone and go back to monitoring his computer. It made him furious that she'd figured out there were cameras in her house. But he had other ways to keep tabs on her, and she hadn't had the sense to have them check her car for tracking devices. Of course, she wasn't driving her car; she was with that fucking detective. Good thing he had put a tracking device on that car, as well. For now, he would allow the conversation to continue, if for no other reason than to find out why he was being forced to listen to the drivel that was bound to be spewed at him.

"To what do I owe the pleasure of this phone call?" he asked, his voice dripping with acid. He would listen, but he didn't have to play nice.

"She has to go. She's starting to become a problem again."

"All in good time, all in good time," he cooed. Fuck if he would let her mess up his plans.

"No, I want it done today. She needs to be silenced."

He had waited a long time to get his hands on Kara; he wasn't going to let this person dictate the timetable he did it on. He would not rush getting rid of her, he could up the timetable and grab her earlier than he had been planning, but he was going to play with her until he got tired of her and kill her or until she died from the games he had planned for her.

"Not possible. Unless you want to get us caught. Is that what you want?"

"You aren't the one who gets to make the decisions here. I am."

"And you going off half-cocked will get us all a nice jail cell. I don't know about you, but I rather like my freedom to do what I want to do."

"I imagine prison would be boring for someone with your tastes." If he wasn't mistaken, he was being ridiculed for his sexual preferences.

"Not going to change my mind that way. We will wait. I won't be able to pull it off effectively without another day to prepare."

"You have twelve hours."

"Can't do it in less than twenty-four."

"Fine, twenty-four. But remember, you know that I have the power to bring this house of cards down, right?"

"Yes. However, you have as much to lose as I do, if not more. So, I suggest you start showing me some respect."

"Oh, no one will ever be able to tie me to you."

"Are you sure about that?" he asked with malice in his voice and disconnected the call.

THE LITTLE BASTARD had hung up. He would have to go. as well. Too many people were involved and everything needed to be put on ice. But not until after Kara Vanderbilt was taken care of. Not a moment sooner. The little sadist thought he could call the shots. Good thing there were other people on the payroll that had a taste for blood. It would make it easier to get rid of him.

There was no way that the blood trail would be linked to anybody but him—no way at all. Every possible connection could be severed, disconnected with clean efficiency. Even if he thought he could dictate what they would do next. He wasn't in control. Never had been and never would be. He was one hundred percent a product of his upbringing and cultivation. It would be best for him to remember who had been given him what he had.

28

Caleb left the meeting and headed out to his desk where he'd left Kara. Except she wasn't sitting at his desk where she'd been filling out a statement with a uniform. Panic filled him as his head whipped around the room. He knew deep down that she wouldn't leave the building, but he couldn't contain the panic that was welling up inside him. He hurried into the hallway and ran into Brad O'Grady, one of the street cops.

"O'Grady, have you seen Kara?" Brad looked at him slightly confused. "Petite, auburn hair, green eyes?"

"Real knockout?" Caleb glared at him until he looked at the ground. "Yeah, I saw her a few minutes ago."

"Where?"

"She was over by the breakroom. I think she was getting something to drink."

Caleb practically ran to the breakroom and breathed a deep sigh of relief when he saw Kara seated at a table talking to Quinn from A Place to Hope. Both women were smiling; they were so intent on their conversation, they didn't hear him approach until he was right next to Kara. She tipped her head up at him and turned that megawatt smile on him, and he was officially sunk. But his face must have shown a different story because her smile cracked and then vanished altogether.

"Caleb, what is it?" she asked, standing up.

"Nothing, nothing. I just ..." Unable to help himself, he pulled her into his arms. "I just got scared when you weren't at my desk. God, Kara, I freaked out. I..."

"Hey, look at me." He looked at her and saw his future in her eyes. "I wouldn't have left without a police escort; you know that, right?"

"I do. It just terrified me. I love you too much to lose you." Her eyes got wide when he spoke the words that had been tearing him apart, trying to get out. Now that he had said them, he felt so much better. But when she didn't say anything, he instantly regretted his spontaneity. "I'm sorry. I know it's crazy, I mean we just met. But, I know how I feel..."

Suddenly, her mouth was on his, effectively cutting off any further words that would have escaped the babbling brook that his mouth had become. She kissed him with a fierce intensity. He could taste salt, and when he broke from the kiss and looked at her, he saw that her cheeks were stained with tears.

"Kara..." She placed her fingers on his mouth and smiled.

"I love you, too, Caleb Montgomery; to hell with it being too soon. If I've learned something in the last few days, it's that life is meant to be lived, and I wasn't. I won't hide my feelings, not when I know how I feel."

A smile of relief broke out on his face, and he kissed her nose. He was lost in her eyes when someone cleared their throat. Blinking, he came back to reality and remembered where they were. Right. The breakroom of the police station. He looked around the room and saw no less than six of his co-workers with shit eating grins on their faces and Quinn sitting at the table, also with a smile on her face. At least she was attempting to hide the smile; the officers in the room certainly weren't. Quinn stood to leave.

"You two should really get a room. In the meantime, I need to go cool off. Because that was five-alarm hot." She pretended to fan herself as she touched Kara's shoulder and nodded at the officers who were all lounging in the office. Strangely, they all got up and left without a word. Not a dig, not a cat call, nothing.

"She didn't need to leave. Sorry I interrupted you both; you looked pretty intense when I walked in."

"That's okay, we were done, anyway. And who am I to say no to a kiss like that?"

"You were the one doing the kissing. In front of an audience, too."

"Semantics. You know you wanted to kiss me," she said flirtatiously.

"Babe, I always want to kiss you. I will never not want to kiss you. Even if you make me angry, those lips are just meant to be kissed. By me, only me," he said softly and kissed her again, not caring if someone walked in. The kiss quickly got out of hand and was one step away from getting them an indecent exposure citation when Kara broke from him. His lips instantly felt lost when the contact was broken.

"Probably should tone it down a little while you're at work," she said, breathing heavily, and then smiled a naughty smile, before leaning forward and whispering in his ear. "I missed out on all the fun of being irresponsible when I was young; having said that, I wouldn't be opposed to finding a place for a nooner."

He grabbed her hand and tugged her toward the exit to the back parking lot where they had parked. Once she was in the car and belted in, he leaned over and kissed her again.

"My town house is a couple minutes away."

She giggled.

"In a hurry?"

"You had me at nooner."

She was full out laughing until his hand slid between her legs and under her skirt, seeking out the hot little spot he knew she loved to have touched, effectively cutting off any laugher.

KARA SUCKED in a breath and moaned at the feeling of his hand between her legs. They practically squealed into his parking lot at his house. Like a couple of sex-starved teenagers, they walked quickly to the entrance to his town house. Once inside the door, they began kissing again. His tongue was exquisite in the exploration of her mouth.

She broke off from the kiss and backed away from him, beckoning to him with her finger as she reeled him in, stopping at the foot of the stairs in his two-story town home. Desperate for his skin on her, she tugged at his shirt, pulling it up and over his head. Her mouth sought out his nipples, teasing one with her tongue until he sucked in air and tugged her shirt over her head. With nimble fingers, he undid the front clasp of her bra and tugged it off her, throwing it to the floor with their shirts.

Then she shimmied out of her underwear and skirt. She was standing before him in nothing but her strappy sandals, when she sank to the steps behind her, spreading her legs, inviting him to feast on her. Kara was momentarily struck by the thought that she felt like a wanton woman and then his mouth was on her. Devouring her with his tongue, he slipped a finger inside her, and she arched up against his mouth, crying out in need.

"Oh, unh, please don't stop," she moaned, reveling over that talented mouth as her orgasm built. When he slipped a second finger in, she bucked against him, straining toward the finish line, straining until it felt like she had fractured into a million pieces.

Digging her hands into his hair, she tugged his face up to hers and kissed him feverishly, while wrapping her legs around his hips.

"I need...I need you inside me," she gasped, all shyness gone.

He tugged at the button and freed himself in one fluid motion and then he drove into her. She was still climaxing from the ministrations his tongue had put her through, and as soon as he thrust into her, she called out in undiluted pleasure. He captured her scream with his lips and drove his tongue into her mouth in the same rhythm that his hips were driving his erection into her.

"God. I can't...I need to..." he panted.

In answer to his pleas, she slid her hands under the fabric of the underwear and pants he was still wearing and dug her nails into him, pulling him closer as she arched into him. That was all it took to destroy his resolve to hold on, and he gasped her name as he rocked into her one last time as he, too, climaxed.

Caleb had been holding himself above her with his arms, but momentarily spent, he relaxed, and his full weight came to rest on her. They had made love numerous times since last night and in numerous positions. However, none of those times had he put his full weight on her. For one fleeting moment, Kara panicked. The claustrophobia of being pinned down was too much for her; she took a ragged breath and inhaled his scent.

At the precise moment that she relaxed, he was moving to get off her, sensing her panic, but she wrapped her legs and arms tightly around him, signaling to him that she didn't want him to move. She needed him there, his body on hers; because she needed to know that she could have a normal moment with the man she loved.

"Kara..." he said, cautiously.

"It's all right. I know what I can handle. And I can handle this. What I can't handle is you moving away from me, not after we just enjoyed an incredible moment of sex together."

He nodded and relaxed, but she could tell he was still trying to keep some of his weight off her. When she looked at his face, she could see that he was trying to shut down his emotions. Suddenly, old insecurities popped into her head. Of not being adequate, never being able to be normal. Maybe it wasn't as much fun for him as for her.

"Unless that is, maybe you didn't enjoy it..." she trailed off, feeling embarrassed enough to want to hide under a rock. Suddenly, she felt his body shaking and, confused, she looked up at him, entirely shocked to see that he was laughing at her. "What?"

"You don't honestly believe I didn't enjoy that, do you?" He rolled off her and lay on his back on the stairs, laughing so hard that tears were forming in his eyes.

"I don't understand how that is funny?"

"Oh, honey, I am a man."

"So? What's your point?"

"I just had sex with a beautiful woman, who I didn't even take the time to take my clothes off for, on the stairs of my house. A woman that I just professed my love to and she to me. A woman who has bestowed the honor of trusting me to make love to her. Me. Does that not equal enjoyable?"

"I..."

"Kara, that wasn't just incredible sex. That was mind-blowing sex. A man could go his whole life without ever having sex like that, and you can actually think I wouldn't have enjoyed myself?"

"No, it's just ... I am such a novice, and you, well, clearly you aren't."

"You don't honestly think that was a pity fuck, do you?" he asked, agitation rising in his voice. "I don't want to ever hear you say anything like that. I don't even want you thinking that. No part of me is having sex with you out of pity. I am making love to you because I want to..."

She stopped him when he would have continued, by climbing onto him and kissing him passionately. His softening cock jerked to attention, and she broke the kiss.

"Honey, if that isn't proof right there, I don't know what is. Because Mr. Happy wouldn't be trying to dance so soon if he didn't want to."

Kara stood up with new confidence and with legs on both sides of him, she walked up a couple of stairs and sank back down, leaving her soaked nether regions within inches of his face. With a wicked smile, she stared down at him.

"Well, then, prove it."

With a growl, he dove at her. Moments later, she was crumbling forward, unable to maintain her posture because of the sensations pouring through her. She crawled off him and up the rest of the stairs. She was brazenly naked and not the least bit affected by it. When she got to the top of the stairs, she turned and looked over her shoulder.

"You coming, hot stuff?" she asked, saucily.

"Not yet, but give me a minute or two and I will be." She wiggled her butt and laughed when he charged up the stairs after her.

AN HOUR LATER, they were lying in his bed, snuggled against each other, both satiated for now. Muscles like rubber, he pulled her butt against his groin. Burying his face in her hair, he sighed.

"Mmmm, you smell good."

"I'm sure that I don't smell that great right now."

"Yeah, you do. God, Kara, what did I do before I found you?"

"Sat in a dark room, pining and waiting for me?"

"I think you just might be right about the waiting part and maybe even the dark. Because my world sure seems a lot brighter now."

"I should be asking what you're doing to me? A year ago, I never would have done any of that. Heck, a week ago, I wouldn't have."

"I guess I'm gifted," he said with a smile on his face, before he claimed her mouth in another kiss.

Caleb must have dozed off, because he woke with Kara in his arms, to the sound of his cell phone ringing obnoxiously on the table by his bed. He rubbed the sleep from his eyes. He should be working on this case, but it really was at a standstill. There wasn't much to investigate at this point; all the leads had dried up before Andrea Vincent had been found.

Sighing, he picked up the phone before it went to voicemail.

"Montgomery."

"Caleb, it's Cathy. We just got a tip to go check out an abandoned cabin on the outskirts of town. It might be where Andrea was held. Get your ass here ASAP so we can go check it out."

"Give me fifteen minutes."

"Make it ten." She hung up and Caleb sat there suddenly wide awake.

"What's going on?" Kara asked, the phone call had obviously woken her up, as well.

"A tip just came in about an abandoned cabin outside town. It might be where he held her."

"Let's go."

"Not a chance. You're coming with me to the police station, where you'll wait until I get back."

"I think I'll be safe here. We weren't planning on coming here, so how would he know where I am?"

"He's always a step ahead of us; remember how you told me you wouldn't leave the police station without a police escort? I need you to do this for me or I won't be able to focus. It's the safest place for you to be."

"I understand that, but Caleb, if this isn't a break in the case...at some point, you're going to have to leave me alone. The city can't afford to keep watch over me, and I need to go to work, too."

"I know that, and we'll figure that out when the time comes, but you need to give me a little more time to find this asshole. I can't leave you unprotected. My head will be consumed with worry for you and that makes for a dangerous situation for me in the field."

"I need you to be safe, so I'll go to the station, because I know it is the smartest choice to make. As long as you do acknowledge that this setup will eventually have to change."

"Not today," he growled.

29

Kara was bored. Resorting to reading all the signs in the room, after reading every magazine in the police station, not that there were that many to read, was getting old. She supposed that they didn't have a lot of time to sit around and read when they were at the station. Looking around the room, she saw some large statute books sitting on a shelf and decided it was better than nothing.

She had just sat down with the large volume of laws when her cell phone rang. Glancing at the screen, she didn't recognize the number. Aware that she had failed to program in the hospital phone number, she suddenly worried it was the hospital calling to say something had happened to Ethan. She answered the phone quickly, tension making her muscles tight.

"Hello?"

"Is this Dr. Vanderbilt?" the female voice asked.

"Yes, this is Dr. Vanderbilt. Who is this?"

"This is Suzanne. Uh, Nurse Abfall."

"Has something happened to Ethan?"

"No. Uh, no, he's fine."

"Then what did you need?" Kara asked. She couldn't help that she sounded annoyed. She had been terrified Ethan had a setback.

"It's nothing like that. But this call does have to do with him."

"How so?"

"Well, you had mentioned that you are his healthcare POA."

"Correct. What is the purpose of this call, Suzanne?"

"It's just, well, hospital policy is that we need to scan a copy into our computer system. In case, something was to change, we would need that on file. I should have gotten it from you the night he was brought in. Things were hectic, and I forgot."

"All right, I'll bring it in tomorrow. Thank you."

"Actually, would you mind bringing it tonight?" Suzanne asked, cutting her off mid-sentence.

"I'm afraid I can't tonight. I don't have the time or the means to get there."

"Please." She sniffled. Was she crying? The woman Kara remembered from school and the other night didn't seem like the type to cry over something so silly.

"I just can't tonight."

"I could lose my job over this. After the other day, the way I treated you, well, Dr. Chiglo and Dr. Brenner weren't happy." This time, the sob was audible. Kara didn't want her to lose her job, even if she was unpleasant to her the other day.

"All right. Fine. I will find someone to give me a ride. But I have to go home first. I'm not at home and the paperwork is at my house."

"T-Thank you," Suzanne hiccupped and then hung up.

Inconvenient timing, but it would be more interesting than sitting around here. Kara's mood brightened when she saw Officer Black. Surely, he would be willing to bring her home and then he could leave her at the hospital and she could visit with Ethan until Caleb got back. That sounded far more enjoyable than sitting in the stuffy police station reading statue books.

"Officer Black, would you mind giving me a ride home and then to the hospital? I need to deliver some paperwork, and I thought I could sit with my brother until Detective Montgomery gets back."

"Sure, that won't be a problem," he said.

Kara grabbed her purse, and they started walking toward the

entrance Officer Black had just come through. They were almost out the door when the radio on his shoulder squawked, and he paused to listen. Through the squawk of the radio on his shoulder Kara could only make out the words ten and fifty; it was amazing that Black could understand anything else.

"Copy that. Four seventy-one responding." He glanced quickly at Kara. "Sorry, there's a minor car accident that just got called in. I have to go."

"No problem. I'll just wait."

Kara turned to go back to Caleb's desk and crashed into someone coming from the other direction. The officer caught her before she crashed to the ground.

"Sorry about that. I wasn't paying attention to where I was going."

"No worries. See you later, Officer Black."

Black paused for a second and looked at the other officer.

"Do you mind giving Dr. Vanderbilt a ride to her home to pick something up and then a ride to the hospital? She has some papers she needs to drop off tonight."

"No problem. I was just getting off shift; my car is parked out front," he said, and she followed him to the door as Black ran out the back entrance.

"Thank you so much for giving me a ride home. I really appreciate it," she said as she buckled into the car.

"I hope Detective Montgomery doesn't get upset," the officer said, smiling.

"I'm sure it will be fine."

"I don't know, he seems awfully protective of you."

A flush creeped up Kara's neck and settled in her cheeks. Never had she blushed so much in her life as she had the last couple days. She wasn't embarrassed as much as turned on by the image of Caleb gloriously naked in bed next to her; the image was so vivid that she could feel warmth spread through her at the mere picture in her mind. The faster he got back and picked her up, the better.

"Ah, that's sweet, seems you have it bad for the good detective?"

"Um, that's a pretty personal question, don't you think?"

"You're right. Sorry, ma'am. It's just, well, the blush, it gave it away."

"Nothing to be apologizing about; I just don't like to share my personal life."

"I get that. Cops are pretty tight-lipped, too. Must be a habit picked up from our professions. I imagine being a doctor means you have to be really careful with what you share." He paused, and when she didn't say anything, he continued. "HIPAA, right?" he asked, an awe shucks smile on his face that for some reason raised her hackles.

"Right."

CALEB WAS IRRITATED when he dropped Kara off at the police station and picked up Cathy. That irritation didn't come close to the way he was feeling now that they were at the cabin. Or what was supposed to be a cabin. In reality, it was a deer blind that some hunter had put up on private property.

"We came out here for this bullshit," he said, fighting the urge he felt to kick something.

This case was infuriating with its utter lack of clues or viable leads. His conversation with Kara kept replaying in his head. There was no way he was leaving her unprotected until this killer was found. No. Way. In. Hell. They could work around her job. Mercy Hospital had security. He would just reach out to them. Doctors worked long hours so she would be covered for a large portion of the day, and when she wasn't at work, well, he would be with her as much as possible. Even if it meant his taking a leave of absence.

"You know as well as I do that we had to come out here. You never know what tip is going to pan out, and since we have nothing but dead ends when it comes to this case, we had to at least check it out." Cathy said, sounding equally annoyed. "I get it, I hate spinning my wheels, too. Not to mention, I would much rather be home with my baby and husband versus trudging around out here on a wild goose chase."

He grunted his agreement. This whole situation sucked. There had to be something that was missed, some clue that would lead them to this maniac. Serial killers got tripped up over small mistakes; they had to just find the needle in the haystack.

"I hate feeling like someone is jerking our chain," Brett mumbled. He had come along hoping they would find some evidence.

"It always sucks when we go investigate a 'tip' that turns out to be nothing. I don't understand why people call in crank tips. I mean, do they get off on wasting our time? Don't they know we have a murder case to solve?" Cathy asked.

The blood in Caleb's veins went ice cold when their words finally sunk in.

"What did you say?"

Cathy looked at him, obviously confused by his outburst.

"I hate when someone wastes our time on a wild goose chase. Caleb, where is your head tonight?" she asked.

"Probably on that smokin' hot doctor he's been watching over," Brett said, but quickly changed his joking tune when he looked long and hard at Caleb's drawn face. "What's wrong?"

"Wasting our time...a distraction...getting Kara away from me." Each word drove a dagger into his heart.

"Caleb, you aren't making sense," Brett said, still not quite understanding what he meant.

"Kara doesn't like being a drain on our resources. She knows that we're stretched pretty thin. He knew if I wasn't there to keep her at my side, it would be easier to lure her away."

"Motherfuck!" Brett shouted.

Cathy was already running to the car as Caleb called the police station. He was climbing in and shutting the door and she already had the car moving, Caleb held his phone to his ear with his shoulder as he buckled in. After what felt like forever, someone finally answered.

"Black."

"Officer Black, is Kara there?" Caleb shouted.

"Nope. She had to run home to pick up some papers to run to the hospital."

"You let her go alone?" Caleb bellowed into the phone.

"No, sir." Black's uninterested tone quickly changed, and Caleb could tell he was all ears. "Officer Grisham took her. She was told she couldn't go alone and I got called out on a bogus traffic accident so I couldn't take her. But I made sure she had coverage."

Caleb's stomach sunk. First, the bogus call to investigate the shed. Then a bogus traffic accident. That was two too many coincidences to sit well with him. Fuck!

"Officer Black, listen to me, this is very important. Have you ever seen Officer Grisham before?"

"Well, no, but I assumed he was a transfer. I was about to leave to bring Kara home when the call came in. I had just told her she had to stay there; she turned to sit down and crashed into the guy. I asked if he would mind taking her. He said he was just getting off shift and he would have no problem bringing her home and then to the hospital. Then I left. She should be at the hospital."

"What was his first name and how long ago was this?" The silence on the other end of the phone landed like a boulder in Caleb's stomach. "Black?"

"I'm not sure what his first name was, but his name badge had a J on it."

"How long ago?" When Black was silent, Caleb practically screamed into the phone. "How. Fucking. Long. Ago?"

"An hour ago. Do you want me to call the hospital and make sure she got there?"

Caleb cut him off.

"Description?"

"Tall, six feet one. Slim build. Brown hair. That is all I can give you. I can have them pull up video."

"Do it and call me ASAP!"

"Do you want me to call the hospital, too?"

"She isn't at the hospital. She walked out the door with the fucking killer." Caleb hung up and punched the dash.

"Motherfuck! J. Grisham?" Caleb felt like he was suffocating. "As in John Grisham. The motherfucker has had her for an hour." He was furious, but Black had no reason to second guess someone in a uniform. "We need to go faster." Cathy slammed her foot down on the gas as they got on the highway.

"The bastard thinks he's funny, has quite the sense of humor, doesn't he? Won't be laughing when we get a hold of him," she stated.

Caleb was terrified. There was no way this was a coincidence. None at all and the bastard had her. Not only that, but he had taken her an hour ago. When he got his hands on that son of a bitch, and he would find him, there was no other option; he was going to make him sorry that he touched what was his.

KARA SENSED as much as felt something was awry when she entered her house. *Stop it; you are just spooked because of what happened earlier, nothing is wrong,* she told herself. Samsonite had greeted her at the door, eager to go to the bathroom. She had grudgingly let him out to go to the bathroom without her to watch over him because she wanted to get the papers and get to the hospital as fast as possible. For some reason, Officer Grisham made her nervous. Sam had been given the cue to be on alert with the officer before Kara turned and went deeper into the house, leaving the door open so he could get back in. Telling herself that leaving the door open was why she felt so apprehensive, she walked into her kitchen and stopped short when her eyes landed on her counter top. Something was wrong, something was very wrong. The block on the counter that held all her knives had one ominously empty slot. She knew that there was no way that a knife would be missing.

Why the hell had she left the police station? She knew better than to leave there. At the police station, she was protected. Here, she was vulnerable. What kind of an idiot was she to leave with an officer she'd never met before? Hadn't she agreed with Caleb that it was the safest place for her right now? Why had she let Suzanne Abfall guilt her into leaving the safety of the police station? Fight or flight kicked in, and Kara decided it would be a good idea to leave and go back to the police station because an eerie feeling had settled over her. Not only did she sense something off, but she could feel malevolence in the air. This time, what she sensed was a shift in the air and an acute awareness of no longer being alone in the kitchen.

Being stupid, or perhaps it was just trustworthy, Kara had asked the officer to stay outside and keep an eye on Sam. All she needed to do was to grab the papers in her office, and if she were being honest, she didn't want him in her home. Rushing into the house, she stopped in the kitchen first to grab her bag that had stuff to occupy her while at the hospital and that was when she noticed the knife. Now, the walls were closing in, and Kara just knew she had made a grave mistake.

Kara whistled for Sam, suddenly wanting nothing more than to have him in the house. When thirty seconds went by and she hadn't heard Sam come barreling into the house, panic really set in. Hoping that he was just too far from the front door to hear her, she whistled again and got the same response. Which was nothing.

Frantically, she turned around to face the entryway between the kitchen and hallway, the same entryway she had walked through only moments before, and that she had expected to see empty. However, it wasn't, and she froze to the spot when her eyes locked on a big figure standing half hidden in shadow in the entryway.

"Geez, you scared me, Officer Grisham. I was just grabbing my bag, but I still have to grab the papers. They're in my office. You really could have stayed outside. Is Samsonite all right? Did he run off?" Kara didn't believe that Sam would have run off, not with her in the house, but she wanted to act as normal as possible.

He took a step toward her. She didn't know why, but she took an instinctive step back and then he reached up to his neck and started to peel the skin away. What the fuck! She took another step back and bumped into the island in her kitchen. She felt behind her, hoping to encounter some kind of weapon. Her fingers touched nothing, her OCD had failed her because everything was put away exactly where she wanted it to be. Which wasn't on the island.

Swallowing, she inched down the island, hoping to get to the knife block that was on the other counter. Just as she got to the end of the counter, Officer Grisham pulled the rest of the skin off his face. Only it wasn't skin at all. What it really had been, was a very high-end latex mask used to disguise his face. Everything started to crumble around her as if the floor had just dropped out and she was in a freefall.

Kara felt dizzy as all her blood rushed to her head, bile rose to her mouth, and her knees turned to Jell-O. She slumped against the counter that she'd been navigating around when it seemed as if her knees would buckle and she would no longer be able to hold herself up. Struggling to right herself, she tried to think of an escape route.

The hulking figure took a step into the light, and Kara's world exploded and splintered into a million pieces. The face staring at her was the face of her nightmares and broke into a sinister smile as he took one giant step toward her and watched the fear spread across her face. There was no way she could get by him. She was trapped.

"Tsk, tsk, now you're not thinking of running, are you?" he asked.

The small control she had over herself evaporated as panic took over because standing before her was a man that sounded just like Devon Bristol and looked just like the monster who had abducted her. But if that was the case, he had risen from the ashes of a burned-out car. And as the monster took another giant step toward her, the hysteria she had been trying to control, bubbled up and erupted from her as she sputtered out a nearly incoherent string of sentences.

"You're dead, you died. You can't be here, you can't be here."

Kara swallowed hard, trying to stop the flow of words. She had to do something; she was not going to let Devon get the upper hand on her again. Subconsciously, she remembered she had been inching to the side and had been trying to get to the knife block. Except she had kept going and instead of going to the other counter, she bumped into the kitchen table. The kitchen table that had a heavy centerpiece on it. Without thinking twice and with as much speed as possible, she grabbed the heavy fruit bowl and threw it at Devon with deadly accuracy, hitting him in the head.

She didn't wait around once the bowl connected; as he stumbled backward, she took the opportunity to run around the table, hoping that she would be able to get to the entryway before he regained his composure. But the bowl had been heavy, and she wasn't able to throw it as hard as she had wanted and had subsequently only stunned him. She had nearly gotten around the table when he straightened and advanced toward her. Quickly, she grabbed a chair and threw it at him. Once again hitting her mark, she deftly maneuvered around him.

Sprinting toward the front door, the hair on her neck stood on end when she heard him tearing after her. As she passed the table in her entryway, she grabbed the vase on it, and spun, throwing it at him in one quick motion. Her aim was not as good on the fly, and this time she missed as the vase flew wide and crashed into the wall, shattering glass everywhere. With nothing left in her path to the door, she knocked the table over to try to slow him down.

No time left and no weapons left meant her only chance was to get outside where she hoped she could outrun him long enough to get to a neighbor's house or garner someone's attention. Unfortunately, she had not had time to introduce herself to her neighbors and ask them if they saw anything suspicious to call the police. Of course, in the last few days, with as often as the police had been at her house, they might already be keeping an eye out for suspicious activity. Hoping that was the case, she spun and ran to the door, but stopped dead in her tracks when another man stepped out of her living room and into the foyer. Her realtor, Marshall Abfall, was standing in front of her.

"Marshall? Oh, thank God, please help me." Kara was already frozen, but if she hadn't been, the look in Marshall's eyes would have paralyzed her with fear.

Still, Kara took a step toward him, until he reached up and began to tug at his facial hair on his face. Her eyes drawn to the movement, she noticed the burns on his neck. Burns that the Marshall Abfall she had met the other day did not have. Then after he slowly peeled off his beard, popped out the contacts that had turned his eyes brown, pulled off the wig that made his hair thick and blond and the fake blond eyebrows, he reached into his pocket, where he retrieved a cloth and scrubbed his face until the bronzer he was wearing wiped off.

Before her very eyes the man standing in front of her no longer looked like Marshall Abfall, rather he looked like the man standing behind her, but with burns. Her head started to swim at the implication that the man who sold her the house had just turned into her worst nightmare. No longer paralyzed with fear, she clumsily turned in a circle, taking in both men, who looked identical in every way, except for the burn scars on the neck of the man in front of her, the man who was brandishing her missing knife.

"What …?"

"You are so right; it was definitely worth all the trouble to see her shocked expression."

Dumbfounded, she just stood before them, swaying from side to side, taking shallow breaths. She knew she was hyperventilating, but there was nothing she could do to stop herself. Aware that if she didn't calm herself, she would pass out, she bent over and took in a couple of deep breaths. Both men must have taken this as a defensive move because the one standing in front of her threw her hard against the wall, while the one who had been standing behind her rushed her and held her to the wall. With his body hard against her, she could feel his arousal, as well as the sharp knife, pressed to her neck. Slowly, he ran his tongue from her chin to her temple.

"Don't you move, you fucking cunt. I would prefer not to kill you right now, but I will slice your neck like butter if you so much as flinch. Which would be a dirty shame since we spent so much time planning for this moment. Ten long fucking years, as a matter-of-fact. We would have liked to have toyed with you a little longer before we took you, but our timeline got pushed up." He must have been confident he had her full attention because he loosened his grip enough for the other man to tie her hands and gag her mouth. "Time to take a little nap," he said before he injected her with what she could only assume was the same drug as the last time.

30

Cathy pulled the car up and onto the lawn of Kara's front yard. He noticed two things right away as he barreled out of the car. That there was a large object lying on the side of her house and that her front door was wide open. He sprinted to the front door with Cathy on his heels as Brett ran to what he could only assume was the body of Samsonite. Caleb found himself praying that Sam was all right because Kara would be devastated when he got her back if Sam was gone.

When he rushed into her foyer, he stopped dead in his tracks as he saw the devastation in the entryway. He felt cold-blooded rage rise in him when he saw the destruction, but then he also felt a certain level of hope. She had put up a fight, a good fight, and he didn't kill her here. The monster wouldn't do that because he would want to play with her for a while before he killed her. But he also felt a crippling fear when he the saw drops of blood. Hers or his? He hoped to hell it was his and that she got in a good enough hit to cause him to bleed. There wasn't much blood, which was good and bad. Bad if it was his because he wouldn't bleed out. Good if it was hers because she wouldn't bleed out.

Cathy was calling in the crime scene as Caleb followed the path of destruction into her kitchen. *The fight had started in there, for sure,* he thought as he scanned the room looking for anything that would help him. His eyes alighted on the knives; he noted the missing knife and the lack of it anywhere else in her normally pristine kitchen. The thought that he had taken her by knifepoint made his blood run cold.

Carefully stepping over debris to maintain the scene as much as possible, he saw something on the floor that grabbed his attention. He was crouching over it when Albrecht came into the kitchen.

"Don't touch that!"

"You think I am fucking stupid? This is the woman I love; do you fucking think I would do anything that would jeopardize her safety?" he roared. Taking a deep breath through his nostrils, he looked at Albrecht, and suddenly he was nearly brought to his knees with the emotional devastation he was feeling. "I'm sorry. I just...how is Sam?"

"You have no reason to apologize, I get it. Sam will be fine; he was sedated somehow."

"Good, that's good. What am I looking at here?"

"If I had to guess? That is the face of J. Grisham."

"What?"

"A latex face mask. It looks exceptionally high end and quite expensive."

"Good God, just when I thought we would be able to identify him with the video footage at the police station, we're back to square one, and we have no idea who we're looking for." Caleb stood and scrubbed his hands through his hair. They were well and truly fucked; there was no way that they would be able to find her.

"That isn't the worst of it."

When Albrecht paused, seemingly for no reason, or perhaps to gauge Caleb's well-being, Caleb was so frustrated he saw red.

"For fuck's sake, say it already. I am not going to go off the deep end."

"I think we're dealing with two assailants."

Alarmed, Caleb stood straight; he hadn't even realized he was stooped.

"What would make you think that?"

"There's a wig in the front entrance. Blond."

Black had called from the precinct when they were en route to Kara's house to confirm his earlier description and tell them that he would send a picture to Caleb's phone. The man in the picture from the video was not a blond.

"She always said she thought Devon had an accomplice, but how could there be two here tonight? It should only be his accomplice. What the hell is going on?"

"We can triangulate where her cell phone pinged last."

"Only useful if he didn't throw the phone; he's too smart for that."

Standing with his fingers still tangled in his hair, his mind was locked down with fear. Until a thought hit him. Kara wasn't stupid. She was a fighter, and she would have a plan to make sure that this couldn't happen to her again. And, if, on the long shot it did happen, Caleb knew she would have some sort of backup plan. If she had any plan in place, the only person she would have trusted with the information was Ethan or possibly his Aunt Vanessa or Dr. Chiglo.

Caleb jerked his phone out of his pocket and called Ethan's room, pacing while the phone rang in his ear, until finally Ethan picked up.

"Hello?" he answered, his voice thick with sleep.

"Ethan, it's Caleb. Listen, I need you to help me."

"What's wrong?" Ethan asked, his voice suddenly alert and no longer sounding tired.

"Kara's gone."

"What the fuck do you mean she's gone? As in you had a fight and she left, or you can't find her?"

"He got her, the psycho got her, and I need you to help me, I can't lose her. We can't lose her. I am losing it, brother. I need to know if she had any kind of fail-safe in case of an emergency?"

"Let me think." He paused for a second while Caleb paced. "Her watch has GPS tracking, and her ankle bracelet has a tracking device called Project Lifesaver. I can call Project Lifesaver, and they can tell us her location. It was designed for dementia patients. Normally, they would respond for us, but in this situation, it wouldn't be advisable. She has other tracking devices sewn into articles of clothing. The other items I can track from an app she and I have access to. Her preparedness will pay off, as long as she has one of those items on her."

"That's my girl!" Caleb had known that she wouldn't go anywhere without being able to be found. "Do you have a way to log on to the app and call Project Lifesaver? Do you have your cell phone?"

"No. It was destroyed in the accident. But I can get a hold of Project Lifesaver and page the nurse. I'm sure one of them has a smartphone I can use."

"All right, at least it's a starting point. Call me as soon as you know something." Caleb hung up and waited.

KARA WOKE with a start when a bucket of ice cold water hit her in the face. It took her more than a few minutes to clear her head. Her body ached from being shoved against the wall, but her shoulders were on fire. It didn't take her long to figure out why. The bastards had stripped her down to nothing and had strung her hands up and over a hook hanging from the ceiling of what appeared to be an old worn-down warehouse.

After they had doused her with the ice-cold water to wake her up, she found herself shivering uncontrollably. Logically, she knew she was precariously close to losing her life, yet she wasn't as scared as the last time. Perhaps her body was on the verge of going into shock, but Kara knew the symptoms of shock, and she didn't think that was what was going on. Just when she thought he, or they, couldn't get more inhumane, she was proven wrong. Her mind was almost numb as if it was going into protection mode so that it wouldn't witness the atrocities that they had planned for her. Knowing that her initial reaction wasn't normal, she decided that if she could keep her wits and get out of there alive, she would make an appointment with a therapist immediately.

"Well, well, looks like the bitch finally woke up. How you feeling?" the one with the burns asked.

"W-who are you?" she managed to say through her shivers.

"Seriously, Kara; how does your brother put it? For such a smart girl, you really are quite dumb? I believe you have met us both a time or two in your life. We couldn't help but bump into you, just to prove we could be part of your lives without you knowing. I lost count of how many times we 'ran' into you. In case you're wondering, I am Marshall Abfall. It was such fun selling you your new home. And this strapping young man over there is Devon. Of course, when it suits us, we like to pretend we are one in the same. Thanks to modern cosmetics, it is still manageable even with Devon's scars to pull it off."

"W-who are you really? How are you alive? Ethan told me you burned in the car crash, trying to get away."

"I did burn; my whole torso is covered in burns because of you!" Devon snarled. "But if you're nice, I could forgive you." Suddenly, he was sweet, like night and day.

"H-how was there a body in the car?"

"We had some help with that. Homeless people are surprisingly easy to come by and useful scapegoats. And we were fortunate, they were such eager beavers to tie up loose ends that they didn't even check to make sure it wasn't Devon in that car. I have a feeling that your parents' money may have helped pave the way on that."

"Not that they could have identified me from dental work or fingerprints since the wrong name would come up. Definitely not Devon Bristol."

"What are your real names?"

"Our current names are all that matters, as our birth names really aren't important. But don't worry, we have some time, so we'll fill you in on all the sordid details," Marshall said.

"You had Suzanne help lure me? Your own wife?"

"It was Marshall's idea to marry that bitch. I couldn't really switch with him and share her; she would have noticed the burns, really was a pity. But he had a point; I mean, she really hated you, you know, so she was useful to help us reach our goals. But I suppose you don't know why do you? It really is a funny story. Do you want to hear it? Of course, you do. After all, we have time until our little benefactor gets here. You see, Suzanne Pascoe had an older sister that she idolized. Ever wonder how you were #2 on our list? How about I let you in on a little secret? Suzanne's dear sister was our first victim." Devon laughed and clapped his hands.

"We never left a note on her, though, not that anyone has found her yet. Maybe we should come up with a clever little rhyme right now? How about, *#1 and done, has it just begun?*" Devon laughed hysterically at the rhyme that Marshall had come up with on the fly. Kara felt a cold, damp sweat break out on her skin and her breathing came in short gasps.

"Why would she blame me for her sister? I had nothing to do with her sister being your victim."

"You kind of did. But let's not skip ahead. Anyway, Suzanne hated you for two reasons," Devon said.

"You survived, and you got all the attention. No one paid attention to poor Lucy when she went missing. That whole from-the-right-side-of-the-tracks thing really helped you get attention. But not Lucy; she was barely a blip in the evening news. It only took a little bit of cultivating to get her to really hate you, and later, she was more than willing to help us. Or rather me, her loving husband. Though she just married me because I told her I broke your heart. She thought she was getting the guy who got away. I sure will miss poor, gullible Suzanne; after all, she served her purpose, so she had to be disposed of."

Marshall made a grand gesture to the ground behind him. Until that moment, Kara hadn't taken more than a perfunctory look at the room; her whole attention had been riveted to the two men standing in front of her. Her eyes automatically went to the spot that he pointed to and lying on the ground in a puddle of dark red blood was Suzanne Abfall, her head nearly decapitated from the slice to her throat.

"A bit messy, I know. Couldn't help myself. She had been such a nag the last few days since you came home. Kara this, Kara that. 'How dare that cunt think she can come back and ruin everything I worked for.' On and on until I wanted to strangle her just to get her to shut the fuck up. But I still needed her. In the end, she was just concerned that I wanted you back, which I did, but not in the way she thought. Like I said, we cultivated her hate for you, so nude pictures of you helped make her hate you even more. She was too stupid to realize that you weren't posing in any of the pictures, and the fact that I left them in such an easy spot to find. What a dipshit. Still, she went ballistic!" He roared with laughter.

"It was quite visual when he sliced her neck—the fountain of blood. A bit much. But, I couldn't be happier that she's gone," Devon said, pouting. Clearly, he didn't like sharing his brother with her.

"Anyway, as I was saying, my brother and I had to change identities about twelve years ago because of some past indiscretions. Lucky for us that we are good at disappearing, not so lucky for you, I suppose. Anyway, who really cares about you, right? We had some help disappearing and were told to come here. When we got here, our great benefactor wasn't all that pleased, even if we had been told to come here, but in the end, was willing to help us lie low awhile until we got our ducks in a row," Marshall said.

"The plan was to lie low for a while, but as it goes, we needed money, so we joined your daddy's staff. Between the two of us, it didn't take us long to figure out that your daddy liked to wander through the gray areas of life. So, a new plan was formed. We decided to let your father catch us doing something dishonest. That way he would think he had us under his belt. Our benefactor was very helpful in the planning," Devon added.

"Of course, he had no idea there were two of us; being an identical twin has its benefits. At least it did until the night he 'caught us' trying to skim money from the campaign. Getting your father to fall for it was like taking candy from a child. We turned into his go-to guys. It was perfect. I could do his dirty work, and Devon would be standing by his side, the perfect alibi."

"And then there was the ultimate goal. Taking your daddy for all he was worth. It was perfect. We told him how the polls kept coming back with him losing because of family values. We made everything look very official. It was hilarious because he was actually winning in the polls, he was just behind in the family value portion. He didn't take the time to read the rest of the report. Weirdly trusting, wasn't he? Anyway, your father was obsessed with power, and we knew it. We knew he would do whatever it took to become governor," Devon continued. "Your *mother*," acid dripped from the word, "wanted it, as well."

"The seed was planted. Along with a couple of nicely placed, but quite fake, newspaper articles left on his desk, talking about a not-so-local politician and the fight to find his missing daughter, it was all we needed to get the ball rolling. The good press the guy was getting was more than your father could handle. He wanted that good press," Marshall said.

From that point, the story was his to tell. Devon took a back burner to Marshall and began getting their devices of torture ready for action. Kara tried not to focus on the table with all the scalpels and other odds and ends. She knew they wouldn't mess up this time, and her only way of surviving was to stall until hopefully, the police could figure out where they took her. She knew that Caleb and Ethan would be doing everything they could think of to get her back.

"H-how did you know about the girl that was m-missing?" she asked between shivers, even though she thought she knew the answer.

"Well, it was little Lucy, of course. We did have to doctor the article; her father wasn't even in the picture, much less a politician. We almost got caught with her. She was a little indiscretion of ours that got out of hand, and the cops were closing in on us, so it was make tracks or go to prison. And, well, we just couldn't have that, could we?"

"I s-suppose not."

"Don't patronize me. I'm pretty smart myself, you know."

"You might be smart, but it doesn't make you any less of a sociopath," she whispered.

"That too. We ended up having to change our identities after that. Which turned out fine, since she was our trial run. Then there was you, beautiful Kara, so perfect in every way. You were really the one that led us to the realization that we have a certain taste for young women, a taste that has to be satisfied." *Trial run? Why would he need a trial run?* Her blood ran cold when she saw the smirk on his face.

"Can I taste her, Marshall; let me just have a taste of her. None of the others have tasted as good as her," Devon said, his voice sounding more unstable by the second.

In the blink of an eye, gone was the sane sounding Devon from earlier, and in entered the one who was clearly fighting mental illness; the one she had spent time with those four days. Here was the man who didn't quite have all his lights on, the one who claimed to have loved her.

"It was so much fun with you ten years ago. Poor Devon hasn't had as much fun since. Of course, he spent a lot of time recovering from the car accident. Tell me, all those years ago, could you tell the difference between the two of us?"

"Yes." It all made sense now. The two personalities. Devon, the man who came professing his love, nuzzling and cuddling with her after he raped her. And then there was Marshall, the man who tortured her mercilessly for four days.

"Be honest, who was better?" Devon asked, sounding like he was a jealous lover.

When she didn't answer, Marshall struck out at her with a crop that had materialized in his hands.

"Answer him, you filthy bitch."

She had to think fast and come up with something, anything that would give her time to be found.

"I c-can't choose. Devon was loving and fulfilled all of my wants and needs. While Marshall, you were so creative and attentive, constantly trying to teach me knew things."

Kara didn't know how she had managed to come up with those words; she knew she wasn't close to sounding believable. Another strike, this time from Devon, who was holding what looked like a flogger. He was staring at her with lust in his green eyes. Devon had never struck her with anything but his hands before; Marshall was the one who enjoyed the different apparatus, but Devon seemed to be enjoying himself now.

"I see you haven't gotten very good at lying in the last ten years." Marshall spat the words out.

"Devon, why are you doing this? You were always so gentle with me."

"Why? Why? I did everything to protect you, to keep Marshall from killing you. But if I couldn't keep you, the only way it could end was with your death. No one else could be with you, only us. Even that college boy we paid wasn't able to finish the job."

"Wait, what? You paid Max to sleep with me?"

The world was spinning out of control again. Everything she had been, and everything she had done, they had a role in. For one split second, Caleb's face floated in front of her eyes. Blinking slowly, she shook her head. No. They didn't have anything to do with Caleb; Caleb was honest, pure, loving, and kind. Nothing that they were. As if reading her thoughts, Devon struck out at her. She had to bite her lip from crying out in pain, and the taste of copper filled her mouth.

"You're thinking about *him*!" he shrieked, striking her again and again, until he finally was exhausted from the effort and she was hanging limp from the beating. She needed to find a way to stall and keep him from beating her again. They needed time to find her.

"Why did you need a trial run? Who was the trial run for?" Her voice was weak, and she hated it.

"You," a third voice offered from the shadows. Kara had to swallow the acid that was pushing its way up her throat, as her mother walked out of the shadows and into the light.

"Ah, lovely, our benefactor has finally graced us with her presence," Devon said, happy once again.

31

Ethan had been able to track Kara quickly, thanks to the ankle bracelet and Project Lifesaver. It had taken longer to get the SWAT team ready to converge on the abandoned warehouse than it had taken to locate her. It had also taken longer to convince his captain that he could be part of the operation without being a hindrance. In the end, he knew that Bob only let him be part of the takedown because he knew Caleb wouldn't listen if he told him to stand down. Not when the woman he loved was in harm's way.

Now that they knew where she was, they were in the process of trying to get "eyes" on the room she was being held in. Caleb felt like he was about to lose his mind. Kara was in the hands of a monster, and he was standing within distance of the building she was being held, but he was being told to stand down. It went against every instinct in his body to stand there and do nothing, when he wanted to charge into the building and be her knight in shining armor—or at the very least, rip the throat out of the person who took her.

Ethan had been given a radio so he could be updated on the situation. As much as he tried to convince the hospital that he was fit enough to leave, it was a no go. In fact, Dr. Chiglo was so concerned that Ethan would try to sneak out, that he had a security guard stationed at his door. Caleb had to smile at the thought of Ethan locked down, but then the smile disappeared, because if the roles were reversed and it were Taylor, well, it was safe to say that Caleb wouldn't find being sequestered in his hospital room as a very funny situation.

Shaking his head to focus himself, Caleb moved like liquid night toward the hulking dilapidated building. At some point in its existence, the building had been a shoe factory but had long ago closed up shop, apparently in a hurry, because there were still decaying shoes all over the grounds, and he had to be careful not to trip over the rubbish.

He came to rest at the predetermined spot that had been agreed upon. At this point, they didn't want to get too close until they knew what they were walking into. Once the recon was in, they would assess and decide on how to proceed. But they wanted to be close to the entry points in case danger to her life was imminent and extraction needed to be done quickly. For now, they felt Kara was still alive. She had to be alive. There was no other option available to him. In such a short time, she had become an integral part of his world, and he didn't know what he would do if she was taken from him. He had to do everything in his power to get her out of that building and into his arms.

For one brief, but undeniable second, Kara had thought her mother was there to save her. Instead, her mother stood staring at her with evil in her eyes. One look at the expression of malevolence on her mother's face right now and that little spark of hope disappeared. As she looked at her mother, something she said replayed in her mind. *You got one thing right; I would have preferred you died. If he would have done his job right, you would have...*

"If he would have done his job right..." she whispered.

"You were so angry, you didn't even pick up on my slip up."

If ever Kara thought her mother loved her, she knew now, more than ever, that it was all a lie. There was never any maternal love. Her mother had always treated her as competition. As if Kara was vying against her mother for her father's attention until eventually, her father started to ignore her to make his life easier. When her mother should have been teaching her important things while she was growing up, she had treated her coldly.

However, in a tiny corner of her heart, the little girl left in Kara had hoped she had been wrong, that there was some way to reach her mother. She had hoped that someday her mother would reach out and hug her and tell her that she loved her. She knew now that would never happen. Her mother was exactly what she had already known her to be, a coldhearted snake. Even so, she had to try to reach her.

"Mother, if you ever loved me, please help me." Even though the weakness was mostly pretend, she hated the sound of it in her own voice. Kara found herself holding her breath, waiting for her mother to do or say something. She didn't expect her to laugh cruelly, but it was exactly what she did, and the sound sapped the hope that was left out of Kara.

"Come now, dear, you are incredibly smart and very intuitive, you always have been. So, how about we all do each other a favor and, for once, be completely honest. I don't love you. I never have. As a matter of fact, I despise everything about you. Surely, you must know that by now." She spat out the hateful words with a sneer on her face.

"The sad thing is, I always knew you didn't love me like you should have. I just never knew why."

"You want to know why? I think I can manage that before I let Marshall and Devon get rid of you like they should have ten years ago."

Grudgingly, she nodded her head yes. If nothing else came from all of this, she would die knowing why her mother hated her so much. Still, she couldn't die letting her mother think she was a weak little girl. Lifting her chin, she stared her right in the eye.

"Yes, *Mother*, why don't you enlighten me?"

Constance Vanderbilt clapped her hands.

"Magnificent, such bravado, even while facing death. I tell you what, boys, if you want to hold onto her for your stupid anniversary, you can, but you need to move far away. All ties to me would be severed, think about it; you can have her for a full year and enough money to be comfortable. Hell, you can keep her indefinitely; I don't care if you kill her. I just don't want her escaping."

"Fuck you ..."

"So crass. Oh well, what do you expect from a little bitch born of a whoring mother?" She laughed as Kara's eyes widened at her insinuation. "That's right. You aren't spawned from me; you were spawned from your whoring father and the underage little trollop he had working as his secretary at the time."

"You're lying." But Kara knew she wasn't lying. It all made perfect sense. The complete and utter lack of compassion, the way she would catch her father looking at her sometimes, and the way the brief spark of love would be extinguished by something her mother would say or do. The fact that Ethan was doted on, while she was ignored. How she looked like her father and Ethan, but nothing like her mother. "No, I understand now. Ethan is yours, but I am not."

"Correct."

"But, how ... why did you raise me?"

"I couldn't let that little cunt ruin everything I had planned for my future. I'm not saying it was easy raising you; it was a hardship. After all, you look remarkably like her. You know your father couldn't—can't—keep his dick in his pants, especially around the younger ladies, and even some men. Isn't that right?" she asked, looking at Marshall and Devon.

"We can attest to that," Marshall said, winking at Kara. "I prefer women, but in a pinch..."

"Indiscriminate sex is Stanley's thing. He doesn't care who it is; hell, I think he would screw a donkey if it was willing. He has a kinky side. I mean, he likes me to spank him, slap him, and basically dominate him in bed. Which doesn't bother me; after all, I like sex, too. I especially like to be rough during sex. I might not love him, but he lets me go as far as I want, the rougher, the better. However, I wasn't going to let his sex addiction ruin what we had. I like living in the Governor's Mansion and being the wife of someone with that much power."

Kara found herself laughing, actually laughing, at the craziness of what she was hearing come out of her supposed mother's mouth.

"What are you laughing at?" she spat at Kara.

"You are a freak show. My father cheats on you over and over, and you stay with him. What a weak person. You think you're strong, yet you aren't. Not really. A strong person would have left."

"Weak? I controlled your father, I called the shots. Thanks to Devon and Marshall, you will die a tragic death; they will once again get away. We will mourn the loss of the daughter we had finally reconnected with. The sympathy will be worth the effort to get rid of you."

"You are truly crazy; you know that, right? You stole me from my mother, as a pawn, all for power and prestige?"

"I didn't steal you. You were legally bought, and no one was the wiser for it. I pretended I was pregnant. Enough money can pay off the most moral of doctors to forget that I had an emergency hysterectomy during the delivery of Ethan."

Kara didn't care to hear anymore, but as long as her mother was talking, it was giving them longer to find her. Even if Marshall and Devon weren't going to kill her right away, she didn't want them to move her to another location.

"If you didn't want another child, why would you want to raise me?"

"I had wanted another child. Just not you. But it wasn't meant to be, so I was fine with the one I had. Then we found out about you because that little bitch honestly thought your father would leave me for her. After I told her to be on her way, I realized it might be advantageous to have another child. The perfect little family, older son, younger daughter. An idea was sparked. I thought I could fake loving you a little better, and maybe I could have if you didn't look so much like her. If only you would have looked more like your father, like Ethan."

While she spoke, she paced the floor in front of Kara, her Jimmy Choo heels clicking on the floor. As Kara stared at her, she realized that her mother was on a precipice. about to tip over the edge into lunacy. While she still maintained her perfect facade, there was a spark in her eye that showed her that Constance Vanderbilt had completely lost it.

"You came so suddenly that I was forced to have an at-home birth, with no drugs. We were so thankful that you were safely here," she scoffed.

"What happened to my mother?"

"She sold you without blinking an eye. She really had no choice; after all, at the tender age of seventeen, she had twin boys who were only one and a newborn to care for. She couldn't afford to feed another mouth, especially after she lost her job for fucking her boss."

Kara gasped at the meaning of her words.

"That's right; Devon and Marshall are your brothers. Born from the same whoring cunt, fathered by the same cheating bastard. I couldn't have another child, but nothing was stopping her from having child after child." Kara couldn't hold back the bile; she vomited at the realization that her brothers had raped her. After she emptied her stomach, she glanced to her brothers, who were smiling cruelly at her.

"You knew? All this time, you knew, and you still did those things to me?"

"Our mother killed herself shortly after you were born. The weight of having sold you was too much; you were more important to her than we were." Marshall said the words so forcefully that spit flew from his mouth. "The woman who raised us wasn't what one would call a nice person. She beat us relentlessly. Molested us. She especially loved to toy with Devon. Constance rescued us from her when we were fourteen. We owe everything to her; anything she asks of us, we will gladly do."

His voice had become strangely monotone, and that scared her more than anything. It was as if he was reciting a prepared speech, but he wasn't selling it well. Constance was oblivious to the change in his voice. As he spoke, he walked toward her mother and slowly wrapped his arms around her. She wound her arms around his neck and kissed him passionately. The embrace wasn't romantic, and it was not sweet, but it was disturbing to watch the woman who raised her with her hands entwined in the hair of the person who had tormented Kara.

Kara once again felt sick to her stomach as her brother stuck his tongue into the mouth of the woman who she had once thought was her mother. Devon walked up behind Constance and ran his hands up her ribs, around to her breasts, where he ripped the shirt she was wearing open and reaching into her bra, he tugged on her erect nipples until she moaned in pleasure.

"You disgust me. You're animals, every one of you!" she shouted.

They ignored her shouts of disgust and continued to make out; in fact, it appeared her reaction was encouraging their tryst. Kara squeezed her eyes shut and tears leaked down her face. The image of the two monsters, who she had just found out were her brothers, undressing the woman, who until a few minutes ago she had considered her mother, albeit a terrible mother, but her mother nonetheless, was more than she could handle.

"Open your eyes, you little cunt," Marshall yelled at her. "Get a good look at us fucking your mommy. Oh wait; she isn't your mommy, is she? Watch as she takes us from both sides, and remember what it was like to have us inside you. Because once we're done with her, the fun begins. Now that you know there are two of us, and now that Devon isn't fixated on you, the games we have planned will be so much better."

She shook her head, refusing to open her eyes and witness the sight of them with Constance. But she could still hear the grunts and groans of their copulation. There was no way to cover her ears.

"Open your eyes and look, or I will buttfuck your boyfriend before I kill him," Devon roared. She shook her head and whimpered. "Now!"

Reluctantly, she opened her eyes to the exhibitionism in front of her. Her stomach knotted as she watched the gyrating sweat-soaked bodies. It was a horrific thing to witness the erotic scene. Kara squeezed her eyes shut tight and swallowed the bile back once again.

"Little sister, open your eyes!" Devon singsonged to her. "I want you to remember we will always love you the most."

Her gaze dropped to the ground, and out of the corner of her eye, she saw something that made her feel moderately better. She still had her ankle bracelet on. For some reason, they hadn't removed any of her jewelry, and the most important piece was on her. Knowing that she was still wearing the bracelet that would allow the police to find her meant that help was eventually coming. Kara knew in her heart that Caleb would do anything to find her and that even if it would upset Ethan and set back his recovery, he would do so to get her back.

Resisting the impulse to keep her eyes shut, she forced herself to look. If it would keep them happy and give Caleb the time to find her, then it was worth it. But as soon as she opened her eyes, something registered as off about the scenario she was watching unfold.

Sure, they were still in the throes of passion, but something wasn't right. Constance had allowed them to tie her hands behind her back and was spread eagle on the ground with Devon on top of her, but Marshall had removed himself from the moment, and Constance was completely unaware of the shift, and it was too late for Kara to do anything to stop it. Marshall took hold of her mother's head by the hair, tugging her head back slightly to expose the neck. Constance was still in the moment and thought it was all part of rough sex. Marshall tugged a little harder to get her attention; clearly, he wanted her to know what was coming, as with his other hand, he pulled the knife across her neck. Kara let out a blood-curdling scream.

Constance Vanderbilt had known that she was going to die while one of the boys she had taken advantage of was still thrusting into her. As Kara screamed, she watched the blood that had sustained the life of the woman she had been meant to love and had come to hate, drain out of her and spray all over Devon.

The severity of it all felt like it was crashing down on her. She felt the gravity in the room crushing her and slumped, literally hanging by her bindings. Nothing could have accomplished as much with as little effort as this had. She hung limply in the disgusting prison she had been shackled to; the prison where she would lose her life because she was suddenly certain that there was no way Caleb would find her in time. If he had called Ethan, they should have been able to get the coordinates of her whereabouts quickly, and the police would be here already. Shouldn't they storm the building? Would they wait until the right opportunity presented itself to charge in, and if so, how much longer would it take?

Defeated. Broken. Looking to the ceiling, she began to whisper *The*

Lord's Prayer. The monsters that were her brothers heard her, and it seemed to agitate them. She smiled a grim smile and recited it again, louder this time, defiance sparking inside of her.

As they advanced on her, scalpel in Marshall's hand and rope in Devon's, she continued to pray. There was nothing they could do to her. Nothing they hadn't done. She would not let them win by seeing her fear. So, she prayed. She let peace and calm claim her. Out loud, she asked God to help Ethan and Caleb understand.

Marshall was visibly furious as he pulled her down from the hook she was attached to, but Devon seemed to be devastated at the mention of Caleb. Marshall thought he was no longer fixated on Kara, but he was wrong. If Marshall had seen the expression on Devon's face, he would have been furious. Kara found it disturbingly sad. If he wasn't a coldhearted, sadistic monster, maybe she would have cared.

As she slid to the ground, she saw something reflect in the warehouse from outside the window. A light. Just a flash, then another. Her heart soared; either the cavalry was here, or the angels were waiting to guide her to heaven.

Then she saw it again. Blink, blink, blink. Stop. Blink, blink, blink. Stop. The cavalry was here. They knew she could see them, but Marshall and Devon weren't looking. A single tear leaked from her eye as the room erupted in chaos.

32

Caleb felt like he was going to jump out of his own skin. Standing outside the decrepit warehouse while waiting for the go sign from the captain was almost more than he could take. He didn't want to push his luck. They didn't want him here; he was too close to this. They wanted him with Ethan because they were both too emotionally involved. But, the fuck they were going to stop him. They weren't going to sideline him when Kara's life was in danger. Not while she was in the hands of that sadistic madman.

"We have eyes on the prize," Santiago's voice said in Caleb's ear piece. SWAT had positioned themselves around the perimeter of the building and had finally gotten eyes into where she was being held. He was desperately waiting for some news from them, so when he finally got some intel, he just about collapsed with relief.

"Roger that, can you take out the subject, without hurting the prize?" asked the captain.

"Negative."

"I need visual, what can you see?"

"There is one deceased woman on the floor and three subjects standing in front of the prize. The prize is alive and well."

Define well, Caleb wanted to know. *Did well mean untouched or did it just mean breathing?*

"Did you say three subjects?" Caleb asked.

"Roger."

"Hold your position for now; we need to know what threat they pose." Bob's voice was tense as he issued the order.

"Copy," Santiago said.

"Fuck that! Sir, with all due respect, we can't leave her in there and wait to see what they are going to do!" Caleb whispered into his mic. He couldn't scream, even though he wanted to do that very thing.

"Stand down, eight seventy-four, or I will pull you. Copy that?" Bob was furious, and when Caleb didn't respond, he repeated, "Copy that?"

"Yes, sir. But even if I lose my job, I won't wait much longer. Those motherfuckers are unpredictable."

Caleb took a deep breath to center himself. He wanted to charge into the building, but he knew that wasn't a good idea. Yet, every cell in his body was telling him they couldn't wait much longer. Every second that she was in that room with those three people was one second too many.

"I need more detail, tell me what else you're seeing," Bob demanded.

"Two males, two females. Female one, the prize, is naked and tied up. The two male subjects look strikingly similar, either twins or at the very least they are related, one male has burn scars on his neck."

"Devon Bristol ..." Caleb whispered, his stomach twisting in a knot.

"Female two? Friend or foe?" Bob asked.

"Unknown. I can't get a visual on her. She has her back to the window...here's something familiar, wait, she's turning around...shit..."

"We need intel, what did you see?" Caleb asked, jumping on the mic before his captain could say anything.

"Female two is Constance Vanderbilt. Oh, sweet Jesus..." Santiago broke off.

Caleb had felt momentarily happy and worried that Constance Vanderbilt was there, happy because she could help, worried that she was also a hostage. But then he felt his blood pressure rise at the tone of Santiago's voice.

"We need to know what's going on," Caleb growled.

"Female two is not a friendly, repeat, not a friendly. Female two and both male subjects are," he cleared his throat, clearly shocked, "undressing. It's apparent that they are familiar with each other," Santiago said.

There was a prolonged moment of silence as everyone absorbed what he had just said. They were undressing, familiar with each other, sweet lord almighty. Had her mother really done this? Had she been part of it all along?

"I think we need to move. They aren't letting her out of there alive," Mueller piped in when Santiago stayed silent.

No shit, Sherlock, Caleb thought. Kara had been right all along; there definitely was more going on than anyone had ever suspected. No sooner had Mueller said that than a blood curdling scream, one he recognized as Kara's voice, split the night. Caleb felt his heart stop beating for one brief moment in time.

"Intel! Who was the source of the screaming?" snapped Caleb, somehow managing not to charge into the building.

"The guy without the burns just sliced the throat of Constance Vanderbilt. She's dead," Santiago answered.

"We need to move. They just killed the governor's wife. Whether she was involved, we just hit a shit storm of epic proportions. These men will not let her go; right now, they don't know that they're surrounded. We have the element of surprise," Caleb pleaded.

"Eight seventy-four, copy. Four eighty-four, stay in position. Team one, take the back entrance, two go in, one covers their flank. Team two, take the side entrance, two in, one cover the flank. Team three, take the front entrance. Eight seventy-four, stay where you are. Do not move a muscle."

Yeah, fat fucking chance, thought Caleb. 874, which was his badge number, was most certainly not sitting this one out. Caleb began to move toward the front entrance. He was as quiet as SWAT and just as skilled. In fact, he had a conversation with Ethan in recent weeks about joining SWAT, which was made up of other detectives throughout the police force, but they hadn't decided yet. If he still had a job after today, he would be applying.

"Eight seventy-four, damn it, hold your position."

"With all due respect, sir, I am just not going to do that. The woman I love is being held in that building. She is naked, cold, and scared…"

"Stand down!" he cut in.

"No! There are two dead women in the room with her. One of the women is her mother. The amount of time we have is limited; let's not waste it arguing over this because I will not sit with my thumb up my ass." Caleb softened his voice and added, "Sir, you can trust me, I will not do anything that will put her in harm's way. If I do, I will hand in my badge."

It was the God's truth because if something happened to her, and if it was because of something he caused, he would not be able to live with himself.

"Don't make me regret this eight seventy-four. Team one, friendly coming in behind you."

"Copy." Mueller's voice came over the ear piece. "Get your ass down here; we go on three. Make sure to cover our six."

Caleb could barely hear Mueller through the mic, but he could hear him enough to know what he needed to know. He flew into position, and on the three count, they silently entered the building. Kara was being held in the center of the building. They had the schematics of the building, so they knew the layout. Other than the offices in the back, the main part of the building was one large open area. Santiago had gotten a visual through from a neighboring rooftop by looking through the front window. When they entered, they found low watt lamps lighting the way. One thing was for certain: the two men holding her were not dumb.

Low wattage lamps would draw less attention. Just because the warehouse wasn't used for its intended purpose didn't mean that it wasn't a potential useful home for a squatter. There were other abandoned buildings in the area, and they all were prone to squatters. Holding Kara in the very center of the building helped ensure that it would be harder to hear her screams. Not that most of the people hiding out in these buildings would do anything about someone screaming. More than likely, they would ignore it. They would assume someone was high on drugs, and if they thought it was someone being attacked, they still wouldn't get involved. They'd just be happy it wasn't them.

Soundlessly, they hurried through the debris toward the center of the building; they were low and fast coming in. Once they got close, Mueller stopped, turned, pointed to his eyes and pointed to the dark space in front of him. and then he vanished around the corner of a stack of boxes that had been left behind. Then Kingsley followed, Caleb behind him. They found themselves in another long labyrinth because of all the junk that had been left there when the owners had vacated the building. If it hadn't been for the lamps, they would have had no idea where they were going.

Coming up behind Mueller again, they waited as he held up three fingers—Mueller indicating they would go on three. Slowly, he lowered his fingers, and when on the last finger he shoved his shoulder into another wall of boxes, dropping to his knees once he was through and in the center of the building. Kingsley and Caleb rushed in behind him, covering him as they entered the room.

Then everything was bedlam as the other teams breached from the other entrances they had come through. Shouting ensued from all vantage points as they yelled at the two men to drop what was in their hands and get on their knees. As the other men secured Devon and Marshall, Caleb quickly scanned the room looking for Kara, his eyes lighting on Constance Vanderbilt and then the body of the nurse he'd met at the hospital. He wasn't sure the connection, but there would be time to find out.

Then he saw her and rushed to her side. As he moved, he grabbed a shirt off the ground, obviously the one her mother had been wearing, and draped it over her. Tears were streaming down her face as she tried to sit up and he gently pushed her back down to the ground.

"Just lie still for a moment, let me check you over."

"I'm fine. I'm a doctor, remember? Just a lot of bumps and bruises." After she sat up and he was certain she wouldn't tip over, he helped her into the blouse, which had to be held shut because the buttons had been pulled off when one of the men had apparently ripped it from Constance's body in the throes of passion. Once the shirt was on, he pulled her into his embrace. Inhaling her scent deeply into his lungs, he felt whole once again.

"God, I was so scared. Get me out of here, please."

"Let's wait for a stretcher."

"No. I want out now. I can feel a panic attack coming. I need fresh air."

Seeing her struggling to get to her feet, Caleb gave up arguing and stood reaching down to help her up. Once she was standing, he wrapped her in his embrace again. She trembled in his arms and then he felt her stiffen, the tension in her body had the hair on his neck standing on end. Kara reached for the gun at his waist and pulled it, pushing him out the way in one quick movement. He felt something solid hit his back over and over and the air rush out of him as he landed on the ground. What the fuck...?

Before he could register what was happening, he heard muffled shouting as Kara unloaded the clip in his gun. His ears were ringing as he turned to see the body of Devon Bristol slump to the ground, blood spilling from wounds that were center mass. Before he hit the ground, he was already dead. Marshall was also on the ground, his hand on his neck, trying to stop the flow of blood from the wound. With the amount of blood spilling between his fingers, the wound would most certainly be fatal if he didn't get help and fast. Yet, no officer rushed to his aid.

Civic duty or not, they were all hoping the taxpayers would be saved the time and expense of a trial. Adrenaline coursing through him, he still didn't register what had caused the pain in his back, and he didn't have time to think about it as he watched Kara standing in a daze, holding his gun, and then she shook her head, and he could see she had regained control.

K ARA SNAPPED out of her trance, set the gun on the ground, and rushed to the side of the man who had abused her. The doctor in her beat out the victim, and she knelt beside Marshall and tried to pinch the artery that had been nicked in his neck. She didn't want to save him, and in all honesty, she didn't think she could save him. That didn't mean she would sink to the level of her sadistic brothers. She was a better person, no matter how hard they had tried to ruin her humanity.

"Always...the...perfect...girl..." Blood coated his teeth as he struggled to speak, making him seem even more sinister to her.

"Fuck. You."

"Ah...the girl...has bite...after all..."

"You should do us all a favor and shut up," one of the officers said from above her. "Ma'am, I strongly encourage you to step away from the suspect."

Paying no heed to the words coming from the officer, she continued to apply pressure to the neck wound, knowing it was most likely too little and too late.

"I don't know if I can save you, but it doesn't mean I won't try, you bastard. What kind of doctor would I be if I did?"

"My...sis...ter..." The word was faint as he began to lose consciousness. Kara was aware of every eye in the room on her.

"Knife!" someone shouted.

Kara instinctively slid to the side, her finger slipping on the artery as the nearest officer wrestled the scalpel out of Marshall's hand, which had gone slack after he had used his last bit of strength to try to stab it into her throat. Regaining her composure, she clamped her fingers back on the artery in his neck, but it was too late. The brother she never knew she had took one last, stuttering breath. The sound of the death rattle always sent chills down her back; it was no different this time, and then he was gone.

Bowing her head, she closed his eyes, not out of respect, but because she couldn't stand to look into the eyes of that monster and see familiar eyes—her eyes—staring back. Looking at him now, the resemblance was obvious. Marshall and Devon, or whoever they were, were identical twins, and they looked remarkably like Kara. She dry heaved at the thought. If she'd had anything left in her, she would have retched right there.

Falling back on her hands and backside, she crab walked as fast as possible away from him, only stopping when she backed into a wall. Except it wasn't a wall. It was Caleb; his warm hands were on her, calming her, but something was wrong with him. His motions were choppy. That realization was all it took to get Kara back in her groove. Whipping around, she turned to look at him.

"What is it? My God, were you hit?" A newfound panic swelled in her. No longer was she acknowledging her ordeal; rather, she was assessing the man in front of her. His face was pale, but there was no blood. "Caleb, answer me. Were. You. Hit?"

"It hit the vest, in the back. I'm fine. Probably a bruised rib or two, just having a hard time with my range of motion."

"Humor the ER doctor; remove your gear so I can take a look." As she issued the order, she checked his vitals. "Now that the scene is secure, can you bring in a stretcher for him?" she asked over her shoulder at one of the very muscular men wearing tactical gear.

"I'm not being wheeled out on a stretcher, the vest stopped it. Stop fussing. It did its job."

"Let me be the judge of that. Take. Off. Your. Shirt."

"Never thought I would see a guy argue with a gorgeous woman asking him to get undressed," came a retort from behind her. She knew it was to reduce some of the tension in the room, so she smiled tightly.

"Stuff a sock in it, Mueller," Caleb bit out.

"Vest. Now."

"Man, are you bossy." He undid the Velcro of the vest and tried to shrug out of it, but when Kara saw the pain it was causing him, she gently placed her hands on his, effectively stopping him, so she could take the gear off for him.

After his chest was bared and she saw no wounds, she walked

around to look at his back. She sucked in a breath when she saw the very easy to discern bruises starting to show from a cluster of bullets that had hit him in the back. Thank God for the Kevlar. As tenderly as possible, she probed the area around the bruising.

"I don't think any ribs are broken, but I want to have an X-ray done when we get you to the hospital."

"Maybe you can get a sponge bath from one of the nurses," came another wisecrack from the men in the room.

"Geez, guys, you're a bunch of comedians. Anyway, the only person giving him a sponge bath is going to be me." Kara winked at Caleb as she came to stand in front of him. Fully in control of herself once again. The roller coaster of the last several hours had taken a toll on her, but she was strong enough to weather it.

"That was one hell of a shot. Who took them out?" Caleb asked, his face tight.

"That would be the doctor assessing your sorry ass right now. She shoved you out of the way, hit the one with the burns several times center mass a split second after he got a couple shots off at you. The other one saw him get the gun and was hit in the neck when he tried to dive in front of him. I'm Aaron Mueller, damn pleased to meet you." Smiling from ear to ear, he shook Kara's hand.

Both found themselves amused by the expression on Caleb's face.

"That was an expert shot. I take it you…"

"I go to the shooting range regularly. I'm not a fan of guns, in my line of work all you need to see is one GSW, I am sure you understand that feeling. Anyway, I also understood there might be a need for the skill one day. Seems I was right."

Caleb shook his head and wrapped his arms around her. Even though she could tell he was in pain, he hugged her tightly.

"So, doc, am I going to live to see another morning with you in my bed?"

"You seem fine, but I'm still going to insist on a full assessment when you go to the hospital." When he opened his mouth to protest, she raised her hand, effectively silencing him. "Notice I said when not if? No need to be a tough guy."

"I'm fine. But if it'll make you feel better…"

"It doesn't matter if she's suggesting it; I'm ordering that you go to the hospital. Even if you were wearing your Kevlar vest, I want you looked at," barked Captain Bob Wickman, who had just walked into the room to survey the carnage. "We're going to need to know what went on in here, but it can wait until after Montgomery gets looked at."

"Cap, I'm not going if she stays here…" Caleb began to protest.

"Like I said, it can wait until after you're looked at. I assumed that she would go with you as she needs to be looked at, as well. No arguments from you, you broke rules earlier, don't let me forget that I gave you a pass on that." And then he walked away to talk to Mueller.

Kara took that to mean it was time for her to escort him to the hospital since he clearly wasn't going to go without her. Linking her fingers with his, she leaned into him and led him out of the blood-soaked room, out of the building and outside, where it was going from night to day, and the sun was rising in the distance, turning the sky multiple shades of pink. Inhaling deeply, she felt free for the first time in ten years.

33

After numerous tests and X-rays, Dr. Chiglo had given him the all clear, and he gratefully accepted a scrub shirt to wear. He'd had enough of hospitals for a few days; he couldn't imagine how Kara could spend her days here after spending so much time in the hospital as a patient.

"I hear that Dr. Chiglo has cleared you to go," she said, smiling as she came through the door into his room.

"Affirmative. How about you?"

"I was cleared a while ago. Other than some abrasions and a few cuts and bruises, I'm fine. Trust me when I say that this was nothing this time around. Anyway, I went upstairs and visited Ethan for a bit. Good thing, too, because in the chaos, they had neglected to update him that I am okay."

"Uh-oh. I imagine he was about to take out the security guard."

"Yeah, just a little bit. Good news is he refrained from hitting Charles over the head, who, by the way, is a very nice man. Even better news is that Ethan is doing really well. Better than really well. Good enough he should be able to get out of here in another few days. The swelling has gone down, and his CAT scans look good. All great news."

"How are you, really?" he asked as he pulled off the hideous gown and pulled the scrub shirt over his head, wincing from the pain it caused to do such a simple act. How had she gone through what she had? He felt like a freight train had hit him. He was obviously a wuss compared to her. After he pulled the hem down, he looked up and saw her frozen, staring at him, mouth agape. "What?"

"Uh, nothing. I just...you are so magnificent. I didn't think after today...I was worried...that I wouldn't be able to...you know. Be attracted to you or anyone ever again." Her cheeks flamed crimson, and he found it adorable, but his heart broke when he thought about how she had worried that all their progress had been for nothing.

"Honey, it's okay, we'll just take things slow again."

"No. You don't understand," she said as she advanced on him—her hands suddenly were under his shirt, touching him gently. He shivered at the contact before she stood on her tiptoes and then her mouth was on his.

"It appears that I absolutely don't understand. Maybe you should explain it to me?"

"I want to devour you right now. I want to get lost in you, I want to feel—I don't know, good. Make me feel good, Caleb." Her hands were all over him, and he was having a hard time focusing, but he knew this was not the right location. Regrettably, he pushed away from her, and when he looked at her, he felt his chest constrict with panic. He could see the wheels turning.

"Kara, don't do that. I want to devour you, too, and the only reason I stopped..." He paused and put a finger under her chin, lifting it until she looked at him, really looked at him. "...is because we're in the ER of the hospital you work for. It would be a little bit of a problem if one of your co-workers walked in."

With a jerk of her head, she let him know she understood, but that she wasn't happy about it.

"Let's compromise," he said, lightly pecking her lips.

"I'm listening," she said.

"My captain doesn't know that I was cleared to go and they're probably at the scene still. So, we have some time. My place is close to here, and yours is a crime scene still, how about we go to my place, and I prove to you that you can still enjoy me?"

"Deal, but I have a request."

"Anything. You can ask me anything, and it's yours."

"I don't want to go back to my house. Ever. Which is a shame, since I really loved it. But I can't. I'm moving forward, and I can't walk into that house and let memories assail me at every turn. Not only did one of those bastards sell me that house ..." She noticed his confused expression and paused taking a deep breath before continuing. "The other guy, the one with the neck wound, he was my realtor, Nurse Abfall's husband, Marshall Abfall."

"But it didn't look anything like him...shit, the second disguise."

"Yep, anyway, I just can't go back there. So, I was thinking..." She paused.

"What were you thinking?" He nuzzled her neck.

"Does your place allow dogs?"

"Regrettably, no. But my lease is almost up."

"Perfect. How about we find a new place that's just ours?"

"That does sound perfect. Now, about that enjoying-me request?"

"I'm totally game to go back and show you that they didn't break me. I get to take charge; you, patient, and me, doctor. Doctor says you need to take it easy."

"Sounds to me like the doctor is planning on taking advantage of the situation."

"No. I only plan to take advantage of you."

TWO HOURS LATER, they were showered and sitting in the conference room. After several hours at the hospital and the couple spent in bed, he had assumed they would be the last ones to the debriefing, but they'd beaten them there and had to wait for about a half hour before anyone showed up.

"Sorry for keeping you waiting, Montgomery. We definitely want to tie this one up and move on," Bob said when he came bustling in the room with a bunch of other people behind him.

"We can't really move on until you find the other victims if that's even possible."

Sadness filled her at the thought of all those other women going through what she had; only, they didn't get to have a chance to move on, because of them she intended on making the rest of her life count for something. They deserved better, and she would give them better.

After everyone found a seat, they all looked at Kara, who was lost in her thoughts until Bob cleared his throat. She jumped at the sound and then smiled uncomfortably.

"Sorry for startling you, I just said your name, and you didn't respond."

"Long day, I was just internalizing. Sorry about that."

"You have the right. I just thought that we could start by you filling us in on what was discussed before I entered the scene. One of the officers said that one of the suspects whispered something about his sister before he died. Do you know where to find her? Maybe she'll be able to shed some light on the inner workings of her brothers," Bob said.

"I don't think that's going to be much help, and he was just answering my question at the time."

"Question?" Gloria asked.

"I had said what kind of doctor would I be if I didn't try to save him. He answered by saying, my sister." It was her turn to clear her throat, and she paused, uncomfortable with the words forming in her mouth. *Time to pull off the Band-Aid,* she thought. "I'm his sister, their sister. I just found out, my mother was the one to tell me that she isn't my mother after all." A single tear slid down her cheek.

She was mesmerized by how white her knuckles were because she couldn't stop staring at her hands. No one shouted out in disgust, and Caleb's hand came up and linked fingers with hers, successfully calming her and stopping her from making fists with her hands. She had been clenching her hands so tightly that her nails, which she kept short, had dug rivets into her palms.

When she dared to look up, she saw sadness, but not disgust. Sucking in air, she told an abbreviated version of the story that had been told to her only hours ago. No need for them to know all the details; it wouldn't change anything. She had already told Caleb everything, and he had agreed with her that the facts, in an abbreviated format, were good enough.

"Apparently, my father is prone to affairs and had twin sons with a woman who worked for him—a very young woman. She had to have falsified papers to make her old enough to work for him as I was born to her when she was seventeen, and the twins were already one, according to my mother. My father was their father, as well. They were my full siblings. Ethan and I share the same father, but not the same mother. I told him when we were at the hospital. I hope that was all right?" she asked, though she really didn't care.

Ethan came before anyone else, except maybe Caleb, and she had also told Caleb. She had to make sure that he could still look at her the same way after finding out that her own brothers had kidnapped and raped her.

"We understand your need to tell him. This is a detail we will do our best to keep out of the press."

"It is what it is. I can try to hide it, but I want to find out who my mother is and find her family. Maybe they'll want to know who I am. They didn't raise the twins, so maybe there is no other family. Anyway, my father and Constance bought off my real mother and got me in return. Sometime after that, the woman who gave birth to me was devastated by selling me and killed herself."

Another tear slid down her cheek; she angrily swiped it away.

"They were raised by a cruel woman who molested them and beat them. Constance Vanderbilt 'saved' them. Suzanne Pascoe, aka Suzanne Abfall, helped lure me to my house so that Marshall Abfall and Devon Bristol could grab me. I don't know their real names. In answer to the question I know you will have, yes, Marshall sold me my home. However, he disguised himself. He must have faked all the information he sent me, because the website, business card, it all had pictures of him with the disguise on. I would imagine that he didn't walk around with a disguise all the time, but I don't think even his wife knew what he really looked like. I should have had Ethan do a background check; I'm usually over-the-top cautious. But I didn't think it was necessary, he was just selling me a home."

"How did you get his name?" Bob asked.

"I asked my friend, Dr. Vanessa Brenner. She said one of her co-workers had a husband who was just starting out as a realtor and would appreciate the business. I think they'd hacked into my computer throughout the last ten years, they must have seen that I was researching homes here. But they couldn't have known I would decide the task was too much with my working such long hours at the last hospital I worked for. It was in conversation that I mentioned looking for a house; she knew that I had accepted the job offer and needed one fast. I think it was just luck on his end that I contacted him."

"Unless he became a realtor and had his wife talk up how he was starting out and needed help in front of the doctors on purpose. Depends on when he became a realtor," Bob said.

"I don't know, it takes a while to get the certification. Unless he just faked his credentials," Caleb offered.

"Everything about them was fake. I would buy that his being a certified realtor was, as well. Anyway, they weren't ready to make a move and take me, but their 'benefactor,' otherwise known as Constance Vanderbilt, forced them to hurry up and grab me. She was behind the original abduction, and I was not supposed to have survived. She told them they could keep me as long as they wanted, as long as I never got away. She hated me so much because my father had an affair and I think she really loved him until the affair, maybe even after. But she was haunted by seeing my face day after day because I look just like my mother. It must have driven her to madness; I believe she really loved him until then. They killed Suzanne after she fulfilled her purpose. They killed Constance Vanderbilt because she had victimized them, as well, and I think they thought it would hurt me. It didn't hurt me to the level they expected; she was never really a mother to me."

Pinching the bridge of her nose, she sighed heavily.

"Maybe that makes me a bad person that I couldn't feel anything but disgust when she died. There was just no love between us; there never had been. I mean, she fucking had me abducted and wanted me murdered."

"How did Suzanne tie in? I mean, why would she help lure you to your house?"

"Her sister was their first victim. Her name was Lucy Pascoe, and they said she was their trial run. I was much more high profile so I would be harder to abduct. They knew they would have to practice. Suzanne hated me for surviving; she hated me for getting the news coverage, though the news coverage didn't really help me out of that hellhole. I did that. Mr. Stanford did that, and he didn't own a television. He does now, though. I don't understand why all these people hated me. I didn't even know Suzanne, not really."

Caleb rubbed his thumb across her wrist over and over, soothing her.

"What are the chances she would marry her sister's murderer?"

"It wasn't a coincidence. Years later, Marshall orchestrated meeting Suzanne. Sold her some story about how he dumped me, and I was still heartbroken over it. I don't know if she even loved him. She just wanted to best me somehow, as some sort of twisted tribute to her sister, I suppose. The whole thing is so twisted."

Another tear leaked down her face.

"They told me they got a taste for young women after me. Though, apparently, they didn't mind men or older women either, at least sexually. However, when it came to rape, torture, and murder, it was always young women. My God, they were so twisted by the environment they grew up in, by their genetics. I don't know. But they weren't ever going to change. They raped and tortured their sister all out of jealousy and rage. They said that she loved me more than them. Even if she killed herself, it doesn't mean she loved them less than she loved me. It just meant she couldn't handle the guilt. It wasn't like she had a choice. She was forced that hand."

More tears, a steady stream now, were dripping down her cheeks and sliding into her hair. Kara had stopped trying to wipe them away.

"My father will tell me her name before I walk away from him forever. He may not have known that my 'mother' was behind this; he had to have at least suspected something wasn't right, but he wasn't innocent. My real mother deserves to have a visit from her daughter, even if it's only to her grave. I'm pretty certain she would have raised me better than those two did. Then again, a pack of wolves would have done a better job."

After they were done with all the loose ends, Kara walked hand in hand with Caleb out of the conference room. Bob stopped them, and they stood much like they had only a few days before.

"Kara, I hope I see more of you. But for better reasons. If it wasn't for you, we might not have found Andrea's killer. I can go to bed tonight, her parents can go to bed tonight, knowing that the monsters that killed their baby are dead."

"You don't need to thank me; I only wish I could have stopped them all those years ago. Maybe I should have slit Devon's throat that day. He was sleeping, and I could have done it. Maybe Marshall wouldn't have killed another ten women without his sidekick."

"I doubt it. I think that you handled the bullshit hand you were dealt well. There is no room for second guessing. You got yourself out of there, because of your will to live and their mistake you lived. They learned from their mistake with you and made sure it didn't happen again."

"I think you're right on that. But I'll always wonder if I could have done more. If Devon would have died, maybe Marshall would have come for me sooner."

"If you had killed him, what would you be now? Could you live with yourself? You couldn't even stand by and let Marshall die; you tried to stop the blood flow. The other detectives told me that much."

"I didn't do it out of the kindness in my heart, though; I wanted him to die, but I wanted him to live because I hoped that he could lead us to the other bodies. I don't know. Even though I tried to save Marshall, in the end, I killed them both today, and I will sleep better tonight for it. What does that say about me?"

"That you did what you had to do. No one will judge you for that. Devon had pulled Officer Montif's weapon. It was an oversight on Montif's part to let Devon get the weapon. But, he thought with that many officers in the room…well, he just didn't think that it was something he needed to worry about."

"Mistakes happen. Go easy on him. Those two men, my brothers, they were resourceful and unpredictable, as well as devious and cunning. A veteran officer could have easily made the same mistake as Officer Montif; he just happened to be in the wrong place at the wrong time."

"He is pretty green. But he'll need to go through some more training."

Bob opened his arms, and Kara walked into them.

"Thank you."

"For what?" he asked.

"For understanding. For being here. For not firing Caleb. For everything. He told me what he did back there, how he hadn't listened to directions. Go easy on him, too. He was just protecting me."

"I know. What we do for those we love," he said and pulled away.

"You knew?"

"Hell, everyone knows. That boy has been wearing his emotions on his sleeves since you pulled into town. Any time one of the other officers looked at you, well, I thought it might come to blows, but he also let it slip to me at your house." He laughed and walked out of the room.

Kara turned and looked at Caleb, her brows arched.

"Come to blows, huh? Nice of you to tell your boss before me."

"Listen, I know you're a beautiful woman and all, but that doesn't mean I like to share, and I definitely don't like all those assholes out there ogling you. As for slipping up to my captain? Maybe I should have told you first, but at the time, I didn't even know that's where my feelings were headed until I said them out loud to him."

"Ogling me." She laughed long and hard over that.

"Is that all you got out of that?"

"Who says ogle, anyway…?"

Caleb took two long strides toward her and silenced her laughter with his mouth. After a thorough tasting of her lips, he pulled back and gazed down at her.

"How about we go get Samsonite and go home?"

"You're sure you still want to live together?"

"Nothing would make me happier. Well, maybe one thing."

"Seriously, what has it been? A whole hour since we made love?"

"That wasn't what I was talking about."

"Then what were you talking about?"

He looked uncomfortable for a moment and ran his hand through his hair before kissing her until her toes tingled.

"Live with you; hell, I want to marry you. You got a problem with that?"

"None. None at all."

EPILOGUE

Kara took a deep breath and let it out; Taylor smiled at her reassuringly in the mirror. It was crazy that they had only met six months ago and already they were such close friends, practically sisters. Taylor was an inspiration to Kara, and Kara only hoped she was an inspiration to her. If anyone had asked all those months ago what her future held, she would have told them that she would be the attending physician at Mercy Hospital, and that was all. She would not have predicted the future she found herself standing in at that moment.

She smoothed her hands down the ivory fabric, reveling in the intricate beadwork of the bodice, exquisite craftsmanship in each stitch. With another deep breath, she looked at herself in the full-length mirror. The woman staring back at her was not the woman she had seen in that mirror not so long ago. The woman staring back at her was more confident than she ever thought she could be.

Her hair was elaborately done, and her makeup was meticulous. It was the most beautiful she'd ever felt, and she was finally confident in her own skin. All it had taken was one man to teach her that there was good in life, the man who was about to become her husband. A few had thought they were crazy for getting married so soon, but those people didn't really know what they'd gone through to get to this point.

A light tap sounded on the door, and Taylor, who happened to be her maid of honor, squeezed her shoulder before turning to see who it was.

"It's time," came the voice of James Montgomery, who had in so many ways became a surrogate father to Kara. His whole family had taken her into their lives as if she had always been a part of it. "Are you ready?" he asked.

She turned and smiled at him.

"My God, Kara, you are beyond radiant. Seeing the changes over you in the last months, I will forever be proud of Caleb for making you so happy and forever grateful to you for helping us see that we were not giving our little girl the benefit of the doubt. If that boy of mine ever hurts you ..." James trailed off. "Well, let's just say, I raised him better than that."

"I have no doubts in my mind that you did. Taylor, well, you would have gotten through to them eventually. Right?"

"I'm not so sure." She laughed, and James beamed at the sound.

"Everyone is seated, and it's time. Bob is outside, waiting to walk you down the aisle."

"Last chance to back out; are you sure you want to help him walk me down the aisle?

"Honey, I had to beat a bunch of men off with a stick to get that honor. William was willing to carry your train, for Pete's sake! I can't wait to do you the honor."

After the news broke of what her father and Constance had done, her father resigned as governor. Technically, he didn't have to. There was nothing he could be charged with. While his wife could not be charged with any crime because she was dead, they still wanted to make sure he had nothing to do with it, and after a thorough investigation, they were certain that he had not known that Constance was behind it all. Judging by his reaction when they told him about Marshall and Devon, he didn't know that he had fathered twin sons. Therefore, even though he may have been complicit in the delay of the ransom being paid, in the end, it didn't matter because the ransom was never supposed to ensure her release. Constance had thought that she had covered all her bases.

However, she didn't realize that Kara was as strong as she was. She thought her an unworthy opponent. Even so, Kara had prevailed, and Ethan and she had moved on. Their father had retreated quietly in the night. She had no idea where he was, and if she had known, she wouldn't have invited him to the wedding. Maybe someday, if he tried, they could repair things, but she doubted it.

In the end, he did tell her the name of her mother. It wasn't difficult to track down her family. The family that her mother had run away from after becoming pregnant with the twins. Her father had given her the job after she came begging for help. She'd found someone to falsify documentation so that she was older, but Constance had still found out how old she was.

Kara's grandparents were thrilled to meet her and horrified by what had happened to her. Since her mother, whose name was Natalie, had cut all ties with her parents, they had no idea about the children she had borne. What they did know was that Natalie was murdered and hadn't committed suicide, like Constance had told Kara. It wasn't a very hard assumption to make to figure out that Constance had killed Natalie.

Before Natalie died, Constance had gotten her to sign over guardianship of the twins to her. It appeared that, from there, Constance had given the twins to a woman to raise. Whether she knew that the woman was a monster remained to be seen, but Kara felt Constance did know. In Kara's mind, her mother placed her brothers in a terrible environment so they could be conditioned and she could be their savior.

Most of the puzzle pieces fell into place after that. They were still searching for a couple of the women but were hopeful they would find them. As the months passed, James and Evie had become such an important part of Kara and Ethan's lives. Therefore, it was logical to have James walk her down the aisle.

Taylor and Ella were already like the sisters she never had, and both would be standing up with her today, along with Quinn and Vanessa, who had said she was entirely too old to be a bridesmaid. But Vanessa couldn't refuse Kara. Grayson, Ethan, Brett, and William were all groomsmen. With little Ava and Alex being the flower girl and ring bearer.

Shaking herself, she hooked her arm with James's and walked to the door. Taylor fidgeted with the train and then grasped her hand before walking out to go get ready to walk down the aisle.

"Ready, little lady?" Bob asked.

"More than you'll ever know."

"Just one thing, before we go in there, there is something I want to ask of you," James said.

"All right..." she said, bewildered at the tone his voice had taken. He actually sounded nervous.

"After we get done in there, I will consider you my daughter. I already do. So, I would appreciate it very much if you would call me Dad. Evie would also like you to call her Mom. You have made Caleb so happy. Before you, there was a piece of him not quite complete. You have helped with Taylor more than we could have ever dreamed was possible. We all love you so much. Can you do that for me, for Evie and me?"

"I don't think that will be a problem, Dad," she replied. Tears were in her eyes as they walked through the door. "Did you ask Bob to wait outside so you could ask me that?"

"Guilty as charged," he answered, laughing.

Kara found herself laughing through the tears. She walked to Bob who was standing by the double doors and placed her hand on the arm he offered. Two of the most amazing fathers she had ever met would walk her down the aisle. She considered herself to be very lucky for that. The double doors opened, and she got her first glimpse of her soon-to-be husband. No longer ashamed when she cried and not caring if she messed up her makeup, she took the first step toward the future she'd wanted for so long.

In a single blink, she was standing before him. Caleb's father gently kissed her cheek and wiped away a tear before placing her hand in the crook of Caleb's arm; Bob shook Caleb's hand and kissed her other cheek before he took his seat. On shaking legs, she and Caleb walked the additional two steps to face their pastor. Before she knew it, they had exchanged the agreed upon traditional vows.

At the rehearsal the night before, they had been told that the rings would be exchanged next, but instead of the pastor signaling for the rings, she looked at Caleb and nodded her head.

"Caleb asked me if he could say a few words to Kara."

"This has been a whirlwind. From the moment I knocked you on your butt, I knew you would be a force to be reckoned with and that I needed to pay attention. And I did. You have made me the happiest man by merely being a part of my life. Now, I consider myself the luckiest man I know, because you are about to become my wife. I promise to love you forever, even when we fight." There were some giggles in the audience, loudest of which was little Ava. "But even if we fight, I promise to make you happy, because you deserve every drop of happiness I can give you."

Kara smiled into the eyes of the man who had brought her from the edge of darkness and despair and led her into the light.

"I will love you always, Kara."

Her lips trembled as she whispered, "I will love you. Always."